Praise for
Mortal Friends

"In *Mortal Friends*, Jane Stanton Hitchcock takes the reader into the elite and little-known world of Georgetown, where the powerful of Washington reside. The plot is rife with deception, betrayal, adultery, mad men, and murder most foul. I had a great weekend with this book."
—Dominick Dunne

"A dazzling, wicked murder mystery that unmasks most of Washington, which may never be the same."
—Bob Woodward

"*Mortal Friends* is at once witty, sophisticated, and chilling—imagine Edgar Allan Poe and Edith Wharton collaborating on a mystery. This novel had me guessing and turning the pages until the very end, and even then, I was surprised. Nobody else out there writes, or entertains, like Jane Stanton Hitchcock."
—Susan Cheever

"*Mortal Friends* is a brilliant mix—an expertly paced novel of suspense and a cutthroat comedy of manners. In Jane Stanton Hitchcock's expert hands, these Capitol killings show D.C. society for what it is— Deliciously Criminal."
—Linda Fairstein

"Jane Stanton Hitchcock's *Mortal Friends* rips the curtain off the world of Washington and its social cutthroats and power players. With elegance and panache she delivers a glittering cast that will keep readers up nights turning pages. A master plotter, Hitchcock has outdone herself. I adored this book."
—Marie Brenner

MORTAL
FRIENDS

Also by Jane Stanton Hitchcock

The Witches' Hammer
One Dangerous Lady
Social Crimes
Trick of the Eye

MORTAL

a novel

FRIENDS

Jane Stanton Hitchcock

A V O N

An Imprint of HarperCollinsPublishers

A hardcover edition of this book was published in 2009 by Harper-Collins Publishers

HarperCollins books may be purchased for educational, business, or sales promotional use. For information please write: Special Markets Department, HarperCollins Publishers, 10 East 53rd Street, New York, NY 10022.

FIRST AVON PAPERBACK EDITION PUBLISHED 2010.

Designed by Kathryn Parise

Library of Congress Cataloging-in-Publication Data is available upon request.

ISBN 978-0-06-117371-4 (pbk.)

10 11 12 13 14   OV/RRD   10 9 8 7 6 5 4 3 2 1

For Jim, who brought me to Washington

No woman has ever told the whole truth of her life.
—ISADORA DUNCAN

A country cannot survive on the impropriety of its wealthiest classes.
—SENATOR ZACHARY GRIDER

MORTAL
FRIENDS

Chapter 1

Violet Bolton loathed concerts as much as she loved murder. Crime was the only real music to my best friend's ears. She always invited me to the opening of the Capitol Symphony because she needed someone to laugh with, and her husband, Grant Bolton, never laughed if he could help it. But on that chilly September evening when it all began, Violet definitely had murder on her mind.

The Symphony Ball is the highlight of the Washington fall season. Violet had to go because she and Grant were big social deals in town—not flashy, fun, publicity social, but solid, blue chip, discreet social—a couple whose presence at a big occasion was noted by important people. I loved this evening. Violet hated it. I couldn't afford to shell out the thousand bucks for a ticket. Violet couldn't afford to let her true feelings show. I went. She paid. The arrangement suited us both perfectly.

The three of us—Violet, Grant, and I—sat together in the seventh row of the orchestra, listening to Mahler's Second Symphony.

"*Maahhh-ler*. So heavy. Reven, tell me why they can't just play show tunes and fuggetaboudit?" Violet whispered to me.

I stifled a giggle, and Violet let out an involuntary guffaw. A man in the row ahead of us ostentatiously shifted in his seat, and Grant gave us one of his stern hall-monitor looks. Grant was Mr. Straight Arrow. No, actually, he was more like a totem pole: tall, wooden, and joyless. I never quite knew when he liked something, but I always knew when he didn't. And he didn't like it when Violet and I misbehaved in public.

As the third movement of the symphony began, I scanned the

glittery crowd, wondering if *he* was there. Violet was thinking the same thing because she surreptitiously pointed to the guy in front of us and mouthed the words, "Serial killer." She was kidding, of course, but it was titillating to think that someone we might actually know *was* a killer.

This being Washington, and Washington being the capital of ambition, there are a lot of killers around here, believe me. I imagined quite a few people in that audience would be capable of murder if they thought it would advance their careers, or keep them in power. But at that point in time, as they say, there was a real, hands-on murderer on the loose—the "Beltway Basher," as he was dubbed by the press. Over the course of the past three years, four young women had been molested and bludgeoned to death in parks around the District. They all had apartments around the Dupont Circle area. Three of the women had worked on Capitol Hill. One had famously been involved with a congressman. There were rumors floating around about a serial killer who was possibly a big shot, possibly in politics, probably a man of wealth and power, hiding in plain sight in Washington society.

I'm fascinated by crimes in which I could see myself as the victim. Not that I *literally* see myself as a victim, mind you, but I think we all wonder how we would react in a really dicey situation. As the symphony played on, I thought back on my life, wondering if I'd ever known anyone who'd committed murder, or been an accomplice to one. That had always been a question in my mind. Would I recognize evil if it came close?

The music ended to rapturous applause. Jed Jimson, the slick chairman of the Kennedy Center, walked out onto the stage into the spotlight. A tall, silver-haired man of sixty, Jimson always looked irritatingly smug. He adjusted the standing microphone, then gazed out at the audience as if we were guests in his living room.

"Well, friends," he began with the folksy confidence of a talk show host, "was that a great concert or what?"

Jimson turned to applaud the orchestra sitting at ease behind him. As the audience enthusiastically joined him, he swept a hand toward the wings. Leonid Slobovkin, the temperamental conductor of the Capitol Symphony, walked out from behind the curtain, gave a stiff bow, and retreated out of sight.

Jimson went on: "Ladies and gentlemen, the Kennedy Center is not only the cultural center of Washington, D.C. It is also America's cultural center. Built in 1967, this great complex is now well into middle age and, like many of us here tonight, showing the effects of long service to this country. . . ."

Polite laughter.

"As all of you here know only too well, we're always trying to raise money for our beloved center, which is in dire need of a face-lift."

Uncomfortable titters.

"Thanks to many of you, we've had success in maintaining our wonderful symphony orchestra as well as our ballet, opera, and theater companies. But we have not had sufficient funds to begin the vast construction project that is necessary to adequately house America's busiest center for the performing arts."

As he cleared his throat, Violet nudged me and whispered, "Here it comes."

"Tonight I have a very special announcement to make. . . . It is my great honor and pleasure to tell you that the Kennedy Center has just received an historic grant for the purpose of refurbishing, renovating, and adding on to the complex. . . ." He paused for effect. "A gift of *One . . . hundred . . . million . . . dollars!*"

A split second of silence was followed by gasps from the audience, then a cascade of applause. Over the clapping, Jimson cried, *"Yes! Isn't that amazing?"* so loudly that feedback screeched over the sound system. No one cared. The applause continued until Jimson shushed the crowd.

"And now I want to introduce you to the exceptional person whose foundation has made this historic gift possible. . . ."

He paused again, milking the moment as if it were the announcement of an Academy Award. Finally, he said, "Ladies and gentlemen, please say a warm thank-you on behalf of the Kennedy Center, on behalf of the American people, and on behalf of all of us here tonight to Ms. Cynthia Rinehart! Cynthia, will you please stand up?"

Jimson thrust his arm forward and pointed down at the orchestra section. A spotlight hit the middle of the fourth row. A woman stood up and turned to face the auditorium. As the applause grew louder, she seemed to brace herself, as if she understood that she was now the focus of attention, curiosity, and more than a little envy. She was no beauty, but she was striking. With her pale skin, bright green eyes, and russet hair, she was exotic and sleek—an Abyssinian cat among the dowdy squirrels of Washington.

I took special note of her chunky diamond earrings—Rocks of Gibraltar on prongs—clearly designed to illuminate her bank account as much as her face. They were the sorts of jewels that draw the attention of people who usually notice little else but themselves. She had a voluptuous body that she simultaneously advertised and hid under a tight-fitting black dress, slim at the hips, straining across the bust. An enigmatic smile fluttered on her lips, as if she relished both the spotlight and the ill will. Along with everyone else, I craned my neck to get a better look at this woman who had, like Athena, sprung full-blown out of nowhere onto the Washington social scene.

"She's too young to be so rich," I whispered to Violet.

"Oh, she's not that young. But she *is* that rich. She does business with the bank. Anyway, you'll love Cynthia. She's terrific." Violet had mentioned Cynthia Rinehart a couple of times in passing, describing her only as this "really interesting woman" I absolutely had to meet.

"She's totally self-made," Violet continued with admiration. "Something to do with the insurance business. I'm not sure exactly what. But she's all gung-ho about philanthropy."

Apparently, Cynthia had already given money to several worthy causes around town—including Trees of Georgetown, one of Violet's pet projects.

"I need to introduce her to some cool women before she gets into the wrong clutches," she added now. Violet fancied herself the town's social arbiter.

Of course, we all knew that after that night Cynthia Rinehart wouldn't need any introductions from Violet or anyone else. The world would be at her feet. Let's face it, a hundred million dollars brews a hefty pot of instant friends.

———

On our way to the gala dinner, the Boltons got waylaid by some muckety-mucks. As president of the Potomac Bank, Grant was always getting waylaid by muckety-mucks who wanted to talk to him about the economy and interest rates and other really dreary stuff. Dutiful Violet stood by her man, as always, chatting amiably with people she both liked and disliked so that even I couldn't tell which was which. I always marveled at the way Violet could disguise her true feelings and maintain a pleasantly social facade.

I went ahead, on patrol, searching for a cute new face, someone I could possibly date or just have a decent conversation with. Unfortunately, this evening was mainly Washington's A-list, meaning that nearly every man there was older, married, world-weary, and political— definitely *not* the crowd in which to find a fun boyfriend.

The large white tent in the South Plaza was dotted with dozens of round tables of twelve, set with musical instrument centerpieces and sparkling votive lights. Not the best decorations, but I'd seen worse. Much worse. I plowed my way through the dressy crowd, wishing that Congress would ban pastels. Black-tie Washington is a sartorial stew of bad clothes and good jewels—a little like London. You can always count on a few bra straps hanging out. Up until quite recently, well-dressed women were suspected of being superficial.

I was trolling along when I ran into my old pal Carmen Appleton, the sassy, savvy special events director who organized the best parties in town, including this one. Clipboard in hand, she breezed past me with little more than a curt nod.

"Hey, Carmen! How's it going?" I called out.

Carmen stopped dead in her tracks, whirled around, and assumed a divalike hands-on-hip posture, obviously itching to get something off her chest.

"It seems that God's latest gift to philanthropy isn't happy with her seat," she said in her famously throaty, cigarette-stained voice. "She wants to be at the *head* table. So guess who has to quickly scamper around like Peter fucking Cottontail, switching place cards and telling certain nitro- glycerin-tempered people they aren't sitting where they thought they were sitting . . . ? And you know what fun that is in this town!"

"Who are you bumping from the head table?" I asked.

"Try the schnauzer, Maestro Slobovkin, and his lovely wife."

"*No!*"

"*Yes!* Orders from Jimson on high. Where does the hundred-million- dollar gorilla sit?"

"*Anywhere she wants!*" we sang out in unison. Flashing me a furious grin, Carmen hopped on.

It's one thing to complain about your seat in Washington, and quite another to get it changed. Only people with real clout got that.

Obviously, giving away a hundred million dollars was now as clout-worthy as holding high political office. Maybe more so.

I made the rounds, doubled back, and spotted Violet talking to Cynthia Rinehart. Several people were hanging around them, angling to ooze their way into the conversation. Clearly, everyone was anxious to meet this woman. But the two ladies were acting like royalty, focusing solely on each other in a vacuum of self-importance. I marched over and crashed their airspace. I wasn't shy when it came to Violet. I'd known her far, far too long to be intimidated by such pretensions. To her credit, Violet immediately introduced me. Cynthia shook my hand with a noticeably firm grip. She was a little coarser-looking up close. She wore a lot of makeup. However, she did have an undeniable magnetism, amplified by her direct manner.

"Well, hi there!" she exclaimed in a voice tinged with a slight southern accent. "Violet here tells me you have a fabulous antiques shop! Tell me your name again?"

"Reven Lynch," I said.

"*Reven* . . . ?" Cynthia repeated thoughtfully. "What kind of name's that?"

Now, everyone who knows me knows the story of my name. I've been teased about it ever since I was a kid. I have a pat response, which has the added advantage of being true.

"I was basically a mistake. My parents never thought they'd have me. Hence, the name Reven is 'never' spelled backward," I explained with my customary self-deprecating laugh.

People usually laugh with me. Not Cynthia. She furrowed her brow, like she disapproved. It was the first time I'd ever gotten such a reaction. I was a little disconcerted.

"Family joke," I muttered.

"Such a pretty name . . . ," she mused. "That is, if you don't know what it means."

"Oh," I said, rather at a loss for words.

"See now, like *rêve*, in French, means 'dream,' " Cynthia went on. "So here's a thought: Why not tell people you were a dream-come-true instead of a goof?"

I looked at Violet. Violet looked at me and raised her eyebrows.

"But you like being a goof, don't you, Rev?" Violet said with mock seriousness.

"Definitely. And you like being goofy, don't you, Violet?"

"Love it!"

We burst out laughing like the demented schoolgirls we were at heart.

Cynthia stared at us like we were nuts. When it was clear we didn't give a damn what she thought, she attempted to laugh with us. But Violet and I go back such a long time and we have so many private jokes that it's a closed shop, if you know what I mean. We had that conspiratorial thing between us that only old and dear friends can have. You can't beat time and history for friendship, particularly after a concert when Violet was in a mood to laugh at anything and nothing. Her laughter was infectious. Finally, we shut up, whereupon Cynthia pointed a red-nailed finger at me and declared imperiously: "I like you." It had the ring of a royal decree.

"Gosh, that means the world to me," I said with an absolutely straight face. I could feel Violet trying desperately not to start laughing again.

Cynthia went on: "I'm buying a house, and I'm gonna need a lot of stuff. You have a card?"

"Not with me."

Cynthia opened her diamond-studded clutch, took out a card, and handed it to me. "First rule of business: Always carry a card."

"I forget to on social occasions," I said.

Cynthia looked around the room. "Oh, honey, this is no social occasion. I betcha there's more business getting done here in this room tonight than'll get done in the whole of Congress next week!"

"How about next *decade*?" Violet said. "They're so pathetic, poor old Congress. All they can pass is wind!"

I laughed. Cynthia didn't crack a smile. Apparently she had no sense of humor. Of course, my father used to say that people are only taken as seriously as they take themselves and that a woman with a sense of humor will never get as far as a woman without one. But people without a sense of humor aren't much fun to be around, no matter how far they've gotten. Violet had a wicked sense of humor. It was the first thing that drew me to her back in the day. I couldn't imagine why she liked this woman and, more to the point, why she thought I'd like her.

When we went off to find our tables, I asked Violet point-blank, "Why do you find that person amusing, pray tell?"

"Cynthia? First of all, she's doing a great deal of good for the community."

"Oh, *puh-leeze* . . . It's me. *Hellooo!* You sound like a politician!"

I knew Violet well enough to know what a line of B.S. that was. Violet couldn't have cared less if someone was doing "good for the community." There were many socialites who did a lot of "good for the community" who Violet avoided like the plague because they were heavier than cheese fondues.

I stared at her, and she finally owned up. "Okay, well, her foundation is doing a lot of business with Grant's bank."

"Aha!"

"And Miss Cynical, I'm thinking of *you*," she quickly added. "Wouldn't it be nice if Cynthia bought a house and wanted *you* to decorate it? Last time I heard you could use the business. So just like her and zip it for your own good!"

As I watched her trip off to her table, confident in her own quiet way that she was in complete control of her world, I thought—not for the first time—how lucky I was to have Violet for a friend.

But that was the last night when all was what it seemed to be.

Chapter 2

At dinner I found myself seated between an empty chair and Bob Poll. Bob was one of those ageless rakes with thick salt-and-pepper hair, a military bearing, and a decade-defying face with a lot of traction on it. He could have been forty; he could have been sixty. It was impossible to tell. But judging from his success and the length of time he'd been a prominent figure in Washington, he was probably closer to sixty. Poll had made a fortune in local real estate, then parlayed his wealth into high social standing by donating often and generously to the city's most prestigious institutions. He was on the board of the Kennedy Center and the opera, but he also advised and funded other, less well-known charities, which made people inclined to respect him. He was good company, and he had a smooth way about him. The rumors of a dark side made him even more intriguing.

"What a nice surprise," Bob said as I sat down, giving me a whiff of his musky whisky breath.

Bob passed for an eligible bachelor even though he'd been involved for a number of years with Melody Hartford, an attractive lobbyist. Everyone assumed that Bob and Melody would eventually marry, but that didn't prevent him from flirting with other women, and occasionally stepping out with them.

"Hey, Bob, how're you doing?"

"Actually, better than expected." He paused to unfurl his napkin.

"Oh? What's wrong?"

He cleared his throat. "Well, I've been involved with a woman for a while . . ." He said this like I was the only person in the Western world who didn't know who he was dating.

"Melody Hartford," I interjected.

"Right. I forget that everybody knows everybody's business here."

"No, just everybody's pleasure," I said with an insincere smile.

"Well, my pleasure and I just broke up."

"You broke up with Melody?" I was genuinely surprised. "But she's here tonight. I saw her."

"Not with me."

"Wow. You guys were together a long time."

"On and off."

"You'll get back together," I said with conviction.

He looked at me askance. "What makes you say that?"

"How many times have you broken up before?"

"Too many."

"People always break up more than once. In fact, a lot of people break up right before they decide to get married," I said.

"Right. And those are the people who get married when they should get divorced. We got divorced first and saved ourselves a pre-nup."

"I'm sorry to hear that." I was actually being quite earnest.

"Don't be *too* sorry," he said.

I could see why Bob was catnip to women. He was flirtatious. Yet he gave the impression of always being slightly amused, as if he understood it was all a game and he was inviting me to play.

He glanced over to my right, where there was an empty seat. "Who's your date?"

I handed him the place card. "Senator Grider. He's not my date."

"Zack Grider. Powerful man."

"Is he? I don't know him. But then, I'm so pathetically apolitical."

"Grider's chairman of the Finance Committee."

"That's nice. What does the Finance Committee do?"

Bob looked at me askance. I couldn't figure out whether he found my naïveté charming or just plain stupid.

"It's basically like the Ways and Means Committee—maybe a little less powerful." I stared at him blankly, waiting for him to elaborate. "It looks after tax, trade, and health policies."

"I see."

"Boring, right?"

"Doesn't thrill me," I said.

He paused, staring deep into my eyes. "So what *does* thrill you, Reven Lynch?"

"Questions like that," I replied sweetly, lying through my teeth. The corn was high and ripe. But at least he was interested enough to actually ask me a question about myself, as opposed to a lot of the men in Washington, whose idea of getting to know you is talking about themselves and then asking you what you think of them.

"What thrills *you*?" I said.

He thought for a moment. "Serious answer?"

"Please."

"Danger," he said with a teasing grin.

"Interesting. Are we talking physical danger, skirting-the-law danger, or just any old kind of danger?"

Bob leaned back in his chair and tapped a fist to his stomach—meant, I supposed, to show that underneath the dress shirt and cummerbund were six-pack abs. "Anything that causes this hard old gut to contract."

"And when's the last time that happened?" I asked him.

"When you sat down beside me," he said in a low, suggestive voice.

I managed to keep somewhat of a straight face, thinking what utter and complete bullshit.

"That's quite a line," I said.

"You like it? I've got more."

I couldn't quite figure him out. Was he toying with me, flirting with me, teasing me, what? It had been so long since a man had appeared interested in me that I was flattered. Bob was very attractive in an over-the-hill-movie-star sort of way. He was one of those men who present a challenge. They're like mercury. Just when you think you have them pinned down, they scatter in a thousand directions. I was intrigued.

We batted the whiffle ball of inane conversation back and forth straight through the appetizer. Senator Grider obviously wasn't coming. That's so typical Washington. You invite senators and congressmen at your own peril because they don't show up half the time. They use Congress as an excuse. But then nothing ever seems to get done in Congress. You tell me.

Bob got antsy way before dessert. Many high-powered men can't sit still for long. They come, they see, they conquer—not necessarily in that order. He wanted to move on. Halfway into the entrée, he asked me if I wanted to "cut out" of the party. I said sure. Why not? I found Violet to tell her I didn't need a ride home, that Bob was taking me.

"Where's Melody?" she whispered.

"They broke up."

Her eyes brightened. "Go for it," she said.

As Bob and I walked out of the hall together, I caught sight of Melody Hartford, who looked quite a stunner in a low-cut red sequined dress. She stood staring at us from a distance, quivering like a flame. Bob acknowledged her with a slight nod of his head. She didn't flinch. We walked on.

"Um, I think your former girlfriend is watching us," I said.

Bob seemed unfazed. "That's her choice."

"Are you sure she knows you've broken up?"

"Oh, she knows."

Bob Poll's hunter green vintage Rolls Royce was idling outside the center. A thuggish-looking driver in a heavy black overcoat and chauffeur's cap got out of the car and lumbered around the front to open the door for us. His face was pockmarked, his neck thick as a tree trunk.

"Maxwell, this is Miss Lynch," Bob said.

"Mrs. Lynch," I corrected him. "I've been married."

Maxwell may have looked like a rutabaga, but he had a nice warm smile. He tipped his hat to me and said, "Mrs. Lynch," as he helped me into the car. Bob and I settled into the plushy back seat. Bob threw a dark green mink and cashmere throw over our legs.

"Very chic," I said, stroking the luxurious blanket.

"I had it dyed to match the car."

"Where to, Boss?" Maxwell asked, eyeing me in the rearview mirror. I bet he'd seen quite a few women in my seat.

"Just a minute. You tired?" Bob asked me.

"Not particularly. No."

"Want to go for a drive?"

"Sure."

"Drive around, Maxwell," he said without elaboration.

We sped along the parkway next to the darkly glistening Potomac River. As we passed the Jefferson Memorial, glowing like a big iridescent pearl against the midnight sky, Bob took hold of my hand and said, "Beautiful city, Washington."

"Yes, indeed. Pierre L'Enfant did a great job." His hand was warm.

"So, Reven, you're one of those people I know but don't really know . . . and I'd like to know a lot better," he added.

"How many times have you said that to women in the back of this car?"

He punched his chest and feigned hurt. "Oof! You got me! But you can't deny we've been flirting with each other for years."

"You flirt with everyone. It's part of your mystique."

"My mystique? I have a mystique, do I?" he said like he knew full well he did.

"Yes. You know that."

"Not really, no. What is my mystique?"

"Oh, that you're flirtatious and you like beautiful women and you're good company and . . ."

"And . . . ?"

"That you have a dark side."

"A dark side," he said, amused. "That's good to hear. I sound interesting."

"Yes, you do. . . . So what happened with you and Melody? Why'd you two really break up?"

"Honest answer? Mel's a great girl. But there are certain things about me she couldn't or wouldn't understand. And I need a woman who will understand those things."

"Like what kinds of things?"

He squeezed my hand. "What say you and I get to know each other a little better? Then I'll tell you, if you're still interested."

Well, I was definitely interested—which was a *really* bad sign. If I'm interested in a guy, trust me, he's a bounder-in-waiting no matter how good he looks at first. My mother always told me I was a "bad picker." And once I had this shrink who said to me: "Reven, when all your bells go off for a guy, don't run, *gallop* in the other direction!" A freaking *shrink* told me this—that's what a bad track record I have.

It was a typical first date, filled with flirtation and falsity. Long ago, I figured out that dating is like campaigning: you don't reveal who you really are or what you're really up to until you get elected. But that night I could feel myself being inexorably drawn to Bob Poll. Don't you love the way that sounds? Being *inexorably drawn* to some-one. God help me, I'm such a romantic. I'm sure that's what a lot of women say just before some guy bashes their skull in.

Chapter 3

The next morning Violet called me at the crack of dawn to dish the party and to find out how things had gone with Bob Poll. I told her nothing much had happened and that he'd dropped me off at my house.

"He was a perfect gentleman . . . unfortunately," I said.

"Did he ask you out again?"

"No."

"He will. Mark my words."

Although Violet had lived like a nun before she met Grant, there was something about being happily married that made her think she knew everything there was to know about relationships. She and Grant had been married for fifteen years. They had one child, a tow-headed boy named Grant Bolton III, called "Tee" for the third, so he wouldn't be confused with his father or his grandfather. When Tee was a baby, Violet constantly showed him off as if he were an accessory: Tee on one arm, designer bag on the other. Sometimes I felt she acted like the boy was the proof of *her* legitimacy, rather than the other way around. But she was justly proud of her little "nuclear family," as she referred to it. And like any good friend, she wanted me to settle down and be as happy as she was. She was always trying to fix me up or advise me on my relationships.

Violet suggested we go for a jog and talk about a "game plan" to get Mr. Poll more interested. We agreed to meet at our usual starting point: the entrance to Montrose Park. I made myself a cup of coffee and checked out the newspaper before heading outside. Cynthia

Rinehart's one-hundred-million-dollar bequest to the Kennedy Center had made the front page of the *Washington Post*. In the Style section was an account of the Symphony Ball along with several pictures of the attendees, including a picture of Cynthia in conversation with Violet (I was visible in the background), and one of me and Bob Poll in a tête-à-tête at dinner. I cut that one out to save.

———

Georgetown is like a little gingerbread village with its colorful row houses, narrow streets, stately shade trees, and postage-stamp front gardens. Everything's within walking distance, but nearly everyone has a car, so parking's a bitch unless you have a garage. I don't. I'd rather rent a car than give up a parking space. I live in a narrow yellow row house on P Street between Twenty-ninth and Thirtieth. It's only a few blocks away from my shop on Wisconsin. I bought it years ago, right after my husband and I got divorced and before the real estate market took off, and it's now mortgaged to the hilt. It's a cozy little place, painted in bright colors, furnished with comfy sofas and chairs, plus what's left of the antiques and paintings from my parents' estate. Over the years, I've been forced to sell off most of the best pieces to keep afloat. But I try not to dwell on the past.

That morning, the sun was out, the sky was blue, the air was crisp, and the leaves were fire-licked with brilliant autumn colors. It was a gorgeous fall day. Or maybe it wasn't. Maybe it was overcast. Maybe I just thought it was gorgeous because, let's face it, nothing beats the prospect of a new romance for lifting one's mood. And I was thinking about Bob Poll.

Sure, I knew his reputation. Who didn't? It was almost a joke. Violet once said Bob was like the Washington Monument: "A big phallic symbol you can visit but you can't move into." He was a lady-killer. So what? I mean, we all love lady-killers because they're such a challenge. You always think you're gonna be the one to tame him. It usually doesn't work out that way. But, hey, you gotta have hope.

I walked up Thirty-first with a new spring in my step. At R Street, police cars were racing up and down the block, lights flashing. I wondered if some political bigwig was in the neighborhood, or if there'd been an accident. The possibility of a terrorist attack crossed my mind because terror was at the back of all our minds these days. When I

turned the corner, a chaotic scene of police cars, officers, and specta-
tors greeted me. Judging from the grim faces, I figured something
horrible had happened. I asked a guy walking his dog if he knew what
was going on.

"They found a body in the park," he said, and quickly moved on.

I walked off in search of Violet. She emerged from the middle of a
small crowd, trotting toward me in a state of high excitement.

"The Beltway Basher has struck again!" she cried breathlessly.
"He's killed another woman. They cordoned off the whole park!"

"Oh, my God! Are they sure it's the same guy?"

"It's gotta be him. The police aren't talking, but I just ran into this
reporter who gave me the scoop," she said.

I was pretty sure she hadn't just run into a reporter who voluntarily gave her the scoop, as she put it. I was pretty sure she'd mowed
down some poor hack and tortured the details out of him. When Violet wanted something, she got it. And there was nothing she wanted
more than info on a good, juicy homicide.

Violet was a serial killer buff. It was her hobby, after gardening.
She watched every single forensic show on television and read anything she could get her hands on that involved murder, although true
crime books were her favorite. Some people read passages of poetry
and prose aloud to friends. Violet read me descriptions of gruesome
deaths and twisted minds.

Thanks to her, I knew more about sado-sexual psychopaths than I
ever wanted to. The fact that one was now on the loose in Washington
was music to her ears. If the Beltway Basher had indeed struck again—
and in our very own neighborhood, of all places—nothing would stop
Violet from ferreting out every last grisly detail of the crime.

Apparently, a dog off its leash went snuffling around in the woods
and exposed the body. According to Violet, whose account I took with
a pillar of salt, the victim was lying facedown in the dirt. Her head was
"split open like a ripe melon oozing pulp," and her bare buttocks were
peeking out from a pile of rotting leaves, "like a pair of moons." Her
words. The rampant glee in my friend's voice was vaguely disconcerting but not unexpected. Violet had absorbed every scrap of information
that was available pertaining to the prior murders. She was convinced
we had a "local Ted Bundy" on our hands. Ted Bundy was Violet's all-
time favorite serial killer because he was so "talented." Also her word.

"Ted pioneered so many of the clever ruses they all use now—like feigning an injury and removing the door handle from the passenger side of his car so the victim can't escape," she said with disconcerting admiration.

But what seemed to intrigue her most about him was that his persona was the exact opposite of who he really was."Ted Bundy was handsome, charming, and lethal—just the kind of man *you're* always attracted to," she once said to me, much to my dismay.

Violet, who had miraculously transformed herself from an ugly duckling into a swan, hated it when people were judged solely by their looks. Ted Bundy confirmed her view that you never really know who people are. "Very often, the prettier the person, the uglier the inner monster," she asserted.

I must admit that I too was fascinated by these current crimes. However, Montrose Park was a little too close to home for me, if not for Violet. It was shocking and scary to think that a killer had come so near. This was Georgetown, for heaven's sake—fashionable, gentrified Georgetown—the social heart of our nation's capital! Things like this just didn't happen here. Except now they did.

"Just think, Rev, that could have been us!" Violet exclaimed, as though the idea titillated her more than it frightened her.

The police weren't letting anyone into the park. Television crews had arrived, and the crowd was growing. Naturally, Violet wanted to stick around. She was like a rubbernecker at the scene of a traffic accident, desperate to get a glimpse of the gore. But I saw no point in all this crepe-hanging. I figured I'd hear all about it on the evening news. And, frankly, the evening news was as close as I wanted to get.

Chapter 4

Lynch Antiques occupied three floors of an old brick building on Wisconsin Avenue between P and Q Streets. My aim was to create the kind of chic, eclectic environment where one could either find the perfect little gift for a special occasion or furnish a whole house in one fell swoop. The front rooms on the first floor were like drawing rooms, crammed with furniture, paintings, chandeliers, and bric-a-brac of all different styles and periods—everything from seventeenth-century Russian icons to a Tony Duquette paper screen with coral finials. The stock ranged from good quality to decorative junk. The second floor was mainly dedicated to tableware and fine linens displayed on antique dining tables and beds. My office was there too—a small back room overlooking a small back garden. The third floor was storage.

The front door bell tinkled as I walked into the shop. Rosina Alvarez, my manager, looked up from her computer. She didn't even wait for me to take off my coat before she said, "Bad news."

"You heard about it already?" News really did travel fast these days.

She held up a sheaf of bills and fanned them in front of me. "These are way past due."

Rosina had the face of a madonna and the sales skills of P. T. Barnum. She was nothing if not direct.

"I take it you don't know there's been a murder in Montrose Park," I said.

"There's gonna be one right here if you don't pay these bills *today*."

"Did you hear what I just said? They found another woman murdered right up there in Montrose Park. I jog there all the time."

She shrugged. "See why I don't exercise? It's too dangerous."

"That's five women he's killed now. Montrose Park is right around the corner. You don't think this is serious? This is really serious."

"Don't obsess. It's bad for your blood pressure, and it doesn't help anything."

Rosina could be so irritating at times, mainly because she was the most unflappable person I knew. She wasn't an obsesser like me. She took life one step at a time and didn't waste energy worrying about the future or regretting the past like I did on an almost daily basis. But she was also young.

"Obsessing comes with age, like wrinkles. One day you'll obsess, just like I do," I told her.

"I doubt it," she said flatly, handing me the stack of bills.

I gave them a cursory glance.

"You know what? I'm just not going to worry about these right now. It's a gorgeous day out there—murder notwithstanding—and guess what? I'm *happy*!"

Rosina shook her head. "Oh-oh . . . I hope he's rich and he has a house he wants you to decorate."

She knew me so well. She knew I had a new man in my sights.

"Don't be such a smart-ass," I said.

"Why not? Someone around here has to be smart about something."

She went back to the books, and I poured myself a cup of muddy coffee from the communal pot. I headed upstairs to my office on the second floor. Sitting behind my desk, I sipped my coffee and stared out at the back garden, dotted with wrought-iron furniture and whimsical stone statuary—the outdoor stuff I couldn't fit inside the store. It usually looked like a graveyard to me. But today it seemed as amusing as a country fair.

I started sifting through the bills. They weren't so amusing. Lynch Antiques was always in the red. I was born with a good eye, and I could never resist a beautiful piece of furniture or a wonderful old painting. I referred to myself as the Grand Acquisitor, and I was always broke. Plus, the whole antiques business had been in the toilet lately, which made things twice as bad. All the dealers were complaining about it.

I felt like ripping up the whole bunch of bills and just throwing them into the air like confetti. But instead, I began the tedious process of arranging them according to which of my creditors was less likely to put a contract out on me if I stiffed them yet another month.

About a half an hour later, Rosina buzzed me and told me to come downstairs.

"I can't. I'm in the middle of committing suicide," I told her.

"You will want to live when you see what's down here."

When I got downstairs, Rosina was playfully peeking out from behind a monstrous vase filled with red roses, which she had placed on the center table.

"He must be rich," she said in a singsong voice, handing me a card.

I opened it with great anticipation. The note read: "Loved being with you last night. Bob." It wasn't handwritten. It was typed on a florist's card. But I didn't hold that against him. I knew he was a busy man. If I'd held anything against him, it would have been the bright red roses, because they are so prosaic and predictable. But you can't have everything.

Rosina wanted to know who they were from, and when I told her they were from Bob Poll, she immediately said, "What happened to Melody Hartford?"

Rosina faithfully read the Reliable Source column in the *Post*, and social magazines like the *Washingtonian, Capitol File*, and *Washington Life*. Bob was always in them, usually with Melody on his arm—but sometimes not. I told her that they'd broken up.

"He's available now. He took me home from the Symphony Ball last night," I said.

Rosina rolled her eyes. Her reaction was predictable. She'd lived with me through so many boyfriends, she was entitled to be a little skeptical. I seemed to have a knack for finding guys who were either newly divorced, getting divorced, or fresh out of some torturous long-term relationship that had left them scarred and unable to commit. Though this might be a description of half the men in the world, it was always the half I seemed to find.

Since my divorce umpteen years ago, all my romances had had an oddly similar trajectory: a whoosh of enthusiasm followed either by a fast puncture or slow deflation. There was always a nail in the tire somewhere. But one must live in hope, and I was absolutely thrilled to get those roses—bloody red as they were. Quite frankly, I didn't appreciate Rosina's uh-oh-here-we-go-again face, dismissing me like I was a third-party candidate with no hope.

I tried to explain to her that when you're single and my age, you can't be too choosy, that most of the men I met either were married or had been in some kind of relationship before me. It was almost unavoidable. But Rosina was twenty-four, not forty-three like me, and she was blissfully engaged to a twenty-eight-year-old contractor who was probably her first beau. What the hell did she know about life?

"Don't be such a pessimist," I told her. "As my father used to say, 'It only takes one.'"

"And my father used to say, 'Don't drink at a poison well.'"

What the hell *that* meant, I have no idea. Nor did I ask.

I called Violet to tell her about the flowers.

"Red roses and a typewritten card, right?" she said.

"How did you know?"

"Everyone knows Mr. Poll's MO, darling. He sent my friend Linda Hawthorne red roses for twelve straight days. Get set for the onslaught. He's after you."

"What happened with Linda Hawthorne?"

"He dumped her. But she's such a pain in the ass, who could blame him? That doesn't mean he'll dump you if you play your cards right."

"And how do I play my cards right, pray tell?"

"Don't sleep with him right away. Think of yourself as Anne Boleyn. Hold out as long as you can until you get the ring."

"And then what? He beheads me?"

"At least you'll have the crown. . . . Oh, and FYI, Miss Montrose—? I actually saw them take away her body. Someone told me they think she's been dead for at least a week, and you know what that means."

"No, what?"

"That we probably jogged past her a couple of times."

"Jesus."

"Don't you just wish *we'd* found her? How exciting would *that* have been? Huh?"

"You are so sinister," I said.

———

Rosina left work early that day to go on her endless hunt for the perfect wedding dress. I manned the front of the shop. A few people dropped in to browse or shoot the breeze, including a couple of my fellow shopkeepers. Everyone was talking about the murder. Toward the end of the day, a rather somber-faced African-American man with dreadlocks walked in the door while I was talking to another customer. He was kind of attractive. He wandered into the next room. I excused myself and followed him. He stood with his hands behind his back, gazing up at one of the paintings on the wall. He was dressed all in black—black suit, black shirt, black tie. A diamond stud twinkled in his left ear. He was not my usual customer.

"Can I help you?" I asked.

"Thomas Wootten . . . helluva painter," he said without looking at me.

"I'm impressed. You know your art."

"No. But I can read," he said, pointing to the small white card on a nearby table: "*Horn, King George's Stallion*, by Thomas Wootten, 1795."

"Oh. My assistant must have just typed that up. It should be tacked up under the painting. Thanks for noticing," I said, affixing it to the wall.

"It's my job to notice things. . . . Detective Gunner, D.C. Police Department," he said, showing me his ID.

"Reven Lynch." We shook hands. "Gunner . . . Great name for a detective."

He shrugged as if he'd heard that one a million times before. "So this is your place. Very nice," he said, nodding his approval.

I was pretty sure he'd come about the murder. But I didn't want to appear rude, so I said: "Are you looking for something special, or are you just browsing?"

"You hear about that murder up in Montrose Park?"

"Are you *kidding*? Who hasn't? It's all anyone's talking about. I always go jogging in that park. It's really scary. You think it's that serial killer again?"

He didn't answer. "So how long have you had this shop?"

"Uh . . . oh, I guess about eight years now."

"How's business?"

"These days not great. The whole economy is screwed. But I'm surviving."

"You from Washington originally?"

"No, New York. Can't you tell, darling?" I drawled, striking a pose. He looked a little mystified. I don't think he found me all that amusing.

Detective Gunner had the style of a hip-hop star. He was around five-ten, a little taller than me—a neat, compact man, who obviously took great pride in his appearance and the way he dressed. He looked a little worn out, though—kind of like his shirt, which was crisply pressed but faded from wear.

"Well, I'm just kinda canvassing the neighborhood. You don't get a lot of murders in Georgetown. You happen to remember anything odd or out of the ordinary in the past week or so?"

"Nope. It's all been just business and gossip as usual!" I said cheerily.

"Hear a lot of gossip, do you?"

"In this shop? Are you kidding? I hear *everything*. For some reason, when people are browsing around together and talking, they don't think other people are listening. But, trust me, I am!"

"If you hear anything interesting, give me a call, will you?"

He took out a card, wrote his cell phone number on the back, and handed it to me.

"Thanks for your time," he said.

We shook hands again. There was no arrogance about him, no swagger—only a hint of weariness in his lively dark eyes, as if nothing in the world could surprise him except perhaps an act of pure kindness.

Chapter 5

After that opening salvo of roses, I didn't hear from Bob Poll again, which was a little surprising, not to mention disappointing. Every time the phone rang, I thought it might be him. It never was. Ten days later, I was upstairs working in my office when Rosina buzzed me and said in a coy voice, "You have a visitor." I was sure it was Bob. I checked myself out in the mirror and took my time walking downstairs. I didn't want him to think I was anxious. When I reached the ground floor, Rosina pointed to the back room, where Detective Gunner was examining a Japanese screen.

"You didn't tell me he was so cute," Rosina whispered.

I felt slightly deflated that it wasn't Bob, but I didn't let my disappointment show. I walked over and greeted him warmly.

"Detective! Good to see you again."

"Hey, Ms. Lynch. Nice screen. Edo period?"

"Yes. You have good taste."

"I like Japanese art."

"I'll give you a good deal. I've had it awhile."

"Nah. . . . Thanks anyway. Look, uh, is there somewhere we can talk privately?"

"Follow me."

I showed him upstairs to my office. He sat down on the couch and declined my offer of coffee. I sat behind my desk, folded my hands primly, and said, "So what can I do for you?"

He pulled a picture out of his pocket and handed it to me. It was a snapshot of a woman. It looked like the photo on a driver's license.

"You recognize her?"

I studied the picture for a long moment.

"No. Who is she?"

"Her name is—*was*—Nancy Sawtelle."

"Oh, my God! Is that—? That's not the woman who was murdered up in Montrose Park, is it?" He nodded. I took a closer look at the photo. "Wow. Poor woman."

"You never saw her around here?"

"I don't remember her. You can ask Rosina."

"Unfortunately, it's the only shot we have of her. The autopsy pictures aren't usable for identification."

"That bad?"

"Yeah," he said softly, sliding the picture back into his pocket.

He slumped back on the couch. He seemed tired.

"Sure you don't want some coffee or something? Water? A soda?"

"No, thanks. Know what I'd like?"

"What?"

"A tour of the shop."

"Really? Are you interested in antiques?"

"Kinda. You mind?"

"Are you kidding? I'd be delighted."

I had fun showing Gunner around. It wasn't every day I met someone who was genuinely interested in learning about some of the pieces I had in stock—not to buy them, but just to know about them, what drew me to them, how and where I'd acquired them. Just when I was ruing the fact that I'd ever gotten into the antiques business to begin with because I was in such debt, Gunner came along to remind me how much I loved my little shop, and how proud I was of it. Besides, as we walked from room to room, I felt he was sizing me up as much as he was the furniture, and I felt kind of flattered. He was cute, like Rosina said.

After the tour, we went back upstairs to my office, and this time he accepted my offer of coffee. He asked me how I'd gotten into the antiques business. I told him that I used to be a decorator, but that I'd always wanted to open a shop.

"I like being my own boss," I said.

I asked him how he'd gotten to be a detective. He said, "When you grow up where I grew up, you've basically got two choices: you're either with the law or against it. My older brother was against it. He got shot. I figured I'd try the other route."

Gunner wasn't too much more specific about his background, but we did talk about some of his cases. He seemed most proud of the work he'd done several years back on the Beltway sniper case, in which ten people were shot and killed and three others critically wounded while they were minding their business, doing mundane things like mowing the lawn, pumping gas, or getting on a school bus.

"Everyone was looking for a white guy in a white van. Then it turned out to be two black guys in a blue car. But we got 'em," Gunner said.

He proudly showed me a newspaper clipping featuring a picture of himself among a group of officers as they arrested Lee Boyd Malvo, the young sniper.

"That's me," he said. "Second from the left in the back row."

He looked a lot younger then, even though it wasn't all that long ago. When he left the shop that day, I'd kind of wondered why he'd dropped by.

In the weeks that followed, Gunner came to visit a few times just to shoot the breeze. Rosina joked that it was because he had a crush on me, and I joked that it was because he had a crush on her. But in truth, it didn't really seem as if he had a crush on either of us. He was simply interested in getting to know me as a friend. He wanted to know all about me, what my background was, where I'd gone to school, how I happened to wind up in Washington. I told him that I'd lived here briefly when I was a young girl. My father was a lawyer with an international practice. He and my mother moved down to D.C. for a brief period of time in the early '80s so he could open a branch of the firm here. We had a house in Kalorama with a pool and a garden. I had wonderful memories of the place and moved here after design school. It was a cheaper, gentler place to live than New York—much less competitive and hard-edged, provided you weren't in politics.

Gunner said he'd seen my picture in a couple of magazines at various social events. I think he was impressed. At least, he said he was. The social world seemed to intrigue him. He was always asking about the parties I went to and the people I knew. I got invited to a lot of big parties, ones you didn't necessarily have to pay for, and I asked him if he ever wanted to tag along. I thought he'd be a cool escort. But he declined.

Then one afternoon he came in, asking to speak to me in private again. I showed him upstairs to my office. He clearly had something weighty on his mind. He fidgeted a lot and looked sheepish.

"Look, I, um . . . I haven't been totally honest with you," he began.

I went on alert. "You haven't?"

"Nope." He flashed his dark velvet eyes at me and expelled a hard sigh, like this was difficult for him. "Fact is, I need your help."

"I'm listening."

Gunner explained that he was part of a "special task force" assigned to investigate Nancy Sawtelle's murder, as well as the four other murders the police suspected to be the work of the Beltway Basher. By this point, I knew quite a lot about "Miss Montrose," as Violet had dubbed her. The papers had reported that Sawtelle fit the same general pattern as the other four women. She was a brunette who was bludgeoned to death in a wooded area and who maintained an apartment near Dupont Circle. The one difference was that she was older than the others by some twenty years.

As I said, I've always been more interested in crimes where I could have been the victim, so this one utterly fascinated me. Not only was Nancy Sawtelle around my age, she'd been murdered in a park I frequented, a park whose tranquil beauty was the setting for dog walkers, joggers, family outings, and the innocent routines of daily life.

"How can I help you?" I asked him.

"Well, I've been coming around here with kind of a purpose in mind."

"Oh?" I said warily.

"You go to a lot of these society events, and you're friends with a lot of fancy folk, right?"

"I guess."

"The guy who's doing these girls . . . ? We have reason to believe he's someone in your world—you know, so-ci-ety." *So-sigh-a-tee*, he pronounced it, with a wink in his voice.

"Yeah, we've actually heard that too."

He perked up. "You have?"

"Yeah. There's been this rumor going around for ages that the Belt-way Basher's a big shot. My friend Violet and I are always joking about it. Maybe it's because of that intern who was killed years ago. You know, the one who was supposedly having the affair with the congressman . . . ? So the police think it's some powerful guy too?"

"Could be. We haven't had much to go on up to now. But we may have caught a break. . . . Look, I'm gonna tell you something I'm not supposed to be telling you. Can I trust you?" He held my gaze for a long moment.

"Yes, you can," I said solemnly.

"Well, even if I can't, I don't really have a lotta options here," he said, like he was talking to himself. He hesitated another moment, then said: "We found a calendar in Nancy Sawtelle's apartment. She was tracking this guy she identified as 'X.' "

Gunner went on to describe the calendar as "one of those month-at-a-glance wall jobs with pictures of harp seals and leopards and all kinds of adorable endangered shit on it." He said that Nancy Sawtelle had written entries in the little individual day boxes, like for example, "X @ KenCen" or "X @ Smith," which he thought stood for the Smithsonian. He showed me how she always used the "internet A," as Gunner called it. He figured she was stalking some guy, and the guy she was stalking could very well turn out to be her killer. He said the police didn't know a whole lot about Nancy Sawtelle. Her fingerprints didn't show up on the national data-base. All they knew was that she'd moved to D.C. about eight months prior to her death. She'd rented a small apartment near Dupont Circle, and she'd had a couple of jobs waiting tables.

"This calendar is key," Gunner went on. "The guy she was track-ing . . . ? He goes to a lot of social events. She's got him at the National Gallery, the Phillips, the Folger, the Smithsonian. But there's only one place where he went where we know that *all* our other victims went too—"

"Where's that?"

"The Kennedy Center. Her last entry reads, 'X @ KenCen.' That was the night of the Symphony Ball."

"Oh, my God, I was *there*!"

"I know. I saw your picture in the paper."

"But how do you know this guy she was tracking is your serial killer?"

"We don't. But it's still one helluva link. And, frankly, at this point it's the only new lead we got."

"So, assuming that this guy *is* the killer, you think he met all these women at the Kennedy Center?"

Gunner shrugged. "Met them, saw them, invited them there maybe. I hear tell some of these guys like to have their girlfriends go to the same events as their wives. Gives 'em a charge. You ever hear that?"

"I told you I hear everything in this shop."

"That's what I figured."

"Why don't you make a list of the events she marked in the calendar and compare it to a list of the people who attended those events?"

Gunner smiled for the first time ever. The smile lit up his face and made him look years younger. He said gently, "Now, why didn't *I* think of that?"

I got the point and felt stupid for suggesting it. "Okay. So you've already done that. Don't you have any suspects?"

"A few . . . *hundred.*" He sprang up from the couch and paced around. "Shit! It's like all you same damn people go to all the same damn parties all the same damn time! Don't you guys ever get sick of each other?"

I chuckled. "You have *no* idea."

"Well, I need to *get* an idea because I believe there's a stone cold killer hiding in plain sight in this town."

"Oh, I can think of several! Some of them are in power."

"All kidding aside, Reven, those rumors you all have been hearing may be true. This guy may actually *be* a prominent person—someone you know, or know of."

I sank back in my chair. "Wow. . . . This isn't a joke, is it?"

Gunner reached into his jacket pocket and pulled out four pictures he'd cut out from magazines. He laid them down on the desk in front of me, one at a time, in a row. Each picture was a group shot of some partygoers, the kinds of photos that appear on the glossy patchwork pages of *Capitol File* and *Washington Life*. In each photo, the head of one girl in the group was circled in blue ink. None of the circled girls was identified by name in print. Each girl just happened to be standing near some celebrity or social couple who were the photographer's real target and who were mentioned in the caption below. The circled girls were unidentified—just four more anonymous pretty faces on the fringes of a big social event. Gunner didn't have to tell me who they were.

"The dead girls?" I said.

He nodded. "Murdered in the meanest way. See what they all have in common?"

"They're all cute young brunettes wearing bad dresses? Sorry!"

"What the *pictures* have in common."

I studied them more closely. "I don't know. . . . They're group shots, party pictures. . . . All in the same magazine? I don't know."

"Where are all these parties?"

I looked again and recognized the unmistakable red carpet in one, the giant columns in another, the gift shop in another.

"The Kennedy Center," I said.

"That's correct. So we got Nancy Sawtelle's calendar and we got the Kennedy Center. And those are the only two leads we have."

Gunner added Nancy Sawtelle's driver's license to the group. He pointed to each picture in turn. "Bianca Symonds . . . Maria Dixon . . . Liza Cooley . . . Dinise Shevette . . . Nancy Sawtelle . . . These girls had names. They had lives. Now they're gone," he said, as if that really meant something to him.

He collected the pictures one by one with care, like he was gathering flowers. He sat back down on the couch, slowly sifting through the bunch before putting them back in his pocket. I didn't say anything. I just watched him. He wasn't detached and matter-of-fact like some detectives you see on TV. These murders seemed to have affected him very deeply. I felt sorry for him.

"I don't know how I can help you, but I will if I can," I said.

"Okay, look, I got a hunch. But in order for me to play it out, I gotta get to know a lot more about society and society people. Right now that world's got glass around it. You all are just a bunch of colorful fish swimming around in this big old aquarium. I don't have any idea who the real players are. But *you* know that world. You know who the really important people are—not just the ones who get their pictures in the paper. You know how things really work."

"Unfortunately, I do. Social life may look like it's all jewels and clothes and parties. But actually, it's helmets, guns, and trenches. Trust me, it's a war zone."

"Like life," he said. "But you gotta know the lies of a world before you can find out the truth."

"I guess."

"So . . . you know what a confidential informant is?"

"A CI? A snitch? Indeed I do," I said proudly. "My friend Violet Bolton has taught me all the crime slang."

"Oh, yeah? She interested in crime, is she?"

"Violet? She's a crime addict. She should have been a detective."

"That right? Well, I need a snitch—someone who'll report back to me on all the social stuff going on in Washington. The dirt. Who's doin' what, and who's doin' who."

"And you think I can do this?"

"I know you *can*. The question is, *will* you?"

"Sure!"

As thrilled as I was with my ersatz Mata Hari assignment, I confessed that I didn't think there was a whole lot going on at the moment—that is, no new affairs or social wars I could think of. But Gunner wasn't deterred. He told me to start with the Symphony Ball, telling him who was there and what the event was like. I gave him a blow-by-blow. Told him about Grant and Violet. Told him about Cynthia and the big donation. Naturally, I mentioned Bob, but I didn't go into detail, since I hadn't heard from him since getting those damn roses.

When I finished, Gunner said, "You know a lot more than you think. You're just used to it all, so a lot of things don't seem strange to you like they do to me. Think of me as a visitor in a foreign country and yourself as a native. You gotta explain things to me that you take for granted."

"Yes, but very often visitors see things the natives don't," I pointed out.

"Let's hope."

When Gunner was getting ready to leave, I joked I was pretty sure I didn't know any killers, but that there were a few people I wouldn't mind killing.

"Yeah? Like who, for instance?"

"Like come into my shop on a Saturday afternoon and take your pick."

He tried to look appreciative, but I knew he didn't think that was funny, especially under the circumstances.

"I won't come here again," he said. "We'll meet somewhere else. I'll let you know where. I have your word now, right? No telling anyone about me or that you're helping me, okay? Trust me, no one likes the police snooping around in their business."

I'm not sure why Gunner chose me except that I was accessible. I had a shop. He hung around. It was fairly easy for him to get to know me. And besides, I wasn't really *in* society, but more on the fringe. It was true I knew most of the players and had my picture taken at big events because of the shop and because I had a certain standing, I guess. But it was mainly because a few of the gossip columnists and editors were my pals and my customers. Also, unlike politicians and most socialites, I had nothing to lose by talking to him. So talk I did, without reservation or fear of reprisal.

At the front door, he paused and said: "Remember, Reven, people never expect evil to look like them."

Woo woo. That sent a creepy chill right down the old spine.

The instant Gunner left, Rosina asked me what we'd been talking about all that time. When I told her, "Antiques," she just laughed.

Chapter 6

Gunner made me swear to keep our relationship a secret—which I did. Swear, I mean. I didn't keep it to myself. I told Violet. I told Violet everything. Violet told me everything. We were best friends, after all. We gabbed to each other on an almost daily basis, dishing the dirt, no holds barred. Years ago, we made this pact never, ever, *ever, ever* to repeat any of the stuff we told each other. If half of what we said to each other ever got out, there would have been a lot more murders in Georgetown.

Her reaction was predictable. She said, "If he wants to know about Washington society, how come he didn't ask *me*?"

It's true that Violet was a much bigger deal in town than I was. It was also true that she would have given her eyeteeth to be a detective's confidential informant, particularly one who was working on a serial killer case. I knew the implied superiority in her comment was unintended. However, it was moments like this that reminded me of how much things had changed since Violet and I first met.

I'd known Violet Bolton—Violet McCloud, as she was called then—since our days at Wheelock Academy, one of the last of the "all girls" schools in the country, located just outside of Providence, Rhode Island. Wheelock was not a great school by any standard. My father compared it to an odd-lot house on Wall Street, because it was known for accepting troubled or less than stellar students. To be honest, my grades never reflected what I think of as my intelligence. I was always more creative than analytical. Wheelock was the only boarding school I could get into at the time.

Violet was my roommate for three grueling years in that gilded detention center. I couldn't help but feel great loyalty to my companion in adolescence, a grim, unsteady, and altogether miserable phase of life. We were all of us in a chrysalis, waiting to take flight. I was a butterfly. Violet was a moth.

I was a star back then, if I do say so myself. The fact that I was the only girl from New York didn't hurt. It meant that I enjoyed a certain celebrity among my peers right off the bat. They thought I was more sophisticated. I was—at least, I convinced them that I was. Sophistication was a language I claimed to speak with absolute fluency. And who could dispute me? It was rather like saying: "I'm an expert on Chinese poetry of the tenth century, *and you prove I'm not!*" I dropped all these sophisticated New York names, and the girls loved it because New York was this big, shimmering Oz of a city they were all dying to go to and to which I actually belonged.

Not only that, I had all the accoutrements of sophistication: my very own gold Dupont lighter (which I'd filched from my mother), fashionable clothes, purchased from the best New York department stores, and loads and loads of pretentious conversation that no one at Wheelock dared challenge. I wasn't nearly as secure or informed as I made out, but my classmates didn't seem to notice. Some of those girls were so provincial they didn't even know what an astringent was. I told them flatly: "*I'm* an astringent."

An adoring clique of girls listened to me night after night as I regaled them with tales of delicious decadence and debauchery in the Big Apple—all the product of my youthful imagination. I was seductive, no question. But I was also very nice to everyone, which is why people liked me. And to be honest, I was gorgeous—a Valkyrie among trolls. Being gorgeous somehow made me a natural leader. Nor did it hurt that boys found me attractive. I was the first girl in my class to be invited on a college weekend—the Harvard-Yale game—by a Harvard senior, no less.

Violet McCloud showed up at Wheelock in our sophomore year. She was from Natick, Massachusetts, a town whose great claim to fame at the time was that it was the home of Tampax. Needless to say, compared to Natick, New York was the clear winner in the cosmopolitan sweepstakes. Violet was a very odd girl, which is probably why they stuck us together as roommates, because I was so popular and she was such a geek. They thought I'd help her along. And they were right.

Violet was smart as a whip, but clumsy—one of those girls who's either tripping over her own feet or getting under yours all the time. Her thick mole-colored hair looked as if someone had put a bowl over her head and cut around it. Her face was pudgy and very pale, but her eyes were sharp and blue, like two sapphires stuck in the middle of a tapioca pudding. When she first arrived at school, she was very unhappy and gloomy, and she cried all the time. I called her "my little rain McCloud." She made no effort to fit in, and our classmates roundly shunned her. I didn't much like her either at first, and I was pissed off at the school for sticking me with her.

However, I soon discovered that Violet had this wonderfully macabre sense of humor, which I really appreciated, even if others didn't. She had honed the art of amusingly gruesome conversation, and she could really make me laugh. Despite her flaccid appearance, she was sharp as a tack, and she never missed a trick. I learned that her quirky personality had a lot to do with all her problems at home. She told me her father had left her mom for a gym teacher half his age who worked in the local high school. Violet was wounded and mortified by the whole situation, which is why she never invited anyone home with her on vacations and also why she hated to go home herself.

God help me, I always love an underdog, so I insisted she be included in the cool group of girls, of which I, of course, was the undisputed leader. Everyone understood that if you were mean to Violet, you had to deal with me.

Throughout our three years at Wheelock, Violet and I became inseparable. People would see us walking together and say, "There goes Reven and her handmaiden." We looked like a champagne flute and a Toby jug. Then I went off to the prestigious Rhode Island School of Design to study art and interior design. I wasn't sure what I wanted to do, but I knew it would definitely be something creative and probably earth-shattering. Violet applied to five colleges but only got into one: DePaul University in Chicago. The day of our graduation from Wheelock, I think it's safe to say that there was no doubt in anyone's mind, including my own, that I would sail through life and Violet would sink like a stone.

But something happened. Or didn't happen, as the case may be.

With so many possibilities open to me, I found it hard to choose one particular path or one particular person—if you don't count my brief marriage to a painter, which ended in a quick divorce. Just when I got a foothold somewhere, I balked, thinking something or someone better would come along. I drifted along under the mistaken impression that my youth and beauty would never end, and that I would succeed in life just because everyone said I would. I felt entitled to great things, whereas Violet was always astonished when anything good happened to her. She beavered away, one step at a time, forging a path that was actually leading somewhere. I was just going with the flow, as we used to say.

Even though we lost touch for a few years after graduation, I always knew what Violet was up to because of the long and detailed entries she sent in to *Passages*, Wheelock's alumnae bulletin. No one wrote in to our "Class Notes" more frequently than Violet. And no one had more positive news. It was almost as if she wanted to make up for her rank unpopularity by showing everyone there was indeed life after boarding school.

I followed Violet's career—from her graduation magna cum laude from DePaul University, to the University of Southern California Law School, to her pro bono stint on the Osage Reservation in Oklahoma, to her move to Washington, D.C., as an environmental lobbyist on Capitol Hill, with interest and, I have to say, hefty amounts of incredulity. I never thought that Violet, a moody, mousy girl, had it in her to do so unbelievably well—and honestly, much better than yours truly.

I was the one who had a series of unsuccessful careers tethered to a string of ghastly boyfriends and one brief marriage, while Violet not only distinguished herself on the work front but managed to snag Thomas Grant Bolton Jr., the handsome and wealthy heir to the Potomac Bank, thus becoming a young grande dame of Washington. The irony was that I actually introduced her to Grant, who was an old beau of mine. Violet now had a family and a settled life, while I was divorced and childless. My biological clock, once ticking like a time bomb, lay unexploded in the dust of failed relationships. Go figure.

I like to think that I haven't changed all that much since our school days. I'm still a tall, willowy clotheshorse with long legs, an ample bust, and a luxurious fizz of golden hair. (Okay, I dye it.) But Violet is vastly improved. When she first came to Washington and looked me up, I almost didn't recognize her. She'd completely transformed herself from the pudgy, mousy girl I'd defended all through boarding school. She was actually good-looking, if a tad overdone for D.C. She'd lost weight and made the most of her body through exercise. Her sharp sapphire eyes were no longer mired in a pudding face, but the most striking feature of a slim and very attractive woman. Plus, her quirky personality lent a certain charm to her face, so that the more you got to know her, the better looking she became.

Though Violet was working as an environmental lobbyist, she didn't know many people. I introduced her to my friends. After she met Grant, she was desperate to fit in. Her clothes left a lot to be desired. She had this one brown suit with green flecks in it that made her look like a diseased tree frog. I introduced her to Lisa, a personal shopper at Saks, who refined her look. I also took her to Ury's Hair Salon, where Sara, a great stylist, reshaped and colored her hair. Violet adapted to her surroundings with astonishing speed and compliance. She was a quick study. I watched her assemble her new image, piece by piece, imitating the style of people she admired and taking the advice of those she respected—mainly me. I had her looking like an appropriately elegant Washingtonian in a matter of weeks.

Still, the ongoing mystery to me, of course, was how Violet had done so well for herself while all my natural looks and sparkle had failed to secure me a better perch in life. It slightly irritated me when she went on and on about Grant and what a wonderful husband he was. I sometimes wondered if I hadn't made the biggest mistake of my life by not grabbing him for myself when I had the chance. But Grant just wasn't my type.

I'd grown up around boys like Grant Bolton Jr.—stiff scions of privilege who felt burdened by their wealth and were constantly trying to overcome the improbable hardship of too many advantages. He was a workaholic even way back then, desperate to prove himself on his own and show the world he wasn't simply another rich man's son, but a contender in his own right. Grant was too boring for me in those days, too much of a WASP, too uptight, and too repressed. I was looking for someone much more exciting and interesting, an uninhibited lover with a wild sense of adventure and a streak of glamour—a shit, in other words.

I could hardly believe it when Violet and Grant fell in love, even though I was the one who fixed them up. It was the most tepid, uninteresting courtship you could ever imagine. The only real sparks came from Violet's determination to get Grant. I was there. I saw that steely one-track mind of hers steaming toward him like smokestack lightning.

You want my honest opinion? I believe the main reason Grant married Violet when he could have had his pick of artful beauties was because she was simply so determined to get him. I watched her tailor herself to fit his needs as well as the needs of his family. I marveled at how quickly she understood that Grant wanted a wife who would not outshine him as his heritage had always done, but who would also complement that heritage by fitting neatly into the Bolton clan and advancing its interests. Knowing how much Grant valued his parents' opinion, Violet also courted them almost as skillfully as she courted Grant—particularly his mother, Lorraine "Rainy" Bolton. Grant always wanted to please his parents, daunting as that task often was.

The fact that Rainy Bolton liked Violet right off the bat was a huge plus. Rainy considered herself an infallible judge of character. She was renowned for her snap judgments about people. Her word was law to Grant, who once said to me, in all seriousness, "Mother can't admit she's wrong, therefore she never is."

Violet knew how to be deferential without appearing sycophantic. Rainy loved it that Violet was so community spirited, yet she didn't put herself forward in any way. In Rainy's eyes, it was important for her son to marry a substantial person, but definitely not "a show horse," as Rainy termed people who flaunted their accomplishments. Rainy was the star of the Bolton family, and she was determined to remain so. Rainy didn't like me on sight, and she immediately took to Violet. Grant, eager to please his mother, took to Violet too. His mother's approval may have been the decisive factor in his decision to marry her.

Back in the day, I never could have imagined that my handmaiden in boarding school would become my queen in real life. Our roles had totally reversed. I sometimes think that had fate been kinder, or had I been less picky, I, not Violet, would be Mrs. Grant Bolton now. But fate had other plans for me, and as my divorce lawyer used to say, "You must start from where you are, not from where you wish you could be." And right now, I was in debt and hoping for a phone call from a man I knew to be Lothario incarnate. Not the greatest place in the world—but not the worst.

Chapter 7

Later that week, Violet came into the shop with Cynthia Rinehart in tow. It kind of irked me to see them so palsy-walsy together, but I understood that Violet had a weakness for celebrities, and Cynthia was definitely the celebrity du jour. Celebrity or not, however, Cynthia seemed to understand that Violet was socially influential, a good person to cultivate if you wanted to break into the older, more permanent social circles of Washington, which included most of the city's big philanthropists.

I figured the two of them had come in to browse around, but in fact they'd come with a definite purpose in mind. Violet proudly announced to me that Cynthia had just bought Gay Harding's old house. I was stunned.

The late Gay Harding, heiress, philanthropist, and kingmaker, was the last of Washington's great grande dames. Her locally televised funeral at the National Cathedral some years back was tantamount to a state occasion. Set back on six acres of prime real estate on R Street, her house had been sold to a dot-com billionaire from Virginia who never moved in. It had been discreetly on the market for the unheard-of sum of fifteen million dollars for a couple of years now. This purchase was clearly part of the tsunami Cynthia was riding into Washington.

I congratulated Cynthia and told her how much I loved that house. At which point, Cynthia asked me if I wanted to decorate it for her.

"Violet says you're the best," Cynthia said. "And that's good enough for me. You interested?"

This was like asking a starving person if they'd be interested in a banquet. Violet knew all about my financial woes, of course. She'd offered to help me on several occasions, but I wouldn't hear of it. The "neither a borrower nor a lender be" credo had been drummed into me since childhood by my parents. However, Violet knew full well that a big decorating job like this was the answer to all my debts, and I was grateful she'd strongly recommended me to Cynthia. Violet was truly my best friend.

"I'm interested," I said brightly.

I'd only taken a couple of decorating jobs since opening my shop, because I just didn't have the time. Neither was as major as this one, but they'd both turned out extremely well. The clients were pleased, plus I'd managed to make some extra money because I was able to furnish the jobs with some of my own stock. Monetary benefits aside, however, I knew it would be fun to redo Mrs. Harding's old house, not to mention a big feather in my cap.

We all agreed to meet at the house that afternoon. As Cynthia browsed around the shop, Violet took me aside and asked me if I'd heard from Bob Poll. When I told her I hadn't, she said that she and Grant had taken a table for the PEN/Faulkner evening at the Folger on Friday night. She suggested I call Bob and ask him if he wanted to be my date.

"Sometimes you have to give these guys a little push," she said.

Call me old-fashioned, but I never think it's a good idea to call a man when he hasn't called you first. That doesn't mean I haven't done it, of course. I rationalized calling Bob by remembering he'd sent me those roses. He seemed to enjoy the company of social heavy hitters, and the Boltons certainly qualified as such. I knew that Grant would put together a good table, with a sprinkling of political luminaries as well. I bit the bullet and called Bob's office, since his home number was unlisted. I was put through to his secretary, an officious-sounding woman who clearly thought of herself as Cerberus at the gate. When I asked to speak to Bob, she asked me who I was, why I was calling, if "Mr. Poll" knew me, and so on. I answered her questions politely and issued my invitation. She said that she was sure that Mr. Poll had "something on his calendar that night," but that she would "pass along" my request. She asked for my telephone number and my e-mail address, "just in case Mr. Poll doesn't have them."

I told Rosina what I'd done. Naturally, she thought it was a bad idea. "You should always wait for a man to call you. Otherwise you set a bad pattern."

I didn't really disagree with her, but I had to defend my action. We were arguing back and forth about the merits of women making the first move when the phone rang. It was Bob's secretary, Felicity, as she introduced herself. She informed me that "Mr. Poll would be pleased" to attend the dinner with me and that he would "have his chauffeur" pick me up at my house at six thirty sharp on Friday evening. They had the address.

"See how fast he got back to me," I said to Rosina after I hung up.

"*He* didn't. His secretary did. Not a good sign."

Rosina was like a freaking soothsayer. Still, I was pleased.

———

As I walked over to Gay Harding's house that afternoon, I wondered if Cynthia was aware that Violet had her own little history with that property. Right after Mrs. Harding died going on ten years ago, her heirs put the house on the market. Grant and Violet wanted to buy it. But Rainy Bolton had been a great friend of Mrs. Harding's, and for some reason she considered it unseemly for her son to own such a well-known property. She famously proclaimed: "That house will always be Gay Harding's house, no matter who owns it."

At the time, Violet suspected that her mother-in-law was just jealous and didn't want her son to have a grander house than she did. But Violet saw this as an opportunity to further ingratiate herself with the Boltons, so she sided with them against Grant, which I thought was a big error. Violet explained she had her reasons, however, and I have to say it was impressive watching Violet tell Rainy that she too didn't think it was appropriate for her and Grant to own Gay Harding's house, when all the while I knew she coveted that house more than anything in the world. Violet was a master at not letting her true feelings show.

Grant got back at Violet years later after the house came on the market again for fifteen million dollars and he refused to buy it for her, even though she begged him to and even though he loved it too. By that time Rainy's opinion didn't matter to her so much.

Grant told Violet, "Yes, I love it. Yes, I want it. And yes, I can afford it. But I'll be damned if I'm going to pay fifteen million dollars for a house I could once have bought for six."

———

The Harding house sat in the middle of a big wooded lot on the corner of Twenty-ninth and R, directly across the street from the old Oak Hill Cemetery and Montrose Park. I arrived first, and believe me, I checked to make sure no one was lurking around in the bushes. It was impossible to forget that a murder had occurred very recently and very nearby—practically across the street. The four-story limestone was in pretty bad shape. Withering ivy had clawed its way over most of the facade, and untended bushes mushroomed throughout the grounds.

Gay Harding had been a friend of my parents. Gay and my mother always stayed in touch, even when my parents moved back home to New York. When Gay heard that I'd moved to Washington, she invited me to several of her parties. At first the high-powered company terrified me, and I felt very out of place. But Gay made me feel right at home. In fact, it was at her house that I first met Grant Bolton and his parents. I don't know if she'd purposely wanted to fix us up, but Grant and I did wind up having a few dates.

I was standing on the front steps recalling those carefree days of my youth when a black stretch limo pulled into the gravel driveway. Violet and Cynthia got out. Stretch limos were not remotely Violet's style, and we exchanged a knowing glance as she walked up to the house. Cynthia looked around the grounds like a conqueror surveying captured territory. The three of us paused in front of the door with its antique brass lion's-head knocker while Cynthia fumbled for the key in her large crocodile bag. As she opened the door, Violet joked, "Shall we carry you over the threshold?"

"No one carries me anywhere, honey," Cynthia snapped. "I go places all by myself."

Violet and I just looked at each other. This gal had no humor. None. Nada. Zero. Zippo. But she did have this great house, which tells you something.

It had been several years since I'd been there. The interior reeked of mildew and neglect, a sharp contrast to the delicious aroma of baking apples that had once greeted visitors in autumn. My mother told me how Mrs. Harding had ordered her chef to keep a pot of apples simmering on the stove in the fall so their delicious scent filled the air. Run-down as it was, there was still an aura of Old World grandeur about the place. We walked through to the famous living room, whose walls had once been described as "the color of burnt roses" by Folly Pritchard, another Georgetown socialite, also gone.

In its heyday, that room had been the social pinnacle of Georgetown, packed nightly with testosterone, power, and ambition. Everyone who was anyone had come to Gay's famous salon—presidents, heads of state, senators, congressmen, cabinet members, ambassadors, supreme court justices, journalists, television personalities, philanthropists, socialites, top military brass, business leaders, as well as Gay's pets of the moment, many of whom, like myself, had no special perch on the rungs of power, but were simply people she liked. Gay was grand enough to entertain anyone she pleased.

The warmth of those parties had chilled into history. The living room's once voluminous gray curtains hung in shreds from the windows, like silk spaghetti. The place was stately but sad, like a decrepit dowager in a tattered dress. Aside from a few pieces of insignificant furniture, the only thing that remained from the old days was Gay Harding's portrait above the mantelpiece. Draped across a beige velvet sofa, wearing a blue dress, a long strand of pearls, and a cool gaze, she epitomized the elegance of a bygone era. But the artist had captured her steeliness as well.

As we studied the portrait, Violet said: "Here's an interesting fact. The man who bought this house from Mrs. Harding originally insisted that her portrait 'convey,' as they say in real estate lingo. Apparently, he needed the painting here to remind people whose house it had once been—as if anyone could forget."

"Trust me. People forget," Cynthia said.

"I hope not. It was such a magical time," I said wistfully.

Cynthia turned around and glared at me with something akin to belligerence.

"Let me offer you another perspective. It was all very well and good to be Gay Harding in those days—or any of those snooty Georgetown hostesses. But try being just about anyone else. *Forget it!* Those gals were a bunch of tough old birds, from what I've heard. If they didn't like you, *God* couldn't help you. Know what I'm saying?"

I actually did know what she was saying. Gay and her set wielded an immense amount of social power. Everyone wanted to be in their orbit. They were a social junta—revered and feared at the same time.

"Her picture's gotta go. Time to clear out the cobwebs and bring some new life to this old town," Cynthia said.

"How about a portrait of *you* up there?" Violet said. I knew she was putting Cynthia on.

Cynthia shrugged. "Maybe. At least people would be looking at the future, not the past."

Violet looked at me and rolled her eyes. Cynthia may have been her new best friend, but that didn't mean she particularly liked her.

As we toured the rest of the house, it became clear that Cynthia was about as interested in decoration as I am in campaign finance reform. Her attitude was basically "Do it and call me when it's done." She only had two firm requests.

"Give me some tradition—you know, some antiques that look like they came from my great granny, 'cause Lord knows I don't have any of my own, and that's what they seem to go for around here," she said with a gleam of defiance. "And some good shades. I hate light. Particularly in the morning when I'm trying to sleep."

"You and Grant." Violet sighed.

Grant Bolton was a neurotic light hater. He carried a roll of duct tape when they traveled to seal the edges of the windows and block out appliance lights in hotel rooms. The glow of a cell phone was like a klieg light to Grant. Ten years ago, when I helped Violet do some minor decorating, I'd blitzed their bedroom with expensive, handmade, lightproof shutters. I told Cynthia I'd order the same ones for her if she didn't mind the cost.

"You can either have those shutters or a private plane," Violet remarked.

"I'll have both," Cynthia remarked. "Money is no object."

I hadn't heard those words in a while, and they were music to my ears.

When Cynthia was inspecting another room, I took Violet aside and told her rather excitedly that Bob Poll had accepted my invitation to the PEN/Faulkner evening. Violet threw her arms around me and gave me a big hug.

"That's fabulous! We've got a great table. I'll seat you next to him so you can work your wiles."

Chapter 8

Friday evening, Maxwell, Bob's chauffeur, picked me up in front of my house, at six thirty sharp. I settled into the creamy leather back seat of the Rolls next to the neatly folded green mink throw, feeling pampered and, admittedly, quite excited. I was looking forward to the evening. I'd made a special effort to look my very best, and though I do have my off nights, this wasn't one of them. I wore a clingy midnight blue velvet sheath and swept my hair up in a soft chignon. I wanted to look elegantly sexy. I checked myself out more than once in my compact mirror and thought, I may not be as luscious as Melody Hartford, but Bob won't be ashamed to be with me.

We swung by to pick up Bob at his office downtown, in one of the big modern buildings around Fifteenth and M. Maxwell had telephoned Bob just as we were about to arrive. He was waiting outside, dapperly dressed in black tie with a black cashmere coat thrown over his shoulders and a long white silk scarf hanging around his neck.

"There she is," he said to me as he climbed into the car. "Maxwell take good care of you?"

"Very good, thanks."

He kissed me on the cheek and sat down with the green mink blanket between us. Maxwell started driving without having to be told where to go. This was obviously a familiar routine to both of them. I casually wondered if Bob ever picked up a woman himself or if he always sent his driver. However, now was not the time to inquire.

"I'm going to let you in on a little secret," Bob said as we drove along. "I was already going to this dinner. I always take a table. Good cause. Nice evening. But when Felicity told me you'd called, I asked a friend to fill in for me because I wanted to sit with you."

I was flattered, except that I was dying to say, "If you wanted to see me so much, how come you didn't call me and invite me to this evening yourself? How come I had to call you?" But I didn't. I just took the compliment as it was obviously intended.

———

The cozy little Shakespeare Theatre was packed. This was the big PEN/Faulkner gala, where a group of writers read short little pieces on a common theme. The theme of the night was love. I was certainly in the mood for that. Bob and I sat with Violet and Grant in the third row. Cynthia was seated next to Grant, and there was an empty seat next to her. I asked Violet who the missing body was, and she said, "Senator Grider. But God knows if he'll show up."

The writers droned on. Finally it was over, and we all trooped into the famous Old Reading Room, a scholar's paradise, designed to look like the great hall of an Elizabethan house. Many round tables set with pretty spring flowers filled the tranquil, opulent space. There was never any need to decorate that room for parties. The carved oak paneling, Renaissance tapestries, mammoth stone fireplace, and treasured stained-glass window depicting the "Seven Ages of Man" speech from *As You Like It* were sumptuous decoration enough. Dinners in this room were somehow enhanced by the depth of knowledge it contained.

The Boltons had put together a good group at their table. Nearly every table included one of the twelve writers; we drew the estimable Dorrit Dearing, whose reading had been one of the best received of the night. Her rumpled, myopic husband, Milton Dearing, was a professional bookbinder. Then there were Roland and Peggy Myers. Rolly Myers was a prominent African-American lawyer, known as "the eminence noir" because of his influence in the highest precincts of power. Peggy was president of the Capitol Symphony, and a good friend of mine. There was also Jean Herrend, a prominent congresswoman, and her husband, Sanders Herrend, an influential businessman who had built his own center for the arts, the Herrend Auditorium, which everyone agreed was an architectural and acoustical triumph and a great addition to the artistic community. Finally, there was Senator Grider, who was obviously meant to be Cynthia's date. Heavy hitters all.

Violet had assured me she was seating me next to Bob Poll. But somehow the place cards got switched around, and I found myself between Senator Grider and Milton Dearing. Cynthia had landed on the opposite side of the table, between Grant and Bob Poll. I didn't like this one bit. She looked almost elegant in a black satin suit and very little jewelry, more toned down than usual, in keeping with the bookish nature of the event. Cynthia was younger and richer than I was, not to mention a budding celebrity. In other words, tough competition.

To make matters worse, Senator Grider was a no-show—*again*. I was stranded with only Mr. Dearing to talk to. While I found him to be a gentle, thoughtful man, he was obsessed with the subject of bookbinding. After a short time, I grew quite bored. There's only so much one can hear about natural adhesives.

Meanwhile, Cynthia held forth. Both Grant and Bob looked quite enthralled with her. She was clearly not afraid to speak her mind in a town where the men do most of the talking. Her competitiveness seemed to invigorate all the men at the table, except perhaps good old Mr. Dearing, who kept droning on about glue. Bob stared hard at Cynthia as she spoke, looking as if he were either fighting gas or an erection.

I flung Violet several hapless glances. She shrugged and shook her head in dismay as if to indicate she couldn't understand how the place cards got switched around.

Halfway through the entrée, Senator Grider finally arrived. He went around the table, introducing himself, shaking hands with everyone, looking deeply into their eyes as he repeated their names, then quickly moved on, like a good politician.

"Long, tough session," he announced as he sat down beside me.

"Well, now you can relax," I said.

He didn't answer. He ordered the waiter to bring him a Diet Coke and launched into a conversation with Congresswoman Herrend, whom he seemed to know. Myopic Mr. Dearing and I had just exhausted another facet of his craft, namely gilt tooling, and I grabbed the opportunity to change the subject.

"So what else are you interested in—aside from bookbinding?" I asked him.

He had launched into the joys of calligraphy when I noticed that Senator Grider was sitting up stiffly, staring straight ahead, as if he were mentally twiddling his thumbs. I politely tried to draw him into our conversation.

"We were just talking about what interests us, Senator," I said.

"Uh-huh," he said, supremely uninterested.

"Aside from politics, what interests you?" I asked him.

"An early night," he said.

Senator Grider had the sturdy, weatherworn look of a farmer. His brown hair was combed in pencil strings over a balding pate. He wore square wire-rim glasses and an air of earnestness coupled with determination. His closely set lead gray eyes glinted with judgment. His lips were as thin as straw. I suspected there was precious little humor under that stern veneer of righteousness. He seemed more blunt than grim, however, so I went on.

"You know, the last time I was seated next to you, you didn't show up," I said.

"Uh-huh."

"Last month at the Symphony Ball? Do you remember?"

"Nope."

The minute his main course arrived, Senator Grider attacked the Cornish hen as if he hadn't had a decent meal in days. The bookbinding man was engaged in conversation with his other dinner partner, so I made a few more stabs at polite conversation with Grider. He returned my questions with grunt answers and continued shoveling in the food. Talking to this man was like talking to hay.

Finally, after several rebuffs, I said, "Don't they feed you in Congress?"

That got his attention. He put down his knife and fork, leaned back in his chair, and fixed me with an inquisitive stare. Taking a slow, deliberate swig of Diet Coke, he asked, "So, what's the story with this shindig tonight?"

"You don't sound as if you enjoy these *shindigs* much," I said, putting as distasteful an emphasis on the word as he had.

"Want the truth?"

"Oh, please don't do anything that's against your principles," I said.

"Well, that sure tells me what you think of politicians."

"Actually, I try *not* to think of them if I can help it," I said.

He raised an eyebrow. "Truth is, I hate these things. Big waste of time, most of 'em."

"I see. So why do you come?"

"To have a look-see. Always important to have a look-see in my business."

"Okay, well, let's try and make this a nice evening for you. What do you want to talk about?"

"Anything but politics," he replied.

"Good. Because I don't know anything about politics."

"My dear young lady, this town is full of people who don't know anything about politics and who talk about nothing *but*. Talking heads with nothing to say."

"Young lady, eh? I'm so flattered."

"Which half is incorrect?"

"I plead the fifth. So what state are you from?"

He froze for a split second as if I'd slapped him. "*Nebraska*," he said, like it was a fact any schoolgirl should know.

"Guess what state I'm from?" I said playfully.

"Ignorance," he replied, without missing a beat.

"Ha. Ha. New York. Originally. Are you a Democrat or Republican?" He shook his head in perturbed disbelief. "Don't take it so personally. I don't know what party anyone's from."

"Know what party the president's from?"

"Don't make me answer that."

"You better not be one of these people who complains about the country all the time."

"What do you mean?"

" 'Cause if you don't make it your business to find out who's running the country, you have no business complaining about it. Who'd you vote for last election?"

"I never vote. It only encourages them, as they say," I said, staring him down.

His straw lips twitched into what seemed to be his version of a smile. He cranked out a rusty hinge of a laugh.

"Very funny," he said, mirthlessly.

Senator Grider was the human equivalent of string.

Throughout the dinner, I kept glancing at Bob, who was talking a little too animatedly with Cynthia. I was careful never to let him catch my eye. But I was irritated that Violet hadn't switched us at the beginning of the meal. Now it was too late.

Toward the end of dinner, Douglas Reed, the president of the Folger, ambled up to a standing microphone in front of the cavernous stone fireplace to thank the writers and all of us for supporting PEN/Faulkner. At the very end, he said, "And now I have a surprise announcement. I'll be brief because I can't compete with all the great writers here tonight. But what I have to say will enhance the future of writers everywhere. The Cynthia A. Rinehart Foundation is donating ten million dollars to our beloved Folger Shakespeare Library! Cynthia, will you please come up here and say a few words?"

Cynthia rose from the table, accompanied by strong, appreciative applause. Senator Grider popped up like a periscope. His chilly eyes focused on her as she snaked her way through the room. At the microphone, she assumed a pious position, hands folded, head slightly raised, as if she were addressing angels in the rafters of that vaulted room. She launched into a speech about philanthropy, calling it "global goodness," and how it had always been her dream to be a writer.

"But my talent lies in giving, not writing," Cynthia said earnestly.

Grider leaned in and whispered to me: "She the one just donated all that dough to the Kennedy Center?"

"The very one," I whispered back.

"Generous gal," he murmured, narrowing his eyes.

I remember thinking I wouldn't have wanted Zachary Grider squinting at me like that. He watched Cynthia wend her way back to her seat. She was stopped en route by a few people offering her their congratulations. Grider didn't take his eyes off her until she sat down at our table again. Then he turned to me and said, "You know her?"

"Kind of. She's just bought Gay Harding's old house, and she's asked me to decorate it for her."

"You a decorator, are you?"

I explained that I hadn't been a decorator for years, that I owned an antiques shop, but that the offer to decorate Mrs. Harding's old house was just too tempting to turn down.

"So this Rinehart gal bought Gay Harding's old house, did she?"

"Yup. She paid fifteen million dollars."

Grider didn't respond, but I sensed a file drawer opening in his brain.

"My wife liked to decorate. Wouldn't let her decorate my office, though."

"Why not?"

"I don't like knickknacks. She was a great one for knickknacks, my wife was."

Everyone at our table congratulated Cynthia except for Grider, who sat there like a big old hayrick without uttering a word. He stood up abruptly and announced to the table: "Folks, I've enjoyed my evening. Pleasure to be with you all. Good night."

"Happy lawmaking," I said with mock cheer.

He reached inside his pocket and handed me his card.

"You ever want to visit the Senate, give me a call."

Soon after Senator Grider left, everyone got up. Bob Poll walked over to my side and whispered, "You've made a conquest."

I looked at him askance. "You *must* be kidding. Senator Grider's as dry as a dust bowl."

"I don't mean him. I mean me."

———

On the way home in the car, I made reference to Cynthia—something about how she was "the girl who had everything."

"Everything except the ability to listen," Bob countered. "She's a little too full of herself for my taste."

I was so relieved to hear this, because I assumed that she'd charmed him. Bob was more eager to talk about Senator Grider.

"I've never seen Zack Grider so taken with a woman," he said.

"If you call that taken, the old toad. . . . What happened to his wife? He alluded to her in the past tense. Are they divorced?"

"Nope. He's a widower."

"I'm sure he bored her to death."

Bob laughed. "See? You're irreverent. I bet he loved that. A breath of fresh air. So many of the women we sit next to at these events are dull because they're so careful."

"How do you mean, careful?"

"Well, say they're married to an important man, or they hold some big job, they have to tread cautiously. Don't forget this is Washington. Anything you say will be repeated and held against you. That's why so many people act like they're on a job interview or in front of a camera. . . . Take my word for it, Grider's smitten with you. And he's a powerful man. I was getting a little jealous."

"That's funny, because I was getting a little jealous of you and Cynthia. You looked like you couldn't take your eyes off her."

Bob chuckled. "That's because I was in disbelief. I never met a woman who sounded more like she was running for office with no office in sight. No . . . she's a ball-buster, but that figures. Shy women don't make fortunes, believe me."

It was nice to think that Bob had been watching me as much as I'd been watching him. I couldn't wait to tell Violet that the seating had worked out so well, since Bob was turned on by Grider's attentions to me.

We pulled up to my house. Maxwell came around and opened the door for us, and Bob walked me up to my front door. I let him kiss me good night, and I have to say that he took my breath away. Still, I didn't ask him in.

"What are you doing for dinner?" he asked.

"When?"

"How about for the foreseeable future?"

I thought he was kidding.

Chapter 9

He wasn't. . . . For the next month, Bob Poll gilded me with so much attention I was practically glowing in the dark. I'm talking about bright gold glittery attention the likes of which I hadn't received since I was a luscious babe in my twenties. Roses every day, dinners every night, evenings at the Kennedy Center, receptions at the National Gallery, the Phillips, the Corcoran, the Smithsonian, the National Portrait Gallery.

Bob didn't enjoy the cultural part of the evenings as much as he did the social part. He was much more interested in the intermissions than in the shows. He liked to mix and mingle and be seen. He actually looked forward to the big gala dinners most people dreaded. I was just the opposite. I loved the shows far more than the socializing. It was such a treat seeing Claudio Piccere and Norma Jessup sing *Aïda* at the opening night of the Washington National Opera. Although when Bob leaned in and whispered to me, "I wish they'd shut up and die already. I'm famished," it kind of broke the spell.

However, when Bob saw how much I loved the arts, he made an effort to discuss the productions we saw rather than treating them as tiresome preludes to a party. My efforts to get him to appreciate culture were not always successful. I caught him nodding off during the Bolshoi's splendid production of *La Bayadère*—but the minute I gently nudged him, he roused himself, grabbed my hand, and kissed it gently, as if to thank me.

For the first time in what seemed like an eon, I was having fun. I'd forgotten what it was like to get all dressed up and go somewhere glamorous on the arm of an attractive and important man. The juices were flowing. I was basking in the fun. If I wanted to see a certain production or exhibition, I merely had to mention it to Bob, and that night we had tickets. Bang—just like that!

Every time Maxwell drove us up to the front of the Kennedy Center or the National Gallery or just about any place, people stopped and stared at that fabulous hunter green Rolls and then at us as we got out. We always had the best seats in the house and the best tables at gala dinners. We were photographed and written up in the columns. The number of "important" people who suddenly took an interest in me was staggering. People who barely knew me, people who wouldn't have spit on me before, now made beelines across crowded rooms "just to say hello." All because I was dating Bob.

I told Violet how much I liked Bob and how my status in life had suddenly changed because I was seeing him. She said wisely: "Listen, Rev, when there's a new queen on the horizon, people want to jump on her golden coach so she won't forget them if she makes it to the throne. And you may make it. Just don't sleep with him."

In between the obligations of this hectic social life, Bob and I managed to wedge in a few cozy dinners at good restaurants where we swapped heavily edited versions of our life stories. I knew the unexpurgated versions would come later when we got to know each other better. Bob's thumbnail sketch was that he'd been married once and had two grown children, a boy and girl, of whom he was obviously fond and proud. The boy owned a large organic farm in Kentucky; the girl was a dermatologist in California. He was loath to talk about his first wife. When I asked him why he'd gotten divorced, he simply said, "We were married young and grew apart"—a safe, stock answer upon which he refused to elaborate.

Another taboo was Melody. When I broached the subject, he absolutely refused to talk about her—which Violet assured me was a good sign.

"When they talk about the exes, it means they're not over them," she said confidently.

Bob asked me quite a bit about my own life, which was a novelty right there. Most of the men I'd dated in Washington were only interested in talking about themselves—what Violet and I dubbed the "I-I-I" syndrome, pronounced *Aiyaiyai*. I could call Violet after a date and say simply, "Aiyaiyai!" and she'd know exactly how the evening went.

I glossed over the topic of my ex-husband, putting a humorous cast on our doomed marriage. "I thought he had talent. He thought I had money. We were both wrong." Enough said.

Bob seemed very interested in the fact that Grant had been an old beau of mine, and that I'd actually introduced him to Violet.

"Grant's a rich, good-looking guy. How come you didn't grab him?" he asked me.

I explained that talking to Grant was like playing tennis against a backboard. I always felt like I was getting my own shot back. I refrained from telling him about a sexual encounter I had with Grant, much as I would have liked to, as it explained a lot.

One night not too long after we started dating, Grant had invited me back to his house after dinner. In the midst of some hot and heavy petting on the couch, he got up and excused himself. I sat in the living room, flushed with passion, I admit, anxious for him to return. Half an hour later with no sign of him, I went searching for him. I went upstairs and found his bedroom. The scent of pine air freshener filled the room. The bed was neatly turned down. A wrapped condom lay atop a pillow. Grant's suit and tie were hanging on a silent butler stand in the corner, his shoes and socks placed neatly underneath. I heard tap water running and called out to him. Grant emerged from the steamy bathroom, toothbrush in hand, all showered and combed, wearing pajamas and slippers. He said, "Your turn. I ran you a bath."

Well, that just kind of killed the mood, if you know what I mean.

Whenever I thought I'd missed an opportunity by not snagging Grant, I consoled myself with the memory of that night. But deep down, I knew that Grant never would have married me under any circumstances. I was much too outspoken and willful to accommodate the never-ending social ambitions of the Bolton family. The truth is, I didn't care all that much about social life, unlike Violet, who helped cement Grant's social status at every turn. Besides, Rainy didn't care for me. She thought me frivolous and flighty. That fact alone was the kiss of death for any hopes I might have entertained.

———

Ignoring Violet's sage advice, I slept with Bob about two weeks into our dating frenzy. I won't go into detail. Let's just say he was competent, and Rosina asked me if I was using different makeup. After that, we always made love at my house, not his. He clearly didn't want his space invaded, although he was very proud of that oversize glass box overlooking the Potomac. He never failed to drop the name of the award-winning architect who had designed it, which was completely lost on me.

His house reminded me of an airport terminal. The decoration was modern and minimal, with lots of leather, steel, and Plexiglas furniture and a few obsessively chosen knickknacks—like the twisty, rainbow-colored Chihuly glass sculpture on the coffee table in the living room and the brass sculpture of a rhinoceros on the mantelpiece in his bedroom. He had four Warhol soup can silk screens in the dining room, plus some other contemporary art I didn't quite appreciate. The whole place was cold, not cozy. And much too neat. Bob loved order. The first time I went there, I threw my coat on one of the two clear Plexiglas hall chairs, and he immediately hung it up. The house wasn't my style, but it was stylish in its arctic way and certainly an anomaly for Washington, which is still mired in mahogany for the most part.

Like any best friend, Violet was eager for my happiness. She wanted me to find true love and settle down like she had. While I knew she disapproved of me sleeping with Bob so soon, I also knew she was rooting for me. Over the years, she'd fixed me up with several candidates, none of whom ever seemed to work out. But that didn't stop her from trying. The minute I told her Bob was courting me in such a big way, she was thrilled. "He's ready. You're ready. You're perfect for each other. It's all perfect!" she said.

While I appreciated her optimism, I felt it was slightly suspect. When Bob was dating Melody, Violet used to say things like, "I pity that poor girl. Bob's never going to marry her. Plus he's kinda weird, dontcha think?" In the past she'd often referred to him as "Kinky Bob" because of the rumors about his "dark side." But the rumors weren't that specific. They were just free-floating, run-of-the-gossip-mill rumors. Then when Bob started dating me, Violet completely changed her tune about him. She obviously didn't want to put a damper on things, unlike Rosina, who made the unwelcome observation that Bob was a little *too* attentive.

"Like he is trying to forget someone else," were Rosina's exact words.

I paid no attention. I teased her that she was just jealous because I got to ride in Bob's Rolls Royce, and I knew how much she loved that car. Rosina used to stand and stare out the window like a starstruck fan whenever Maxwell pulled up in front of the shop.

"Before he breaks up with you, will you ask him to give me a ride?" she asked me.

I countered: "After I *marry* him and you're my maid of honor, I'll *buy* you a Rolls of your very own."

That shut her up.

Rosina's skepticism notwithstanding, I was in heaven—floating on top of the universe, enjoying every second of this unexpected midlife romance. I remember sitting in my office having just ordered the fabric for the curtains in Cynthia's dining room, thinking how well things were going for a change. I had a fabulous new man, a great new project, and I was feeling really good about myself and about life in general. Of course, that's just the time you know you're gonna fall and break your neck . . . or someone's gonna break it for you.

Chapter 10

The media frenzy over the murder in Montrose Park had finally died down. That didn't mean Violet's passion for the subject abated. She scoured the Internet and obscure publications for scraps about the murder. Finally, she announced to me in dismay, "I think the case has gone cold." She wasn't the only one. I'd seen Gunner earlier in the week, and he seemed disheartened as well. I tried to amuse him with funny social stories, but he was clearly brooding about the case.

"It's like waiting for a personal terrorist attack," he said. "It's gonna happen. We just don't know how or when."

Everyone was on edge. There were still warnings posted to avoid jogging or walking alone in Montrose Park. Only Violet was ready to brave the woods again. I forbade her to go alone. We took little forays into the forest on our jogs, but we were cautious. Even Violet turned around before we got in too deep.

The next big thing that happened was that Cynthia flew Violet and Grant down to Acapulco on her private plane for a "Rinehart Retreat," which Cynthia described in the press as "a conference to discuss global giving." Apparently, it was more productive to talk about world poverty in a rich resort.

I was surprised Violet and Grant went. The Bolton family was usually much more low key, preferring to keep their philanthropic efforts private. Violet came back from the three-day trip raving about all the famous people she'd met. It sounded like a mighty impressive group—including former heads of state, Nobel Prize winners, and plenty of what Violet called "celebrity tinsel."

That Saturday, a big article appeared in the *Washington Post*, entitled, "Charitable Trailblazer: Cynthia Rinehart and the New Philanthropy." A large color picture of Cynthia took up nearly the entire front page of the Style section. She was standing in front of the Kennedy Center with her arms outstretched like she was inviting the world into her own private house. It was a puff piece, describing the origins of Cynthia's fortune and her philanthropic plans.

What I found most interesting was how Cynthia arrived on the scene out of nowhere with scads of money, and everyone just took it for granted that she was on the up-and-up. Like Violet, people had only the vaguest idea how she made her fortune. No one in Washington seemed to care that much where Cynthia's money was from— only that there was a ton of it, and that she was giving it away.

When that article came out, we learned how brilliant she was. Violet had told me that Cynthia made all her money in the insurance business. But it was *how* she made it that was so interesting. Her chief claim to fame was the invention of a specialized policy that defrayed the cost of hospice care, allowing the children or close relatives of a dying patient to take out a loan secured by the patient's estate.

Although I didn't particularly like Cynthia, after I read that article, I have to admit that I admired her. According to the piece, she had grown up dirt-poor in a tiny little town in North Carolina and worked her way up from scratch. She described how her dad got cancer and lingered for months in a hospice facility. His illness wiped out the family's savings. She called it the "formative experience" of her youth.

After graduating from college with a degree in accounting, she went to work for a big insurance company in Charlotte, where she dealt with other families who had also been devastated by the prolonged illness of a loved one. She then created a specialized insurance plan specifically designed to cover only hospice care, and formed her very own company. I didn't understand all the technical aspects, but clearly it was a brilliant and innovative idea. The fact that she figured out a way to save families from the extra burden of being financially ruined by an emotionally debilitating situation was particularly impressive. This niche market turned out to be a bonanza. Her little company expanded and became extremely profitable. She sold it to one of the big insurance carriers for a few hundred mil, which she immediately put into a foundation. A real American rags-to-riches success story.

The piece went on to describe Cynthia's budding "philanthropic empire," which included her Rinehart Retreats, her unprecedented one-hundred-million-dollar bequest to the Kennedy Center, and her bequest to the Folger, as well as several "smaller but significant" bequests to other charities and institutions around town. It mentioned that she had bought Gay Harding's house and that she was quickly establishing herself as "a queenpin" in the charity world, as well as in Washington society.

Cynthia was quoted throughout, but the gist of all her comments was summed up at the end of the piece when she told the reporter:

> *Do I think I'm entitled to special perks because I give away millions of dollars? You bet I do! I've put Washington on the philanthropic map. Before me it was a swamp of penny-ante contributors. I'm out to make a difference in the world, to lead the way by giving much and giving often. Call me a trailblazer.*

Violet called to ask if I'd seen the article.

"How could I avoid it? Tell me something: You think Gay Harding ever called herself a trailblazer?" I asked her.

"I doubt even Daniel Boone ever called himself a trailblazer," Violet said testily. "It's just ridiculous. People should never talk to the press unless they have to."

"Is Cynthia upset with the piece?"

"Are you kidding? She's *thrilled*. I just talked to her. She just forges ahead. That's what I love about her. She's so positive about everything. And she sent me a gorgeous shawl from Pianissimo."

"How come?"

"To thank me for all I've done for her. I mean, I've introduced her to everybody. Senator Pomador's going on her board, thanks to me. And you know he's going to bring some heavy hitters with him. I got you to do her house. And, to be honest, not only have I seen to it she's in the right hands, I saved her from some really clunky clutches."

Violet saw herself as a kind of puppet mistress and a power behind the scenes. She liked to think that if anyone wanted to make it socially in Washington, they had to pass muster with her first. Though she pretended to loathe publicity because the Bolton family ostentatiously cultivated a low-key image, she never missed a chance to promote herself as one of Washington's younger doyennes.

There were certainly splashier, more exciting hostesses in town, like Nouria Sahala, the gregarious wife of the Otanni ambassador, and Corinna Huff. But Violet set embassy social life apart from what she thought of as "real" social life, run by "cave dwellers" like herself—in other words, those whose fates and fortunes were as fixed as the sun and unaffected by a change of political power. Corinna Huff was in a class all by herself because she was married to the grand old man of the Senate, Barkley Huff, and they had the best house in Washington as well as the widest circle of influential friends in both politics and the media. Violet was a good deal younger than Corinna, and her group was less glitzy. But she could produce stars at her table—particularly philanthropic and political stars. Being married to the president of the Potomac Bank gave her a lot of clout. The influential Senator Pomador, chairman of the Appropriations Committee, was a case in point.

I have to admit that Violet's friendship with Cynthia irked me on a number of levels, the chief being that she didn't seem to see the Cynthia I saw. Cynthia treated Violet very differently from the way she treated me. Of course, Violet wasn't working for Cynthia, and I was. However, even when you work for someone, they shouldn't treat you rudely. Just the opposite, in fact.

Any time I made a date with Cynthia to meet me at the house to show her a piece of furniture I'd had especially carted in for her approval, either she would keep me waiting for two hours, or else she wouldn't show up at all. It was impossible to pin her down. When I asked her what color she wanted the library, she said firmly, "Red." "Any particular shade of red?" I said, and she replied, "That's what I'm paying you for." So I chose a warm red with a little blue in it, so it didn't veer into orange. When she saw it, she had a fit, insisting that she hated red libraries and had specifically instructed me to paint it green. There was no point arguing with her, so I had it painted over. Then she screamed about the green being the wrong color. She constantly found fault and ignored what turned out well. She never paid her bills on time. It was a trial working for her.

In short, Violet didn't see the tantrums and the dismissiveness and the contradictions. There was also Cynthia's irritating refusal to talk to me in person, instead making me deal with her crisp-voiced secretary,

Ms. Fisk. But I've found that when a close friend gets involved with a new person, it's best not to interfere or make derogatory comments. Let them find out for themselves if the friendship is or isn't worth pursuing. My theory has always been, what they do to one they will do to another. I just decided to sit back and wait.

———

Bob invited me to be his date at the new British ambassador's "Dinner for Friends," the quaint name given to a dinner where many of the people were strangers to the recently arrived couple. I knew that Violet was going too, and I suggested we have lunch so she could fill me in on the new ambassador and we could discuss what we were going to wear and all that sort of thing. It was always fun for us to be invited to the same events—even more fun now that I was with Bob and not scrounging around for a date or going as an extra girl.

Unfortunately, at the last minute she called to cancel our lunch because of some emergency committee meeting. Violet was an eleemosynary workhorse, serving on numerous boards and always at the beck and call of all kinds of charities and worthy causes.

"Then I'm going home to collapse before the dinner," she announced just before she hung up.

I decided to go over and do some work at Cynthia's house to fill the time. At noon, I was in the dining room, trying to decide between the three orange stripe samples the painter had left, when I heard the front door open and shut. It was the weekend, and no one was supposed to be there. I went on the alert, in no small part because the house was so near Montrose Park. Everyone in Georgetown was wary. I suddenly had a terrible feeling that I was in danger—due, I'm sure, to the fact that Violet had instilled in me a great fear of the stealthy ways of serial killers.

"They hunt for human game," she said. "If they're clever, and they target you, you're dead, believe me."

With Violet's words ringing in my ears, I stood very still, listening closely while planning my escape. Needless to say, I was vastly relieved when I heard a peal of laughter and recognized Cynthia's voice. I figured she was there showing off the place to yet another person she wanted to impress. What luck, I thought. I can finally grab her to come take a look at the paint samples in person, rather than having to arrange an appointment through Ms. Fisk—or worse, facing a repeat of the library fiasco.

I was on my way to say hi when I heard the other voice more distinctly. It was Grant. I knew that mid-Atlantic accent and scratchy drawl of his anywhere. I don't know why, but something told me not to let on that I was there. I paused and listened to their insinuating sonatina laughter, which quickly segued into a fugue of low moans. Tiptoeing down the corridor, I peered around the corner into the front hall. I could hardly believe my eyes.

Grant—totem-pole, steel-rod-up-his-you-know-what, mega-WASP, withholding cheapskate Bolton—had morphed into an undulating porn star! His pants were down, Cynthia's skirt was up, and the two of them were on the floor, going at it like a couple of ferrets. Seeing Grant make such passionate love was like watching a science fiction movie. In fact, I was so shocked that all I could think was what a good thing it was that I'd just had the place steam-cleaned, or else they would have been fucking in a sea of dust.

I slipped quietly out the back door, praying to God they wouldn't hear me. When I hit the street, my mind felt like a railroad station with trains pulling in and going out on fifty tracks. How was I supposed to handle this? Violet was my best friend. She and Grant had been married, what? fifteen years? They had the "perfect" marriage. And now, suddenly, in waltzed Morgan le Fay to wreck the whole thing—and *I'm* the one who had to find out about it? It wasn't fair. I don't want to know this, I thought. But how could I un-know it? How could I erase that terrible image and all its implications from my mind?

I walked back home in a stupor, wondering how long their affair had been going on. I pictured the four of us standing together at the Symphony Ball. Had it started back then? Before then? Was it a new development? Had Cynthia ordered those lightproof shutters for Grant?

One thing I was pretty sure of was that Cynthia had set her cap for Grant, rather than the other way around. I sincerely doubted that Mr. Unexcitement would have dared to make the first move. But how was that mummy of a man going to resist Cleopatra? However it started was ancient history; it was now going great guns, if that floor show was any indication.

To blab or not to blab, that was the question. Do I tell my best friend that her husband is an unfaithful bastard? Forget the fact that Grant was having an affair with Cynthia, my financial savior, who now owed me a ton of money? I couldn't even begin to focus on that aspect of the situation, although I have to admit the thought crossed my mind. The thing I really had to examine was my relationship with Violet.

I loved Violet like a sister, perhaps even more so because there was no sibling rivalry between us—just pure, unadulterated friendship. The bonds of adolescence never entirely dissolve. When she and I were together, we felt young again and laughed a lot, in that schoolgirls-at-heart sort of way that magically erases the passage of time. We were lifelines to each other's youth, guardians of our shared memories. We filled in each other's blanks and spoke the shorthand of true friendship, which takes up where it left off, no matter how long the gap in between, and is always bigger than the sum of its parts. I couldn't bear to see her hurt.

But . . . but, but, but . . . nothing counts until after the but. . . . I have to confess I felt a tincture of glee in discovering there was a crack in Violet's perfect life. Actually, crack doesn't cover it. Grand Canyon is more like it. Hard as it is to admit, I got a perverse pleasure in knowing that all those times she held Grant up as a paragon among husbands, making me feel like a jerk for having tossed him away myself and tacitly proclaiming herself the smart one for grabbing him, there was something rotten beneath the surface of their marriage that she herself wasn't aware of.

Strangely enough, this was the moment where I finally admitted to myself that I was a little jealous of Violet—not because I wished her any sorrow, but only because my own life hadn't gone as planned.

I wondered if that made me a terrible person. Possibly. But I had to acknowledge that aspect of my feelings, because my next step was so important. Should I tell her about this or not?

I tried to put myself in Violet's position. If I were she, would I want to know if my husband was cheating on me? You bet! I'd want to know as soon as possible so I could kick the bastard out before he kicked me out—or at least start stockpiling information for my lawyer.

But I wasn't Violet.

Even knowing her as well as I did, I still had no idea how she would react to the news that her perfect marriage was a sham and that her new best friend was busy seducing her husband. And all this coming from me, her oldest friend . . . ? If I told her, would she kill the messenger? If I *didn't* tell her and she eventually found out that I'd known all along, would she hate me? If I didn't tell her and she *never* found out, would it always be the big pink affair in the room between us? Would I be able to go to dinners and parties with Violet and Grant and Cynthia and simply *ignore* what I knew was going on under everyone's nose? Would this omission constitute a betrayal of sorts?

I wondered if there was a remote possibility that Violet knew about this affair and just hadn't told me. I doubted it, even though I knew Violet to be an extremely artful dodger when it suited her. She could look people she hated in the eye and make them feel as if they were her bosom buddies if she thought they would be useful to her charities or to the bank. We always joked about how duplicitous she could be in pursuit of a good cause. I was sure that was one of the reasons Grant had married her; he knew her ambition would always trump her honesty. It was probably why she'd become friends with Cynthia to begin with, because Cynthia was doing business with the bank. Still, bank or no bank, I was sure Violet would never condone an affair, and that she would have told me if she had any suspicion that Grant was cheating on her. That's not something you can keep from your very best friend.

I was dying to talk to someone about it, someone who could help me figure out what I should do. If it had been anyone else's husband, I would instantly have called Violet, sworn her to secrecy, and discussed the whole situation with her. But now I had to be very careful who I confided in. This secret was a dirty bomb. Any leakage would have dire consequences.

I knew one thing for sure: if Violet ever did find out about the affair, and the fact that I'd known about it all along without telling her, she would look back on that period of time using the psychological equivalent of a twelve-gauge pump-action shotgun—aimed directly at yours truly.

Chapter 11

That night, I dressed for dinner at the British Embassy with a heavy heart. I felt like I was going to a funeral. The inevitable Maxwell pulled up in front of my house promptly at seven. It was raining lightly. He rang the bell and stood outside, waiting for me on the stoop, a big, black umbrella in hand. I opened the door. His jowly white face gleamed out of the dusk like a pockmarked moon. He held the umbrella over my head as he escorted me to the car.

"Dismal night," I remarked—and I wasn't just referring to the weather. He didn't reply. I didn't expect him to.

Maxwell and I never said much to each other beyond hello and good night. By now, the routine was familiar: he always glanced at me in the rearview mirror, presumably to make sure I was comfortable. I always smiled at him. He always smiled back. Then he drove on. He was attentive and correct, yet careful not to intrude. The perfect chauffeur.

The green mink blanket was folded neatly on the seat. I absently stroked the fur, dreading the evening ahead. I debated whether or not to tell Bob about the situation. Here again, I had to question my motives. I asked myself if I truly wanted his opinion or if I just wanted to confide a secret to him, hoping it would act as a catalyst to somehow deepen our own relationship.

Bob and I had been seeing each other practically nonstop for over a month—which may not seem like a long time in the scheme of things, but when you're at these older bat ages and time is precious, it's a significant investment. We were still skimming the surface. Bob didn't like to talk about personal things. I kept hoping for that "watershed moment," when we'd open up to each other and take the relationship to a whole different level. But it never seemed to come. I knew I couldn't push it, so I just decided to relax and have fun.

Now I had something serious on my mind. Perhaps this was the time to find out if he could be of some real emotional support to me. By the time we reached his office, I'd pretty much decided to take the chance and confide in him.

Maxwell pulled up in front of the building. He spoke on the phone for a moment, and then turned back to me. "Mr. Poll apologizes, Ms. Lynch. He's running late."

That was actually the most I'd ever heard Maxwell utter at a clip since Bob and I started dating. I was anxious, so I started up a casual conversation to calm my nerves.

"How long have you been driving for Mr. Poll?" I asked.

"Five years," he replied without turning around.

"This must be a wonderful car to drive."

"Oh, yes, ma'am," he said emphatically, patting the steering wheel. " 'Course, she requires a lot of maintenance—just like all you beautiful ladies."

I asked him if he was from Washington, and he told me he was from Seattle originally. I remarked that he was a long way from home.

"Yeah. I miss it sometimes. 'Specially this bakery I lived around the corner from. They had the best chocolate chip cookies," he said.

"Oh, I love chocolate chip cookies. There's a farmer's market up in Bethesda that makes fabulous chocolate chip cookies. I'll bring you some."

"Thank you, ma'am! Though Lord knows I don't need 'em."

Maxwell reminded me of a jolly uncle.

I asked him some more about the car, just to make conversation. Of course, what I really wanted to ask him was how many of his boss's women he'd looked at in that rearview mirror, and what he thought of them all. I wanted to ask him if Bob acted any differently with me than he did with the others. I wanted to ask him about Melody Hartford and what the real story was there—what she was like, and why she and Bob had broken up. I wanted to ask him who else Bob had dated.

If anyone knew the secrets of Bob Poll's life, it would be his chauffeur. There was also Felicity, of course, the incongruously named secretary who arranged his schedule with dour efficiency and who Bob referred to as his "Chief of Staff." I actually spoke to her more than I spoke to Bob about our plans. But Felicity probably never laid eyes on most of the women she arranged dates for, including me, whereas Maxwell was on-site. He'd met us all in person. I sensed that old Maxwell was a loyal soul, however, and that I wouldn't be able to maneuver him into a personal conversation about his boss. So we just kept talking about the car.

Bob emerged about fifteen minutes later, wearing a tuxedo, patent leather pumps, the long white silk scarf around his neck, and a gray cashmere topcoat draped over his shoulders. Maxwell ushered him to the car, holding the umbrella over his head. Bob apologized for being late, then fell ominously silent.

"The embassy, sir?" Maxwell said.

Bob nodded curtly. He always took my hand when we were in the car, but that night he didn't. He stayed close to the window on his side with his legs crossed, the dark green mink blanket almost like a barrier between us. I knew something was wrong, and that made me even more nervous.

"Can I ask you a hypothetical question?" I said.

He paused, then turned to me, looking distracted.

"Sure. What's up?"

"Okay, let's say you found out that the wife of a very close friend of yours was cheating on him. What would you do?"

"Nothing."

"You wouldn't tell him?"

He shrugged and looked contemptuous. "God, no."

"Why not?"

"Men don't tell each other that kind of stuff."

"Do women?"

"A lot more than men."

"What makes you say that?"

"Because it's been my experience that women can't wait to break up their friends' relationships," he said with a bitter chuckle. "You gals are always egging each other on to leave us guys. You're always telling each other there's something better out there."

I got the feeling he had a specific case in mind.

"Is that what Melody's friends told her about you?" The question flew out of my mouth. I regretted it the second I asked it.

"This is your hypothetical case, not mine," he snapped.

"Okay, so you wouldn't tell him—even if you knew his wife was making a fool of him?"

"Maybe he knows she's having the affair. Maybe he doesn't mind. Maybe it turns him on."

"There's a revealing comment," I remarked.

"I don't think people's sex lives are anybody's business but their own. The last time we made a big deal about an affair, it cost the country a billion dollars, made us the laughingstock of the world— and to what end? Anyway, you can't prove it unless there's a video cam in the bedroom . . . or DNA on the dress, of course. . . . So who's your girlfriend?"

"What girlfriend?"

"The one with the unfaithful husband who you can't decide whether or not to tell."

"Very good."

"You're not subtle," he said. He didn't say it gently or jokingly. He said it rather cruelly. I turned away.

He reached across the blanket, took my hand, and kissed it. "I'm sorry. I'm sorry. Please forgive me. I have a lot of things on my mind right now. I didn't mean to be so dismissive. How can I help you?"

"I don't know. I think I'll have to figure this one out for myself."

He cast the blanket aside and moved in close to me, putting his arm around me. "You look beautiful tonight."

"Thank you. Can I ask you a personal question?"

"You can ask. I may not answer," he said sweetly.

"Were you ever unfaithful to your wife?"

"Why do you want to know?"

"Okay. You don't have to answer."

"I don't mind answering. I just want to know why you want to know?"

"Because . . . I guess I'm trying to understand what drives two people apart."

He spoke as if he were talking to himself. "It's much more interesting to try and understand what binds two people together. Why we stay with each other is much more of a mystery than why we don't."

"So why do people stay together?"

"I guess it's different in every case. The only thing I know is that it's hard to stay married. You gotta work at it. Marriage is work, work, work. People just get sick of the job."

"Did you get divorced because there was someone else?"

He thought for a moment. "No . . . no one in particular, that is. Just kind of everyone in general. I got to a point where I figured I'd done the best I could for my kids, and I wasn't getting any younger. To be honest—I wanted to be a kid myself for a while."

"How did your wife feel about that?"

"Angry. Hurt. Resentful. But she got over it."

"How?"

"Partially through the biggest divorce settlement the District had ever seen up to that time. I remember she said to me, 'Suing well is the best revenge.' "

"So are you sick of marriage?"

Once again, I could have kicked myself the minute I said this, because what I was really asking him was whether our relationship was going to wind up at a dead end, or whether he was thinking in permanent terms.

He hugged me closer. "You know what you're really asking, don't you? If I'm serious about you . . . about us. And I want to tell you right now, honestly, truthfully, to the best of my knowledge . . . I believe I am."

"You *believe* you are?"

"I wish I could give you assurances. And I think I'll be able to in time. Haven't we been having fun together?"

"Yes." I shut up. The conversation was veering into emotional quicksand. I glanced at the rearview mirror, where Maxwell's beveled eyes were fastened on us. He looked away.

"Relax," Bob said.

I nestled into the small of his arm as we drove in silence. I stared out the window. The buildings shone like wraiths in the misty night. Between my dilemma with Violet and the gaffe with Bob, all my insecurities were kicking in. I knew I had to pull myself together for the evening ahead.

Chapter 12

The British Embassy is the crown jewel of Embassy Row. Designed by the great architect Edwin Lutyens, its vast Queen Anne country house pretensions are reminiscent of the glory days of Empire. As we drove up to the right front gate, Maxwell rolled down the window and announced to the guard checking off names on a list, "Mr. Robert Poll and guest."

"Sorry, sir. I don't see his name on the list," the guard said. Maxwell had him check again, to no avail.

Finally Bob rolled down his window and said to the guard, "Is there a problem here?"

"Terribly sorry, sir, I don't see your name on the list. Have you some identification?"

Bob didn't like being asked for identification. He considered himself enough of a wheel in Washington that people should know who he was without proof. And he certainly wasn't used to being omitted from the entrance list. I saw he was getting agitated, and he'd hardly been in the best of moods to start with.

"Look, I'm Bob Poll. I've been here many, many times."

"Yes, sir. I'm terribly sorry for the inconvenience but I'll just have to check."

Bob pulled out his wallet, took out his driver's license, and handed it to the guard.

"A moment please, sir," the guard said, walking off to confer with a second security guard nearby.

Bob sat silently with clenched teeth, staring straight ahead. He was seething.

"I'm surprised you even carry a license, since you never drive yourself," I said to try and break the tension. He didn't laugh.

The guard finally came over, handed Bob back his license with apologies, and waved us on. Bob jammed the card back in his wallet and rearranged his neck like his collar was too tight.

"Obviously a new man," he said irritably.

Maxwell drove the car up the driveway and turned left into the stone porte cochere. Bob and I got out. I checked my coat in the ladies' cloakroom, freshened up, and met Bob outside the vestibule. Together we climbed the wide stone steps of the double-sided staircase under the painted gazes of George III and Queen Charlotte imprisoned in their huge gold frames—a little tweak at the Colonies. We reached the landing, where we walked down the wide hallway, picked up our seating cards from Araminta Upton, the embassy's fresh-faced, fun-loving, very "county" social secretary, and joined the reception line. Marge Horner was in front of us. Marge was the widow of Henry Horner, a big campaign contributor and former ambassador to Luxembourg. I wasn't surprised to see her there. I'd heard Marge had already latched on to Constance Morely, the new British ambassador's wife, barraging her with invitations and notes, as was her custom.

Marge Horner had made a career of courting the wives of important new ambassadors the minute they arrived in town, while they were too green to know who was who and what was what. Her favorite ploy was to give a tea party for the ambassador's wife. Marge would then be invited to the embassy to meet the ambassador, the real object of the hunt. Violet called her "Spiderwoman" because once Marge snagged the unsuspecting couple in her sticky web, she never let them go.

Marge was a largish woman with silvery blond hair. Tonight she was wearing a voluminous white evening gown that made her look either like a galleon in full sail or a duvet cover, depending on the angle. She certainly never had much use for me, who she considered to be "just" an antiques dealer and therefore not powerful in the spheres to which she aspired. We were not each other's cup of tea, but since we occasionally found ourselves brewing in the same pot, we were usually coolly cordial to one another.

Tonight, however, she gave me a warm hello and a kiss on both cheeks, which was odd, considering she was a great friend of Melody Hartford, Bob's ex-girlfriend. It was well known that Marge had done everything in her power to help Melody land Bob. I was sure that it irked her to see him with me, and that to cover it up she was giving me an overly saccharine reception. Aside from that, there was always the possibility that *I* might land Bob. It was so like Marge to hedge her bets. I saw through her, and what's more, she *knew* I saw through her, but we both pretended otherwise. She moved on, accosting Bob with air kisses and chatter.

When she thought I wasn't paying attention, she whispered to him, "Melody's here," thinking I wouldn't hear her. But I did. I watched Bob's face very closely, on the lookout for any telltale change of expression. He nodded without much interest, I was pleased to see. Marge chirped a parting remark to both of us and moved on in the line. I sidled up to Bob and whispered, "I heard that."

"What?"

"What Marge said . . . that Melody's here. Did you know she was going to be here?"

He seemed slightly nonplussed by the question. Once again, I felt like kicking myself. I didn't want to sound clinging, but I was sure I did. This whole thing with Grant's affair had thrown me off my game. I felt off-balance and anxious.

"Mel's a big girl," he said. "She can go where she wants."

His response, coupled with his initially foul mood in the car, raised my suspicions. I felt a knot forming in the pit of my stomach.

The line inched along, and we finally reached Sir James and Lady Morely at the head of the small reception line. With her luminous, fair complexion and bobbed brown hair, Lady Morely, a slender woman in her forties, had the classical look of a cameo. However, a soft sheen of sorrow undercut her cheerful party demeanor. No matter how much she smiled and laughed and talked, her large blue eyes seemed silted with sadness. The source of her sorrow was well known: years earlier, she had lost her only child to a rare disease.

Sir James, a thin, gray-haired man with owlish looks, seemed a little uncomfortable in this social situation. People said he was an exceptionally talented diplomat who was more at ease at the negotiating table than the dinner table. He was older than his wife, and he looked at her almost like a proud parent, even though it was she who seemed more at ease in their grand surroundings.

Bob held up the line as he lingered for a chat with Sir James. I wondered if this was an attempt to make up for us being detained at the entrance. I went on ahead and waded into the sea of guests in the library. Melody Hartford was practically the first person I saw—mainly because you couldn't miss her. She stood out in the largely drab crowd in a too-low-cut black dress and too-high spike heels. She looked like an elegant slut. Her plump, bright red lips seemed to throb like a juicy heart. She stood, wineglass in hand, holding forth to a small group that included Marge Horner and two men I didn't recognize but who looked like a pair of salivating hounds. I saw Marge nudge Melody surreptitiously when I came in. They both pretended not to notice me, just as I pretended not to notice them.

I breezed passed them, dying for a friendly face. I spotted Violet across the room, waving at me to join her. Under normal circumstances, I would have been relieved to see her. I would have rushed right over to dish about Marge and Melody. But tonight, when I saw her standing there between Grant and Cynthia, I froze. I literally couldn't move. Fortunately, a waiter passed by, and I grabbed a glass of wine from his tray. I drank about half of it before marching onward toward the menacing triumvirate.

Violet looked like a pretty pastry in a dress of tiered ecru lace. Cynthia, on the other hand, was sleek in a stunning purple satin number and her Rock of Gibraltar earrings. Grant was his usual totem-pole self—wooden, expressionless, with his arms crossed like a barricade in front of him, watching others dance around him. I couldn't erase the image of Grant and Cynthia going at it on the floor.

"Well, if it isn't Dream Girl!" Cynthia cried out as I joined the group. I was so fucking sick of that joke.

Grant was palpably more ill at ease than usual that night. I could barely look at him, much less say hello. He immediately excused himself to get us drinks—a ridiculous ploy, since we all had drinks in our hands. Cynthia was obviously uncomfortable too. When Violet started talking about the Beltway Basher, Cynthia's eyes wandered, and she dashed off to talk to some bigwig. Violet stared after her.

"You'd think she'd be more interested in that case, since her house is right across the street from Montrose Park," Violet said. I knew from her demeanor that she didn't have a clue what was going on between Cynthia and Grant. "Any news from your detective?" she asked.

"Not a peep."

Violet shrugged. "The case has probably gone cold. . . . You saw who's here, right? Melody Hartford. You see those big tits hanging out of her dress? Men don't like that . . . *much*," Violet said with a sarcastic little laugh.

It was a joke, but I couldn't even smile. Violet studied me for a second. "What's the matter? You look pale," she said.

"Nothing, I just, uh . . . Bob was in a foul mood when he picked me up. That's all."

"So how are things going with you guys?"

"Fine."

"Have you had your 'watershed moment' yet?"

"No. We're still kind of skimming the surface. . . . How was Acapulco?"

"That's right; I haven't really talked to you since we got back. That was an amazing conference. Cynthia was fabulous. You should have seen her. What a star! And I love what she's doing."

"Which is what exactly?"

"Making all these famous, self-important people understand that they are *nothing* compared to the world's ills and that we all have to start taking responsibility for the planet. Philanthropy is the new pink!"

I didn't laugh. Violet took a step back and stared at me. "What's with you tonight? You feeling okay?"

"Actually, I have a headache."

"Want an aspirin? I always carry them for Grant."

"No, thanks. I took something right before I left. . . . So you and Grant are okay?"

Violet cocked her head to one side. "What a strange question."

"Well, it's just that with all that traveling and stuff. I just thought you might be tired or something . . . you know."

"I was exhausted. But I've recovered. And Grant is like the Energizer Bunny. He went out to the club today and played golf. Then he had meetings all afternoon. He never stops." If she only knew.

Violet paused and assessed me again. "Look at me," she ordered.

"What?"

"*Look* at me."

It was hard to look her in the eye, but I managed. She pointed her index finger at my chest. "Revennnnn . . . you're hiding something from me, and I know what it is," she said in a singsong voice.

"What?" I held my breath.

"I bet your detective has told you something you swore not to tell anyone, right?"

Relief surged over me.

"No, I told you. I haven't seen him in ages."

Violet looked concerned. "Then what's with you, Rev? I know you're upset about something."

I certainly wasn't going to tell her what was really on my mind—at least, not there, not then. I was fumbling around for an excuse when I noticed Melody flounce over to Bob and say a flirtatious hello. She batted her eyes at him and stuck out her breasts until they were practically sitting on his chest.

"I'm worried about that!" I said, nodding toward Bob and Melody.

Percolating with forced gaiety, Melody was a little too vivacious, like a woman desperately pretending not to care. The more she pretended not to, the more it was clear she did care—very much. The question was, did Bob? He didn't appear enthralled, nor did he seem eager to get away from his old flame.

"I see your point," Violet said. "Or rather, I see her points."

We laughed grimly. For the moment, at least, I was able to transfer some of my anxiety onto Bob. This got me off the hook with Violet, except that now I had yet another thing to worry about.

"If I were you, I'd go over there and stake your claim," Violet said.

"He'll think I'm jealous."

"You are, aren't you?"

"Men don't like possessive women."

"Come on, I'll go with you." She grabbed my arm.

We walked across the room together like we used to do at school mixers when we saw a cute boy in the stag line and Violet was too embarrassed to approach him all by herself. Only then it was *me* guiding *her*. Violet never had the courage to approach a boy on her own. Unfortunately, the boy always wound up falling for me, not her. It was sad. But she never held it against me. It was just the way things were.

The second we approached, Bob reached out, grabbed my hand, and said, "Mel, you know Reven Lynch, don't you? And Violet Bolton?"

We all exchanged constipated hellos. Bob then put his arm around my waist and tugged me in close, clearly declaring his allegiance to me. But the move was so jerky and awkward that the drink in his other hand spilled on the rug, giving rise to a round of edgy laughter, then an abysmal silence.

I'm not good with silence. It makes me much too nervous.

I glanced around the wood-paneled library with its shabby genteel décor, and said in a fluttery voice, "Well, the Empire certainly isn't the only thing the sun has set on. God, how I'd love to get my hands on this room!"

"Really? We were just talking about NATO expansion," Melody countered in a condescending tone.

"I'll bet," Violet muttered under her breath.

To our collective relief, dinner was announced and we all joined the slow migration toward the ballroom. Just before entering, I was pulled aside by Araminta Upton. Jolly, convivial Araminta really ran the show, especially when the embassy was transitioning from one ambo to another. She'd always been very kind to me and often invited me to large dinners when they needed an extra woman.

"You've been requested," she said, with a knowing little smile, then quickly walked off before I could inquire by whom.

———

Bob and I were at separate tables. His was way off to the side of the room. Just before Bob took his seat, he walked over to me and whispered, "I'm in Siberia." I didn't really care where I was seated, but placement obviously meant a lot to Bob, who didn't appreciate any diminishment of his own self-importance and who was very aware of Washington pecking orders. I watched him as he went to find his seat three tables away from mine. His eyes were focused on the ambassador's table, where Melody was heading. When she stopped at the head table, Bob winced. I couldn't tell if he was still interested in her, or if it was merely the fact she was seated better than he was.

I looked around to see where Violet, Grant, and Cynthia were sitting. Cynthia was seated at Lady Morely's table, along with Grant, but not beside him. Violet was at a good table nearby. I was standing there in a kind of stupor, wondering how many people in that room were hiding secrets or pretending to be something they were not, when who should come and offer to pull out my chair for me but Senator Grider. I'd forgotten all about Araminta's comment that someone had requested me, but the minute I laid eyes on his dour farmer's face, I knew it was he.

"No Congress tonight?" I said as we sat down.

"All work and no play makes Zack a dull boy. Get it?" he said with a hopeful little smile.

"I got it. Zack, that's you, right?"

"That is correct."

He was so corny it was kind of disarming in its own blunt way.

"What's new in the Senate?" I asked.

"Do you care?"

"Uh, no. Not really."

"Then why'd you ask?"

"Because this is a dinner party, and we have to make conversation."

"No, we don't. Trouble with people is, they always think they have to talk. Know what the world fears most?"

"Another designer handbag?"

"Nope. Silence. If we had one mandatory Silent Day a month in the Senate where everybody had to just sit and think, you can bet your boots there'd be a lot less haggling and a lot more action."

"Why don't you propose it?"

" 'Cause it'd take too much talking." He cranked up that rusty-hinge laugh of his.

I picked at the appetizer, which was described as roasted red and yellow peppers and foie gras terrine. Grider eyed me as he wolfed his down.

"You don't look as fresh and carefree as the last time I saw you. Got something on your mind?" he asked.

I thought this was pretty perceptive, but I wasn't ready to answer his question honestly.

"Did you request me?" I said.

"Yup."

"How did you even know I was going to be here?"

"Got the list. Saw your name. Had my secretary call up."

"And why did you request me?"

" 'Cause I like you. Why else? You gonna ask me why I like you? I'll tell you. You're pretty. You pretend to be dumber than you are, which is a welcome change from most of the people around here. You're not in politics, so I don't have to talk shop. And you remind me of my late wife when she was young. She always said what was on her mind. You could either take it or leave it. She didn't give a hoot. That answer your question?"

"Yes, but I'm curious. If she was so outspoken, how did you get elected? I thought politicians' wives had to be as careful as the candidates."

"First time I ran for office, I told her, 'Flora, say what's on your mind, 'cause if they elect me they're gonna be stuck with you.' She did. They did. I've been in the Senate twenty-seven years."

"Your wife's name was Flora?"

"Yup. She was pretty as a rose too. Know what kind of flower you remind me of? A daffodil."

"That's too bad. I think I'd rather be an orchid. A lovely hothouse orchid."

"Nope. Daffodil. What do I remind you of?"

I drew back to appraise him. "A great big ear of corn."

"Yellow corn, white corn, Indian corn, Kandy Korn? What kinda corn you got in mind?" he said without missing a beat.

He looked dead serious for a second before a dry smile twitched across his straw lips. His gray eyes twinkled at me. Grider was a disarming combination of sternness and whimsy. I couldn't help but like him. We talked straight through the entrée, and I suddenly realized that he'd actually managed to get my mind off my current problems.

During dessert, Sir James tapped his glass and rose to his feet. He made a toast welcoming us all to the embassy at this "Dinner for Friends." Then he introduced Dr. Ranvaneer Singh, a special guest who he said would tell us about "a subject that is very near and dear to Constance's and my heart: childhood lupus."

Dr. Singh was a short, stout, bearded man in a neat white turban who explained what childhood lupus was and described some of the advances being made in the field. He lauded Lady Morely's Childhood Lupus Foundation, which, he reminded us, had been started in memory of her deceased child. He spoke in a lilting Indian accent, reminding us all that death is where it all ends up, no matter how much we eat, drink, and make merry. It was rather a strange speech which had little to do with the evening. When he finally sat down, people looked as if they'd been drenched by a hard rain. We all thought that was the end of it when, suddenly, Lady Morely stood up and tapped her glass.

"I had not planned to say anything," she began in her clipped British accent. "But something so extraordinary has happened that I must share it with all of you here tonight. . . ."

An expectant hush filled the room as we all wondered what joy could brighten the gloom of Dr. Singh's speech.

Lady Morely went on: "The Childhood Lupus Foundation has received a most generous pledge of *one million dollars*—from Ms. Cynthia Rinehart!"

My heart sank. I immediately focused on Violet across the room. She was giving Cynthia the thumbs-up sign. Cynthia stood up as everyone applauded—everyone except Senator Grider, that is. He crossed his arms, sat back in his chair, and looked impassively at Cynthia as she gave her stock speech about the importance of philanthropy in today's world.

"I put my money where my heart is," Cynthia said finally, looking soulfully at Lady Morely, who would have burst into tears if she wasn't English. The English know how to stow it in public.

As soon as Cynthia sat down, I leaned in and said softly to Grider, "What do you think of her?"

"Never met her. You're the one decorating her house, aren't you? What do *you* think of her?"

I'd forgotten that I'd told him that, and I was surprised he remembered. I knew I had to be careful what I said now.

"I, um . . . well, working for someone is different from knowing them socially—"

"First time I've seen you shy about speaking your mind. How come you don't want to tell me what you think? Don't you like her?"

I paused, then said firmly, "No. I don't."

"How come?"

I actually thought about telling him she was having an affair with my best friend's husband, but I refrained. Instead, I said, "She's imperious and self-important. She thinks she's God's gift. She has her own agenda, and I don't trust her as far as I can throw her."

"She'd be right at home in the Senate. Sounds like a few of my colleagues," he said. "Can I ask you a question?"

"Sure."

"How does she pay you?"

"By check probably . . . when she does pay me," I added slyly.

"She owe you money?"

"A little."

"Personal check?"

"I think so. Actually, I'm not sure. She might do wire transfers. I leave the bookkeeping to my assistant, Rosina."

"You mind taking a look?"

"Okay. I'll let you know. Why is it important?"

"It's important how people pay for things in life."

I suddenly wondered if Grider had requested to sit next to me for reasons other than the ones he stated. Did he have a hidden agenda as well? Was he really just after information about Cynthia?

"Like to see you home, if I may," he said.

"I'm sorry, but I'm here with someone."

"Who?"

"Bob Poll. You know him, don't you?"

Grider nodded up and down, up and down, with a fixed expression on his face. He looked like one of those dolls you stick on a dashboard whose head slowly bobbles as the car starts to move. At that moment, Bob stood up and signaled to me he wanted to leave. He rose before either the ambassador or Lady Morely, which was considered an act of lèse-majesté. He started walking out of the ballroom. I had no choice but to follow him.

"Sorry, Senator, I have to go. It's been interesting talking to you."

"You're not a hothouse flower, you know. You could grow in a nice plain field."

I had no idea what he meant, but I suspected it was his idea of a flirtatious remark.

Chapter 13

The minute we got into the car, Bob started ranting about the evening. He didn't hear Maxwell when Maxwell said, "Where to, sir?" So Maxwell just started to drive.

"Worst dinner I've ever been to at the Brits!" Bob fumed.

He criticized everything. The food: "Inedible. A drawback in food, dontcha think?" The company: "Second-raters, all of 'em." The ambassador: "Doesn't understand the first thing about Washington. God help the Queen." Even the flowers got a hit. He referred to the pretty, colorful mixed bouquets as "tacky FTD deliveries."

I didn't agree with Bob about the evening or about the charming new ambassador and his wife, but his anxiety struck a chord in me. I felt sorry for him and the fact that he let his feelings show over a stupid social slight—i.e., seating him in the Falklands while his ex-girlfriend got London. If anyone was at fault for this, it was Araminta Upton. Minta's jolly demeanor hid a canny talent for arranging some truly diabolical seating assignments. If she didn't like you, you'd know it the minute you sat down. I guess she didn't like Bob.

When he finally calmed down, I put my head on his shoulder and snuggled up to him. His mood changed on a dime.

"I'm sorry. Thanks for putting up with me," he said.

Maxwell tried again, and Bob told him to drive to my house. I finally got up the courage to ask him the question I'd been dying to hear the answer to all night: "So did you know your former girlfriend was going to be there?" I said it lightly, teasingly, so it wouldn't sound as desperate as it felt.

"Mel? No, I didn't know."

No Academy Award for him. Of course he knew. That's probably why he was in such a foul mood when he picked me up. But I didn't press the point. I asked him if he wouldn't mind raising the glass shield between us and the driver. I didn't want Maxwell eavesdropping. Bob flicked a switch, and the partition glided up.

"How much does Melody know about us?"

Bob shrugged. "Don't know, don't care."

I studied his face for a long moment. "You *really* don't care?"

"You care more than I do. I'm with you. I'm happy I'm with you."

"Are you really?" I knew I sounded insecure. I was.

He stroked my hand. "You don't trust men at all, do you? Why is that?"

"Experience, I guess."

"And you've been hurt," he said matter-of-factly, like it was par for the course.

"Let's just say . . . disappointed."

"You know, I'm doing my best to remedy that. I really am." He sounded so sincere.

"I know."

"Are you saying I don't pay enough attention to you? Because if that's the case, I'm gonna pay more attention to you. I'm gonna pay so much attention to you, you'll get sick of me."

I smiled. He really was being adorable. "No, it's not that."

"What is it then?"

"Okay, well, it's just that we never seem to go beneath the surface. We're always sort of skimming along on top of the wave. You know what I mean?"

"Not really."

"It's kind of hard to explain because you're so attentive and wonderful, and it's such fun being with you. But . . . it's all kind of one note. On one level."

I felt him deflate. "I'm sorry you feel that way."

I gripped his hand tighter to reassure him. "Look, I really want this to work out for us, Bob. You make me so happy, and I think I make you happy."

"Yeah, you do."

"But right now I don't feel as if we're getting to know each other any better—just *longer*. If that makes any sense."

Bob clenched his jaw and turned away, humming with agitation. He stared out the window. The whole evening seemed to have derailed him somehow. We drove in silence for a long time, with Maxwell sneaking peeks at us in the rearview mirror.

I didn't know what else to say. I was kicking myself for having said too much already. I thought I'd succeeded in plunging Bob back into his black mood. When we pulled up in front of my house, Bob walked me up the steps to my front door. I invited him in for a drink. He accepted. One thing led to another, and before I knew it we were in bed.

That night the sex was wilder than it had ever been. Afterward, instead of him getting up and leaving, we talked. It was the moment I'd been hoping for. He told me all about Melody and how painful it had been to break up with her, but how he just didn't want to marry her, and she told him to take a hike. He told me how he was terrified of commitment, and how he didn't want to make another mistake. He told me about his arid marriage, and how he started cheating on his wife right after their first child was born. We talked about his childhood—his distant, pious mother and his controlling, abusive father, who demeaned him constantly and made him feel inadequate no matter what kind of success he had.

I told him a lot about my own life too. The miracle was that he listened. I confessed how weird it felt that things just hadn't turned out for me the way they were supposed to, given all my early promise. I admitted I was a little jealous of Violet because she'd started out with so little and made so much of her life, whereas I'd started out with so much and let all my opportunities slip through my fingers. I thought about telling him about Grant and Cynthia, but I decided against it. This was our watershed moment. I didn't want to pollute it with other people.

We talked for a good two hours. At the very end, I said tearfully, "I just can't seem to get it right." Bob took me in his arms, kissed my tears away, and said tenderly, "Until now."

God, what a moment. I felt so safe with him. And I knew I could help him too, because for all his money and power, he was actually quite a lonely man. I asked him to spend the night, but he very sweetly said he had to go.

"It's almost two. Big day tomorrow. I've got this business thing I'm working on. Forgive me?"

I put on a bathrobe and saw him downstairs. As we reached the front door, he took me in his arms one more time and said, "I'm not good at expressing myself. I want things to work out between us, Reven. I really do. Just give me some time, will you? And trust me a little. You're wonderful. I love being with you. I love you."

The magic L-word! And I didn't have to say it first or coerce him into saying it. He'd said it all on his own, with no prompting.

Naturally, I replied: "I love you too, Bob."

He blew me a kiss at the door. Even though it was chilly, I stood on the threshold and watched him trot down the steps toward the waiting Rolls. He tapped the passenger window to wake up Maxwell, who was asleep in the driver's seat. Bob got into the car and waved at me as they drove off into the night.

Did I love him? I certainly loved the idea of him. And I really loved that he loved me.

Or so he said.

Chapter 14

My phone rang the next morning around eight. I was semi-awake, having tossed and turned all night, thinking about Bob as well as the horrible triangle of Violet and Cynthia and Grant. I hoped it was Bob calling to tell me he couldn't sleep either. But it was Gunner.

"You up?" he said.

"Sort of. Why?"

"Can you meet me? It's important."

"Come on over and have a cup of coffee."

"I'd rather not. Can you meet me up at the Oak Hill Cemetery ASAP?"

"You're kidding. The *cemetery*?"

"Unless you can think of somewhere more private around here. It's important. Please."

Only for Gunner would I have dragged my ass out of bed to go to a cemetery! I layered up for the cold and walked briskly through the bustling streets of Georgetown. Garbage was being picked up. People were on their way to work. As I crossed R Street, I glanced at Cynthia's house, thinking of what had transpired there. I finally reached the cemetery. The main wrought-iron gates at the entrance were padlocked. But the smaller side gate, usually locked at that hour as well, was ajar, just wide enough for me to slip into the grounds.

It was a dull gray winter day. I spotted Gunner a short distance away, standing in front of the small Gothic stone chapel. He was wearing a black coat and black knitted cap, walking around and rubbing his hands together to keep warm. He saw me and waved me over.

"What exactly do you have against the indoors?" I said as I reached him.

"Come on, let's walk. It's too damn cold to stand still."

"And whose fault is that?"

Gunner looked exhausted, like he'd been up for days. He shoved his hands deep into the pockets of his coat. White puffs of our breaths were visible as we strolled through the sprawling, hilly terrain. Grand mausoleums, stone statuary, and large crosses loomed over the more modest moss-covered headstones. The ground was damp.

"What's the big emergency?" I asked him.

Gunner flung me a sidelong glance. "How serious is it with you and Bob Poll?"

I was amazed by his question.

"How do you know I'm going out with Bob?"

He didn't respond. That was typical Gunner. He used silence as a weapon, knowing that nervousness or impatience would always get the better of me.

"If you want to know the truth, I think we're pretty serious about each other. Why?"

"Ever hear of a club called King Arthur's?"

I groaned. "Not only have I heard of it. I've actually been there."

"When?"

"A couple of years ago, I guess. This smarmy PR guy took me there on our first and, I might add, *last* date."

King Arthur's was an upscale "gentleman's club" on M Street. It consisted of a long bar and a large, dimly lit room, packed with small round tables and their cargo of lone men watching a naked girl gyrating around a pole planted in the center of a tiny, bright stage. I remembered how the music had scorched my ears, how my date had stuck a twenty-dollar bill into the bra of the waitress who brought us our drinks, and how he'd ogled the curvy dancer in the diamond G-string as she dipped and twirled around his fantasies. I knew I was in real trouble when four off-duty strippers came to pay homage to my date, like chickens paying homage to the fox.

I'd never been to a strip club before. The atmosphere was strangely antiseptic. Every so often, a man got up from his seat and wandered over to the little stage to ogle the naked, dancing girl. Touching was forbidden, so the two caressed each other with their eyes until the man rewarded her by stuffing money into the white satin garter around her leg, an ersatz nosegay blooming with dollar bills. I got really bored watching these zombie guys come and go in turn. There was no talking to my date, not only because the music was too loud but because his high-speed Internet attention was focused elsewhere. It was not an evening I remembered with any fondness.

"Don't tell me you dragged me out here at the crack of dawn to ask me if I'd ever heard of King Arthur's?"

"Not exactly. What'd you do last night?"

"I went to the British Embassy."

"With Bob Poll?"

"As if you didn't know. Are you following him or me?"

"What'd you two do after you left the embassy?"

"We went back to my house, if you must know."

"Know where he went when he left you?" Gunner asked.

"I do now . . . King Arthur's, right?" Gunner nodded.

"Nancy Sawtelle worked at King Arthur's as a hostess for eight weeks when she moved to D.C. I have a hunch the guy who did her goes to that club. I've been going there on and off, checking out the scene. They don't know I'm a cop. Last night, your friend Mr. Poll shows up there at two in the morning. And I see it's not the first time he's ever been there. They all know him—bouncers, bartenders, waitresses, strippers. He's treated like King Arthur himself."

I felt sick. It threw my whole relationship with Bob into question.

"Well, he's always been rumored to have a dark side. So he's into strippers. So what?" I said, trying to act nonchalant when in fact I was mortified.

"So I'm already looking at Mr. Poll because I can put him at the Kennedy Center parties with the murdered girls. Last night I see him at King Arthur's, the club where Nancy Sawtelle worked. You do the math."

I stopped short. "Whoa! You're not seriously suggesting that Bob Poll is your serial killer?"

"I don't know. I'm just saying it's a coincidence that this one guy happens to go to the two places where every one of the murdered girls either worked or partied. And it's not like these two places are a natural fit. I mean, we're not talking about going to the Kennedy Center and the National Gallery or the Phillips Collection. We're talking about the Kennedy Center and King Arthur's. High culture and low life. How many people span those worlds?"

I guffawed. "A lot more than you think, trust me."

"Maybe. But Poll's the one I'm looking at now."

"Well, it wouldn't be the first time I'd fallen for a killer!" I said lightly.

Gunner glared at me. "You think this is *funny*?"

His intensity scared me a little. "No."

"Yeah, you do. You think it's a game. I'm gonna bring you some autopsy pictures so you can see how funny those girls look after this guy's gotten through with them."

We walked on.

"I'm sorry. I don't think it's funny," I said after a time. "I just know Bob, that's all. He may be a serial flirt, but he's no serial killer."

"Uh-huh. . . . You sure about that?"

"Absolutely, positively. He's not the type."

"There is no type. Psychopaths can be very charming. How do you think they get their victims—by looking like what they really are? Ted Bundy looked like the all-American boy with a bright future. That's what made him so goddamn dangerous: no one could believe he was the *type*."

"You sound exactly like Violet. She loves Ted. And she thinks there's a serial killer lurking around every corner."

"Well, I got news for you. There's one lurking around here."

"It's not Bob."

"You ever talk to him about these murders?" Gunner asked.

"No."

"He know about me?"

"*No.*"

"Make sure he doesn't find out. . . . Do me a favor?"

"What?"

"Next time you and Mr. Wrong get together . . . ? Ask him casually about the murder in Montrose Park. See how he reacts."

"What if he kills me?"

"Then I guess you won't be getting back to me."

"Ha. Ha. You know, I'm not sure I like you, Gunner."

"Yeah. And you wanna know *why* you don't like me?"

"Why?"

" 'Cause I'm a nice guy. What is it with you girls who only like bad boys? Huh? Can you answer me that? Bob Poll's a bad boy, Reven. Don't fall for him."

I didn't want to tell him I had already fallen.

"Can I ask you something?" I said.

"Shoot."

"What did Bob do when he was at the club?"

"Sat down. Had a drink. Talked to a few of the girls."

"That's not so bad, is it?"

"You tell me."

I had to admit, it wasn't a great sign after our particularly intimate night. We continued on in silence.

"I'm finding out all this stuff I don't want to know," I said, after a time.

"Like what?"

"Like Grant Bolton and Cynthia Rinehart are having an affair."

"How do you know?"

"I saw them going at it on the floor of her house yesterday afternoon."

"They see you?"

"No, thank God! I got out of there fast. Violet's my best friend. Last night we were all together at this dinner at the British Embassy. Grant's making a fool of her, and she doesn't have a clue. I don't know what the hell to do. Should I tell her what's going on or not? What do you think?"

"I can't comment on that."

"Why not?"

"That's your world, not mine."

"Cheating husbands are universal, don't you think? Sometimes I think they make the world go round. I'm just asking you for your advice. If you were in this situation, would you tell a friend if his wife was cheating on him?"

"Probably not."

"Would you want to know if you were the one being cheated on?"

"I don't know."

"By the way, are you married?"

"I was."

"So why did you get divorced, if I'm not being too personal?"

"I didn't get divorced. My wife died. And that's as personal as I'm gonna get. Can we change the subject?"

I felt bad. "I'm sorry. . . . It's just that I'm really upset about this situation, and I don't know what to do. Now you come along and tell me Bob's into strippers—"

"You better pray that's all he's into."

We stopped in front of an old stone mausoleum with the name HOLLIS chiseled in big bold letters above the entrance. It was a big, dank tomb with eight crypts lining the interior, four on the bottom, four on top. Whoever designed it had thoughtfully provided a low stone bench to the left of the entrance where mourners could sit down and take a rest. The iron grille door was ajar. A heavy chain lay on the ground beside a broken padlock. Vandals had gotten in and sprayed white paint swirls over a couple of the crypts.

Gunner closed the door and wound the heavy chain around the bars, fastening it with the broken padlock, trying to make it appear secure.

"No respect," he said.

"No," I agreed. And I wasn't just talking about the mausoleum either. We sat down on the bench. I finally said, "Okay, I'll ask Bob about Miss Montrose."

"Thanks. I'm curious to hear what he has to say."

Gunner looked around and decided this was a good place for us to meet. It was off the main path, isolated under a stand of trees. He said we needed a code name so we could text each other in one word if either of us wanted to come here and talk. I suggested "Usherville" because the dank tomb could have been a stage set for "The Fall of the House of Usher."

"We'll make Usherville our little place, shall we?" I said as a joke.

Gunner shook his head. "I wish I had your innocence."

Chapter 15

When I got back home from the cemetery, I couldn't stop thinking about Bob going to that strip club. Violet called to ask if I wanted to go for a jog. Well, she didn't exactly ask. She said she'd be over to pick me up in ten minutes. Under normal circumstances, I would have enjoyed a nice run with her so we could rehash the previous night's dinner, assessing the new ambassador and his wife and their entertaining style, as well as poking fun at Marge Horner and a couple of other barnacles at the party. But today I was afraid to see my old friend—afraid of what I might or might not say. I still hadn't made up my mind whether or not to tell her about Grant.

"You look exhausted," Violet said when I opened the door.

"Big night," I said. "Let's get going."

As we jogged up Thirty-first Street, I told her about my watershed moment with Bob and the early-morning meeting with Gunner.

"*Ewww*. Bob went to a strip club after that?" she said with distaste.

"I know. I'm ill. I feel like I should break up with him right now."

Violet stopped dead. "Don't you dare! He probably just went there for a drink, to unwind."

"You think so? Really?"

"Look, you're having a great time with this man. He obviously cares about you. He just told you he loved you, for heaven's sakes. Are you going to let this one little incident that you're not even supposed to know about color the whole relationship? Give the poor guy a break, for heaven's sakes."

Violet's words calmed me down. That's the power of friendship. She could have taken a totally different tack that morning. If she had, who knows? I might have broken up with Bob right then. But I think Violet understood that deep down I wanted to be convinced his behavior wasn't all that terrible, just a "guy thing," as she put it. She told me to forget about it. That was easier said than done. But I was falling in love with the guy and when you fall in love you can easily make excuses for really dicey behavior.

"Well, there's another little matter too," I said. I told her Gunner's theory.

She burst out laughing. "Talk about good news, bad news. Good news is you finally find a guy. Bad news is he's a serial killer! How TV movie of the week is that?! You can sell your story to the networks!" Violet said with great glee in her voice.

"I didn't say that! I just said Gunner's interested in the fact that Bob could have been in the vicinity of all five girls, that's all. He's not accusing Bob of being the killer."

"Well, we always heard Mr. Poll had a dark side," Violet said.

"My question to you is: Do I tell Bob about Gunner or not?"

I thought this was a rather clever way of asking Violet what she would do if she were in possession of a sensitive secret.

She slowed down. "Seriously? The key question is, Do you think Bob could possibly be involved in these murders? Because if you do, then you can't tell him about Gunner. And you certainly shouldn't be going out with him. Do you think he's involved?"

I may have answered a little too quickly when I replied, "No! It's ridiculous!" The instant I said this, I felt hesitant. "Still, that visit to the strip club gives me pause. Not the fact that he went there, but the fact that he went there last night—after we'd had such an intimate time together."

"I told you to forget about that. It's probably an old haunt and the only place he could think of that was open at that hour," Violet said. "You promised Gunner you wouldn't tell anyone about him, didn't you?"

"Yeah. But I told you."

"Oh, that doesn't count. I'm your best friend. Anyway, if Gunner's such a great detective, I'm sure he suspects you've told me about him. He's gotta know you well enough by now to know you can't keep your mouth shut."

"Thanks a lot."

"Okay, so ask yourself this: Is there any advantage in telling Bob?"

"Not really. But keeping a secret from somebody can ruin a relationship if they find out later on that you've been hiding something from them."

I studied her closely to see how she'd react.

"I think some secrets are better kept," she said.

"You do? Are there things you'd rather not know?"

She hesitated. "Let's put it this way . . . there are probably some things we're all better off not knowing. I know there are things I'd rather not tell," she said dramatically.

"Such as?"

She paused. "I cheated at golf the other day with Rainy."

"You didn't!"

"She always cheats with me. I thought, Today it's my turn."

"I don't believe you."

"Okay, well, I *almost* cheated. I thought about it, then I chickened out. . . . Did I ever tell you I was a spy and that I did things for my country that I can never ever talk about?" she said.

"Please, Vi, I'm not in the mood today," I said.

Violet made up for being such a straight arrow by inventing all kinds of glamorous personas for herself.

We trotted into Montrose Park, down the wide paved road leading into the woods. People had been warned not to go too deep into the park until they caught the killer.

"We should turn around," I said.

Violet didn't reply. A devilish look came over her face. I knew that look from boarding school. She got it whenever we were about to do something illegal, like smoke a cigarette or sneak off campus to grab a sandwich at the local deli.

She picked up the pace and beckoned me to follow her.

"Come back! It's not safe!" I cried.

"Chicken!" she called out and kept on running.

I certainly wasn't going to let her go into the woods alone—not with a killer on the loose. I ran after her, very aware that no one else was around.

"Where the hell are you going?" I yelled.

"*You'll see!*" She veered off onto a narrow trail.

I followed her along the path to a clearing, where strips of tattered yellow crime scene tape dangled from thin metal rods planted in the earth. We stopped short, panting from the run, staring out at the bleak ground. I immediately understood where we were.

"Oh, my God," I whispered.

"This is where they found Miss Montrose. She was right over there," Violet said, pointing ahead. Her mischievous glee had evaporated. She looked pale and solemn.

"Jesus, I thought it was over in the other direction, near Whitehaven."

Violet shook her head. "No. It was here."

We stared at the scene for a long moment. I imagined Nancy Sawtelle, lying facedown in the dirt—violated, soiled, and bloody. The leaves rustled. The tapes fluttered in the breeze. I felt a chill of evil. Violet and I looked at each other. I knew she felt it too. We both turned at the same time and ran away as fast as we could.

When we were walking home, I asked her how she knew the exact spot. She told me the police and forensic teams had been there for days, combing the whole area.

"I snuck up there a couple of times to watch them," she said.

In order to diffuse the grimness we both felt, Violet made a joke, as was her wont.

"Here's the thing: serial killers never get up in the morning and think, What shall I do today? They get up and say, '*Who* shall I do today?' You kind of have to admire their sense of purpose."

I smiled in spite of myself. But then a terrible image flashed through my mind. I saw Bob standing over a girl in a field with his arm raised and a club in his hand. In one swift and mighty blow, he cracked her skull open. When she turned her bloody head, it was me.

Chapter 16

The next night, Bob took me to a black-tie opening at the National Gallery. Maxwell called for me as usual, and we drove to Bob's office. I was nervous about seeing Bob. Gunner's unwelcome revelation about the strip club had taken the whole day to really sink in, but sink in it had. I wanted to know why he'd gone there. Was it just to relax? Or was there someone special there he wanted to see? I couldn't very well ask him without betraying my relationship with Gunner. But it was very much on my mind when Bob got into the car and gave me an affectionate kiss hello.

"How's my girl?" he said, settling into the back seat.

"Fine."

"This should be a fun evening."

"I thought last night was a fun evening," I said, throwing a little chum in the water.

"Parts of it were, anyway," he said.

"Guess what Violet and I did today?"

"Let me see. . . . You planned an invasion."

"We went jogging in Montrose Park. She took me up to see where that poor woman was murdered."

"What poor woman is that?"

"Don't you remember that woman who was murdered in the park a couple of months ago? The one they think was the victim of the serial killer."

Bob shrugged. "They think everyone's the victim of a serial killer. Frankly, if there were that many serial killers around, we'd all be dead."

"Don't you believe they exist?"

"In Hollywood more than anywhere else. They're on the major villains list: Nazis, terrorists, the CIA, rich white guys, and serial killers. Where would movies be without them?"

His amused nonchalance was no great relief to me. On the contrary, it made me wonder if I'd had suspicions about him that I wasn't admitting to myself.

"I can't believe you didn't read about it. It was all over the papers."

"I probably did, but you know what? I try to put that kind of story out of my mind. It's mental pollution."

I stared out the window at the passing night, trying to make up my mind whether to ask him the next question. Finally, I turned and asked him, "Did you mean what you said last night?"

"I don't know. What did I say?"

"That you loved me."

He feigned surprise. "Did I say that?"

I didn't answer. I just nodded. I didn't much care for his coyness.

"Then I must have meant it," he said, pulling me in close. "You mustn't be so insecure, Reven. Let things take their course. Don't worry so much."

I laid my head on his shoulder, and we drove the rest of the way in silence. As we pulled up in front of the East Wing at the National Gallery, I realized that the partition in the car was down and that Maxwell could hear everything I'd said. I was a little embarrassed. That was the thing about Maxwell. He was like a fixture you forgot was there. I wondered if he'd been paying any attention, or if he just tuned out and drove. As he gave me his hand to help me out of the car, I thought I detected a sympathetic smile on his large round face and a look of compassion in his eyes. He'd surely been listening, and I think he felt a little sorry for me. This was the first time I got the sense that Maxwell wasn't just a fireplug with a hat, but a person who took more of an interest in his boss's life than he let on.

———

Bob held my hand as we entered the East Wing of the National Gallery. We paused for a photographer, who snapped our picture and asked for my name. Unlike the guard at the British Embassy, he knew who

Bob was. We walked on into the airy garden atrium, with its multi-pyramided glass ceiling, pale stone floor, and large, whimsical Calder mobile dangling overhead. We headed one flight up, where the dinner was to be held. The many round tables covered in pearl gray tablecloths and set with lush white flower centerpieces and silver candlesticks softened the angular impact of the majestic modern space.

The evening was in honor of the opening of the Dan Flavin retrospective. Before dining, the guests were invited for a private viewing of Flavin's innovative neon sculptures. A large placard hanging on the wall just outside the entrance to the show rooms read "DAN FLAVIN, 1933–1996," in bold red letters. Underneath, printed in smaller black type: "*This exhibition was made possible by a grant from the Cynthia A. Rinehart Foundation.*"

My heart sank.

As Bob and I ambled through the maze of rooms, each one glowing with a work of Flavin's elegant fluorescent art, we discussed the pros and cons of buying a Flavin for his dining room. We walked into a room where several railroad tracks of glowing neon tubes climbed the walls and snaked across the ceiling, showering us in a cool but intense red light. I was enjoying the somewhat hallucinatory effect when I noticed another couple at the far end of the room. It was Grant and Cynthia, staring at each other like Romeo and Juliet, their faces bathed in the red glow. Suddenly, the room was less like a cool shower and more like hell.

Had Bob noticed them? If he had, he made no sign of it. He was busy staring up at the red railroad-tracked ceiling.

"Think red would be good in my dining room?" he asked me.

That neon night belonged to Cynthia. Dozens of people came up to her to congratulate her on the exhibition. Many more people knew her now. She was becoming a real power player. She appeared to be in a good mood because she was even civil to me, the minion decorator. At one point she said to me, "We wanna get one of these in the house," meaning a Flavin. All I could think of was her and Grant doing the horizontal cha-cha on the hall floor. The image was engraved on my retina like an etching on glass. I could see through it, but it was always there.

Meanwhile, Violet stood by, basking in the reflected neon light of her protégée. I overheard her talking to one of the guests.

"You know, when Cynthia first suggested this show, some of the old fuddy-duddies around here didn't want it. They don't think light is art. But she persisted—with a little bit of help from me and Grant, of course," she said with a wink. Violet never missed a chance to subtly remind people that Grant was a trustee of the National Gallery, and his father had once been the president.

"Cynthia's like a shot of adrenaline for this town," she went on. "She won't let sleeping dogs lie, that woman," Violet said with pride.

I thought of one sleeping dog Cynthia had woken up with a vengeance.

We sat through an interminable dinner. Just before dessert, Rutledge Price, the director of the National Gallery, stood and introduced Cynthia as "the woman who made this evening possible." Another grant. Another speech. Another party.

Cynthia took her kudos, then introduced a heavy metal band who sang so loudly the Calder mobile shivered. Not a great choice for that staid, older crowd. Bob remarked that the only upside was that a lot of them were pretty deaf anyway. Still, many people left, including Bob and me. I waved good-bye to Violet, who was boogying away in her seat, snapping her fingers, having a high old time, gloriously oblivious to the treachery around her.

I felt physically and mentally depleted by the time I got home. Even Bob noticed that my mood was subdued. He asked if I was feeling okay. In fact, we were both a little reticent. If a relationship was two steps forward, one step backward, we were in the midst of a backward step. He kissed me good night at the door. It was clear that neither of us felt in the mood for anything more. As I got into bed, the only bright side to the evening I could think of was that Melody hadn't been there to stoke up old memories.

Chapter 17

A couple of days later I had lunch at Café Milano, a chic, airy restaurant in Georgetown. By day, Café Milano was almost like a private club where we all went for lunch and where we were bound to run into people we knew. Dinner was the same. Starting at around ten at night, however, the place transformed into a glitzy singles scene. A younger, hipper crowd congregated at the restaurant's long bar, drinking and flirting to strains of loud music. Violet and I often speculated on what the array of gorgeous girls in their halter tops and skinny jeans did for a living, since we never saw folk like that during the day. "You can bet they ain't working at Brookings," was Violet's line.

My lunch date today was Peggy Myers. As president of the Capitol Symphony and the wife of Rolly Myers, an influential power broker around town, Peggy went everywhere, and she was privy to a lot of gossip. Rolly had worked his way up from modest roots, but Peggy came from a grand old African-American family of doctors, lawyers, and intellectuals going back generations. Her sense of elegance was innate, not merely a patina she had acquired. Her one failing was that she was too discreet. Still, we were such good friends that I could usually read between the lines of her diplomatic lips.

I was curious to know if she'd heard any whispers about Grant and Cynthia, particularly since Cynthia was around the Kennedy Center a lot, and Peggy was there too on account of the symphony. I was trying to artfully steer her around to that subject when who should loom over our table but Marge Horner.

"Mind if I join you girls until my lunch date arrives?" she said, sitting down before we could object.

I flung Peggy a beleaguered look and ordered another glass of wine. We started one of those conversations about the various ambassadors and their wives, which embassies gave good parties, and which ones were to be strictly avoided. It was a little dicey talking about these things with Marge, because Marge wasn't considered what Corinna Huff deemed a "safe" person. Corinna divided the world into "safe" and "unsafe" people. Safe people were comprised mainly of her glittery, high-powered group of friends, people around whom she felt comfortable and could say anything without fear of its being retailed to the gossip vendors around town. Unsafe people were those who threw scraps of information to bigger dogs in order to further their social prospects.

Marge Horner, who lived to repeat gossip because she thought it stamped her as an insider, was definitely an unsafe soul. She blurted out rumors and secrets under the guise of deep concern. She also had that irritating knack of reminding people they'd once said something they clearly regretted—like having spoken ill of a candidate they were now supporting, or having criticized a hostess whose hospitality they were currently enjoying.

Marge brought up the evening at the British Embassy, mainly to let us know she was now a good friend of the Morelys. Or so I thought. But then she mentioned that she had been sitting at Violet's table, and that there had been a discussion about the Beltway Basher.

"Violet regaled us with all the gory details about the crimes. It was the most un–British Embassy conversation you can imagine," Marge said.

"That's Violet," I said.

"Isn't it?" Peggy said with a smile.

Marge leaned in toward us and lowered her voice. "I was so shocked to hear that she and Grant are separating," she said with intrusive concern.

Marge Horner's information was like secondhand smoke—that is to say weak, but just as deadly.

"Who told you that?" I said angrily.

She drew back. "Oh, I don't know. I forget."

When I pressed her as to where she'd heard this horrible rumor, she got very fluttery and evasive. She maintained she didn't remember, but I didn't believe her.

"Think, Marge. It's important. *Think.*"

"I told you. I forget. I just heard it, that's all. You hear things. I don't keep notes on who said what. I'm sorry I mentioned it. I feel terrible now."

What a lie. She didn't feel terrible in the least. Marge knew I was Violet's closest friend, and Marge had had it in for Violet ever since Violet gave a birthday party for one of the new cabinet wives and didn't include her. Hell hath no fury like an uninvited guest, I always say.

I stared at Marge for a long moment with narrowing eyes, viewing her like a rival government agency, with hefty amounts of suspicion and disdain. She finally took the hint, stood up, and announced she was moving to her table to wait for her lunch date to arrive.

"I said I was sorry," she muttered as she left, sounding about as sincere as an indicted lobbyist.

Peggy was ominously silent after Marge's abrupt departure. She tried to avoid my gaze by sipping her wine.

"Don't tell me . . . you've heard this too, haven't you?" I asked her.

"Oh, you know what this town's like, Reven," she said dismissively.

Coming from Peggy, this was a clear yes. It was obviously a subject she didn't want to get into. I reflected on the tricky syncopation of a long marriage. I knew for a fact that most of my married friends had lived through periods of infidelity—either on the part of the woman or the man. These dalliances were rarely spoken of and not generally known. They were tense moments that passed, after which adjustments were made and new rhythms set. A good marriage, like a good friendship, has to be larger than the sum of its parts.

But here's the thing: if Marge and Peggy knew something was up, it meant the tom-toms were beating. It was one thing for me to know what was going on, and quite another for the whole world to sit and watch while Grant and the Trailblazer made a fool of dear Violet. By the time coffee arrived, two things were clear: I'd had one too many glasses of wine, and I needed to pay someone a visit. Before I went ahead and ruined my friendship with Violet by telling her what I knew, I would go to the source of all this angst. I looked at my watch. It was just past three. The bank didn't close until five.

———

The Potomac Bank was located in an ersatz Greek Revival building on the corner of Wisconsin and M Street. Its golden dome is a Georgetown landmark. Grant took over the building some years back from the now-defunct Briggand's Bank, whose owner had been indicted for money-laundering. Grant always wanted to have his office there, even though the bank's corporate headquarters resided in a towering office building in Chevy Chase. Grant liked the golden dome, the comfortable Georgetown atmosphere, and being able to walk to work.

I helped him decorate the place, preserving as many of the original fixtures and fittings as possible. The brass-barred teller cages, brocade curtains, mahogany furniture, and thick burgundy carpeting were heavy and old-fashioned, yet oddly soothing—like visual oatmeal. Grant believed his customers felt more comfortable in traditional surroundings. He was projecting.

As I walked toward M Street, I stared up at the famous golden dome, which cast a dull gleam against the overcast sky. It was like my brain—a dull gleam in my overcast head. The four glasses of wine at lunch may have had something to do with my decision to confront Grant that afternoon. But it was also the fact that I'd known the man for ages. We'd dated. I'd introduced him to Violet. He was now hiding Cynthia, a weapon of matrimonial destruction. Before a war started, I felt I had to try and reason with him first. I was just tipsy enough to think I could wing it.

I'd been to the bank many times. I breezed past the tellers and bank officers seated at their desks and took the elevator to the second floor. Grant's secretary, Mrs. Madden, a gaunt, tightly wound, silver-haired woman with all the charm of a paper clip, was just coming out of his office. Grant and I caught sight of each other as she was about to close the door. I edged past her and sailed into the room. I knew by the look on his face that I was about as welcome as a bank inspector.

"You can't go in there without an appointment!" Mrs. Madden cried.

Grant interrupted her. "It's all right, Maddy. Close the door, please."

Grant's spacious office spread out over half the top floor of the bank. The wood-paneled room, with commanding views of Wisconsin and M Street, looked more like a library than a corporate office. The floor-to-ceiling brass bookcases were filled with sporting books. Two original bronze Remington sculptures of cowboys on bucking broncos flanked the picture window. A large partners' desk floated like a big wooden crate in a sea of deep green carpeting.

Grant moved stiffly, as if he was wearing a suit of armor. He sat down on the leather swivel chair behind his desk, indicating with an awkward hand gesture that I should take one of the armchairs opposite him. He crossed his arms tightly in front of him and said, "To what do I owe this unscheduled visit?"

I'd prepared a flowery lead-up in my head. But when I opened my mouth, the Imp of the Perverse just popped out. I couldn't help it.

"Grant, I know you're having an affair with Cynthia Rinehart."

Grant was stunned for a moment. And so was I, for that matter. I couldn't believe I'd just blurted it out like that. He got all huffy and indignant, sputtering away like a double boiler as he denied the accusation. He demanded to know where I'd gotten such a "preposterous idea." I watched him like I was watching a movie, the wine having imbued me with a curious detachment. Finally, I had to interrupt.

"Stop!" I cried, holding up my hand. "I was *in* the house. I saw you two going at it on the floor."

That shut him up. He reddened to the shade of his burgundy blotter and stared at me like he couldn't believe what I'd just said. His face was a kaleidoscope of torment. I softened my tone.

"Look, I know this is none of my business. But Violet's my best friend. I introduced you guys. I care about you both. Talk to me, Grant. What's going on with you?"

After a long pause, he said: "Are you going to tell Violet?"

"That's the last thing I want to do. You think I want to hurt her? That's why I'm here. Word's getting out, Grant. Marge Horner knows about you two, for Christ's sakes. And let me tell you, if Marge knows, you may as well put it on YouTube."

Grant shot up from his desk, shoved his hands in his pockets, and strode over to the window. He stared down at the street for a long moment, then said, "I think this may be a bad-luck building. The guy who owned it before me went to jail."

"These days they don't put you in jail for adultery—at least not here. If they did, the whole country would be locked up."

" 'Stone walls do not a prison make, nor iron bars a cage,' " he said morosely. "That's practically the only thing I remember from English class."

Grant was a little too earnest and uncomplicated to be a tragic figure. But he was clearly having a Hamlet moment of angst and indecision. I sensed he was itching to talk, so I let him talk. He told me that Cynthia had come to see him initially to open an account. By the time she left his office, he was hooked. She kept coming back, ostensibly to discuss her "mission statement," and other things pertaining to her foundation. I gathered from what he said that her mission was less about a statement and more about seduction.

"I always thought that love was something you had to work at, that it took time," he said. "But with Cynthia . . . I don't know. It just kind of happened. I feel drunk when I'm around her. Dizzy, off-balance, and yet totally grounded, like I could take on the world. . . . As much as I care about not hurting Violet . . . ? I kind of *don't* care when I'm with Cynthia, if you know what I mean. It's hard to explain."

I actually could have explained it to him. Grant was like an adolescent boy who had just gotten laid by a pro.

He refused to tell me exactly when the affair began, but I sensed it had been going on quite awhile, and that far from abating, it was heating up. That day in the house might have been an example of its intensity. I asked him if he was seriously contemplating leaving Violet. He hesitated for a nanosecond too long, then said weakly, "I haven't really thought about it," in such a way as to make me think he'd thought of little else.

"Violet's the mother of my son. I owe her a lot. My parents adore her. I can't leave her. I can't. . . . But you know what?"

"What?" I braced myself.

"I've been thinking about other people my whole entire life. Maybe I need to start thinking about *myself* for a change. Maybe it's time for me to take care of *me*—yours truly, numero uno," he said, tapping his chest with his index finger.

This sort of infantile psychobabble certainly didn't sound remotely like the Grant Bolton I knew. It sounded to me like pap spoon-fed to him by his sexy mattress partner.

Instead of challenging him, I said, "You're right, Grant. You do need to think of yourself. And you need to think about your whole life, not just one aspect of it."

"I know. I'm trying not to see Cynthia. But she keeps calling me. She's so hard to resist. You know why she bought Gay Harding's house?"

I wanted to say, "So you two could have a convenient place to fuck?" But I refrained.

"Why?" I asked innocently.

"Because I mentioned to her how much I love it and how we almost bought it. All she wants to do is please me. . . . Jesus, I'm so confused."

So I was right, I thought. Cynthia had ordered those light-proof shutters for Grant. I then tried my best to convince him that the sturdy bonds of loyalty were truer than the gossamer threads of the illicit. In other words, he couldn't have his cupcake and eat it too. As I spoke, he kept giving me these woeful little nods, like a schoolboy being chastised. He interrupted.

"Let me ask you something, Reven. Have you ever done something . . . something you couldn't control? Like on the spur of the moment you just acted impulsively, and that thing changed the course of your whole life because you suddenly realized you were another person? Someone you never thought you were? Never dreamed you could be . . . ? I don't know. Am I making any sense?"

"Yes. Listen, Grant, we've all done things we wish we hadn't, made choices we didn't even know were choices at the time. But that doesn't mean we have to stick by them. In life, you find out who you are gradually, not all at once. You made a bad choice, okay? But you can still get out of it."

"You don't understand. I can't. I've done something irrevocable here," he said.

"I know it feels like that now. But trust me, in a few months you'll be over it."

"I wish that were true. You don't know how much I wish that."

Grant assured me he was going to do some "very deep soul searching." And although I didn't think his soul was exactly the place he needed to search first, I left his office feeling rather pleased with myself, knowing I had done everything in my power to keep Violet's marriage together and her happiness intact.

Grant's infidelity was no longer merely a secret I was hiding from Violet; it was a bomb I was protecting her from. Our friendship had changed once more. I had the upper hand again. Only unlike our school days, Violet would hopefully never know it.

Chapter 18

Gunner drifted in and out of my life at this point. He called to check in occasionally, and whenever he wanted to see me in person, he texted me with the word "Usherville" and the time, and I'd meet him at the Hollis mausoleum. We usually met in the morning or the evening when the cemetery was closed. I once saw a grounds-keeper in the distance, but he ignored me. I figured Gunner had received permission for us to be there.

There was no new news about the serial killer, but Gunner was obsessed with Bob Poll. He always asked me how my relationship with Bob was going. I was very honest with him. I told him I was seeing Bob nearly every night and that things were very easy and pleasant between us, but we'd reached a kind of plateau and I didn't quite know how to move us forward.

"Count yourself lucky," Gunner said.

I, of course, was curious to know from Gunner if Bob had been back to the strip club. Gunner said he hadn't seen him there again, but he'd found out that Bob had not only dated several of the girls, he'd paid for one of them to go to graduate school and for another to have breast implants. There was no evidence that Bob and Miss Montrose had ever known each other, although Bob had frequented the club during the time she worked there. Gunner didn't seem reassured when I told him Bob had made light of serial killers, telling me they were basically Hollywood villains.

"You keep expecting this guy to take off his mask. He won't, unless he gets you in a situation where he wants to," Gunner said.

It was on one of these walks that Gunner told me that they had located a safety deposit box belonging to Nancy Sawtelle. It contained over a hundred thousand dollars in cash.

"Wow. What does that mean?" I asked him.

"Could mean any number of things. Maybe she had a sugar daddy. Maybe she was blackmailing someone. Or maybe she was just thrifty," he said with a snicker.

Gunner asked me how my "pal" Violet was doing, and I told him I'd gone to the bank to confront Grant about his affair with Cynthia.

"Still haven't told her yet, huh?"

"Nope. But people are talking, and I wanted Grant to know that," I said.

"So's he gonna give her up?" Gunner asked.

"Who knows? All I know is that every time I see Violet, I feel so guilty I can hardly stand it. And when I see the three of them together, I want to throw up. I have no idea if I'm doing the right thing not telling her."

"You've known her a long time, right?"

"Ever since boarding school."

"What does she think of Bob Poll?"

"Violet? She just wants me to be married and happy like her. Or like she thinks she is. She used to say Bob had a dark side."

"Maybe you should listen to her."

"Violet thinks everyone has a dark side," I said, joking.

"She may be right," Gunner said.

———

One mild late-winter evening as we were walking in the graveyard, a long and plaintive howl pierced the evening air.

"Sounds like a wolf," I remarked.

"A werewolf, if it's around here," Gunner joked. "You know there's a theory about werewolves."

"Oh-oh. . . . Let's hear it."

"When Ted Bundy was in prison on death row, he was interviewed by one of those profilers from the FBI. The profiler described Bundy as being a kind of engaging guy. He said Bundy talked about the murders like they'd been committed by another person. 'The Entity,' Bundy called himself."

"The Entity? That's creepy."

"Yeah. He was able to distance himself from the crimes by referring to himself as another being, apart from himself. That was Bundy's way of maintaining control and not losing his cool—except for this one time. The profiler asked Bundy a question that embarrassed him."

I guffawed. "What embarrasses a serial killer, I'd like to know?"

"It was something gross like how Bundy masturbated in front of the heads he'd cut off."

"Ugh!"

"Anyway, according to the profiler, Bundy lost control. His features physically changed, and his body gave off this putrid smell. He started sweating and panting, and his eyes looked like fire. The profiler said he was really terrified to be in the same room with the guy, 'cause he'd finally gotten a look at the real monster. This is what his victims saw."

I made a mental note to tell Violet this story, assuming she didn't already know it. She loved stories about Ted.

"So what's the theory?" I said.

"A lot of people believe that the whole werewolf myth got started with a real-life serial killer—some guy who hunted in the Balkans hundreds of years ago who seemed supernatural because his crimes were so horrific and they couldn't catch him."

"That's very interesting."

"All serial killers are werewolves, only most of 'em don't need a full moon to morph into monsters. They have their own little moons inside them."

"Here's a Ted Bundy story for you. Violet told me that Ted went to Lake Sammamish one summer day with his arm in a sling. He approached eight women, asking each of them if she'd help him unload a sailboat from his car, which was parked a little ways away. Five of the women said no. One of the women actually walked with him to the car, but when she saw there was no sailboat, she fled. Two women said yes. They both disappeared without a trace that day. Months later, their skulls were found in the woods near the lake."

"That's a famous story," Gunner said.

"But here's the thing: I've often wondered what I would have done if he'd approached me. Did those six women who got away sense that he was evil? Or were they just lucky? Would I have gone with him? Would I recognize evil if it came so close?"

Gunner stared at me. "What do you think?"

"That's just it. I don't know. I don't think any of us really knows until it's too late."

"Oh, I think some of us can make what's called an educated guess," Gunner said.

"Which means I should be wary of Bob Poll."

"You tell me."

The howl came again. This time, Gunner lifted his head up and howled back at the top of his lungs—a long and plaintive howl, just like the distant one. It was a pretty weird moment.

"Are you guys communicating?" I joked, trying to diffuse my sudden unease.

"Nah . . . Just kidding around, is all. Barkin', tryin' to make them listen to me. . . . Story of my life."

Chapter 19

The night of the Golden Key Awards, as they were called, Bob came to pick me up in person for a change. I was pleasantly surprised when I opened the door and saw him standing there instead of Maxwell. He asked if he could come in for a drink. He said he had something he wanted to give me. We were having a glass of wine when he pulled the robin's-egg blue box out of his tuxedo pocket and handed it to me.

"I hope you like it," he said.

I recognized the Tiffany wrapping and pretended not to be as excited as I was. We hadn't made much emotional progress since he'd told me that he loved me that one time. But we were coasting along at a good clip, and I instinctively felt this present was a declaration of more serious intentions on his part. I opened the box and pulled out a gold bracelet made of small, square links with a slide-in clasp—nothing super extravagant and not really my taste, but still quite nice. The fact that he gave me a gift was much more important than the gift itself. I put it on and made a big fuss over it. I kissed him and told him I'd "thank him properly" for it later on. After we finished our drinks, Maxwell drove us to the Kennedy Center.

I confess I've never really cared much for the Kennedy Center architecturally. The big marble box with its gaunt metallic columns somehow reminds me of a government building in the People's Republic of China. But that night, gleaming against a lapis lazuli evening sky, it struck me as very elegant. I kept fingering my bracelet and holding it up to admire it, not just because I wanted Bob to understand how much it meant to me, but because it really did mean something to me. I figured he was a man who just couldn't express his feelings easily, but that didn't mean they weren't there.

As we pulled up to the front entrance, a huge white stretch limousine was disgorging its cargo just ahead of us—Moby Dick in a sea of black catfish. Cynthia stepped out of the car, followed by Braden Boyd, a tall, gangly, dapper man-about-town. A former ambassador and dedicated public servant, Braden always reminded me of Ichabod Crane. Like Bob Poll, he had been divorced for many years, and he looked like he was ripe for the picking, but dream on. He always outran the pack of single Washington women snapping at his heels. Like Bob, Braden was known to enjoy escorting high-profile ladies of all ages, however, and it was interesting to see him with Cynthia—whose profile now was as high as a head on Mount Rushmore. I watched her sashay into the Kennedy Center on Braden's arm. She was wearing a long emerald green satin gown, an ermine capelet, and an air of entitlement. She acted like she owned the place. And in a way, she kind of did.

This gala was being held to celebrate the Cynthia A. Rinehart Foundation's first annual Golden Key Awards. Life-size color photographs of the evening's honorees, resting against huge gold easels, stretched the length of the long hall leading down to the Grand Foyer. Large gold letters hanging overhead proclaimed this to be the "WALK OF ACCOMPLISHMENT." The honorees were collectively identified as "KEY PLAYERS."

When Bob went to pick up our tickets at the box office, I strolled down the hall, looking at the photographs. It was a group of celebrities, all of whom were famous, and a few of whom were accomplished. Then I came to the one honoree who wasn't particularly famous or particularly accomplished—unless you count owning a bank: Grant Bolton. I knew Grant was going to be honored because Violet had mentioned it, even though it was supposed to be a secret. She was very excited about Grant being included in such exalted company.

Grant was posed sitting behind his desk at the bank, with his hands clasped in front of him and a vaguely pained expression on his face. Carmen Appleton sidled up alongside me. I hadn't seen Carmen in months—not since the Symphony Ball. She looked up at Grant's picture and said in her husky voice: "God, I hope he's sitting on a toilet, 'cause he sure looks like he needs to go—if I may be so crude."

I laughed because it was absolutely true. All the old-time movie star lighting and smooth grooming couldn't soften Grant's constipated smile.

"He seems a little out of place in this star-studded group, don't you think?"

Carmen sang softly, " 'It's not for me to say . . . da, da, da, da . . .' "

This was ominous. I couldn't quite figure out whether she was implying that Grant had somehow bought his way into the event or, worse—did *she* know about Cynthia and Grant?

"Are you trying to tell me something?"

"Oh, Miss Reven, how I would just *love* to tell you so many, many, many, *many* things. . . . But unfortunately, I must run off now and try and accommodate the never-ending demands of our great benefactress, who is tonight's lovely hostess."

She knew something—no question.

"Does anyone know what these awards are all about?" I asked her.

Carmen raised her large brown eyes to the ceiling and thought for a moment. "Egomania?" she said coyly.

She trotted on, then turned with an afterthought. "Oh, and by the way—I seated Ms. Hartford *waaaay* far away from the head table, so you and Mr. Wonderful won't have to see her carrying that big huge Statue of Liberty torch for him."

So Melody was there. Did Bob know that? All my anxieties ambushed me anew. I fingered the bracelet to reassure myself that he loved me. *Me*. That bracelet was the tangible proof.

"Your former girlfriend's here," I said to Bob teasingly when he walked up with the tickets.

"Yeah, I know. I just saw her," he said casually. "Come on, let's get our seats."

I surreptitiously checked myself out in my compact mirror to make sure I was still looking my best. My face had definitely lost its glow.

———

The evening was a people-watching smorgasbord with all forms of celebrity life represented, "sports to nuts," as Violet said. Everywhere I looked I saw a famous face.

"I'm the only person here I don't know!" I joked to Bob.

He didn't laugh. I don't think he liked being reminded I wasn't as prominent as some of the other ladies he'd escorted—particularly not at a party where you're ranked by how many hits you have on Google. It was times like these that I sensed his bristling insecurity more than ever.

We had good seats near the front of the theater. But, as usual, Bob complained they weren't the best. I caught sight of Melody Hartford's bouffant hair and even more bouffant bust three rows ahead of us to the right. I was on alert. When the curtain went up, the evening's fourteen honorees were seated onstage in front of a large movie screen. Cynthia walked out from the wings to hefty applause and stood in front of the microphone at the center of the stage.

"Welcome, everybody, to the first annual Golden Key Awards!" She looked radiant in the spotlight, and her delivery had become even more polished and self-assured. "There are top people in every field," she continued. "But it's my belief that you are only as good as you give. The Cynthia A. Rinehart Foundation is pleased to honor those people who have not only achieved a great level of success but who have also given generously of their time and resources to a variety of worthy causes around the globe. I call them my Key Players, because they and people like them have made a real difference in the world. This is the first ceremony of what I hope will become a long and important tradition here in Washington."

Cynthia seemed right at home on stage. Her jewels of mass destruction—a diamond and emerald necklace and earrings to match—sparkled under the bright spotlights. Grant was the only one of the honorees who didn't look at her as she spoke. He sat staring into space, seeming vaguely catatonic.

Cynthia introduced the first honoree, a reality television star who recently emceed a telethon for victims of diabetes. The auditorium darkened, and a short movie about the star's life played on the big screen. When the lights went up again, Cynthia delivered a few more platitudes, then asked the star to stand up. She hung a big golden key on a blue ribbon around his neck. As the audience applauded, and it was clear we were going to have to endure this little ceremony fourteen times, Bob leaned in and whispered to me, "*Long* night ahead."

Totem-pole Grant was much more ill at ease than the other honorees, most of whom were famous or semi-famous and thus accustomed to the spotlight. The little movie of his life made much of the Potomac Bank's charitable activities in Washington. I was rather surprised Grant had agreed to participate in this kind of event—or that his parents had let him agree to it—simply because the Boltons had always prided themselves on strict privacy. The Bolton seniors' patron saint of philanthropy was Andrew Mellon, who built the National Gallery and donated it to the nation along with its core collection of paintings from the Hermitage, yet declined to call it the Mellon Gallery in the interests of modesty and genuine humility—a decision that seems like science fiction in today's world of eleemosynary egos.

I caught Bob glancing in Melody's direction a couple of times. To be fair, I couldn't really tell if he was looking at her or just looking around because he was bored.

At the dinner, Bob and I were seated near enough to the head table so I could see the action. Each table had an honoree. Grant was at Cynthia's table, seated on her left. It would seem an odd choice to many, given the fact that she could have selected someone far more famous among the honorees. The Secretary of Commerce was on her right.

I studied Grant and Cynthia closely. They barely exchanged a word the entire night. That's when I knew for sure they were still seeing each other. People who are having an affair never talk to each other at parties. It's always the first clue. I caught Violet's eye at one point and gave her a little wave. She didn't wave back.

At our table, Peggy Myers, who can talk to the soup, was doing her best to charm Bob, but he'd sunk into a really foul mood. I wondered if it had to do with Melody being there, or if it was merely the result of enduring this endless, boring evening. I waved to him across the table and pointed to my bracelet to let him know how much I loved it. He nodded back with a halfhearted smile.

During dessert, the soft piped-in music grew increasingly loud. Suddenly, strobe lights started flashing and a troupe of actors in animal costumes bounded into the room from all sides. Lions, tigers, giraffes, monkeys, and zebras danced around the tables. They were soon joined by human trees, bushes, and flowers. In a few short minutes, we were smack in the middle of a papier-mâché jungle with the entire cast of *The Lion King* singing "Can You Feel the Love Tonight."

Bob lowered his head, closed his eyes, and massaged his temples as if he had a major migraine headache.

We got out of there well before they began the next number.

———

On the way home, Bob was totally preoccupied. I wasn't exactly buoyant myself.

"So what'd you think of the evening?" I said.

"On the Richter scale of dismal? I give it a nine," he said flatly.

"What are people supposed to do with those golden keys?"

"Hang themselves."

"You watch. Cynthia will wind up giving philanthropy a bad name," I said.

"Just as long as she doesn't give another party I have to go to."

"Next year you'll get a key."

"I'm attending a funeral that night, trust me."

We pulled up to my door. Bob declined my offer for him to come inside and asked me to sit with him a moment in the car. He raised the partition and spread the green mink blanket over our laps. Clasping my right hand in both of his, he said he had something to tell me. His tone was so serious and his manner so earnest that for one brief and shining moment I actually thought he was going to propose.

Silly me.

"So . . . you sure you like your bracelet?"

"I wish you'd come in and let me show you how much."

"I'd love to, but I've got a big day tomorrow, and that evening kind of put a nail in the old coffin. You mind if I don't?"

"No, of course not. How 'bout I make you a delicious dinner tomorrow night, and we rent a fabulous movie and just spend a really cozy evening at my house? I won't wear anything but this," I said, holding up the bracelet.

"That sounds fun. But I'll have to postpone it."

"Oh? Why?"

"You really like that bracelet, don't you?"

"I love it. Didn't you see me admiring it all during dinner?"

"Well, enjoy it. You deserve it. You're a great gal, Reven. Do I make you happy?"

"You know you do."

He leaned over and kissed me gently on the mouth.

"Listen, I have to go out of town for a while on business."

My heart dropped. "Oh?"

"I'm looking at a couple of properties."

"Where?"

"An undisclosed location," he said, teasing. "Don't worry. I'll call you every day."

"So when will you be back?"

"Not sure."

"Are we talking a day, a week, a month—twenty to life?"

"Closer to a week, I'd say." He stroked my hand. "You have such soft skin. . . . So . . . enjoy your bracelet and be patient, okay?"

"Not one of my greatest virtues."

"I'll call you. Promise." He kissed me again.

A dark shape loomed up at the window. It was Maxwell. He opened the door and helped me out. Bob stayed in the car. Maxwell saw me to my door. I told him to wait a second. I quickly ran inside and got the tin of chocolate chip cookies I'd bought for him at the farmer's market.

"I've been meaning to give these to you," I said.

"Golly, you're so kind. Thank you so much," he said, averting his eyes as though he couldn't bear to look at me. I sensed he felt sorry for me.

I waved good-bye to Bob, then went into the house. I stood for a long moment in the dark hall, reflecting on the evening.

You know that sinking feeling you get when you know you've lost something—not just misplaced it, but really lost it? That's exactly how I felt. I told myself I was being paranoid. I switched on the light and examined the bracelet again. It looked cheaper than it did before.

Chapter 20

Ididn't hear from Bob the next day, or the next, or the day after that. I tried calling him at home but there was no answer, and his cell phone went to voice mail. I even got up the courage to call his office, knowing I would have to speak with the icy Felicity. She told me that "Mr. Poll" was "out of town," but that she would be sure and give him the message that I had called. I clung to that gold bracelet as proof he still cared for me.

Later on that week I met Gunner at Usherville for a briefing session. Gunner had become like a kind of shrink to me, someone I could confide in without fear of betrayal. When I got there, he was sitting on the stone bench in front of the mausoleum, absorbed in a book. The instant he saw me, he shoved the book into his coat pocket.

"Whatcha reading?" I asked, sitting down beside him.

"Nothin'."

"C'mon, Gunner, I want to know what detectives read."

I held out my hand. He pulled out a ratty little paperback from his pocket and handed it to me reluctantly. It was called *The Book of Five Rings*.

"Never heard of it," I said.

"Great book."

"What's so great about it?"

"For one thing, it teaches you how to have patience."

"Boy, I should read it then." I absently leafed through the pages without really looking at them. "I haven't heard from Bob in a few days," I said, glancing at Gunner out of the corner of my eye. He didn't say anything—purposely, no doubt. "I know you don't like him, but look what he gave me." I showed him the gold bracelet. "Isn't it pretty?" Gunner gave it a cursory look, and still didn't say anything.

"He had to go away on business," I explained.

"Oh, yeah?"

"I'm sure he'll be back soon, and I'll hear from him then. Don't you think?" Gunner shrugged. "Tell me something, would you give someone a gold bracelet if you didn't care about them?"

He chuckled. "I couldn't afford to give them a gold bracelet if I *did* care about them."

"But you do think I'll hear from him, right?"

"He's your boyfriend. You tell me. . . . So how's your girlfriend Violet doing?"

"I don't know what to do about Violet. I can't talk to her anymore."

"I take it you still haven't told her."

"About Grant? No. We were all at the Kennedy Center last week. Cynthia gave Grant this stupid Golden Key award."

"Yeah, I saw that in the paper. Nice picture of you and Mr. Wrong."

I ignored the comment. "Cynthia put Grant next to her at the dinner. Poor Violet just sat there looking adoringly at Grant with the patented Nancy Reagan stare, totally oblivious to what's going on right under her nose. It's excruciating for me. I agonize about whether to tell her or not."

"You think he's still seeing this Rinehart woman?"

"Absolutely. They didn't say a word to each other all night. That's always the tip-off. I'm worried this is going to wreck my friendship with Violet." I glanced up at the crypt. "I wonder who the Hollises were."

"General Matthew P. Hollis was a Civil War hero. Fought for the Union. There's a lot of Civil War dead buried here."

"Really?"

"Yeah. It's your neighborhood. Don't you know about this place?"

"Not much, I'm afraid."

Gunner gave an amused shrug. "It's interesting how people ignore what's closest to them."

"So tell me about it."

"It actually has a connection to your pal Grant Bolton."

"How so?"

"You know the Corcoran Gallery?"

"Sure."

"In the late 1840s, old Mr. Corcoran bought the original fifteen acres this cemetery's on. Corcoran also founded Riggs Bank, which was taken over by the Briggands in the '80s, and then by the Bolton family when old Mr. Briggand went to jail. It's now part of the Potomac Bank, if I'm not mistaken."

"That's exactly right. Grant thinks he's in a bad-luck building because Mr. Briggand got caught."

"You know the little stone chapel there as we come in? That was designed by James Renwick, the guy who designed the Smithsonian Castle and St. Patrick's Cathedral up in your former neck of the woods. It's called the Renwick Chapel."

"How do you know all this?" I asked him.

"I was interested. Aren't you interested in the history of Georgetown, owning an antiques store and everything?"

"I have a few other things on my mind at the moment."

"Did you know your friend Gay Harding's buried right next to that chapel?"

"Yes, *that* I knew. . . . Tell me something, Gunner. Do you think this bracelet's some sort of consolation prize?"

"I don't know. What did the good Mr. Poll have to say for himself?"

"I have a bad feeling."

"How do you mean?"

"I think the bracelet's his way of breaking up with me."

"You should be so lucky." Gunner smirked.

His knowing attitude irritated me. "You keep *saying* that. I know what you're insinuating, and I just don't believe it."

"Then how come you're talking to me about it?"

"You said you wanted to know all the stuff that's going on. Why are you so fixated on Bob?"

"And you're asking me this because . . . ?"

"I don't think you're right, okay? I mean, I really don't think he's capable of anything so terrible, but—"

"*But?*"

"Well, it's just that I don't feel I really know him, even though we've been going out all this time. If he does have this dark side, like everyone says, I'd kind of like to know what it is. I know he goes to that strip club. . . . I mean, do you have any real proof other than your crazy intuition about him?"

Gunner bristled slightly. I'd hit a nerve.

"The other day you told me that story about Ted Bundy. Maybe those girls who escaped being his victims at the lake had an intuition. Intuitions aren't crazy. In fact, they're what separate a good detective from a great one."

"I'm sorry. I didn't mean to offend you."

"It's cold. Let's walk," he said.

We walked in silence for a time. Then Gunner said, "You asked me about that book I was reading. . . . The author, Miyamoto Musashi, once killed thirty guys with a sword in each hand. One to fend off, one to kill. People always underestimated him. And he always surprised them. Know why? Because he saw through preconceptions and conventional wisdom and bureaucratic tyranny right down to the essence of things. He pierced the lies and got to the truth, even though people in his time thought he was crazy. No proof doesn't mean a thing isn't true. You gotta follow your gut. And my gut tells me that Bob Poll is somehow involved in this case."

Our custom was to part ways well before the entrance to the cemetery. I tried to hand him back the book before he separated, but Gunner refused to take it.

"Read it," he said. "You might learn something."

Chapter 21

After that meeting with Gunner, I decided it was time Violet knew about Grant's infidelity before this awful secret wrecked our friendship for good. I often dropped in on her unannounced in the morning for a cup of coffee on my way to work. I left the cemetery and walked over to her house, steeling myself for what was arguably to be the most difficult conversation of my life.

Violet and Grant lived in the same house Grant had when he was a bachelor—a yellow mini-mansion with white columns on the corner of Twenty-eighth and Q. Violet used to refer to it as Tara before she married Grant, when she wanted to show she was not impressed with the grandeur of the place. Maureen answered the door. "The ancient Maureener," as Violet referred to her, was the old housekeeper who had been with Grant since practically his diaper days. She was usually a sunny, if doddery, old sort. But when I said hello this morning, she eyed me with all the friendliness of an enemy combatant. I paid no attention and walked past her to the back of the house.

Violet and Grant always had their breakfast on the sunporch, a room drowning in chintz, large china animals, and white wicker furniture about as cheerful as old bones. I expected to see Grant. But Violet was having breakfast with Peggy Myers. Peggy lived in Kalorama, and it was most unusual for her to be there at that hour of the morning.

"Morning, Peggy. Morning, Violet," I said.

Peggy greeted me but Violet ostentatiously turned her back and stared out the bay window facing the back garden. I tried again.

"Good morning, Violet."

Violet calmly sipped her coffee, refusing to turn around. "Is it very cold outside, *Peggy*?" she said at last.

"Not as cold as it is in here," I said, hoping for a laugh.

Violet slammed down her coffee cup so it clattered on the saucer, and said, "You know, Peggy, if there's one thing I hate above all other things in this world, it's a *liar*." She spit out the word.

It didn't take a genius to figure out that something really bad had happened, and that it somehow involved me. I dreaded to think. I made another stab at communication. Violet not only ignored me, she got up and walked out of the room. Her face looked like tear-stained pomegranate.

I pitched Peggy a hapless, bewildered look. Peggy said simply: "Grant left her."

I sank down in a chair, poured myself a cup of coffee, and asked Peggy to tell me exactly what she knew. She recounted the whole story as it had just been told to her by Violet. Apparently, the night before, Grant announced he was leaving her—just like that. He packed a bag, told her he could be reached at the Four Seasons, and walked out—but not, unfortunately, before dragging *me* smack into the middle of it. He confessed he'd been having an affair with Cynthia and that I knew all about it. He told Violet I'd come to the bank to confront him. I couldn't believe it. Grant wasn't just an asshole. He was the whole intestinal tract.

"He wants a divorce," Peggy said softly.

"Don't tell me he wants to *marry* Cynthia?!"

"Looks that way."

I sprang up and headed for the door. "I need to talk to Violet!"

"Not without a bulletproof vest!" Peggy cried. "She's furious at you."

I whirled around. "Furious at *me*? She should be furious at *Grant*, for Christ's sakes! *I* didn't do anything!"

"You know what they say: the cover-up is always worse than the crime. Why does everyone always forget that?" Peggy mused aloud.

"I didn't cover anything up. I just didn't tell her. An omission is not a lie."

Peggy let out this big guffaw and said: "Oh, honey, you've been in Washington too long!"

I stared at her, feeling totally defeated. "What should I do, Pegs?"

Peggy Myers was the Eisenhower of our little group. Whenever the troops had a dustup, she helped smooth the ruffled egos. She thought for a moment, then said, "I'd let her cool down for a couple of days. She's going to need her friends to rally around. You above all, Reven. Give her some time. Then call."

Very sound, sensible advice. Naturally, I didn't take it. Peggy left, but instead of going with her like she suggested, I marched upstairs to find Violet. She wasn't in that stifling Victorian enclave they called a bedroom—a room so full of knickknacks and bric-a-brac it looked like a thrift shop. She was one flight up, in Grant's dreary green prison cell of an office, sitting staring at a photograph of her and Grant and Tee in a silver frame on his desk.

"Go away, traitor," she said, without looking at me.

"Violet, please let me explain."

"Go away. I have nothing to say to you. *Nothing!*"

She sounded so forbidding, I figured I'd take Peggy's advice and try this another day. I was just about to leave when she swiveled around and started ranting at me. For someone with nothing to say, she proceeded to really let me have it, hardly drawing breath, telling me what a horrible bitch I was for going behind her back and for conspiring with Grant against her. I could see Grant had learned something from all his years in Washington. He'd spun my visit to him like a veteran campaign manager.

Violet accused me of being jealous of her and secretly pleased this had happened because I'd never gotten over the fact that Grant had chosen her over me back in the day. This was revisionist history at its most egregious. But I just stood and took it because I felt so sorry for her and so dismayed that my well-intentioned actions had contributed to her distress. Violet was taking out all her frustrations on me because she couldn't take them out on Grant. I knew I had to be a big enough person to suffer the slings and arrows of a distraught friend, to see beyond the moment to the friendship itself.

Eventually she calmed down—no person, not even Violet, could have kept up that level of rage without spontaneously combusting. It was good for her to get it all out. I think she appreciated my stoic attitude, because when I walked over and put a sympathetic hand on her shoulder, she didn't swat it away. I took that as a sign she was already starting to forgive me. I sat down beside her.

"I'm so sorry, Vi. I just wanted to spare you finding out about it if I could. I knew how painful it would be for you. I've been in *agony* over whether or not to tell you. And, in fact, this morning I decided I would because I knew it was ruining our friendship. I couldn't talk to you like I used to, and you sensed something was wrong. So I was going to tell you, no matter how hard it was. You've got to believe me. Look, I don't know what Grant's told you about our meeting, but I swear to God, I was not on his side. The reason I went to see him was to try and make him give her up. When I left, I thought he would."

Violet didn't respond right away. She looked thoughtful and sad. Finally, she spoke: "This is like when we were back in school, and you protected me. I appreciated it then. And I'll always be grateful to you. In fact, it's one of the reasons I came to Washington, because I knew I could count on you. But we're not in school anymore, Rev. You're not my nurse, and you had no right to play with my life."

It was true, I had been Violet's guardian angel in school because I was on top of the world then, and my word was law. I recalled what my father once told me. He said: "If you look back on your school days as the best days of your life, it means you never really grew up. You always see the world a certain way, no matter how it really is." Dad stopped short of saying that people who constantly reminisced about the glory days of their youth were failures, because he was not a judgmental man. But I wondered if I was somehow living in the past, hoping for those brighter days of my youth to come back in another incarnation.

"What's this going to do to Tee?" she said plaintively. "I can't imagine how he's going to take it."

"He's a strong, good kid. He'll be okay."

"He'll probably blame me," Violet said.

Tee was closer to Grant than he was to his mother, which was another reason the affair with Cynthia hurt Violet so badly. I think she feared her son would take his father's side.

"I'm so sorry, honey. I was wrong. I guess I should have told you."

"I don't know. . . . Maybe not," she said. "I don't know what I'd have done in your place. You did what you thought was right."

"I tried to, but maybe I fucked up. . . . Can you forgive me?"

We stared at each other for a long, emotional moment. I think that Violet and I always saw each other the way we were when we first met. Sure, our faces had crumbled with time, but those older masks couldn't hide our youthful souls or all the things we'd gone through together. Few things are more precious than a good friend of long acquaintance. We were like a little country of two with our own secret history. No matter what happened around us, it was important to both of us to defend that precious turf. I think we both realized this at the same moment because we spontaneously burst into tears and fell into each other's arms, sobbing. We had a good cry, then a serious talk. Scraping the barnacles off a long friendship is a painful but necessary process that often occurs after a shipwreck.

After we dried our tears, Violet admitted she'd hacked into Grant's computer and found all these e-mails between him and Cynthia. Their affair had been going on at least a year, maybe more.

"How did you get his password?" I asked her.

"He's so unoriginal. It's 'Potomac.' Surprise, surprise."

Grant's e-mails were terse and functional, obviously setting times and places of assignations, like "3:00, Rockville," or "4:30, Days Inn."

Cynthia's e-mails were more forthcoming. She wrote things like, "You are all-powerful, the master of your fate and mine," and "I am in awe of your strength and your wisdom. What a brilliant and sensitive man you are! I am totally in your hands." She signed hers "C."

I'm sure Grant believed it when she told him how marvelous he was. Either that, or he just wanted to hear it. In her e-mails, Cynthia came across as a helpless little southern belle, when in fact it was so clear to me she was the puppet mistress pulling his strings.

Violet then pulled up the Web site for the Cynthia A. Rinehart Foundation, which Grant had bookmarked. The screen lit up with a picture of Cynthia standing in front of the Kennedy Center—an enhanced and retouched version of the one that was used for the big article on her in the *Washington Post*. A blue banner floated above her head with "The Cynthia A. Rinehart Foundation" written in gold letters. Off to the side was a list of information links, including "Board Members," "Golden Key Awards," "News and Events," and "The Art of Dying," a nod to the original source of her wealth. Violet clicked on the list of board members, and an impressive array of names came up with pictures and biographies. Senator Pomador headed the field. There was a large picture of the senator, a portly, white-haired man with teeth that looked like tiny tombstones. Violet was about to click on another link when we both looked at each other, and without saying a word, she shut down the computer. We'd had it.

We went back downstairs. Maureen made us a soothing cup of tea, and we sat in the living room. Violet told me she never had a clue about the affair until she and Grant got home from the party they'd gone to last night, and he abruptly announced he was leaving her on the spot. It was so like Grant to think he could avoid unpleasantness by simply packing his bags and withdrawing.

"I threatened to follow him and make a scene unless he told me the whole story. Soup to nuts. When he started talking, he couldn't stop—just like some adolescent kid with a crush who needs to tell you every detail of a first date, including what he ate for dinner and the color of his socks. When he told me *you'd* gone to see him, I felt like I'd been punched in the stomach," she said.

As Violet described Grant's version of our meeting, it was easy to see why she'd gotten the impression I was on his side. He'd twisted my expressions of sympathy to make them sound like I was cheering him on. I set her straight fast and made her understand that I was only thinking of her and how I could best help her.

I still blamed Cynthia much more than I blamed Grant. I told Violet I was sure that Cynthia had made the first move, and probably several moves after that. I pictured Grant as a granite boulder it took many pushes to dislodge. However, once he started rolling downhill, there was no stopping him. I told Violet she'd just have to make it super-tough for Grant to divorce her. It was then she admitted something to me I never knew before.

"I can't make it that tough. We have a prenup." She sighed.

"You're *kidding*. You never told me that."

"I know. I didn't think it was very romantic. I signed it the day of the wedding. It's generous enough. I won't starve."

I recalled the day Violet got married. The four o'clock ceremony took place in the Episcopal church on O Street. I was Violet's matron of honor. Violet wafted down the aisle in a high-necked, old-fashioned dress studded with seed pearls, on the arm of Mr. Bolton Sr. Her own father had refused to attend when Violet forbade him to bring his gym teacher mistress. The church was packed with Grant's friends and relatives, and a sprinkling of Violet's pals—mainly the people she'd recently met in Washington through me.

I remember Violet's mother, a tense and tired-looking woman in a faded blue dress. She sat in a corner during the reception, chain-smoking and looking at her watch. She hardly spoke to a soul. Rainy Bolton was the one who had organized the wedding. The large tent on the back lawn of their sprawling house in Chevy Chase was deco-rated with ivy-covered columns and trellises. Everyone agreed the event was a model of understated elegance. Violet seemed so happy. Yet now I wondered if that last-minute prenuptial ambush had some-how put a crease in the ivory satin memory of that day.

Violet sipped her tea, looking morose. "If I divorce Grant, I go back to being nobody again," she said.

I found this comment as sad as it was untrue.

"You aren't somebody just because you married Grant, you know. You're a wonderful person, Vi. And besides, I know Grant still loves you."

"I have a flash for you. Grant never really loved me."

"That's ridiculous!"

"No, hear me out. I'd only admit this to you, Rev. Grant never wanted a wife in the traditional sense. He wanted a partner in the Bolton firm. I understood that on our very first date, when all he talked about was the bank and his family and his mother. He wanted someone who was ambitious but subservient. I made myself into that person. I had Rainy pegged right off the bat. She wanted a daughter-in-law she could boss around, but one who'd reflect credit on the family as well. I was always careful to kowtow to Rainy, because I knew that Grant would never marry anyone she didn't approve of. Rainy wants to be the star of this family, let's face it."

Personally, I thought Lorraine "Rainy" Bolton was cyanide in a bun. I couldn't stand her. She'd been a pill to me when Grant and I were dating, going out of her way to tell me that I'd have been bet-ter off "getting a real education" rather than going to design school, which she considered on a par with peeling a peach correctly and pouring tea. Thanks, Rainy. The Boltons didn't really respect any-one who hadn't been to graduate school or law school. That's why they adored Violet, of course, because Violet was such an academic achiever. Rainy deemed Violet fit to carry the Bolton colors right from the git-go—but under her command.

"I wonder what old Rainy will think of Cynthia," I said.

"I'm worried about that," Violet said.

"She'll loathe her!"

"I'm not so sure. For one thing, the Boltons consider themselves great philanthropists, and they like people who give away money."

"Yes, but not so ostentatiously. You never hear about the Boltons, because they do it all so privately. That's one thing I really do respect about them. They don't court publicity for their good works. They just donate and shut up about it."

"Don't kid yourself. Rainy *loves* publicity. She just doesn't want to *appear* to love it because she thinks it's unseemly for the family to draw attention to itself. But secretly, she wants people to find out about all the good they've done. Cynthia's her golden opportunity. She'll throw all this reflected light on the family, and Rainy will bask in it while pretending to shun it the whole time. The Boltons will be compared to Cynthia as two sides of the philanthropic coin—the ones who want credit, and the ones who don't. And besides, Rainy's impressed with Cynthia. She's told me so herself."

"Let's see how impressed she is when she finds out what's happened."

"I hope she tells Grant he has to ditch Cynthia. She's the only one he'll listen to, believe me. She can be bossy."

Calling Rainy Bolton bossy was like calling Hurricane Katrina a squall. The woman was a steamroller. She always got her way.

Violet hung her head. "I know Grant's in love with Cynthia."

"No. He's in *lust* with her. It'll burn itself out. You watch."

Violet shook her head and said, "I wish I knew a hit man."

"Right!" I laughed.

Violet glared at me. "I'm serious, Reven. If I could get rid of her, I would."

"No, you wouldn't. Not really."

"You don't know me. I'd do it in a heartbeat if I knew I wouldn't get caught. Wouldn't you—if you knew you wouldn't get caught?"

I thought for a second. "No. I'm too paranoid. I still feel guilty about that comic book I stole when I was in the fourth grade."

"Guilt's not my problem. My problem is, I know too much about forensics," Violet went on. "They get you on the tiniest thing now. Have you heard of 'touch DNA'? If I touch you like that," she said, brushing my arm, "I leave invisible skin cells. They found them on JonBenet Ramsey's pajamas and they matched the other unidentified fluid at the crime scene. . . . Oh, I wish Cynthia was a jogger so the Beltway Basher could have a shot at her." She sighed.

I didn't take Violet seriously when she talked like that. But I did take this situation seriously, and Grant's departure presented real problems for me as well. I was still working for Cynthia. I had that damn house to finish.

"Well, I'm going to quit working for her. I have no intention of making a love nest for those two," I said.

"You're the best, Rev. Thanks for being so loyal."

"I just have to figure out how I quit and get her to pay me the money she owes me."

I was thinking about this when I suddenly had a brainstorm! As I often say, there are four ways to get to know someone quickly: sleep with them, travel with them, gamble with them, and—last but not least—decorate for them. Houses can tell you more than résumés, if you know where to look.

I flicked my eyes onto Violet's and said three words: *"Mary Lou Lindsay."*

Violet flinched and went white as a sheet at the mention of that name. No surprise there. It was like mentioning Dr. Mengele to a concentration camp survivor. If there was one person above all who'd made Violet's life a living hell in school, that person was Mary Lou Lindsay.

Let's face it, hate for hate's sake is a fact of school life. It happened quite a lot at Wheelock, where we were all sequestered for long periods of time without a break. One girl would take a hate on another for no apparent reason. Mary Lou Lindsay was our class hater-in-chief. She was a porky, egregious bully with dung-colored hair and eyes like smoke. She ruled a faction of girls who found her bossy ways and scary gift for mimicry charismatic. She took a hate on Violet the minute Violet arrived in our sophomore year. To the other girls, Violet was just a weirdo they teased whenever she crossed their path. To Mary Lou Lindsay, Violet was a victim to be hunted down in corridors, classrooms, and stairwells, and tortured with taunts and pranks and worse.

True, Violet was quirky and unattractive in those days, which made her an easy target. But Mary Lou's hatred was shimmering—almost sexual in its intensity. She made Violet's life utterly miserable, playing every sort of rotten trick on her, including setting fire to her bed. Complaints to the authorities only made matters worse. Mary Lou was crafty. She could never be blamed for the acts she perpetrated. Like some Mafia don, she often ordered other people to do her dirty work for her.

Finally, it got so bad I took matters into my own hands. I disliked Mary Lou, but I purposely befriended her in order to gain her confidence. She was suspicious at first because I was so close to Violet. Mary Lou and I were biology lab partners, and when we were dissecting a pig, I made some crack about Violet looking like the pig, knowing that meanness was the way to Mary Lou's heart. I pretended to be sick of Violet and purposely shunned her to hang out with Mary Lou.

Mary Lou was thrilled to be my friend, because everyone wanted to be my friend in those days. She was anxious to impress me. She liked to brag that she could drink any man under the table and that she knew enough about mixing drinks to be a bartender. I then discovered that she had a bottle of gin hidden in her locker—information I promptly shared with the proper authorities. Mary Lou was expelled.

People were surprised at how upset she was at being kicked out. Her tough-girl facade crumbled. She ranted and raved that her life was over. She pleaded with the headmaster to give her another chance, saying that her parents had sacrificed so much to send her to a private school and how it meant so much to them that she go to a decent college. Strangely enough, she didn't blame me. She blamed Violet. I figured that was because Violet had been the object of her irrational hatred all along. Old hatreds die hard. I remember her screaming at the top of her lungs down the corridor: *"You're gonna pay for this, Violet McCloud! One day you're gonna pay!"*

Mary Lou left Wheelock, never to be heard from again.

I figured we had another Mary Lou Lindsay on our hands in the person of Cynthia Rinehart, who had set fire to Violet's bed in the metaphorical sense by sleeping with Grant. I told Violet that instead of quitting the job, the thing for me to do was to keep on working for Cynthia to try and uncover something bad about her, something that would put Grant off.

"He likes her now because of the sex and because he thinks she's such a hot shit around town. But what if he found out something horrible about her? He'd leave her in a flash."

We both knew that Grant was a priggish coward at heart, and that ultimately the most important things in life to him were his reputation and the reputation of his family. One of the main reasons he married Violet was because she'd been so squeaky-clean in all areas.

Violet seemed frozen as I shared my brainstorm with her. I asked her if she was okay.

"I was just thinking about Mary Lou Lindsay," she said, her gaze drifting downward. Clearly, neither one of us had forgotten the pains and glories of our early school years. Those memories were etched in our psyches as deeply as a first love affair.

I finally convinced her to see the wisdom of my plan. We called it "Operation Mary Lou Lindsay."

When I thought we'd covered everything, and Violet was feeling better, I started telling her about Bob. She listened to my concerns about him, and my feeling that he was distancing himself from me.

"I still haven't heard from him, you know, and it's been almost a week. Of course, he did give me the bracelet," I said, trying to buoy my spirits. "I shouldn't forget that, should I?"

Violet just looked at me. "You know what your problem is, Reven? You're forty, and you still feel like you're eighteen. When I was eighteen, I felt like I was forty. I never expected life to be anything but hard, whereas you were always shocked when things didn't go exactly your way. You're still looking for some Prince Charming to come and save you from your own existence."

"That's harsh," I said, hurt.

"No. What's harsh is to marry the prince and have him turn into a total toad. Why do you think Princess Diana captured the imagination of the entire world—because she cared about land mines? She *married* a land mine. So did I."

I disagreed with her about Prince Charles, but I didn't feel this was the moment to mention it. I guess there are times when you have to be there for a friend and not immediately expect reciprocation, irritating as that may be. So I forgave her. I was relieved that everything was out in the open between me and Violet at last. Secrets corrode relationships.

It just goes to show you how personal history repeats itself, and how the covert actions of one's youth can become the models of maturity. In a way, Violet and I were right back where we started from: two schoolgirl conspirators angling to bring down a bully.

———

Violet left Washington the next day. She said she was going up to the Millbrook School to break the news to Tee in person. But I figured she just wanted to get the hell out of Dodge. It was going to be interesting to see what the adolescent boy made of all this sexual mischief and betrayal. I wondered what he would think of Cynthia.

Poor Violet was always so vested in maintaining that she had an idyllic life. But now her so-called perfect marriage was over. Just goes to show you never really know how flimsy something is until you watch it fall apart.

Chapter 22

It took about a nanosecond for people to find out that Grant had left Violet for Cynthia. In Washington, communication between federal agencies may be like pulling teeth, but the gossip mill sure knows how to share information. Besides, it was the kind of story that offers welcome relief from political news and reminds us where so much of politics actually comes from—namely, the trials and wreckage of the human heart.

When Violet got back from seeing Tee, she was more depressed than ever.

"Tee says he hates the both of us," she told me. "He doesn't even want to come home on vacation. He wants to go to his friend Daniel's house in Maine."

"He'll get over it," I assured her. "He's a teenager."

"Yeah, just like his father," she said sourly.

Violet had a fairly complicated relationship with her son. While she had doted on him and catered to him when he was little, once he grew up and developed a personality of his own—in other words, started talking back to her—things changed. She grew distant from him, as if she were afraid of him. Even though I knew she loved him fiercely, they didn't seem able to connect. She referred to him jokingly as her "little serpent's tooth." But kids have a way of seeing through jokes like that—not to mention adults. It was odd, but I always got the feeling that Violet was on stage with Tee, never quite herself for some reason.

As far as Washington society went, Violet put on a brave face and tried to act as if the whole thing would blow over. However, this proved difficult. Though people generally agreed that Grant was behaving abominably, many were afraid to take Violet's side for fear of alienating Washington's newest power couple. Invitations dried up, and she was left to wallow in the shame of a very public humiliation.

Aside from Tee, the hardest thing for Violet to deal with was the reaction of Grant's parents. Violet told me that Rainy Bolton had called her to say how sorry she was. Violet was touched by her mother-in-law's concern, and they apparently had a good talk. However, a few days later, she heard from Maureen, who heard it from Winston, the senior Boltons' butler, that Grant had brought Cynthia over to his parents' house for dinner.

"Can you believe they actually *fed* that bitch?" Violet moaned to me. "So much for family loyalty!"

It didn't come as any great surprise to me that the Boltons sided with their son. As Violet had surmised, Rainy was secretly thrilled Grant was going out with Washington's new philanthropic star. Rainy was a stealth starfucker, if ever there was one. While she pretended to shun the spotlight, she never missed an opportunity to step into it when she could, or at least catch its ambient light.

―――――

Meanwhile, I had my own romantic problems. I hadn't heard from Bob in over two weeks. *Two whole weeks*. Not one word. He'd beat a hasty retreat after a constant siege. The abruptness of his silence was jarring, to say the least. Every time the phone rang, I went on alert, hoping it was him, or even the officious Felicity, calling to arrange a date. But it never was. Still, I had faith. I wore the bracelet he gave me every day, refusing to believe I wouldn't hear from him eventually.

Rosina was sanguine about the whole situation. She'd never cared for Bob to begin with. Now that he wasn't calling, she voiced her dislike of him more frequently and forcefully than ever, preparing me for the worst.

I confess that I broke down and called him once. Well, maybe more than once. Maybe a few times. But his cell phone always went to voice mail, and I hung up quickly—except for one time. I left this message that was meant to sound breezy and spur-of-the-moment, but which

I'd actually rehearsed for a good half hour before I made the call. I don't know why I bothered, or what I hoped to achieve. Ever since one of my old admirers tracked me down to the roulette table in the Katmandu Casino in Nepal on New Year's Eve years ago, I've known that when a guy really wants to get in touch with you, he will.

I found a card at Just Paper and Tea, my favorite stationery store on P Street. It had a picture of the Lone Ranger on it. Inside, I wrote, "Who was that masked man?" and mailed it to Bob. I didn't tell Rosina any of this. I couldn't stand the fact that she might have been right when she observed that he was too ardent to begin with. Nor did I tell her that I'd driven by his house a number of times. I figured he'd gone away somewhere, because the Rolls wasn't in the driveway. The Rolls was never there unless Bob was, because Maxwell garaged it near his own house in Rockville so he could look after it.

Rosina told me the only thing she would regret if we broke up for good was that she would never get to ride in that car.

———

I saw Gunner once during that period, ostensibly to tell him what had happened with me and Violet. I told him all about Violet's and my little plan: Operation Mary Lou Lindsay. I said, "Let's face it, life is high school with wrinkles."

I asked him if he could check out Cynthia for us. He kind of laughed without responding. I couldn't tell if he thought my request was ridiculous or out of line or what. It was very hard to tell what Gunner was thinking.

I asked him how his case was going, but he was evasive, as usual. He was more interested to know if I'd heard from Bob yet.

"He's probably still away," I said. "I'm not worried." I held up the bracelet and jingled it in front of him.

The truth is, I was very worried, and quite embarrassed over Bob's radio silence. However, I wasn't going to admit that to Gunner. Nor was I going to tell him that I'd called Bob, driven by his house, and even staked out his office a couple of times. I didn't want Gunner to think I was a stalker—which I kind of was.

One night, when I was feeling low and sorry for myself, I took a look at the book Gunner had given me, *The Book of Five Rings*. Gunner had written his name inside the front cover: G. A. Gunner. When I

. .. .

---

saw this, I realized I didn't even know his first name. I read the translator's preface, which described the book as a military manual that applied Zen principles to the martial arts. More correctly entitled *The Book of Five Spheres*, it was written in 1643 by a disenfranchised samurai named Miyamoto Musashi, a legendary figure about whom very little was actually known except what he wrote about himself in the book. The translator pointed out that a samurai with no master like Musashi had to become his own protector, forced to live by his wits and his skill as a swordsman. In essence, the book was a testament to the power of the individual against a hostile world.

The pages were well thumbed. Gunner had highlighted several passages throughout the text in orange: "*Understand the harm and the benefit in everything*"; "*Learn to see everything accurately*"; "*Become aware of what is not obvious*"; "*Be careful in small matters*"; "*Do not do anything useless.*"

One little section he'd marked rang a bell with me: "*Let there be neither insufficiency nor excess in your mind. Even if superficially weakhearted, be inwardly stronghearted, and do not let others see into your mind.*"

I took this to heart, since my mind was always careening between "insufficiency" and "excess," and because I rarely had an unspoken thought.

After I'd read the book, Gunner struck me more like a warrior on a quest than just another detective doing his job. He seemed to be following the principles of a higher order. He clearly felt some deep affinity with the book's seventeenth-century author. He had underlined the part where Musashi states he killed a man in a duel at the tender age of thirteen and written the words, "*Redemption through action.*" I wondered if Gunner had ever killed anyone.

———

I hadn't heard from Bob in exactly eighteen days when Marge Horner came into the shop. She never came into the shop, except if someone dragged her in after lunch. But if she wanted to enrich my coffers, who was I to argue? Marge's day look was a tweed suit that looked like a horse blanket, a jangly charm bracelet, and pair of ingot-sized gold earrings. I was polite to her—well, civil. She walked around picking up small items—boxes, candles, books, that kind of thing. She surreptitiously glanced at the price tags. If something cost more than twenty-five bucks, she immediately put it down like it was burning her hand.

"Looking for something special?" I finally asked her.

"A wedding present," she said with a curt smile.

I inquired how much she wanted to spend. She said she'd like to keep it under fifty dollars. I told her that was a little tough, but she could get a really nice scented candle in a pretty china cup for fifty-five.

"No candles. I'd like to get something a little more personal."

I asked very innocently who the gift was for, thinking that if I knew them or knew something about them, I could help her better.

"Oh, it's for Bob and Melody," she said casually, as if I already knew it.

"Bob and Melody?" I heard myself repeating. I say "heard myself," because right then I felt like I was in an echo chamber in some alternate universe.

"Yes, isn't it amazing? After all this time? They just snuck off to Virginia and tied the knot. So romantic—eloping at their age. I just found out about it last night because they're giving a big reception at the Hay Adams. I think I need to get them just a *little* something, don't you? Nothing too lavish if there was no formal wedding. You agree?"

I nodded like an automaton. No wonder I hadn't heard from Bob. That son of a bitch was *married*? To *Melody*? It didn't seem possible.

I stared at Marge as she jabbered on about Bob and Melody's on-again, off-again courtship and its "thrillingly happy ending." Out of all the antique joints in all the towns in all the world, she walks into *mine*? Fat fucking chance. She knew exactly what she was doing coming in here, hoping to be the first to bring me these tidings of discomfort and joylessness. I kept my cool, I'm happy to say—in part because I was able to recall Samurai Musashi's sage advice: *Be inwardly strong-hearted, and do not let others see into your mind.*

I advised Marge that I thought the newlyweds would just love a book on Victorian houses, knowing full well how much Bob loathed anything cluttered and old-fashioned. Marge was hesitant. She'd obviously seen his modern, minimalist abode. When I insisted it was the right choice, she said a pointed, "Well, of course, *you* would know."

God, I hated that woman.

Rosina watched us the whole time, no doubt waiting for me to crash into the guardrail. But I just cruised around the shop, slow and steady, wrapping the book, ringing up the sale, telling Marge, "Have a nice day!"—a loathsome, overworked catchphrase I only use with people I really detest.

The second Marge was out the door, I ran upstairs to my office, fighting the urge to cry. I stood staring out the window with my arms crossed, looking back on my relationship with Bob like it was a movie I'd seen rather than something I'd lived through. I was more stunned than upset. The shock of it was just beginning to sink in.

Rosina knocked softly on the open door and entered.

"Can you *believe* he did this to me?" I asked, turning to face her.

"Definitely," she replied.

"I knew you'd say that."

"You want the truth now, or you wanna wait until you feel better?" she said.

"Might as well hit me with it now. I'm down, and I'm not getting up again."

"Okay. Since I've been working here, you've had a few boyfriends, right?"

"Right."

"And they were all different, right?"

"Right."

"*Wrong*," she said firmly.

I hated it when Rosina played these little games, but I was too upset to challenge her.

"Go on." I sank down on the chair behind my desk.

Rosina sat on the couch, arranging her wide red ruffled skirt around her so it looked like she was sitting in the middle of a giant rose. That skirt reminded me of the bushels of garish red roses Bob had sent me in the early days.

"All your boyfriends?" she began. "They look different, but they are all the same. I knew when I met Mr. Poll that he was just another one of them. More smooth, more sophisticated, but he is just like the others."

"In what way?" I asked wearily.

"Because I can see he likes himself more than he likes you."

"How could you see that?"

"First, because everything is so crazy and in a rush. All the flowers and the notes and the phone calls. They are not about you. They are about him and about how much he can impress you. A man who tells you he cannot live without you on the first date is already thinking about his freedom."

"I loved him."

"You didn't even *know* him."

"I did so!" I protested.

"No! What he has done now—going off and getting married without telling you—that is who he *really* is. Because that is an action. The rest is just a long date. You loved the *idea* of him, Reven. You loved the attention more than the man. I can see it when you are going out with him. There is no time for you to think about who he really is, or for him to think about who you really are. You saw each other a lot. But did you ever *know* each other? I don't think so. You were both acting in a play. And now the play is over."

"He told me he loved me. He gave me this bracelet, didn't he?" I said, raising my wrist.

"You don't even like that bracelet. I don't know why you wear it."

"Yeah, well, now I hate it." I took it off and offered it to her. "Want it?"

"No, it's ugly."

I flung it across my desk, where it disappeared into the clutter.

"You wanna know when you *really* fell in love with Bob Poll?" Rosina asked.

"When?"

"When he stopped calling you."

She had a point. Rejection has often made my heart grow fonder. But I still had to defend myself.

"Look, Bob Poll went on a campaign to make me fall in love with him. You saw it. Maybe he was only doing it to make Melody jealous. Maybe he thought he loved me, then realized he couldn't live without her. But whatever the reason, he succeeded."

"No, he didn't. You are not in love with him."

"How do you know?"

"Because I know. I think you are more upset because he didn't tell you. If he had called you and told you about this himself, would you feel so bad now?"

I thought for a moment. I had to admit that Marge's startling road-side bomb delivery had wounded me almost as much as the news itself. Finally, I said, "I don't know."

"If you ask me, I feel sorry for Melody. This is not a man you want to marry," Rosina said. "I'm gonna tell you something I wasn't gonna tell you."

"Great. More bad news."

"This will make you feel better. Mr. Poll . . . he hit on me." Rosina nodded knowingly.

I was truly shocked. But I knew she wouldn't make something like that up. She was very happily engaged to her contractor.

"When?"

"The one time he came into the shop to pick you up for lunch. And that's another thing. He had no interest in your business. That detective is more interested in your store than Mr. Poll. Anyway, you were in your office. I buzzed you to come down. I was looking out the window at his car, and he asked me if I wanted to have a ride sometime."

"That's not exactly hitting on you."

"He said, 'I'll take you for a ride if you promise not to tell your boss.' I thought he was kidding. But then I looked at his face, and I knew he wasn't kidding. Even though I love that car, I would never get in it with him."

"Were you scared of him?"

She laughed. "For me, no. For you, yes. Trust me, he's not gonna be faithful to her. And he will try and come back to you. You watch."

"You think so?" I said, unable to disguise a little feeling of hope in my voice.

Rosina sighed in exasperation. "I can't believe it! Forget about this man! He's not for you. He's not for anyone!"

Rosina was like a sprite, thin and lithe, with large dark eyes, pale skin, and a silky black ponytail. She was only twenty-four, and she didn't have much formal education, but she was full of common sense and a bracing sort of compassion that enabled her to comfort and con-front at the same time.

I took to heart what she said, but when she left to make me a cup of tea, I had a good cry. Did I really not see the true character of the men I dated, or did I just willfully ignore it for some neurotic reason I couldn't even begin to fathom?

I dried my eyes before Rosina came back with the tea. She wasn't a great one for self-pity.

"What should I do?" I asked her, sipping the soothing brew.

"If I were you, I'd call him up and congratulate him. Tell him to get his wife to register here for the wedding presents. We could use the business."

I told Rosina she was too young to understand that when you get to be my age and you meet someone who might be possible for you, you're willing to overlook a hell of a lot. I still couldn't imagine Bob as a serial killer—just a lady-killer. With one more lady down. Me.

Chapter 23

Violet phoned me later that morning. Her voice was somber. "Rev," she began slowly. "I need to tell you something."

"If it's about Bob getting married, I've already heard."

"Oh." She sounded vaguely disappointed. "Who told you?"

"Marge Horner came into the shop, ostensibly looking for a wedding present. She couldn't wait to break it to me. Who told *you*?" I asked her.

"I'm sitting here looking at a tacky invitation to the reception, hand-delivered by the Hunter Green Hornet. Did you have any idea about this?"

"None."

"Well, I never liked him anyway," Violet said.

"You told me you did!"

"I lied."

"Thanks a lot."

"I thought he made you happy. But clearly he didn't, so now I can tell you the truth. I think he's weird. I'm sorry, Rev. I really am."

"Don't be. It's the story of my life, misreading people."

"Why don't you take the day off? Come with me up to Saks. I have a fitting."

I figured, what the hell? Why not? The last thing I wanted to do was stay in the shop and wait on anyone else eager to buy the happy couple a wedding present.

———

Violet picked me up in her blue Volvo, and we drove up to Saks in

Chevy Chase. The whole area had become more gentrified in recent years, boasting a row of glittery new designer boutiques, built to accommodate the fashion needs of a younger, trendier social crowd. Old Guard Violet still went to Saks's famed Fifth Avenue Club, where she found comfort in the cubicle of Lisa Crawford, the personal shopper to whom I'd introduced her when she first arrived in Washington. Lisa, a slim, chic African-American woman with closely cropped hair, had a *Vogue* editor's eye for fashion. If she didn't like an outfit, she would point to it and say, "And that would be a big *no!*" Violet ignored Lisa's sage advice on clothes at her own peril.

I sat on the couch while Violet tried on a snappy navy blue number Lisa had chosen for her. Violet looked great, and Lisa called the fitter. While we were waiting, Violet showed me and Lisa the invitation to Bob and Melody's reception.

"A little tacky, dontcha think?" Violet said.

Lisa, who knew I'd dated Bob Poll because I'd bought an outfit from her when I was seeing him, examined the flimsy card and looked at me sympathetically. I just shrugged and said, "C'est la vie."

Lisa got a kind of knowing look on her face, and intuitive Violet immediately sensed that she had a tidbit of gossip she was itching to tell us.

"What?" Violet said, pointing at Lisa. "You know something. Spill it."

"I don't want to make anyone feel bad," Lisa said, glancing at me.

"I'm beyond caring," I said.

"Okay. . . . Well, you know Once Is Not Enough?"

We both nodded in amusement because Once Is Not Enough, Washington's premier consignment store, was Rainy Bolton's favorite shop in Washington. She loved Inga Guen, the owner. The shop was frequented mainly by style-conscious women who either couldn't afford to buy new designer clothes or, like Rainy Bolton, who could easily afford them but found the hefty prices in retail stores "a scandal." Violet often lied and told her mother-in-law she'd purchased an outfit there secondhand when in fact she'd bought it brand-new, simply because she wanted Rainy to believe she was thrifty.

"I happen to know that Mr. Poll has a running account at that shop," Lisa went on. "He sends a lot of ladies to get designer outfits, and they send him the bill."

"How do you know that?" I asked.

"There's this woman who comes in here who used to work at King Arthur's, that strip club. But now she's married, so she can afford to shop here. She told us that Mr. Poll used to buy her a lot of stuff there, and he sent a lot of the girls from the club there to get clothes from Inga."

"Out of the goodness of his heart, no doubt," Violet said.

Violet and I just looked at each other. Sometimes the most interesting information came from the most unlikely places. Lisa and Inga were not involved in politics or the government, but they probably knew about more sexual shenanigans in Washington than the FBI, simply because they sold clothes and they knew who was buying what for whom and when.

"Honey, you are so well out of that one," Violet said, referring to Bob. "I bet your pal Gunner would be interested in that info."

After the fitting, Violet and I went for a stroll along Boutique Row. I told Violet she absolutely had to go to Bob and Melody's reception, if only for my sake. She said she couldn't face it—Grant would probably be there with Cynthia.

"If you think I want to run into the two of them in front of the whole of Washington, you're nuts. I'd rather go to Iraq."

I told her that was just the time to do battle—with everyone watching.

"I should give you the book Gunner gave me. There's a section called 'Win by Letting Yourself Be Hit At.' "

Violet looked at me askance.

"What book is that?"

I started explaining the *Book of Five Rings* to her, but she didn't seem too interested. She cut me off and said she felt much too humiliated to go to the reception no matter what "some dead samurai said about winning." I have to say I didn't really blame her. I felt so low myself I wasn't even interested in shopping. But Violet said she wanted to buy me a present, so we dropped by the Dior boutique to see if there was anything there that caught my fancy.

Nouria Sahala, the vivacious wife of the Otanni ambassador, was in the back room, trying on an evening gown. We caught a glimpse of her walking back and forth, adjusting the long train. Violet stopped short and ducked away before Nouria could catch sight of her.

"What's the matter?" I asked.

"Come on, let's get out of here!" Violet said, quickly heading for the front door.

I was mystified by her behavior. I knew that Violet and Nouria were friends, and that Nouria always invited the Boltons to her famous parties. The exotic décor of the Otanni Embassy, combined with Nouria's personal warmth and her power-laden guest lists, made her invitations much coveted around town.

I knew Nouria to say hello to. She was an acquaintance rather than a friend. A think-tank wonk I once dated took me to one of her dinners a while back. Nouria had subsequently come into my shop to ask my advice on redecorating the sprawling white living room of the embassy, which was blandly pleasant but lacked the exotic charm of the main reception hall. I suggested a more colorful scheme, incorporating some of the decorative motifs of her country. But nothing ever came of it, because she didn't want to close down the embassy for the time it would have taken to refurbish it. Besides, she was a firm believer that people, not décor, make a party. Nouria had always been very nice to me. When she caught sight of me and waved a warm hello, I couldn't very well avoid her without appearing rude.

"Reven! Nouria!" she said, pointing to herself, as if I wouldn't know. I found that quite endearing. "Come here! I need your opinion. Do you like this dress?"

Nouria was a tall, blond beauty with a sunburst smile and the figure of a runway model. Her clothes were chic and often quite flamboyant. It was generally agreed that Nouria had done more to showcase Arab women's rights just with her outfits and her parties than a bundle of international conferences on the subject. I gave the leopard-print chiffon sheath the once-over. She looked great in it.

"You don't think it's a bit too much?" she asked me.

When I walked into the back room to take a closer look at her, I saw the real reason Violet had hightailed it out of there so fast. Sitting on the couch, also appraising the dress, was Cynthia!

"Well, hi there, Dream Girl!" she said. "What brings you to this neck of the woods? Aren't you s'posed to be working on my house?"

This was the first time I'd actually clapped eyes on Cynthia since Grant's decampment. I wondered if she'd seen Violet. I prayed not, because it was imperative to make her think that Violet and I were on the outs if Operation Mary Lou Lindsay was going to have any chance of success.

I told her I was "just browsing around, taking a break." It was impossible to tell if she believed me.

"Come on, girls, what about the dress?" Nouria said impatiently. She spoke in a swift patter with a light accent.

Cynthia and I both agreed we liked it, and if she liked it, she should buy it. As I was leaving, I heard Cynthia say, "Nouria, honey, let me buy that dress for you as a little gift."

Nouria shot back, "What? Are you *crazy*? I buy my own clothes."

I was pleased that she didn't even thank Cynthia for the offer.

———

Violet was skulking around the parking lot, waiting for me.

"Did they see me?" Violet asked as we got into the car.

"I don't know. I don't think so."

"What took you so long?"

"Nouria wanted my opinion on the dress."

"Did Cynthia say anything to you?" she asked.

"Nothing memorable. But she offered to buy that dress for Nouria," I said.

"You're kidding!"

"Nouria told her to take a hike! She didn't like it one bit, I could tell."

"Bless her little ambassadorial heart! But how cheeky is that? The witch thinks she can just *buy* her way in anywhere!" Violet fumed.

"It's been known to work before," I said.

"Yeah, well, it just goes to show you how much this city has changed. Money never used to mean beans here. Power was all that really counted. But now it's like money has taken over this whole town like a big fungus. Money and power and celebrity have all become the same damn thing. You can't tell the difference anymore."

"They're not the same. It's just more difficult to separate them now because they're all so intertwined."

Violet pulled out onto Wisconsin Avenue. She drove for awhile, then said: "I wonder if Nouria will still invite me to the embassy."

"Of course she will. Nouria's loyal. Don't think like that."

I said this to pep Violet up, knowing full well that divorce was a big eraser for most women, particularly in Washingon. We'd both seen it so many times. Women started off strong when they first went out on their own, then gradually got rubbed off the social page. Violet herself had supported a few hapless ex-wives when they became single, so she knew the score.

She said somberly: "Don't kid yourself. In this town, old ex-wives never die. They just fade away."

Chapter 24

I was embarrassed to tell Gunner about Bob, embarrassed to admit he'd been right all along and that Bob was not at all what he seemed to be. I still didn't believe he was a killer, but the guy definitely had some faulty wiring somewhere; no normal person courts someone the way he courted me then ups and marries someone else—even if she is his old girlfriend.

It was too freezing a day for Usherville, so Gunner and I broke precedent and met at this little café way up on Connecticut. Besides, I needed a drink. I ordered a double scotch—something I've never done in the middle of the afternoon—well, almost never. Gunner had an orange juice. I purposely didn't say anything until our drinks arrived because I didn't want the waiter interrupting us. Plus I needed to drink up a little courage before I admitted my humiliation. I took a couple of swigs of scotch and relaxed a little as the liquor warmed my innards.

Finally, I said lightly: "Well, guess what? You were right. . . . Bob is not the man I thought he was. Turns out he's a complete shit."

Gunner didn't say a word. He just stared at me. I took a few more sips of scotch, trying to avoid his gaze.

Finally, I looked him square in the eye and said, "He's married. . . . He married Melody. The two of them snuck off together and tied the knot. I haven't heard a word from him. Not one fucking word. . . . You'd think he might have told me, wouldn't you? Know anyone who wants a hideous gold bracelet?"

Gunner had no reaction. At first I thought he didn't really understand what I was telling him. He just sat there with his chin jutting out and his head tilted back, staring at me with narrowed eyes and a slightly pained expression on his face, like a big cat being pelted with sleet. It suddenly dawned on me that, on the contrary, this news wasn't coming as any big shock to him.

"Oh, my God! You *knew*. You *knew* he got married, didn't you?" One tiny nod of that dreadlocked head told the tale. "How long have you known?"

He hesitated, then said, "Nine days."

I was horrified.

"*So why the hell didn't you tell me?*" I cried. The bartender glanced over at us, then went back to polishing glasses.

Gunner sighed. "I thought about it."

"You *thought* about it? What stopped you?"

"Nobody knew about it—not even that goon chauffeur. So if I'd told you and you'd reacted and tried to get in touch with him, he'd have to wonder where you got your information. Also, I kinda wanted to see how it would play out."

"*Play out?* What are you, some kind of fucking photojournalist who takes pictures in a war zone and does nothing when someone's about to get shot? If you found out someone was gonna kill me, would you tell me? Or would you just wait to see how it *played out*?"

He didn't respond. Another thought occurred to me.

"You've been following him, haven't you?" He didn't answer. He didn't need to. The answer was obvious. "So was he seeing her the whole time he was seeing me?"

Gunner lowered his eyes. I knew I was right. I drank the rest of the scotch.

"So *that's* why you kept telling me he was a shit—because you knew it for a fact. Although God knows when he got the time to see her. . . . *Jesus Christ!*" I was near tears.

"You're upset."

"Ya *think*?"

"I'm sorry."

I just looked at him. "You know what I'm really upset about? I'm upset about *our* relationship. Fuck Bob Poll. I was wrong about him. It's not the first time I've been wrong about a guy. But here's the thing: I took a look at that book you gave me, and I can tell from all

that shit you underlined that you see yourself as some kind of samurai warrior with this deep code of honor and ethics within yourself.
And yet, and yet . . . when it comes to acting honorably toward me,
you just abdicate all responsibility and decide to wait until it *plays out*.
I don't get it. Can you please explain it to me?"

Gunner paused. "I'm glad you took a look at the book."

"Yeah, well, screw the book! I wanna understand what our relationship is, okay? I mean, you come in and you plunk yourself down
in the middle of my life so that I tell you everything and you tell me
nothing! Is that how it works? Then you find out something that is so
important to me and you don't say a word and I'm just supposed to
accept that, right?"

Gunner spoke softly and deliberately, like he was talking to a child
having a tantrum. "I needed to see how this guy would handle the
situation with you."

"He hasn't *handled* it. I haven't heard a freaking word from that
rat bastard son of a bitch, okay? Not one freaking word! You know
who I had to hear it from? Marge Horner—one of the worst unelected
people in Washington! *Marge fucking Horner*. Spiderwoman. Who
snubs me because she doesn't think that I'm grand enough for her. I
had to hear it from *her*. Whaddaya think of that?"

"I think," he began softly, "that's one way of handling it."

We sat in silence for a time. Finally, I said, "You want to know something?"

"Sure."

"You're just as bad as he is. You just sat by and waited for me to be
humiliated—and I don't mean by Marge. I mean by Bob. If you'd told
me, I would have broken it off first and saved myself. . . . *Oh, never
mind! Shit!*" I buried my head in my hands and lost it.

Gunner let me cry. He leaned back in the rickety wooden chair
with his arms crossed, staring at me. The piped in music started playing
"Stand by Your Man," and it was so ridiculous that it made me laugh—
that weird hysterical laughter you get when you're crying and everything suddenly seems totally absurd and pointless. Gunner handed me a
paper napkin from the dispenser. I blew my nose and wiped my eyes.

"So did you *attend* the wedding?" I asked him facetiously.

He shook his head in amusement. "Wasn't much of one. They went
to the Arlington Courthouse."

"What do you do? Just tail him around all the time?"

"Something like that. . . . Reven?"

"*What?*" I said petulantly.

"Don't envy Ms. Hartford. This is not a man you want to be married to."

"That's what Rosina says. You know what I found out? He has a running account at this upscale consignment shop. He sends a lot of girls there. Girls from King Arthur's."

"Once Is Not Enough," Gunner said.

"You *know* about that?"

"There's not a lot about Mr. Poll I don't know, except the one thing I'd like to know."

"If he's your killer, right? . . . Do you really believe he's a serial killer? I mean *really*?"

Gunner shook his head. "I just don't know. Anyway, I could believe it. I could even know it for a fact. But without proof, it doesn't do me any good."

"No, but seriously. Do you have anything linking him to these crimes, other than your obsession with him?"

"Look, I have my own theory about these crimes, okay?"

"Jesus. You're like a politician. You just say whatever you want to say. You don't answer the damn question."

"I gotta go."

I was so sick of this game. How come I was always the one giving out the info, and he was always the one holding back? I reached across the table, grabbed his sleeve, and said, "Okay, Gunner, here's the deal. Before you leave here, you have to tell me one really personal thing about yourself!"

He cocked his head. "Why?"

"To make up for the fact you didn't let me know about Bob. And because I've had it, okay? Tell me something important and meaningful about yourself right now, or I'm finished. You can get yourself another snitch. And no bullshit. I mean it."

He didn't have to answer me, and we both knew it. But he understood I was dead serious. Either that, or he just plain felt sorry for me.

He finally leaned forward, put both his hands palms down on the table like he was bracing himself, and said: "Okay. . . . My daughter died two years ago, and my wife committed suicide as a result."

Pow! Just like that, without much emotion, like his grief had simply wrung dry. I stared at him, not knowing how to respond.

"My God . . . I'm so sorry," I whispered.

"Thank you." He bowed his head, as if lost in memory.

I touched his hand. He didn't move. We stayed that way—with my hand on his—for quite a long time. We didn't say a word. He didn't look at me.

"Any time you want to talk about it—" I said at last.

"*I don't,*" he said firmly, withdrawing his hand. "Don't tell anyone. Please."

"No. I promise. Cross my heart."

"So . . . You satisfied now?" I nodded. "Good. We still friends?"

"Friends," I assured him.

We shook hands. He stood up abruptly, fished in his pocket, and took out a twenty-dollar bill for the check. He slapped it on the table and said, "Seeya when I seeya."

After Gunner left, I sat for a while, thinking about what he'd said. My own dumb romantic problems paled in comparison with his sorrows. I thought about the miseries people conceal and how they manage to survive. Gunner's revelation explained his odd combination of intensity and detachment. I got an insight into why he liked that book. Discipline is the key to coping with a personal tragedy of such magnitude; otherwise your sanity might gallop away. That book taught you to harness your mind, to control it, no matter what evils assailed it.

I think that was the very first time I felt a real connection to Gunner. I knew I'd never say anything about this, not even to Violet. This didn't feel like gossip or idle speculation or something we could joke about. It felt heavy and ominous, like some great big chunk of darkness.

Chapter 25

When I got back to the shop, Rosina told me that Ms. Fisk, Cynthia's secretary, had called.

"The Trailblazer wants to see you this afternoon," Rosina said.

"That's too goddamn bad. I'm not going. I feel too rotten. Anyway, I just saw her."

Rosina then used her tried and true powers of persuasion: she fanned a handful of bills in front of me.

"She owes you a lotta money. You better go pick up a check."

I forced myself to go, even though I was still mightily upset about Bob. I now had to add him to the long line of charismatic miscreants I always seemed to wind up dating. How could I keep getting it so wrong, time after time after time after time? Was it just that the pickings were so slim that the only guys left were fatally flawed? Or—God forbid—was it me?

Bob was gone, but there was still hope that Grant might be saved from the clutches of the Trailblazer—with my help.

———

The offices of the Cynthia A. Rinehart Foundation were located on the ground floor of one of those ornate old mansions along Embassy Row. I'd never been there before, even though I'd been working for Cynthia for nearly five months. The décor, bland and modern, featured one of those Walls of Narcissism, as I call them, where people hang pictures of themselves posed with every celebrity, politician, or billionaire they've ever met or been in close proximity to. "To Cynthia

Rinehart, with admiration and blah, blah, blah." Signed, Famous Person. Actually, the wall was pretty damn impressive considering how short a time she'd been on the scene. I was amazed at how quickly money had purchased her so many high-powered friends.

Smack in the center of this ego collage was a picture of Cynthia with Grant, the unknown soldier of the group. I remember the moment it was taken at the Golden Key dinner. She was hanging a key around his neck like it was a leash. He looked like a startled owl. It was the only unsigned picture in the bunch.

When Ms. Fisk introduced herself to me, I thought, This *can't* be the Ms. Fisk I've spoken to umpteen times on the phone, arranging deliveries and bill payments and all the other stuff for the house Cynthia couldn't be bothered with. *That* Ms. Fisk had a crisp linen voice that I imagined belonged to a sleek, cool, and tailored sort of person. *This* Ms. Fisk looked like a chaotic troll with thatched hair, a squat physique, and a truckload of attitude.

"This way, please," she said, opening the heavy oak door to Cynthia's office.

Cynthia was sitting behind her desk, and she was not alone. Grant was standing behind her like a concrete stanchion. I wanted to lash out at him for nearly wrecking my friendship with Violet, but instead, I swallowed my anger and said a warm hello to both of them. I acted especially pleased to see him, thinking of the big picture: Operation Mary Lou.

"So, did Nouria get that fabulous dress?" I said brightly to Cynthia, hoping to get off to a friendly start.

She glowered at me without replying. Grant didn't say a word. The two of them stared daggers at me. Cynthia motioned me to sit down like she had a scepter in her hand.

"I'm not one to beat around the bush," she began.

"Wait, please," I interrupted her. "I think I know what you're going to say, and I just want you two to know something first, okay? I don't blame anyone in this situation. This kind of thing happens. I don't think people should take sides at this point. In fact, I told Violet that she just has to deal with it now." I shook a teasing finger at Grant. "You were very naughty to tell her I came to see you."

He shifted uncomfortably from one leg to another, but remained silent.

I continued. "I also told her that it's impossible to legislate feelings, and there's no point in trying to hold on to someone who doesn't want to be with you. She got very angry at me, and the upshot is we're no longer speaking. I just thought you'd like to know."

I waited for a response. Neither of them moved.

"So, to make a long story short," I went on, "I'm really looking forward to finishing the house, Cynthia. I thought it was important that you know that whatever has happened in other areas will not affect my professional commitment to you, because I basically consider all this none of my business."

They still didn't move. Their silence was daunting.

"So, um, I'll need a check today, if that's okay. We're a little overdue."

"Well, Dream Girl," Cynthia began, "I'm very sorry to hear about you and Violet, because Violet's gonna need all her gal pals right now. And we very much appreciate your candor and your understanding, don't we, darlin'?" She glanced up at Grant. He blinked but said nothing. She went on. "However, I find it curious that two women who aren't speaking to each other are going shopping together, because I have always been of the opinion that when women shop, they talk."

I was flummoxed, but I managed a weak comeback. "Well, uh, this *just* happened. Actually, it happened right after I saw you in Dior. Violet and I had a big argument on the way home in the car."

Cynthia smirked. "Nice try. But I will no longer be requiring your services. Ms. Fisk will give you your check. By the way, I've deducted twenty thousand dollars from the bill."

"*What?* Why?"

"Because you've made mistakes in the house, that's why."

"Are you serious? What mistakes?"

"I don't have people working for me whose mistakes I have to bring to *their* attention. People who work for me bring their mistakes to *my* attention before I get wind of them. That's how I know they're working *for* me and not against me. You've made mistakes. There's no point in arguing. You're fired."

I usually insist on half the money upfront when I order an item, to cover my cost. But I'd been tolerant about late payment from Cynthia because it was such a big job and I figured she was good for it. Now she was stiffing me. I was livid. I had absolutely no idea what she was talking about. I challenged her to tell me exactly what mistakes she thought I'd made, but she refused. I told her I was going to sue her if she didn't pay me *all* the money she owed me. She dared me to. We got into a shouting match. She finally stood up and walked out of the room, telling Grant, "Handle this for me, darlin'. I have a meeting at the Kennedy Center."

She slammed the door behind her. I couldn't believe it. I just stood there with my mouth agape. Finally, I said to Grant, "What the hell are you doing with that sociopath?"

He immediately rose to her defense. "She's a tough businesswoman who's made it up the hard way. She doesn't like people taking advantage of her. I've seen the bills. You charge an obscene amount of money."

"You think anything over a dollar-fifty is an obscene amount of money. You're the cheapest man alive!"

Grant was irrationally stingy. I suspected that Rainy Bolton had hung a sign on his balls when he was a kid that read, "Whosoever takes your money, takes these too."

"I'm a banker. I know the value of a dollar," he said.

"Listen, twenty thousand dollars is nothing to her. But to me it could mean the difference between salvation and purgatory. I'll sue her! I will!"

This was an idle threat, of course. How could I afford a lawsuit, when I could barely afford next month's rent?

"I don't know what to tell you, Reven."

I started pacing around, vowing not to go gentle into the bankruptcy night.

"Fine! If she wants war, she can have it. I'm not without friends in this town. I'll get the word out about her, trust me."

"I think I should warn you, Reven. Cynthia is revered in this town. You'd be unwise to challenge her. Just take a look at some of the people on her board."

Grant was right. Cynthia had collected an impressive list of board members, especially the venerable old Senator Pomador. The diverse group of distinguished men and women had been chosen for their impeccable reputations and sterling credentials in order to create an aura of irrefutable probity for the Rinehart Foundation. Still, I persevered.

"Grant, you've known me for more than twenty years. Are you going to take her word over mine?"

Grant crossed his arms in front of him and refused to answer. His WASP heritage had armed him with formidable abilities to stonewall.

"You just better wonder what other lies she's told you. Maybe she hired me because she knew she could stiff me. Ever think of that? Maybe she never had any intention of paying me what she owes me because she knows damn well I can't fight back."

"It's not like she can't afford to pay you. She is simply morally outraged that you would take such advantage of her because you thought she didn't know any better."

"Please! Save the moral outrage for war and global warming, will you? And anyway, that's not true! I dare anyone to go into that house and show me what mistakes I've made!"

Grant's face twitched like he was trying to keep from erupting into a rage. He hadn't changed much in all the years I'd known him. He had been blessed with strapping, wholesome looks that had weathered well. He looked like an aging boy. Yet there was a new hint of cruelty in his expression, brought on, I suspected, by the selfishness of lust.

"What's happened to you, Grant? You used to love Violet. And I thought you cared for me as a friend. What is this woman's hold over you that you've changed so radically? You used to be a pal."

"No, I used to be a doormat. No more! Let me tell you something, Reven. People have underestimated Cynthia her whole life—just like they've underestimated me. I've always done what people said I had to do, what was expected of me, instead of what I wanted to do. Your life goes down the drain in tiny drips when you live like that. Before you know it, you're all dried up. Cynthia's taught me not to wait for the ax to fall. You have to deal with people who stand in your way, not knuckle under to them."

Though Grant sounded like he was talking to himself, trying to justify leaving Violet, I suddenly understood the true nature of his relationship with Cynthia. Sure, it was about sex. But I could just hear Cynthia preying on Grant's insecurities by comparing them to her own. I imagined the in-depth postcoital discussions about how much alike they were, how misunderstood, underappreciated, and unsung—until they hooked up. A Georgetown Bonnie and Clyde. Separately, they were nothing; but together, they were a powerful entity—the "We'll show them as lovers united against the world" form of courtship. I was beginning to understand just how cunning Cynthia was.

"Grant, listen to me, you're one of my oldest friends. I love you, and I love Violet, and—"

He interrupted me. "*Yes*. Some people say you and Violet love each other *too much*."

I just shook my head in disbelief. It was such a ridiculous accusation—one that simply never would have occurred to Grant's pea brain had not some malicious little birdie been a-whisperin' in his ear. Grant's prudish outlook on sex had always mirrored Queen Victoria's when she declared that carnal love between two women simply didn't exist.

"Who is putting these nutty ideas into your head, Grant? As if I didn't know."

"You know, Reven, I've defended you up, down, and sideways in this town, but no more."

"*Defended* me?"

"That's right—defended you. Everyone knows you overcharge. Your shop is twice as expensive as the other shops in Georgetown."

"That's a lie! I decorated your bank practically at cost, for Christ's sakes. You were thrilled with me then. . . . Wait!" I cried, pointing at him. "Did you tell Cynthia I saw you two together in the house that day?"

"No," he said unconvincingly.

"Oh, my God, of course you did! You *told* her. And from that moment on, she's been working on you, figuring out ways to discredit me. Isn't that so? Well? Isn't it?"

Grant handed me the check. "You better take this now and leave, or else you may find yourself in a lawsuit."

It was no use. They had me over a barrel, and they knew it. I grabbed the check and got out of there fast, convinced more than ever that a man in lust is a man in peril.

———

I went straight back to the shop and ordered Rosina to pull up all of Cynthia's bills.

"What happened?" she asked me.

"She fired me."

"Aiyaiyai."

I handed Rosina Cynthia's check. She looked at it and made a face. "Only thirty thousand dollars? She owes us at least fifty."

"I know. But it's all we're going to get from her."

Rosina shrugged. "That's how the rich get richer. . . . And it's a check this time so we have to wait until it clears."

"Let's hope it does clear."

I suddenly thought of Senator Grider, remembering he'd asked me how Cynthia had paid her bills.

"Rosina, how did Ms. Rinehart pay us? Was it by check, bank transfer, what?"

"Always bank transfers. This is the first check."

"You're sure?"

Rosina looked at me like I'd insulted her. "Yes, I'm *sure*."

"What bank?"

"The Potomac Bank."

"Natch! That's how she wormed her way in. Let me see that check."

I took a closer look at the check. It had her name, Cynthia A. Rinehart, printed across the top. "I'll give this back to you later. I want you to go through all of those bills and make sure she doesn't owe us even more money. I'll be in my office if anyone wants me."

"You're sure you want your creditors to know where you are?" Rosina joked.

I went upstairs to my office and found Senator Grider's card. I was ostensibly going to inform him how Cynthia paid me, but my real mission was to let him know that she'd stiffed me for twenty thousand dollars. He was a powerful man. I wanted powerful people to know what she had done to me. I rang the number on the card and got through to a skeptical aide. I left a message for Grider to call me. Before I had a chance to go back downstairs and give Rosina Cynthia's check to deposit, the phone rang. It was Grider himself.

"Want that tour of the Senate I promised you?" he said.

"No, actually, Senator . . . You remember at the British Embassy, you asked me how Cynthia Rinehart paid me?"

"Yup."

"Well, she just fired me."

"Thought you were decorating that castle of hers."

"I was, but no more. It's a long story, but I wanted you to know that my assistant Rosina says that she always paid by wire transfer from the Potomac Bank. I'm sitting here with the only check she's ever given me—the kiss-off check that she handed me today. It's a personal check. Her name's on it. It supposedly covers my expenses to date. All except twenty thousand dollars."

"What happened to the twenty thousand?"

"You'll have to ask her."

Grider paused. "You're saying she stiffed you for twenty thousand dollars?" he asked.

"Well, I hate to tell tales out of school, but that's what it looks like. It may even be more. Rosina's checking her account as we speak."

"Awful sorry about that."

"Not nearly as sorry as I am."

"You might want to sue her, though I don't recommend it. More trouble than worth, lawsuits."

"The fact is, I can't afford to sue her, and she knows that. I'm afraid there's a lot of personal animosity here. She ran off with my best friend's husband, and who knows, this may be a kind of indirect revenge. This is more than you want to know, of course. But you did ask me about her method of payment, and it was wire transfers."

" 'Cept for that personal check."

"That's right."

"Thank you for that information."

"You're very welcome.

"Good-bye for now."

He hung up so abruptly I was surprised. I thought Grider sort of liked me. Guess not. I guess he really was only interested in Cynthia after all.

I went downstairs, handed Rosina the check, and went straight to Violet's house to inform her that our little plan wasn't going to work.

———

It was an unseasonably mild day. Violet was in the garden, repotting some plants. She looked like a real hausfrau in a heavy sweater, a utility apron, and a bandana. When I came outside, she said, "I should probably just let them die, dontcha think?"

"Cynthia fired me."

"You're kidding."

She clapped the dirt off her hands, took off her apron, and led me inside to the sunporch. She got us ice waters, and we settled in so I could tell her the whole story. I told her nearly everything, including how Cynthia had stiffed me for twenty thousand dollars and how I'd told Senator Grider. When I mentioned that Grant was there, she just snickered, but I knew she felt real anguish. She looked like she'd aged about ten years in the space of days. I figured I'd spare her the worst of it—namely, Grant's insane accusation that she and I were more than friends.

"So I guess it's curtains for Operation Mary Lou. No chance of finding the metaphorical bottle of gin in Cynthia's locker now," I said.

Violet was staring at me in an odd way. "Reven? Can I tell you something?"

"Sure."

"If I tell you, will you promise not to think less of me?"

"Come on. What?"

She pulled off her bandana and kneaded it in her hands while she spoke. She was obviously very nervous.

"It's something I've wanted to tell you for a long time. And I've just never had the guts."

"What? Spill it."

"That bottle of gin you found in Mary Lou's locker . . . ? I planted it."

She said this very softly, no doubt to try and lessen the impact. I was stunned. Truly stunned. Finding that bottle of gin and getting Mary Lou expelled was one of the defining moments of my youth. At the time, I'd really agonized about it, and throughout the years, I'd often wondered if I'd made the right decision.

Back then, expulsion from school was a very serious thing. It went on your record and had dire implications for your future, instead of being the bad-girl badge of honor it is today. There were certain offenses that meant immediate expulsion from Wheelock: smoking anywhere except the common room, having an alcoholic beverage on campus, sneaking a boy into your room, going off-campus without permission, and cheating. I was fully aware of the consequences Mary Lou would suffer because of my actions. But I hated the shitty way she treated Violet, so after considerable soul-searching, I informed the dean.

I can still see me and Mary Lou standing side by side in Dean Trowbridge's office that cold February morning. Our housemother, Miss Moore, along with three other grim-faced faculty members, including the stern school physician, Dr. Woodcock (who Violet famously nicknamed "Dr. Timberprick"), were present. First, the dean asked me to tell him how I discovered the bottle. I told him the truth: Mary Lou was changing for gym class. I saw the bottle peeking out of a pile of clothes at the bottom of her locker. I confronted her. She denied the bottle was hers. I said I had no choice but to report her.

Then Mary Lou was asked to explain herself. She swore up and down she was innocent and that someone had planted that bottle in her locker. No one believed her, and no one was surprised she was a secret drinker. In fact, there seemed to be a tacit agreement among the adults present that it explained a lot about her erratic behavior. She cried and carried on like it was the end of the world. I'd never seen this über-bully even close to tears before, and there she was, all hundred and fifty pounds of her, standing in the middle of the floor bawling her eyes out. I couldn't help feeling sorry for her, and maybe even a little ashamed of myself for having nailed her on a first offense.

Then that Salem witch trial thing happened where the dean told her if she admitted her guilt, she would not get expelled because an admission was a step toward repentance. However, if she continued to maintain her innocence, she'd be out on her ear come Sunday. Mary Lou held firm until Dean Trowbridge picked up the phone and started dialing her mother. At which point she hung her head and said, "Okay . . . I'm guilty. The bottle was mine."

Dean Trowbridge gave her a benevolent nod—his benediction for her honesty. The faculty all breathed a sigh of relief and exchanged little smiles of satisfaction, having had their suspicions confirmed by the horse's mouth herself. This was the Wheelock version of waterboarding—confess or die. Then Dean Trowbridge excused us both and told Mary Lou he'd inform her of his decision "in due course."

On our way out the door, she whispered to me: "You know damn well who set me up."

Well, I *didn't* know. And besides, I'd heard her confess!

That Sunday morning when we all came back from church, Mary Lou was trudging down the hall with two suitcases. She'd been expelled.

I remember she looked at me and Violet with her scary, smoky eyes and said, "You'll pay for this." Violet and I just turned away, but I felt bad for her even then.

Over the years, I'd often wondered what ever became of Mary Lou. She never wrote into the alumnae bulletin. For that matter, neither did I. Perhaps she wondered whatever became of me. It all happened a long time ago, but somehow one doesn't forget the dramas of school days, perhaps because they are the first indications of character in oneself and in others. Violet's terrible admission that she had planted that bottle made me reevaluate my decision to report Mary Lou. It also made me think about how cavalierly Violet and I had wrecked a girl's life back then, and how the whole course of Mary Lou's existence may have changed because of what we, two idiot schoolgirls, did to her. I justified my decision by telling myself I was acting in the best interests of a person I cared for—Violet.

Back then, I considered myself a pretty good judge of people. Given recent developments, however, I had to admit there had been times when I'd been misled. I hated the fact that Violet had manipulated me so egregiously.

"How could you have done that to me?" I asked her.

"I didn't do it to *you*," she replied. "I did it to that bitch, Mary Lou. I'm sorry if I hurt you, Rev, I really am. But you know how horrible she was to me. You know she made my life a living hell. I had to do something to protect myself. I had to get rid of her."

"Yes, but you should have told me."

"Maybe," she said, pausing. "And maybe you should have told *me* about Grant."

Touché.

Chapter 26

The Reliable Source column, along with the local magazines—*Washington Life*, *Capitol File*, and the *Washingtonian*—all covered Bob and Melody's splashy reception at the Hay Adams. I still hadn't heard a word from Bob—not that I expected to. But it was galling to see him looking so relaxed and happy in those pictures. Everyone was there, including Grant and Cynthia, who were photographed standing with Nouria Sahala in her leopard-print Dior dress. Marge Horner, wearing a fixed pumpkin smile, popped up in several photos and was quoted as saying she was going to give the couple "an exclusive little dinner" at her house. Even Peggy and Rolly Myers were there, much to my dismay, along with the Jed Jimsons, Kyle Michaels, the artistic director of the Kennedy Center, Leonid Slobovkin and his wife, and many other prominent Washingtonians. Rosina finally confiscated all the magazines because she couldn't stand to see me poring over them and torturing myself.

"People who are attracted to the thing they hate are the most miserable," she said. Wise words.

Cynthia moved into her house—well, Gay's house, as I preferred to think of it. I heard through the grapevine that she got some schlocky decorator from out of town to finish it for her. A blurb in the Style section deemed her "a worthy successor" to Mrs. Harding, saying that Gay would have undoubtedly approved of Cynthia's "ongoing munificence and enrichment of the community."

Poor Violet was now more obsessed with Cynthia than she was with the Beltway Basher—which was really saying something. She

stopped clipping articles about the stalled progress of that investigation and focused on coverage of Cynthia instead. She even stopped
asking me about Gunner, which was fine with me; I couldn't stop
thinking about my last conversation with him, the deep sadness in his
eyes. Violet tracked Cynthia like a bloodhound, which wasn't hard—
the scent of Cynthia's money had left a trail all over town.

Cynthia was like a philanthropic Lady Bountiful, tripping through
Washington, handing out millions to various charities and institutions
like golden apples from a bottomless basket. Everyone wanted to meet
her, to court her, to impress her in order to benefit from her unparalleled largesse. Not only was she giving lavish amounts of money to
charity, she was giving lavish gifts to important people around town—
Chanel bags to congressional wives, cashmere mufflers and designer
ties to senators and cabinet members. The list of recipients was long
and prestigious.

Cynthia referred to herself and Grant as the "It" couple because the
two of them were invited everywhere, including the White House.
She seemed to be at the center of everything, hawking philanthropy
as if it were a new miracle cure. Indeed, philanthropy was a worthy
calling as well as a redemptive force. So powerful was its intrinsic
goodness, it could restore the luster to even the most sullied reputations in short order. When in doubt, give. When in trouble, give.
When indicted, give more.

Though Cynthia was justly proud of the work she was doing, there
was an undeniable arrogance in her manner. Carmen Appleton and
Peggy Myers privately objected to the way Cynthia was throwing her
weight around the Kennedy Center. Carmen, in particular, was fed up
with Cynthia's high-handedness. She complained about it to me and
Violet over lunch at Café Milano.

"Honey, we all know that the people who give the most money get
the best seats. But guess what? I am sick of hearing about it! What
about all of us grunt envelope lickers and floor sweepers? Don't *we*
deserve any credit?"

What bugged Violet more than anything was that so many people
were willing to overlook the fact that, great philanthropist or not, this
woman had stolen her husband.

"She's generous to a fault all right," Violet said. "And trust me, I'm
gonna find out what that fault is."

It was then that Violet confided to me that she'd hired a private detective firm to check Cynthia out.

"How do we know this woman is really who she says she is?" Violet said.

Trust Violet to think of something vaguely shady like that. Her penchant for true crime shows had a practical application at last. Waiting for the report gave her a modicum of hope.

————

Constance Morely came into the shop on a rainy Tuesday. I hadn't seen Lady Morely in months, not since that famous evening at the British Embassy when I imagined Bob was being stalked by Melody, though I now suspected it had been the other way around. Constance said she wanted to buy one of my signature herb-scented candles, and we got to chatting. Naturally, I wanted to avoid the big topics like Bob's marriage and Violet's breakup, so I asked her how her lupus foundation was coming along. She informed me that they'd run into "a bit of a cock-up," as she put it.

"I don't like to talk about it," she said, sniffing a candle. "Thyme?"

"Verbena."

I hardly knew Constance Morely, but she seemed like an elegant, mild-mannered sort of woman, the perfect wife for an ambassador. Those girls had to be at least as diplomatic and discreet as their husbands—though many of them certainly were not. I sensed there was a story there.

The trick in getting more information out of someone is to confide something very personal about oneself first. Nine out of ten times they will reciprocate, or even top you. So I threw a little chum in the water to get her going. I broke my taboo about not mentioning Violet and Grant's breakup. Not only that, I told her how Cynthia had fired me and stiffed me out of twenty thousand dollars, claiming I'd made mistakes I'd never made.

"It you want my honest opinion, the only reason she hired me to begin with was so she could get closer to Grant. Once she snagged him, she didn't need me anymore. That's the real reason she fired me."

Just as I figured, the minute I said this, Constance lowered her voice to a whisper. When those diplomatic girls get going, they can dish with the pros, let me tell you. She told me—in strictest confidence, of course—that right after that dinner at the embassy, Cynthia asked if Constance would introduce her to the prime minister.

"Naturally, I was extremely grateful to her for the generous gift she pledged to my little foundation. So I put her at his table when he came to town," Constance said. "I'm told she's going to present him with one of those Golden Keys next year. And I understand she asked him to participate in one of her retreats."

Constance said soon after that introduction, Cynthia wrote her a letter saying she'd been "overzealous" in her commitment to childhood lupus.

"She apparently met a doctor who doesn't agree with the research Dr. Singh is doing. She did give us fifty thousand dollars, which is a great deal of money, of course. It's just that when you're expecting a million, well . . . We're such a small foundation, and we'd made commitments based on her pledge."

"Can she do that? Just renege on a pledge like that?"

"She didn't sign a formal contract. But even if she had, I'm hardly in a position to sue her. I'm sure you understand."

I certainly did understand. The wife of the British ambassador was not about to get involved in a lawsuit.

"Have you told anyone else about this?" I asked her.

"No. Just James, of course. One has to be so careful in whom one confides in Washington."

"Believe me, I know."

I walked her to the door, past Rosina, who had her nose in the accounts, pretending to mind her own business—a sure sign she'd been eavesdropping. I stood at the window and watched Lady Morely's car drive off, wondering how I could use this latest intelligence to my advantage. I certainly planned to tell Violet. Rosina sidled up next to me.

"I assume you heard everything," I said. "Wasn't I brilliant to get that out of her?"

Rosina shrugged and said slyly, "She didn't buy a candle, did she?"

"You think she *wants* me to repeat that story?"

"Why else would she come here?"

"Are you insinuating I spread gossip?"

"No. I am telling you directly. You should have a blog and call it antiquesandgossip-dot-com. This shop is like a beehive. There is always a buzz here. Not just you. I hear the customers talking. They think I'm not listening, and I'm not supposed to be. But I am."

As Rosina and I were staring out the window, debating the lesser points of my discretion, I suddenly caught sight of Bob Poll's hunter green Rolls gliding past the shop. My heart did a cartwheel. I gripped Rosina's arm.

"Oh, my God! Look!"

"I never got to ride in that car!" She sighed.

The Rolls stopped in front of Bambino, a fancy children's clothing boutique two doors up the block. Maxwell got out and walked around the car. He stood at attention, obviously waiting for someone. I held my breath, expecting to see Bob. But pretty soon, Melody walked out of the boutique carrying a red shopping bag.

Much as I hated to admit it, she looked great. The polished chrome sexpot was history. She was a rich matron in crocodile shoes and a designer suit. She had a soft gleam about her, like burnished gold. She casually handed the shopping bag to Maxwell, who took it with a rigid arm. As she lifted her well-turned ankle and stepped into the car, I was hit by a bolt of envy. Maxwell closed the door behind her and glanced in the direction of my shop. I pulled Rosina back from the window so he wouldn't catch us staring at them.

"You think she is pregnant?" Rosina asked.

"If she is, it's *The Omen*, part three."

Rosina looked at me sympathetically and said: "He will cheat on her. You will see."

As I walked upstairs to call Violet, I thought of my whirlwind courtship by Bob as the dating version of a science fiction movie where the heroine is drawn into an alternate universe with disastrous consequences. Either he was crazy, or I was, or both of us were. In any case, it was over and I hated him, and although I really didn't think he was a serial killer, I liked to refer to him as such.

When I told Violet about Constance Morely's visit and the fact that Cynthia had reneged on her pledge to the lupus foundation, Violet said, "Funny you should mention it, because I just got off the phone with Douglas Reed's wife, who told me that the Folger may have to sue her because she's threatening to renege on her pledge to them."

"Wow. . . . What's going on, I wonder?"

"Maybe she really doesn't have the money," Violet said. "Wouldn't it be delicious if this turned out to be some sort of scam?"

Chapter 27

Rosina took the next month off to go to Uruguay to get married. Naturally, she invited me to the wedding. I wanted to go, but I couldn't afford the time off, plus I had to take care of the shop. She found me a replacement—a sweet, dim young woman named Amber Corey, whose resemblance to Rosina began and ended with her slim figure and dark, pretty looks. Rosina warned me that she didn't know Amber all that well and that she wasn't the brightest bulb on the Christmas tree, but assured me she was honest.

"She used to work at Banana Republic with a friend of mine. He told me she found a dollar in one of the changing rooms and chased the customer halfway up Wisconsin to give it back," Rosina said.

Honesty counts for a lot these days. But as far as I was concerned, Amber's most important quality was that she was available immediately for the price I could afford to pay her. She showed up for work the first day wearing a gold lamé halter top and stretch white pants. In winter.

"Hey, Ms. Lynch, it's, like, so, like, nice to meet you," she said, giving me a limp-fish handshake.

When Violet saw Amber, she whispered to me, "You know how we've always wondered what all those gorgeous girls who hang around the bar at Café Milano at night actually *do* during the day? Now we know."

I was very patient with Amber at first, since she was young and relatively inexperienced, even though she'd worked in retail before. However, having to explain simple tasks to a person who obsessively pasted decals on her fingernails and used the word "like" in every sentence—usually more than once—was definitely not my forte.

"Like okay, I, like, get it now," Amber would say as she examined one of her nails. But then she wouldn't get it, and I'd, like, have to show her how to do it again. And again. And, like, again. The third day she was there, I noticed the tiny tattoos on her ankles. The one on her left ankle read, "Amber," with hearts on either side. The one on her right read, "Corey," with little stars on either side. I joked with Violet that she'd had them put there so in case she forgot her name she could just look down.

The intercom system posed a special challenge for Amber. After a week, she still wasn't quite sure what numbers she had to punch to buzz my office. One morning, she came running up the steps, announcing, "There's, like, this old guy here to see you?" ending that sentence, as she ended almost all her others, with an inquisitive inflection.

"Did you get his name?"

"Oh, I forgot. I'm like really sorry. But he's in, like, this, like uniform . . . ?"

I heaved a weary sigh and got up from my desk. "Try and ask who it is next time, okay?"

"Yeah, sure! I almost did. And then, I, like, forgot?"

I walked downstairs hoping it was the "like" police coming to cart Amber away. I was astonished to see Maxwell standing there in his chauffeur's cap and coat, holding the cookie tin. He was red-faced from the cold.

"Maxwell!" I cried. "How nice to see you!"

He nodded sheepishly. "I'm just in the neighborhood with Mr. Poll, and, uh, I been meaning to return this to you," he said, handing me the tin. "Cookies were delicious like you said. Just like back home. Better even."

"That's so sweet of you, Maxwell. You didn't have to do that."

"I wanted to thank you, ma'am," he said with great sincerity and what I thought was a hint of nostalgia. "You were always kind to me."

He said this in such a way that it made me think that perhaps the new Mrs. Poll was not always kind to him.

The Rolls was parked outside the shop at a meter. I was dying to ask him what Bob was doing in the neighborhood, but I felt awkward mentioning him. Maxwell inquired after Rosina. I told him she was down in Uruguay, getting married. I introduced him to Amber. They shook hands. I couldn't imagine what the staid chauffeur made of Miss Gold Lamé in her halter top, stretch pants, and big hoop earrings. But he seemed to take it in stride.

"Amber, Maxwell. Maxwell, Amber. Amber . . . you see that beautiful car out there?" I said, pointing out the front window to the Rolls. "That's Maxwell's car."

"Oooh, like, wow! That is like so hot!" Amber said, peering out the window for a closer look.

I winked at Maxwell. He was asking me about Rosina and her marriage when Amber said with alarm, "Hey, there's, like, this guy out there, looking in the car . . . ?"

Maxwell rushed to the window. It was Bob, clearly searching for Maxwell. Bob gazed directly into the shop. I wasn't sure if he saw me, but I knew he saw Amber. You couldn't miss her. She looked as out of place as a kewpie doll in a museum. Bob ogled her for a few seconds, then continued up the block in search of his driver.

"Darn, I gotta go!" Maxwell said hurriedly. "Nice to see you again, Miss Lynch."

Maxwell ran after Bob and escorted him back to the car. I could see Bob chewing him out as Maxwell opened the door for him. Just before ducking into the car, Bob glanced back at the shop. I thought he caught a glimpse of me, but I wasn't sure. Amber gave him a little wave.

"That other old guy's real cute," she said. "You know him?"

"I used to."

I watched the car drive off.

"So, like, that's, like, the older guy's car, right?"

"Right." I sighed.

"Really nice, huh? What is it?"

"A vintage Rolls Royce—probably old enough to be your grandfather."

"Cool."

A little later on, Amber came up to my office and said, "Um, Ms. Lynch, I have, like, real bad cramps. You think maybe I could, like, have the afternoon off, if that's okay?"

"Sure. Absolutely. You go home and rest. And if you want tomorrow off, take that too! By all means."

"Actually, I gotta go over to my friend, Julie's, tomorrow, 'cause, like, um, we've got this thing tomorrow night, um—"

"Whatever, hon. You just go. And don't you worry. Come back whenever you feel like it. I'm sure I'll survive without you. Oh, and if you want that cookie tin, feel free . . ."

I couldn't wait for Rosina to get back home.

———

The next day, Amber didn't show up, much to my relief. She didn't show up the day after that either. I was manning the shop by myself, figuring out a gentle way to fire her, when who should walk in but Senator Grider. He was wearing an ill-fitting navy blue suit, a white shirt, and a red-and-white polka-dot tie. He was taller than I remembered, nearly six feet. He had a stringy, taut physique and a lopsided but athletic gait, like an arthritic ex-marathoner. I was surprised to see him, as abrupt as he'd been the last time we spoke.

"Well, well, well, Senator. . . . And what brings you to my neck of the woods?"

"My niece is getting married, and I need to get her a present."

"Great! I can definitely help you there. Do you have a price range?"

"Well, she's my only sister's only child, so I guess I kinda better splurge. Say twenty dollars?"

I paused. "You're kidding, right?"

He paused. "Yup. Just wanted to see if you'd notice. . . . Nice place you got here. Homey. Well, fancy homey. My wife liked antiques. I don't really understand them myself. To me a chair's a chair. Long as you can sit in it comfortably, it doesn't have to look like something you'd win at a fair."

"Shall we look around for a present for your niece? Do you have any idea what she might like?"

"Dorcas is like her mother. No matter what you get her, she's gonna hate it."

"I have a suggestion. . . . Is Dorcas registered anywhere?"

"Registered?"

"Yes. Brides usually register at a certain store to avoid getting things they don't like. They pick out things they need and want, and people buy those things for them. That way everybody's happy."

He guffawed. "Dorcas won't be happy till Judgment Day. But it's a fine suggestion. I'll ask her mother where she's registered."

"Not that I want to do myself out of a sale," I said. "So if you see anything you think she might like, feel free."

He looked down and shuffled his feet. "Truth is, I do see something I like. . . . Well, uh, what I mean is, I didn't just come here for Dorcas."

"No?"

"Nope . . ."

Silence.

"Why *did* you come here? To find out more about Cynthia Rinehart?" I actually knew why he'd come, but I didn't let on.

He cleared his throat. "There's a play on at the Kennedy Center— *Ah, Wilderness!* Like to see it?"

I found his shyness quite endearing.

"When?"

"Thursday night?"

I thought, What the hell? Why not?

"Okay. Thanks. I'd love to."

"You would?"

"You seem surprised."

"I guess I am, kinda. But I'm very honored and happy too. One thing, though . . . I have to meet you there. I can't pick you up. I'm liable to be late, so I'm gonna leave a ticket for you at the box office. That okay with you?"

"That's fine."

"Good. Very good. So, uh, see you Thursday night, then. That's three days from now."

"Yes, I know when Thursday is. Right after Wednesday. See you!"

He paused at the door. "Guess who's from Nebraska?"

"You."

"Aside from me. But anyway, I'm not originally from Nebraska. I'm from Kansas originally, but we moved to Omaha when I was two years old. Fella you'd never think came from the sticks. Guess."

"I just can't imagine."

"Fred Astaire."

"Really? I never knew that."

"Very few people know that. If I could come back as anybody in the whole wide world? Know who I'd come back as?"

"Let me guess. . . . Fred Astaire?"

"Nope, Teddy Roosevelt, trust buster. But after that, Fred Astaire. Fred wasn't a dancer. He was dance itself. Whatever you are, you wanna try and be the thing itself. . . . Who would you come back as?"

"I don't know. I'll have to think about that."

"You think about it and give me your answer Thursday night. And I'll tell you if I think it's a good choice for you."

"I look forward to your opinion."

On his way out the door, Grider did an unexpectedly agile little buck and wing, an attempt to imitate Fred Astaire. As he tapped his way out the door, he tipped an invisible hat to me and smiled. He almost tripped but caught himself, and with a flourish of his hand cried, "See ya!"

Zachary Grider was quirky, awkward, and dour, with flashes of whimsy that were bright and unexpected, like the sun glinting off a piece of rusting metal. The thing I liked about him most, however, was that he was the exact opposite of Bob Poll. I was actually looking forward to our date.

——

Amber didn't show up for work the following day either. I can't say I was unhappy. That was the perfect excuse I needed to let her go. I did call her, however, just to ascertain what her plans were and if she ever intended to show up again. There was no answer at her house. I left a message on her cell.

Gunner came into the shop later that afternoon. I was surprised to see him because of his penchant for secrecy. I knew right away from the look on his face that something really bad had happened.

"*What?*" I said.

"There's been another murder in Rock Creek Park."

"Jesus! You think it's your guy again?"

Gunner nodded. "Oh, yeah. It's my guy all right."

"Have you checked up on Bob Poll? I hope he *doesn't* have an alibi."

Gunner hesitated. "Is there a young woman working here named Amber?"

"Yeah. Rosina's down in Uruguay getting married. Amber's her replacement. Why?"

"Is she here? I'd like to talk to her."

"No. She hasn't been here for a couple of days."

"When was the last time you two spoke?"

"Two days ago. I called her this morning and left her a message. . . . Wait . . . Don't tell me—"

It's hard to explain how I felt at that precise moment—kind of like someone had poured molten lead into me.

"You think it's Amber?"

Gunner shrugged.

"Jesus! Are you *sure*?"

"Pretty sure now," he said.

"Jesus . . . Oh, that poor girl. This is terrible. Oh, my God."

I started to hyperventilate. Gunner took my hand and held it until I calmed down.

"I'm so sorry," he said. "You gonna be okay?"

"I guess."

"Can I get you a glass of water or something?"

"No. I'm fine."

He let go of my hand and began pacing around the shop. "Listen, Reven, I need to talk to you about something. . . . There are going to be a lot of police officers coming around here to ask questions."

"I know. I'm dreading it."

"If they ask you about the task force, you can certainly say you know me and that we've spoken. But I doubt they'll ask, and if they don't I wouldn't bring it up. See, technically, the Park Police have jurisdiction over crimes where the bodies are found in public parks. The Park Police are part of the Department of the Interior, i.e. the federal government. They don't really appreciate our special task force. It's a territorial thing, like the FBI and the CIA. My tree's bigger than your tree—you know. I'd hate for them to interfere with some of my leads."

"I won't say anything. I promise. I certainly won't tell them about Bob Poll."

"I wouldn't. Not just yet."

"But you should know that he saw her."

"Who?"

"Bob saw Amber through the window two days ago. Maxwell came here to return a cookie tin to me, and Bob was standing right outside, looking into the shop. Amber waved at him and thought he was cute."

"Interesting."

"*Interesting?* You know, I'm beginning to think you may be right. You better check and see if he has an alibi, that bastard."

"Don't worry. I'm on it. . . . I gotta go. Remember—keep it simple. Just answer the questions."

"Mum's the word," I said. "But Gunner, I'm a little scared."

"That's why it's so important we don't blow this thing. We gotta get him. And we don't want anyone tipping him off."

The truth is, I was terrified. Death had come much too close. However, I trusted Gunner and felt flattered that he considered me such an important part of his investigation.

———

The next day, officers from the Major Crimes Unit of the U.S. Park Police came to interview me, along with some detectives. I told them everything I knew about Amber, which wasn't much. I said she hadn't worked for me that long a time, and that I knew very little about her. I didn't even know where she lived. I told them she mentioned a girlfriend named Julie and a party she said she was going to. I didn't mention Gunner. They said they'd be in touch.

Amber Corey was considered to be the sixth known victim of the Beltway Basher. Like the others, she was a slim, dark-haired woman who had died as a result of ferocious blunt force trauma to the head and whose body was found partially clothed in the woods of a public park. And, like the others, she had a connection, however tenuous, to Bob Poll.

Chapter 28

If it hadn't been for Violet, I never could have gotten through the next couple of weeks. I think Amber's murder caused me to have a mini nervous breakdown. I forgot how much she had annoyed me and only remembered her as a sweet young woman who was simply trying to do her job as best she could. It's one thing to have a safe armchair read about a serial killer, and quite another to actually feel his breath on your neck. This monster had invaded my life. I couldn't shake the feeling that I might be next. If Violet and Gunner were right about this psychopath, Amber had been picked deliberately, not at random. And if the killer knew her, he knew me.

I told Violet I was terrified to be alone in my house, and she promptly invited me to move into her guest room.

"Until you feel safe," she said.

"I'll never feel safe again," I told her.

Tee was home for the weekend when I arrived at the house. He was the spitting image of Grant—a sandy-haired, fine-featured boy with the same standoffish attitude of his father. He was very polite and respectful, but he generally kept to himself, playing endless video games and texting on the phone. He called me "Aunt Rev."

I was dying to ask him what he thought of the split between his parents, and his opinion of his incumbent stepmother. But he was one of those kids who didn't invite chummy chats with adults. He did, however, seem older than his fourteen years. I think he found his mother and me vaguely amusing. He liked to hear stories about our school days together. Sometimes I got the feeling he was watching the two of us together as if he were watching characters in an old-fashioned play. Aloof as he was, Tee seemed much more sophisticated and savvy about life than we were at his age. Occasionally, flashes of Violet's macabre humor popped out of his mouth. Like the night before he went back up to school, and we all had dinner together. We were talking about the murders when Tee turned to his mother and said pointedly, "Well, at least one person's happy about them. Right, Mom?"

It was so true. The flurry of excitement kicked up by the case was about the only thing that could have taken her mind off Grant and Cynthia.

The media pounced on the story. I got my fifteen minutes in the sun all right—buried alive with honey on my head and a swarm of reporters buzzing around me night and day. I refused to talk to any of them, but I read every scrap they wrote about the case. It turned out that Amber Corey was a party girl with several boyfriends. Police suspected she'd been killed after a party she'd attended in Adams Morgan. One article suggested she'd worked at King Arthur's. I knew Gunner would love that.

Violet was more interested in the way she died.

"She was raped with a foreign object that tore apart her insides, then smashed on the head. Or maybe he smashed her first, then he raped her. Anyway, it's just like all the others," Violet said. "It's definitely the same guy."

I have to say I found Violet's interest in the physical details of the crime a little off-putting. There is such a thing as too much information. I just couldn't stop thinking about poor Amber's last moments. It made me ill, imagining what she'd gone through and the terror she must have felt.

"She must have known not to go into Rock Creek Park alone. . . . That big desolate tract of woods? She was dumb, but not that dumb. It just doesn't make any sense," I told Gunner.

"She was murdered somewhere else and dumped in the park," Gunner confided.

That little fact hadn't been in any of the papers. Neither had the fact that, like all the other girls, Amber had a link with Bob Poll. Given the way Bob had treated me, I was ready to admit I had no idea who he really was and finally take Gunner's suspicions about him seriously. I told Violet that I was coming around to the idea that Bob Poll might actually be the killer.

———

With Tee gone, Violet and I had the house to ourselves. It was kind of like being back in school again, except there was no homework—if you don't count having to watch forensic shows with the hostess. Bill Kurtis of *American Justice* and John Walsh of *America's Most Wanted* were her heroes. *Law and Order* and *C.S.I.* were mandatory viewing.

"Did Grant approve of your preoccupation with crime?" I asked her one night after a marathon of cold case shows.

"He didn't care. Grant didn't notice all that much about me, you know. I remember once I asked him which of two dresses he liked best. I put one on. He looked at it. Then I went back into the dressing room, counted to sixty, and came out in the exact same dress. He looked at me, said, 'The other one,' and went back to his book. He wasn't very interested in me, now that I think about it. I wonder if he really looks at her," she said wistfully.

"It's been my experience that what they do to one, they do to another," I said.

I think Violet liked having me around, and I have to say it was rather wonderful to get up every morning and have someone to bitch about life with. Gunner knew I was living at Violet's house, and one day he called and asked if he could come over and talk to me.

"I've always wanted to see the inside of that house," he said.

"I thought you wanted to keep our relationship a secret," I said.

"From the Park Police. But you can tell your pal Violet—on the way-off chance you haven't already." No fool, Gunner.

"I haven't," I protested weakly. He just let it drop.

Violet was thrilled she was going to get to meet the intriguing detective at last. I knew she'd always been a little envious of my relationship with Gunner. Though he'd already guessed I'd told her about him, I told her to play dumb when she met him.

"For God's sakes, don't let on how much you know," I instructed her.

It was one thing for Gunner to suspect I'd told Violet everything, and another for her to confirm it.

"Fine. And how much does he know about *me*?" she asked.

She gathered from my hesitation that I'd told him everything. I half expected her to throw a fit. But she just laughed.

That afternoon, Gunner came over to Violet's house, and I introduced them for the first time. They shook hands. Violet flashed him one of her queen-at-teatime smiles and said, "How do you do? So nice to meet you, Detective. Oh, love your diamond stud!" She pointed to his ear, as if it were an unexpected touch. I could tell she wasn't fooling him, but Gunner was polite. He didn't let on. He complimented her on her house, the décor of which was what I call "Old World Weary." Rainy Bolton was the original decorator, and the whole place reflected her joyless, juiceless touch. Violet had hardly changed a stick of furniture in the fifteen years since she and Grant had been married, for fear of offending her formidable mother-in-law. It was Rainy's view that serious people didn't care all that much about clothes or decoration.

When Gunner admired the drab but important American eighteenth-century highboy in the hall and asked if she'd gotten it from my shop, Violet replied haughtily, "No, no, that's a family heirloom."

She meant Grant's family, of course, because from what she'd told me, her own family was pretty short on heirlooms, if you don't count lava lamps and avocado green kitchen appliances. She sounded slightly pretentious, which surprised me because she'd always feigned a certain disregard for the shabby grandeur surrounding her. But now that Grant had left her, she clung much more to the physical property of their marriage as evidence of her connection to the Bolton clan.

Gunner wanted to talk to me in private. Violet led us to the library, where we could be alone. Unfortunately, this was the room where the portrait of Grant's maternal grandfather, Colonel Compton, hung above the mantelpiece like a big black cloud. The colonel's eyes followed you around the room no matter where you stood, making you feel guilty about something.

The Ancient Maureener brought us tea and biscuits on a silver tray. I sat on the old leather couch. Gunner sat catty-corner to me on the fraying needlepoint wing chair. I poured us both a cup of tea.

"Any more news about Amber?" I asked him.

Gunner shook his head. "Listen, Reven, I need you to do something for me, okay?"

"Okay."

"It involves answering some difficult questions."

"What kinds of questions?"

"Questions about you and Mr. Poll."

"Go ahead. Fire away."

Gunner shifted uncomfortably in his seat. "How was the sex between you two?"

"I never kiss and tell, Gunner . . ." I paused, just to tease him a bit. "But if you must know, it was okay. Maybe the earth didn't move, but it trembled occasionally," I said coyly.

"Was he into bondage or anything unusual? Any kind of rough stuff?"

"The answer is no. And I know why you're asking."

"Why?"

"Because I know from Violet—our in-house serial killer buff—that when you guys have a suspect, you always want to know what kind of sex they're into. You want to find out if it's anything kinky that might be reflected in the crimes. Right?"

"Kinda."

"Violet told me that when the police interviewed Ted Bundy's live-in girlfriend, she revealed that Ted sometimes liked to tie her up and pretend to strangle her. . . . But that she didn't think anything of it at the time. *Oy.*"

"So Mr. Poll never did anything that made you . . . uncomfortable?"

"Not really. It was missionary madness all the way." Gunner looked thoughtful. "*What?* You're thinking something. What is it?" I asked him.

"Well, I maybe just figured out why he likes to go to strip clubs."

"Why?"

"Let's just say that your Preacher Poll is a little more adventuresome with other types of ladies."

"What do you mean?"

"He likes it rough with strippers. He's been known to rope and brand."

"Not *literally*?"

"Oh, he's a regular cowboy, our boy Bob is. But he's discriminating. He only picks gals who won't talk."

"Well, one of them obviously talked to you."

"Yeah. . . . I guess I'm just a persuasive kinda guy."

As I was thinking back on the sex I'd had with Bob, Gunner said, "So you never felt like you were in any danger."

I shook my head in grim amusement. "No. In fact, I felt safe with him—idiot that I am." Then I suddenly remembered something Bob had said. "But wait! I remember I did once ask him what thrilled him, and he said, 'Danger.' I remember that now."

Gunner cocked his head to one side. "He say what kind of danger?"

"I asked him that, actually. And he said something like anything that caused his gut to contract. But I have to be honest with you. I never felt threatened by him."

Gunner crossed his arms in front of him. "Try a little experiment with me?"

"What *now*?"

"Lie down on the couch, close your eyes, and say whatever comes into your head about Mr. Poll."

"Are you serious?"

"I'm serious."

"You really ought to be a shrink, you know that?"

I lay down on the couch and closed my eyes, like he said. I started venting about Bob and how he'd humiliated me. This didn't seem to be getting us anywhere, so Gunner suggested I be more specific.

"Forget how you feel about him now, and describe a typical date you had with him—from beginning to end. Where you went, what you talked about, who you saw, what you wore, what he wore, what you ate, drank, where you ended up. Say whatever comes into your head, no matter how dumb or insignificant it seems."

I'd had some experience with free association on an analyst's couch. I rambled on about the time Bob took me to the Folger. I chose that night because we'd had such a great evening, and I wanted to show Gunner that I wasn't a complete and total masochist. The man really had made an effort to sweep me off my feet. I didn't just *imagine* the whole damn thing.

I described how Maxwell came to pick me up at my house, as usual, and how we drove downtown to pick up Bob at his office, as usual. I told him about the whole evening—the program of writers at the theater, who was there, what the dinner was like, who we both sat next to, what I was wearing, the man who talked about bookbinding, how Bob held my hand as we strolled through the library, Cynthia's million-dollar pledge, the fact that I'd been worried about him sitting next to Cynthia, and how relieved I was that he didn't seem to like her. In reliving it, I began to feel this terrible sadness welling up inside me. I'd been so happy then. And I was so miserable now.

"It was freezing on the way home," I went on. "So Bob put the green mink blanket across our legs, and—"

"*Stop*," Gunner said. He said it quietly, but urgently. "Repeat what you just said."

"I said it was freezing on the way home, and Bob put the green mink blanket across our legs."

"What green mink blanket?"

"The one he kept in the car for cold weather."

"Describe it."

"It's this gorgeous blanket from Pianissimo. Like a throw, you know? It's dark green mink and cashmere. He had it custom-dyed to match the Rolls."

Gunner was silent. I snaked my head around and looked at him. He was staring hard into space, his eyes burning with intensity, like he was about to ignite.

"*What?*"

"You say he kept this blanket in the car?"

"Yes." I sat up.

"All the time?"

"Yes . . . well, probably just in the winter for the cold weather. It was very cozy. Why?"

"How many times did you see it?"

"I don't know. It was always in the car. Oh, one time it was in the trunk, and Maxwell got it out for us."

It didn't take Sherlock Holmes to figure out that the green mink blanket had something to do with the case. I hadn't been watching all those forensic shows with Violet for nothing. I knew that forensics were pretty much the only way to go these days.

"They found a green hair on Amber, didn't they? I'm right, aren't I? Did they find green hairs on Amber?"

He didn't answer. He didn't have to. I knew it was another detail that had been kept from the public.

I was beside myself.

"Jesus . . . I'm gonna buy a gun," I said.

"No, you're not."

"Yes, I am. They changed the law, and you can't stop me."

"You still need a permit. I don't recommend it."

"Great. So what happens if he comes after me?"

"He won't. He doesn't go after women he knows well. And he doesn't go after blondes. Poll didn't date any of these girls. He only knew them casually, if at all."

Gunner left in a hurry after that, leaving me to cope with the idea that I'd not only dated a serial killer, I'd been jilted by one.

Chapter 29

After I told Violet about Gunner's reaction to the green mink blanket, she was convinced that Bob was the Beltway Basher. We fantasized about the day Mr. Poll was charged, and Melody had to stand by her man in court, wearing a tailored pastel suit, the preferred uniform of wives with publically disgraced husbands. It would be one of the biggest cases ever, Bob was so rich and so high-profile.

Violet said he kind of reminded her of Jack Unterweger, yet another sexually sadistic psychopath I'd never heard of. She gave me an article on the charismatic Austrian journalist and darling of Viennese society who turned out to be a serial killer of prostitutes. Unterweger denied his involvement in the crimes right up until he hanged himself in his prison cell. In a creepy twist, he left proof of his guilt by using the same complicated slipknot on his own noose that the murderer had used on his victims. It was a good grisly read.

"Jack couldn't admit it, but he still wanted everyone to know he'd done it because serial killers are such narcissists at heart—just like Bob," Violet explained. She was the expert. Too much of an expert, in fact.

Much as I appreciated her hospitality, it seemed like every conversation we had wound up with Violet referencing some ghoul who'd taken multiple lives. You try being fed a daily dose of Ted Bundy, Jeffrey Dahmer, John Wayne Gacy, Ed Gein, Andrei Chikatilo, Charles Manson, David Berkowitz, Gary Ridgway, the Zodiac. And lest we forget the ladies: Aileen Wuornos, Nannie Doss, Belle Gunness, Marybeth Tinning, and Sister Amy. I began to have more sympathy for

Grant. I finally put my foot down and told her: "Tell me about dead-heading roses, not people, for a change."

It was as if Violet needed to surround herself with darkness in order to feel better about her own life. I think that's called depression. She was only making things worse by tormenting herself.

I tried hiding the Style section of the *Post* and the various social magazines so she wouldn't see all the parties to which she was not invited. But, perversely, she wanted to know all the stuff that was going on without her so she could wallow in her own exclusion. She went ballistic if she saw a picture of Grant and Cynthia. She kept track of all the hostesses who invited them and not her. She drew up two lists, one headed "The Quick," comprised of friends who kept in touch; the other headed "The Dead," made up of friends she never heard from again.

There were those who tried to maintain friendships with both Violet and Grant during this dicey period—the "Independents," I called them. Some were people I'd always suspected of courting Violet simply because she was married to Grant. Having made such a big effort over her, they were now kind of stuck with her. She clung to them fiercely, like a candidate making sure of her super delegates, calling them up to remind them that they owed their allegiance strictly to her.

Meanwhile, Cynthia made it clear that whoever saw Violet would never see her or Grant again. It didn't take a genius to see that Violet wasn't going to win that competition. President of the Potomac Bank plus major philanthropist versus dumped-on middle-aged housewife . . . ? You tell me.

One of the things Violet was most worried about was being kicked out of her International Club. The International Clubs are basically tony welcome wagons for the wives of ambassadors, senators, congressmen, cabinet members, and important government officials who arrive in Washington and don't know a soul. They give influential newcomers an opportunity to mix and mingle with others of their ilk. The clubs are mainly for out-of-towners. However, they also include a handful of prominent Washington women. It was a reflection of Grant's high status in the community that Violet had been invited to join. She was in the best club, too—the International Neighbors Club Number One, which had the most important ambassadors, or at least the ones with the showiest embassies.

How Violet exulted in being a member of this elite little group! She loved the perks and special excursions, like the private tour of Blair House or brunch at the White House. Members were urged to supply some form of entertainment for the group. Thanks to Grant, Violet took everyone to New York for a private tour of the gold vault of the Federal Reserve Bank. I hinted that I would love to see the ninety billion dollars worth of gold bullion glinting away in cages eighty feet below the streets of lower Manhattan. Friend that she was, she let me tag along. When certain people protested that I was not a member, she ignored them.

She knew that after Grant divorced her, she'd be asked to resign, and there'd be no more social perks and private trips.

"They'll kick me out as soon as the divorce is final!" she confided to me tearfully, citing the wife of a famous journalist who was asked to resign after her husband died suddenly.

Violet had pretended to poo-poo the whole notion of Washington society when she was quietly at its pinnacle. But now I understood just how much it really meant to her. Her desire to hang on to the top rung increased exponentially as she felt herself falling down the ladder.

I felt so sorry for her. I urged her to quit tormenting herself and focus instead on her son and her charity work and particularly on the upcoming twenty-fifth Wheelock reunion, which Violet had agreed to host a long time ago. Many girls who hadn't clapped eyes on each other since graduation were coming to Washington for this monumental occasion.

Over the years, Violet had hosted any number of small events connected with the school—fund-raisers, lectures, musicales, and things of that nature. Why she, of all people, who had loathed and despised Wheelock, would have been the one to carry the torch of school spirit with such enthusiasm was a testament to revenge as much as anything else. These gatherings were opportunities for Violet to show her old classmates how well she had done in life despite her famously rocky start.

But now she was threatening to call the party off. She blamed it on the fact that her plans were up in the air, but I knew it was because she didn't want anyone to see how her brilliant life had suddenly tarnished. After all those stellar entries in the alumnae bulletin, I certainly understood her predicament. It was humiliating. But so what? We all get humiliated at some point or another during our lives. The trick is not to let it make you resentful or defeatist. I told her she absolutely couldn't cancel, that it would be a selfish act.

"Listen to me, Violet. People have made plans, booked flights, hotel rooms, arranged tours of the city. They're looking forward to this event, and there isn't enough time to change the venue. Your life can't stop just because Grant's being such an asshole. And you can't expect other people's lives to stop either," I said.

She was adamantly opposed at first, but after many a long heart-to-heart, she finally agreed to go through with it—on one condition. If I came.

"I don't do reunions," I said flatly.

"Well, I won't do this one without you," she countered. "I need you there to hold my hand."

I reluctantly agreed, figuring I could always back out at the last moment. But I did begin to wonder if what upset Violet most was not that she had lost her husband, but that she had lost her social standing.

———

After two weeks I felt strong enough to go back home. That's when Violet gave me the gun. Grant had a big collection that he used to keep in their country house in Virginia. He had all kinds of guns—everything from antique muskets to modern handguns. Mr. Bolton Sr. had always given Grant a gun for his birthday ever since he was a boy. He took Grant on hunting trips because that's what "real men" did, according to the elder Bolton.

The den of their sprawling house near Middleburg had four Revolutionary War muskets and three eighteenth-century powder horns hanging above the stone fireplace. When they sold the house a few years back, all the guns got packed away and stored up in the attic on Q Street until Grant figured out what he wanted to do with them. Even though guns had been illegal in the District at that time, I doubt Grant or Violet ever gave it a second thought. What were the odds the police would bust in and search the house of a prominent family?

Violet and I went up to the attic, and she opened a small cherry-wood case, where an ornately engraved, pearl-handled gun nested on a bed of blue velvet.

"The Boltons gave this to me two years ago for my birthday," she said with evident pride.

I didn't want to take it at first—not just because Gunner had told me I needed a permit, but because I'd never shot a handgun. I wasn't particularly afraid of guns. My dad taught me to handle a shotgun when I was fourteen. He used to take me skeet shooting at a range on Long Island. I got so I was hitting more clay pigeons than he was. Mom hated guns, and she hated the fact that I liked to shoot skeet. For a while she called me her "little killer," until Dad told her to quit it.

"I don't think this is a good idea," I said, as Violet continued to press the gun on me.

"How'd you like to wake up some dark night with Bob Poll creeping up the stairs and you without any protection? This is a good gun. Grant's practiced with it."

That did it. I took the case with the gun inside and put it in my suitcase, along with a handful of cartridges.

———

My first night home, I got the jitters. Even though we're all packed in closely in our little Georgetown row houses, I was still nervous about someone breaking in. Amend that: I was nervous about the serial killer breaking in. I'd installed an alarm system once upon a time, but cancelled the monitoring service a year ago to economize. The alarm might go off, but no one would come to my aid because it wasn't connected to a central station. I lay awake in bed, glad I had that gun.

At breakfast the next morning, I began the tedious process of going through the stack of mail I'd neglected since Amber's death. Among the bills and circulars, one letter stood out. The second I saw the ecru envelope with the congressional seal on it, I suddenly remembered that I'd stood up Senator Grider! The letter inside consisted of a single scrawled line: "You missed a good show." It was signed, "Zachary Grider."

I felt bad. I really did. But it was an honest mistake. I'd completely forgotten about his invitation in the wake of the murder. I found his card and called to apologize. I left a message with some aide, hoping it would eventually get passed up the ranks, never really expecting to hear from him again.

Chapter 30

Spring was here at last, and there were signs that things were picking up in the trade. Just as life was kind of getting back to normal, Rosina called and told me she and Martin were going to stay in Uruguay a while longer, and when they came back, she was going to work for her husband's contracting firm. I was heartbroken, but I wished her luck and sent my love. I couldn't help wondering if Amber's death had been a factor in her decision. She recommended a friend of hers to take her place.

Polo Martinez arrived at the shop one cloudy morning and immediately brightened my day. Polo had been working in an art gallery on Connecticut Avenue, and he wanted a change. I spoke to him for five minutes and hired him on the spot. Like Rosina, Polo was born to sell. There's nothing like a puckish, raven-haired gay guy with a Spanish accent to charm the ladies and the gents. He was a natty dresser in his designer jeans, driving shoes, Turnbull shirts, and a rainbow collection of cashmere sweaters that he wore slung around his shoulders. He was always on time and always in a good mood—which is more than can be said for myself. It was a pleasure to come to work every morning and see his smiling face.

As I got to know him, I learned that Polo was the Scheherazade of gay Washington. He loved regaling me with endless tales of his illicit trysts and descriptions of the male strip clubs around town, along with the prominent men who frequented them. Even I had no idea how many people led double lives around this town—men and women alike. Polo was not discreet, which I loved.

I was beginning to feel a little more hopeful about life, less apprehensive. Then one evening, I was home alone when the phone rang around nine. I picked it up, but no one was there. I figured it was a wrong number or a computer. It rang again about five minutes later, and the same thing happened. My phone didn't register a number. It just read "Private Caller."

A thought flashed through my mind. What if it was the serial killer, trying to find out if I was home?

It happened a third time, and I just let it ring. When it rang a fourth time, however, I'd had it. I picked up the phone and yelled, "Listen up, you bastard, whoever you are, you better quit calling me or I'm gonna sic the police on you!" I hung up. A few seconds later the phone rang again. I picked it up again and yelled, "*Whaddya want from me?*"

After a slight pause, I heard a soft raspy voice say, "Ms. Lynch?"

"*Yes?*"

"Zack Grider."

I gasped. I was so embarrassed. "Senator! I'm sorry! I've been getting these crank calls, and I thought it was another one."

Without missing a beat, he said: "You don't like politics. You don't like theater. You like Asian art?"

"I *beg* your pardon?"

"You familiar with the Freer and Sackler Galleries?"

"Of course."

"They're having a shindig there tomorrow night. I'm dropping in for a look-see. Like to have you on my arm if you're free."

"Listen, I have to explain about the theater, I—"

"Explain it to me tomorrow night," he interrupted. "Okay?"

"Okay."

"I'll pick you up. Not taking any chances this time," he said with his rusty-hinge laugh.

"Do you know where I live?"

"Yup. Got all that information. Wrote you a card, remember? Just need your e-mail address or fax machine number."

"Why?"

"Gonna have my secretary send you a copy of the invitation with all the particulars."

I gave him my e-mail address.

"Pick you up at seven sharp. Good night. Sleep tight. Don't let the bedbugs bite," he said.

I hung up, somewhat amused. The phone didn't ring again.

————

The next morning I opened the e-mail from Senator Grider's office and found a nice note from his secretary, along with an electronic copy of the invitation for that night's party. It read, "Cynthia Rinehart invites you to a special night at the Freer and Sackler Galleries to celebrate the birthday of Grant Bolton Jr. . . . ." Or words to that effect.

I simply couldn't believe it. It was my impression that Senator Grider didn't know Cynthia or Grant. And what in God's name was Cynthia doing, giving a birthday party for Grant in the first place? And in a museum of Asian art, of all places! How this venue related to a man whose main passions in life were his bank, his fishing camp, and golf was anybody's guess. To Grant, the Far East was the tip of Long Island, and his idea of Nirvana was a hole in one. Was this the hidden Grant—the Grant I didn't know? Or was it simply a vast miscalculation on her part?

And there was another thing: how Cynthia got permission to give a dinner in those galleries was a mystery. Years ago, Violet had tried to organize a dinner there for the head of the Osaka Bank, who had done business with Grant. She even got the Japanese ambassador to intervene on her behalf, but there was just too much rigmarole with the board and everything, so she finally gave up and instead held the dinner at Evermay, a pretty little landmark estate in the heart of Georgetown available for rental. I suspected that Cynthia had once again pledged a ton of money to the galleries, a persuasive tactic that works far better than diplomacy in today's world.

I called Violet, told her about the invitation. I offered not to go if she didn't want me to. Much to my surprise, she was ecstatic. She'd heard about it already. She said: "Go! Wear a videocam and report *everything* back to me!"

Still, I was a little nervous. What would Cynthia do when she saw me there? Not to mention Grant.

————

Senator Grider rang my doorbell at seven o'clock. I invited him in for a drink, but he declined.

"I'll take a rain check, if I may. Don't want you to miss the exhibition." He paused. "Like that outfit," he said pointing to my midnight blue silk dress.

"Thank you. An effort was made."

"Well, then, thank *you*."

He showed me to his car, an old gray Buick, natch.

"I pretend this car is a red Porsche convertible," he said as he started the engine.

"Why don't you just *buy* a red convertible? It doesn't have to be a Porsche."

He cranked up a laugh. "Oh, you're funny, you are."

We started off down the block.

"Senator, let me explain about the theater, okay?"

"Only if you call me Zack."

"Zack . . ."

I told him about Amber. He glanced at me as he drove.

"Oh, yeah, I think I read something about that crime. You're saying that young girl worked for you?"

"Just for a week or so. My assistant left to get married, and she filled in. It was such a shock."

"Oh, I can b'lieve that. Scary thing, murder. 'Specially when it comes close."

"Has it ever come close to you?"

"Well, let's see now. . . . I remember this minister shot his entire family when I was a boy."

"Did you know him?"

"Nope. He lived in another town. But I never forgot it. Man of the cloth doing something like that makes you realize there's real evil in the world."

"Well, they think she was murdered by the Beltway Basher. You've heard of him, right?"

"Who hasn't? I'm not as much of a one-tracker as people think."

"What's a one-tracker?"

"Person who keeps his mind on one track to the exclusion of everything else."

"Well, anyway, I'm sorry I stood you up. I just completely forgot. I've been a little out of my mind."

"Understandable," he said with a nod.

"You should know something else too."

"What's that?"

"About tonight. Cynthia and Grant are *not* going to be pleased to see me there. In fact, she may ask me to leave."

" 'Cause she fired you, right?"

"Right. I didn't know you knew Cynthia."

"I don't."

"Oh. Do you know Grant?"

"Nope."

I looked at him askance. "Then how come you were invited to this party?"

"I'm a United States senator. I'm invited places all the time by people I don't know. This Rinehart gal's invited me to a whole mess of things. She wants to give me some award—a brass ring or something like that."

"A golden key?"

"That's it. . . . Never went to anything of hers before 'cause it didn't interest me. Now I'm interested."

"Why?"

"Oh, just interested to have a look-see, is all. Maybe run into a few elephant bumpers."

"What are elephant bumpers?" I asked, amused.

"People who think they're big shots and only wanna hang out with other big shots. . . . 'Babylon endures wherever human folly shines or human folly lures,' " he said with a chuckle. "Elephant bumpers are always fun to see."

"Well, I warn you. Cynthia's not going to be at all happy to see me. And Grant will probably bust a gut."

"Both of 'em can bust away. Long as you're with me, they'll have to stick it," he said, giving my arm a solid pat.

Chapter 31

The invitation stipulated that guests were to enter through the Sackler Gallery on the Mall side. Traffic was backed up in front of the serene classical building as cars inched their way into the circular cobblestone courtyard. A valet attendant took charge of the Buick and handed Grider a ticket. A guard checking names on a list recognized Grider as we entered the museum.

"Evening, Senator," the guard said. Grider shook the man's hand with genuine warmth. He seemed touched the guard knew him, rather than treating the encounter as a chore.

An attendant took our coats. The guard directed us to the underground galleries leading to the Freer. Grider offered me his arm as we walked down the diamond-shaped staircase together.

The first perk of the evening was the chance to view a special exhibition of ancient Chinese bronzes, which, unsurprisingly enough, had been made possible by the Cynthia A. Rinehart Foundation—a fact heralded by an enormous sign at the entrance to the rooms. We began our tour in the Sackler and continued on through the underground passageway leading to the Freer, where the dinner was being held.

Grider knew quite a bit about Asian art. He was explaining the finer points of a Shang Dynasty bronze brazier to me when I spotted Cynthia striding briskly through the exhibition, breezing by history as if she had only the future in mind. She was wearing a tight, heavily embroidered mandarin-style dress, the breast area of which featured a cutout designed to reveal her bosoms squished together like two large balls of Turkish delight. She ignored all but her most prominent guests.

Luckily, she didn't see me. Grider and I had continued strolling through the exhibition when he suddenly raised his head and sniffed the air.

"Something's burning," he said.

I smelled it too. We quickly made our way upstairs to the Freer's boxy reception room, where the aroma of sandalwood incense was intense. There was a sudden crashing sound, as if someone had knocked over a cabinet full of crystal ware. A few seconds later, another crash came.

"What in the heck's *that*?" Grider said irritably.

Just then I spotted Greg the Spy, as I called him. Greg Boyd was a former schoolteacher who now worked as a majordomo for Couture Cuisine, one of the best caterers around town. In that capacity, he not only supervised big events such as this, he also saw to it that dinners and parties ran smoothly in the private homes of the most powerful people in Washington—including cabinet members, congressmen, the president of the World Bank, and the chairman of the Federal Reserve. He was privy to many sensitive dinner-table conversations. Greg knew what everyone really thought of everyone else, but he was trustworthy to a fault. Since he was way overqualified for his job, I always teased him about being a spy for some covert government agency.

I flagged him down as he was offering a tray filled with champagne flutes to passing guests.

"Greg! What's with the crashing glass?" I asked him.

"That's meant to be wind chimes, but the sound system isn't working right." Greg offered me some champagne, then said to Grider, "Can I get you a diet cola, Senator?"

"Yup, thanks," Grider said. "This is almost as bad as the peacocks, isn't it, Greg?"

"Almost," Greg said with a smile as he walked off.

"What peacocks?" I asked.

"Greg and I were at the opening of this place years ago. They had these peacocks parading up and down the lawn. Two of 'em got into a fight, and there was blood all over!" Grider said with a guffaw. "I told Greg, let's get those birds into Congress, and we can all join in!"

"So you know Greg?"

"Everybody knows Greg," he said. "He was the only one my wife would ever let into our kitchen."

Another crash. Grider and I both cringed.

"Oh, where is Cole Porter when we need him?" I said blithely.

"You like Cole Porter? He was a Hoosier, you know. Born in Peru, Indiana."

"Do you make it your business to know where everyone is from?" I asked him.

"Just people I like a lot. And people I don't like so much."

"Doesn't that just about cover the waterfront?"

"Nope. There's a world full of people I don't give a hoot-owl hoot about."

At the far end of the room, a giant papier-mâché laughing Buddha on a pedestal loomed over the room like a macabre parade float. We went to take a closer look. Our skin glowed blue under the glaucous lights. We looked like a roomful of corpses.

Eight round tables set with brown tablecloths, orange gauze napkins, and black chopsticks surrounded the Buddha. The centerpieces consisted of glazed pink pagodas rising up out of beds of brown moss. These modern sculptures, capped with sloping tops, were slightly reminiscent of penises.

"This looks like a party for an Asian porn star," I said.

"Never been to a party for an Asian porn star, or any porn star, for that matter. Have you?" Grider said.

"No. It was just a little joke."

The Buddha was the only one laughing. The noise, the smell, the lighting, and the décor had dampened both of our spirits. In fact, all the guests seemed to be moving in slow motion, like they were in an aquarium.

I saw Cynthia chatting with several people, but Grant was nowhere in sight. It was getting late. We were all hungry. Then a voice rang out over the crowd: "Quiet, everyone! Grant Bolton is coming! Grant Bolton is coming!"

"Paul Revere at the Freer!" Senator Grider quipped, looking to me for approval. I rolled my eyes. "Didn't like that one, eh?" he said.

"Senate humor, I presume?"

A smiled twitched across his thin lips. He seemed to like it when I teased him.

The crowd quieted down. Grider and I edged closer to the entrance. I wanted to get a good look at Grant. Finally he appeared, looking dapper in a custom-made tuxedo and black needlepoint pumps embroidered in red with his intertwining initials. He remained glacial despite the applause. Cynthia threw her arms around him and cried in a breathy Marilyn Monroe imitation, "Happy birthday, Mr. Bank President!"

"Now maybe we'll get to eat," Grider said.

Cynthia paraded Grant around the room like a show dog. When he caught sight of me, his face kind of crumpled with consternation. The next thing I knew, Cynthia was barreling toward me like a fist.

I nudged Grider. "Oh-oh, here we go."

Cynthia marched right up to me without giving Senator Grider a glance. She said, "Well, if it isn't Nightmare Girl. And just what the hell do you think you're doing crashing my party?"

Senator Grider stuck out his hand. "How do, Ms. Rinehart? I b'lieve you're my hostess for this shindig tonight."

"Who are *you*?" she said, squinting at him in the low light.

"I am the man who accompanied Reven Lynch to this party," he said, then whispered a pointed aside to me: "Presidential humor."

Cynthia looked like she was getting ready to call security to have us both chucked out when the light suddenly dawned. Watching her fury morph into embarrassment when she realized she'd just offended Senator Grider was a gratifying moment. I wished that Violet could have been there. I never thought I'd see the day when Cynthia was speechless, but she was then. She looked back and forth at us several times, as if to say, Don't tell me you two are here *together*?

"I told Senator Grider that you might not be thrilled to see me here, Cynthia. So if you'd prefer us to leave, we certainly will, won't we, Zack?"

Before Grider could respond, she slammed into reverse.

"*Leave?* I wouldn't hear of it! I was rude. I apologize. Forgive me, Senator, for not recognizing you. Reven, since you are gracious enough to be here tonight and accept my hospitality, the very least I can do is to offer it to you with open arms."

She pointed her hand at me like a gun, daring me to shake it— which I did, with a sulfurous smile. She turned to Grider and purred, "Now you, Senator, are sitting next to me at dinner. We mustn't talk now, or we might run out of conversation."

"Doubt it," he said.

Cynthia flitted off to "attend" to her other guests. Grider stared after her.

"Like watching burlap turn to silk," he said.

Cynthia headed straight for Grant, obviously to inform him who I was with. I saw they were having a little tiff. It looked like she was trying to get Grant to come over and say hello to Senator Grider, and Grant didn't want to oblige her, probably because it meant having to face me. I knew he was desperate to avoid me, but it was difficult to do so without appearing rude to the senator.

Cynthia won. She and Grant shuffled over to us. Grant shook Senator Grider's hand and thanked him for coming. Then he said a sheepish hello to me. I just stared at him. He knew what I was thinking. I didn't have to say a word.

Dinner was announced. Cynthia grabbed Grider's arm and pulled him toward the dining area. Grant and I were left alone just as another burst of those breaking-glass-fingernails-scraping-a-blackboard wind chimes crashed over the sound system. I said, "Sayonara, asshole," and moved on to find my seat.

I was placed at the head table between Senator Grider and Mr. Bolton Sr. My place card read, "Guest of Senator Grider." Zach obviously hadn't told them I was coming. Mr. Bolton was standing, waiting for the ladies to be seated. As he turned to shake my hand, he suddenly realized who I was. He froze. He couldn't even say my name. He gave me a curt nod and sat down. I figured that was because I was a reminder that his son was still married to Violet, and that this evening's festivities were hardly in the best of taste.

I admit I was very surprised to see Grant's parents there at all. The senior Boltons were a pair of ruthless pioneers who had reinvented themselves as landed gentry. Grant Bolton Sr. was a robust man of seventy-plus years with iron gray hair and the hardy demeanor of a sportsman. Though he cultivated the style of a patrician to the manor born, he was in fact a tough, snobbish, self-made man who had all the pretensions of Old Money and none of its charm. He had built the Potomac Bank virtually from scratch into the powerhouse it was today.

His wife was seated next to Grant, on the opposite side of the table. Rainy Bolton was a petite and tidy woman who wore her steel-wool hair in a tight bun and her mouth in a smile that looked like a frown.

Her beige silk evening suit was tailored and proper, and purposely plain in the style of Really Old Money. I figured she'd bought it at Inga's. She wore a diamond and pearl choker and earrings to match. I knew from Violet that her mother-in-law's collection of dowdy antique jewelry had not been "handed down" to her from her grandmother, as Rainy claimed, but surreptitiously purchased at auction to look as if it had been inherited. To me, Rainy Bolton was "mutton dressed as lamb and twice as tough," as my mother used to say.

Grant was the apple of his parents' eye—the only son who had been brought up like a prince and who was expected to marry a girl of substance and worth. They thought I was much too frivolous for Grant. But, as I said, I was astonished to see them there; I thought they had really loved Violet, who had done the family credit while posing no threat to Rainy, plus given them a grandson they adored. Maybe Violet was right, I thought. Rainy was a stealth starfucker, and Cynthia was now a big star.

Cynthia monopolized Grider. Mr. Bolton Sr. barely spoke to me, probably out of guilt. There was nothing left for me to do but drink. The appetizer arrived, followed by the first bout of the evening's entertainment: twin brother violinists dueling to see which one could play "Flight of the Bumblebee" faster. Other variety acts punctuated the five-course meal, including six Chinese drummers who were more deafening than Niagara Falls and a bewildering scene from a Kabuki play. By the time the troupe of Korean acrobats showed up, jumping and flipping around the tables just before dessert, I'd had so much to drink I felt sloppier than a half-eaten egg roll. Yet I wasn't quite comfortably anesthetized, so when I noticed that Senator Grider's wineglass was still full, I asked him if I could have it. He pushed it over with a judgmental air.

"You a teetotaler?" I asked him.

"Yes, ma'am, I am."

"Well, then, don't mind me!" I toasted him and drained the glass.

His expression soured. "My wife had a drinking problem."

"Oh, I don't have a problem. I just like to drink! Nights like this, you should seriously reconsider your position on the subject."

Finally, a huge cake was wheeled in on a trolley. It was one of those fantasy cakes: a large pagoda, with "Happy Birthday Grant" written across it in big red letters. Grant rose from his chair to blow out the six candles—one for each decade, and one to grow on. He blew them out in one breath, but they all flickered back to life—trick candles being Cynthia's idea of a joke.

Cynthia got up from her seat and tapped her glass. A chorus of pinging crystal soon silenced the room. She fastened her eyes on Grant, who was seated across the table from her. She wished him a happy birthday and then, in one of the great understatements of all time, she said, "I'm sure that some of you are wondering why I chose this museum to celebrate Grant. . . ."

Not some. *All.*

She launched into a speech about how this was going to be "the Asian century," and the party was not only to celebrate Grant but to mark the opening of the new exhibition, sponsored by her foundation. I may have been a little tipsy, but I got the point: she'd made *another* big contribution to *another* important institution, and this was *yet another* party to show it off. Grider sat with his arms crossed in front of him, his straw lips clenched tight, staring up at her like a farmer with a pitchfork.

———

The valet attendants were all backed up. They took forty-five minutes to bring the car around. By the time I collapsed into the gray Buick, I was utterly exhausted. Grider and I hardly said a word to each other on the way home. He pulled up in front of my house and said, "I hate to leave you after all we've been through together."

"You mind if I don't ask you in for a drink? I'm about to collapse."

"Don't mind at all. Need to get some shut-eye myself. Like to see you again, though. I'm invited to a cocktail shindig at the Otanni Embassy this Friday. Wanna come?"

"Sure. Great. Whatever."

"Pick you up at six."

He walked me to my door. Just as I was about to unlock it, he said, "Like to kiss you good night, if I may."

I was too drunk and too tired to make an excuse. I just lifted my head and closed my eyes. He was an unexpectedly good kisser. I was amazed. I actually enjoyed it. But that could have been the wine.

Chapter 32

The phone rang around eight thirty the next morning. I had such a hangover, it sounded like a fire alarm. It was Gunner.

"Turn on Channel Four right now," he ordered and hung up.

I paid no attention. I rolled over and went back to sleep. The phone rang again. This time it was Violet, screaming into the receiver.

"They got him! They got him! Channel Four! Quickly! They're doing a recap!"

I switched on the television to the Channel Four news. A man with a blanket over his head was being escorted to a police car by about a dozen officers in flak jackets. Jenna Jakes, the local anchor, was on the scene, mike in hand, talking to the camera: "Early this morning, police took into custody a man they suspect is the *Beltway Basher* . . . blah, blah, blah . . ."

I had never recovered from a hangover so fast in my life. I was glued to the set, trying to see if it was Bob Poll under that blanket. They panned back to a long shot, where I thought I saw the Rolls parked on the street. But the shot cut away after a split second, so I couldn't be sure. My chest was thumping so hard.

Violet screamed: "*The Rolls, the Rolls, did you see the Rolls? Did you see it?*"

"I think so. Did you?"

"Yes! I saw it! *It's Bob! It's Bob!*"

Jenna Jakes came back on camera and said, "Martin Wayne Wardell has been charged in the murders of Bianca Symonds and Amber Corey. But authorities believe he's responsible for at least four other murders in the District, murders committed by the man they call the Beltway Basher . . ."

"It's not Bob," I said, deflating.

"No . . . I guess that wasn't the Rolls," Violet said.

"At least they finally got the guy."

Later on that day, I found out that it *was* the Rolls. Martin Wayne Wardell turned out to be none other than the avuncular, cookie-loving chauffeur: *Maxwell!*

Close, but no Bob Poll.

The news had a profound effect on me. I was relieved, but I was also pretty creeped out that he turned out to be someone I'd been alone in a car with umpteen times. He could easily have driven into Rock Creek Park and bludgeoned me to death if he'd wanted to.

I could still see those eyes watching me in the rearview mirror—especially at night, when they were two faint gleams in the darkness. I used to think they were gentle, disinterested eyes, windows to a gentle, disinterested brain. But now I knew they were busy little eyes, sharp little eyes, hating little eyes—peepholes on a hideous world of homicidal madness. They were dark corner eyes, eyes on the hunt, eyes with a plan, eyes fueled by super-octane pain and fear. Serial killer eyes.

Being that close to someone so evil is something you can't really fathom until it happens to you. Violet made me read Ann Rule's book *The Stranger Beside Me*, where Rule describes being holed up for nights on end in a suicide prevention clinic, taking calls on the hotline with her friend and colleague, one Theodore Robert Bundy. Rule couldn't believe it when she finally found out who Ted Bundy really was. Or *what* he really was. How would you like to discover you'd spent many a midnight hour alone with a guy who kept women's heads as trophies? Like Gunner said, "You don't recognize evil if it looks like you."

The corollary to that is you don't recognize evil if it's in familiar surroundings. I know now you can be *this close* to evil and not see it until it's too late. I was so focused on Bob Poll, I wasn't paying attention to anything else.

Violet told me I was lucky I was a blonde. She said that Wardell was an "organized" serial killer, as opposed to a "disorganized" one. Violet knew so much about these fiends.

"The organized ones are the really scary ones because they're very smart and they're very cagey and they know how to blend into your world without you suspecting it," she said.

She also told me they were "as finicky about their victims as gourmets are about food. . . . If a guy likes brunettes, he's gonna hunt brunettes. He probably got one look at Amber, saw she was his type, and bingo! Rosina was lucky she was out of town."

Whatever. I felt I'd dodged a date with death.

I was dying to know what Bob thought.

———

The press went berserk. It was a national story because it involved a serial killer in the nation's capital, who worked for a socially prominent Washingtonian with deep connections in Congress and the White House. Several reporters wanted to interview me, but I kept my mouth shut—not just about Amber, but about the time I'd dated Bob. There were others who didn't. In fact, the only amusing thing that came out of all this was that several women of, shall we say, interesting character blabbed to the press about being alone in that car with Maxwell—revealing, of course, that Bob had taken them out.

Bob was even more into the "high-life, low-life" syndrome than anyone had ever imagined. A gorgeous blonde who identified herself as an "exotic dancer," but who actually worked for a tony D.C. escort service, wrote an article entitled "My Night with a Serial Killer." It wasn't clear until the end if she meant Bob or Maxwell.

"Melody must have loved that one," Violet said.

———

Gunner and I went for a walk later that week—not in the cemetery but in Montrose Park. I congratulated him on solving the case.

"It's nice to feel safe here again," I said.

"Your tip about the green mink blanket. That was the big break," he said.

As we strolled down the path into the woods, Gunner told me they had found a green mink hair on Amber. On the basis of my recollection, they got a warrant to search the car and found the blanket. The hairs matched. There was blood in the trunk of the Rolls. They searched Bob's house and Maxwell's house. They found blood from two of the girls in Maxwell's house. They had their man.

"The fiber evidence was key," Gunner said. "Juries love forensics."

"So you're sure he's the Beltway Basher?"

"Pretty sure," Gunner said.

"Did he confess?"

"Nope. Not even to the ones we got him cold on. Not yet. He's a scary guy."

I looked at him askance. "That's an understatement."

"He's got this permanent smirk on his face, like he's got secrets we're never gonna find out."

We talked a lot about the crimes. Martin Wayne Wardell was from Phoenix, not Seattle, like "Maxwell" had told me. He had a record. He'd served six months in the Central Arizona Correctional Facility on an assault and attempted rape charge against a waitress in 1997. When he got out, he moved to Virginia, changed his name to Maxwell Martin, and somehow got a chauffeur's license and a new social security number. Just goes to show you how easy it is to become someone else. He met Bob at King Arthur's, and Bob hired him as a combination chauffeur and bodyguard. In retrospect it seemed like an unlikely pairing.

The theory was that Wardell had followed Amber after meeting her in my shop. The night of her party, he pretended to run into her after it was over, maybe offered her a ride home in the Rolls, then somehow lured her to his house and assaulted her there. He wrapped her up in garbage bags, put her in the trunk, and dumped her in Rock Creek Park.

"I just can't imagine what her last moments must have been like," I said to Gunner. "Thank God you got him. . . . I think about being in the back of that car. . . . Of course, Violet said I'm not a brunette, so he wouldn't have been interested. But do you think I was ever in any real danger?"

"You never know with these guys. But I think your friend Violet's right. Wardell hunted thin young brunettes. When he saw Amber Corey, he didn't see a lovely young lady. He saw prey."

"I bought cookies for this man, for Christ's sakes! How can I ever trust anyone again?"

"It's hard. If these guys looked like what they are, they'd never get near you. The whole point is, they're chameleons. They appear to be whatever you want them to be. You see him as a nice, kind chauffeur? Nice, kind chauffeur he is. That's how they lure you in."

"Amber never had a chance, did she?"

"Probably not."

We walked along in silence. Something was eating at him. I realized we were heading for the very spot where Miss Montrose was killed.

"Where are we going, Gunner?"

"I just want to see something, that's all."

We finally reached the spot. The crime scene tape was gone now. Thin rays of sunlight pierced the budding spring foliage. The little meadow looked the picture of bucolic innocence, but I still got a chill knowing what had happened there. Gunner gazed out over the scene.

"Bob Poll ever call you?" he asked me.

"Nope. I would have told you."

"So you haven't spoken to him since he got married, huh?"

"Haven't spoken to him, no. But I saw him from a distance that day, when he was staring at poor Amber through the shop window. That's one of the reasons I thought maybe he was the one. And I got those phone calls where no one answered. Maybe it was Bob. I wonder what he thinks of all this."

"Oh, I'm sure he's appropriately shocked," Gunner said with a hint of sarcasm. He was lost in thought, staring at the field.

"You know, for someone who's just solved a major case, you don't seem that happy," I said.

"There's an old samurai saying, 'After victory, tighten the cords of your helmet.' "

"What's that supposed to mean?"

"C'mon. Let's head back." He stooped down, plucked a tiny blue flower from the ground, and handed it to me. "Present for you."

"Thanks." I twirled the little bluebell around in my fingers. "Cherry blossoms'll be out soon. Hope they last this year. Want to go with me when they bloom?"

"No, thanks. I've seen them enough times." He walked on.

Gunner seemed weighed down by something. I figured his reaction had a lot to do with the nature of the job. The homicide police deal with such sadness and horror and wasted lives every day. Maybe after a while, it's hard for them to get excited even if they do solve a case, because they know it's just one tiny chip off the iceberg of evil. But, as always with Gunner, I felt there was something else he wasn't telling me. Something important.

Chapter 33

I come here for the chocolate fountain," Grider said as we stood in the reception line, waiting to say hello to the Sahalas. Rashid Sahala was the ambassador of Otann, a small, progressive, oil-rich Arab state in the Gulf. However, it was his wife, Nouria, who had put the tiny country on the social map. Since their arrival in Washington seven years ago, Nouria Sahala had raised the profile of the embassy higher than the price of oil. She courted important people with enviable determination, yet remained fiercely loyal to her friends, especially when they were no longer in power. Owing to the changes in political fortunes, her larger parties had swelled to the size of football rallies in order to accommodate all the has-beens and the have-nows, as well as up-and-comers who showed promise, and her constant core of close pals.

I saw a lot of people I knew that evening. I waved to Peggy and Rolly Myers, to Molly Raft, an artist and famous Georgetown hostess, to Tessa Winston, whose husband John started the Kennedy Center Honors years ago, to Greta Dalton and her husband Lon, whose small, elegant dinners boasted an international guest list and were a required social stop for any new ambassador in town, to Justine and Lander Marx, who had a billion-dollar art collection in their elegant modern house, and to Nan Liddell, a well-known art dealer who often bought things for her clients in my shop. The dreaded Marge Horner accosted me and acted very friendly.

"Reven! I haven't seen you in ages!" Marge said, immediately turning to Grider. "And Senator, how nice it is to see you too!"

Grider had that do-I-know-you look on his face, but he shook her hand and acted cordial.

"Who's that again?" he asked me when Marge flounced out of sight.

"Someone you want to avoid," I said.

I knew from Violet that Nouria wasn't that fond of Marge, even though Marge was always offering to give her dinners and luncheons and teas. But Nouria was also a kind soul who understood how much social life meant to Marge, so she always included her in the large parties, but never at the small dinners.

Grider and I finally reached our host and hostess, who introduced us to the guests of honor—the Otanni foreign minister and his wife. Nouria made sure that a photographer captured Senator Grider shaking hands with her husband and the minister. Then she posed with all of them herself. She was very good at her job. She said a warm hello to me and pulled me into one of the pictures. Grider said to the photographer, "I'd like a copy of that one, please."

Formalities over, Grider and I wandered into the main entertaining room, a large square space with delicately carved lattice walls. A circular fountain, covered with colorful floral mosaics sat in the center of the tiled floor, its tall spout dribbling water down into an azure pool. Rose petals floated on the water, giving off a sweet scent.

"So where's the chocolate?" I said.

"Different fountain. Follow me."

Grider led me across the room, where a group of guests were crowded around what looked like a pedestal with a basin on top. Protruding from the center of the basin was a spigot spewing out liquid chocolate. Waiters in long white coats stood at attention, holding silver trays filled with juicy fresh strawberries and sliced oranges on long wooden skewers. Grider plucked two skewered strawberries from a tray and held them under the cascading chocolate. In seconds, they were coated in sweet chocolate. He popped one into his mouth and handed me the other to try. The chocolate enhanced the flavor of the strawberry, and vice versa. It was a delicious treat.

"Best dessert in Washington," he said.

Grider helped himself to another chocolate-covered strawberry, then looked around the room.

" 'Scuse me a second. There's someone I need to talk to," he said and abruptly walked away.

I stayed by the fountain to experiment on my own. I was running an orange slice under the chocolate waterfall when another skewer playfully nudged mine aside.

"Ah-ah, no chocolate barging." I laughed, turning around.

The man holding the dueling skewer was Bob Poll. I felt a jolt of something—I'm not sure if it was embarrassment, shock, nostalgia, or what exactly. But whatever it was, I just stood there like an idiot, staring at him, holding the dripping orange slice over the fountain.

"Long time, no see, Reven," he said. "Come on over here and talk to me a sec."

I'm not quite sure why I followed him over to a corner. I told myself it was because I was interested to hear what he had to say about all the events that had transpired since we last met. But it was more than that. I still felt a tug of attraction.

"So how are you, beautiful?"

Beautiful? How long had this guy been married?

"Fine thanks, Bob. How are you? How's married life?" I asked him breezily.

"Unfortunately, it's just how I remembered it," he said with a smirk.

"Do I dare even bring up the subject of Maxwell?"

Bob shook his head. "What a shock, huh?"

"Was it?" I said pointedly.

"Damn right. The guy had great references. He worked for the Dumonts, for Chrissakes. I've been dealing nonstop with the cops and the press. . . . Nightmare. It's been pretty tough on Mel, too. Not exactly the perfect way to start out."

"I can imagine," I said, recalling the tell-all articles written by Bob's ex-girlfriends.

"Listen, uh, I was very sorry about your, uh . . . that girl who worked for you."

"Amber."

"Amber, right."

"You saw her, you know."

"I did?"

"Yes. That day Maxwell came to drop off the cookie tin. You looked at her through the shop window. She thought you were cute."

"I don't remember. I was looking for you."

"I was there. You could have come in."

Bob lowered his voice. "Listen, I, uh . . . I know I should have called you, Rev."

"About Maxwell?"

"No, well, yes . . . but I mean before that. I should have called and told you I was getting married. I feel bad about that."

"Just out of curiosity . . . why didn't you? Were you afraid I'd throw a hissy fit?"

"Let's just say my bride had some jealousy issues."

"*Really?* But you were seeing Melody the whole time we were going out, weren't you?" I knew this from Gunner.

He cocked his head to one side. "Who told you that?"

"Oh, you know Washington. So many little birds with such big mouths."

"I don't know who told you that, but it's not true," he said unconvincingly. "So is this thing with you and Grider serious?"

I stepped back and looked him up and down. "You know what, Bob? It's none of your fucking business."

With that, I turned on my heel and walked off. Out of the corner of my eye, I saw Melody making a beeline for Bob. She didn't look pleased. I turned away. Grider was in a corner, talking to a man I vaguely recognized. They both stood with their arms crossed, tilting slighting toward one another like giant bookends. Grider caught sight of me and waved me over.

"Reven Lynch, Sam Pomador."

We shook hands. "Ms. Lynch," Pomador said with a smile, exposing a set of tombstone teeth.

Pomador patted Grider on the back and said, "Glad we had this conversation, Zack. I'll be seeing you. Nice to meet you, Ms. Lynch." He walked off.

"Who's that?"

"You really don't know who anyone is, do ya? Sam Pomador's one of the longest-serving senators in history. He's the Senate's pro tempore emeritus and a senior member of some very important committees. He also happens to be chummy with your pal, Ms. Rinehart. He's on her board."

"I thought he looked familiar. There's a picture of him in her office. Tell me something, what horse died so Senator Pomador could have his teeth?"

Grider roared with laughter. He sounded like a clanking engine.

"He wants me to go on her board," he said at last.

"Will you?"

"I don't go on boards. It's not in the public interest."

"Violet introduced Senator Pomador to Cynthia, you know. And then he got a lot of influential people to go on her board."

"I'm not surprised. Sam's a persuasive man. . . . Well, I've had my look-see. Let's go get some dinner. You like fish?"

Grant and Cynthia were arriving just as we were leaving. They were part of a large crowd. They pretended not to see us, and we pretended not to see them.

Chapter 34

Tucker's was a simple, no-frills restaurant on Connecticut Avenue, just down the street from Politics and Prose, one of the last independent bookstores in Washington. Grider said he liked it because he could have a meal and then go buy a book, or the other way around if he was dining alone. The home-style eatery had a bar at one end, long wooden communal tables in the center, and smaller tables off to the side. It smelled of homey cooking aromas. The host knew Grider. He greeted the senator warmly and showed us to a table for two in a darkish isolated corner. I sat on the wooden banquette. Grider sat opposite me on a chair. My paper placemat was decorated with engravings of all the U.S. presidents. Grider's placemat featured a map of the United States. Our utensils were folded into red-and-white-check paper napkins. The setting was about as romantic as a fishing camp.

The host handed us menus and took our drinks order. I ordered a glass of white wine. Grider ordered a beer.

"I thought you didn't drink," I said.

"Beer's not drinking. Beer's a food group," he said with a grin.

There were only two appetizers and two entrées to choose from. Grider recommended the iceberg lettuce wedge topped with blue cheese and the whole grilled bass.

"This place is part-owned by a Greek fella," he said. "Trust me, the Greeks know how to grill fish."

Our drinks came. The waiter took our orders, and we relaxed.

"How'd you ever find this place?" I asked him, trying to hide the skepticism in my voice.

"Don't judge a book by its cover," he said. I got the feeling he was referring to more than just the restaurant.

"Saw you talking to your old friend Bob Poll. I was glad to hear he got married," he said.

"Really? Why is that?"

" 'Cause it meant you weren't going out with him anymore. . . . Can I ask you a personal question?"

"Depends." I braced myself.

"You ever get your twenty thousand dollars from the Rinehart gal?"

"No. Unfortunately."

"Oh."

"Why?"

"Just wondering, that's all."

"How come you're so interested in Cynthia?" I asked him.

"She's an interesting gal. She made a big splash with that hundred-million-dollar contribution to the Kennedy Center. Got my attention."

"She got mine when she ran off with my best friend's husband."

"Mr. Potomac Bank. That's what I call a keeper."

"*Please* . . . I hate her, okay? She's ruined my friend Violet's life. She stiffed me. And I'll tell you something else. She makes these splashy contributions, gets all the publicity, then she withdraws them on some flimsy pretext."

Grider's eyes narrowed. "You know that for a fact?"

"Absolutely." I told him about Constance Morely's lupus foundation and the rumor about the Folger. "Violet's keeping track of everything. She's obsessed with Cynthia. She's even got a private detective checking into her background. If you want to talk to someone about her, talk to Violet."

"Uh-huh. What else did your friend Violet tell you about her?"

"Well, it's no secret that Cynthia thinks she owns the Kennedy Center. I guess in a way, she does. You should talk to Carmen Appleton and Peggy Myers about that. They have to work with her. You know what Peggy told Violet the other day?"

"Like to hear it."

"Peggy's the president of the Capitol Symphony, as you know. Well, apparently, Cynthia isn't happy with Leonid Slobovkin, the conductor."

"I'm a symphony goer. I know Maestro Slobovkin."

"So his contract's up this fall, and Cynthia wants Peggy to appoint Nelson Mars as the new conductor. *Nelson Mars!*"

"Who's that?"

"You never heard of Nelson Mars? He's this pop conductor. He'll make Beethoven sound like Beyoncé."

"Who's Beyoncé?"

"Never mind. Nelson Mars isn't the right person for that orchestra, okay? And furthermore, Peggy doesn't want him, and she's the president, so it should be her choice, right? But the Trailblazer is butting in."

"The Trailblazer?"

"Oh, that's what we all call Cynthia because that's how she referred to herself in that big article in the *Post*. She said, 'Call me a trailblazer.' So that's what we call her. Except that she's blazing a trail straight to hell, if you ask me."

The waiter set down our appetizers as I rambled on with other grievances. Grider sat there like a big blotter, chomping on his lettuce wedge, soaking it all in. When I'd finished my spiel, he said quietly, "I don't know why you ladies think Ms. Rinehart owns the Kennedy Center."

"Because she gave them a hundred million dollars, that's why. She who gives the most money *owns*," I said, as if it were obvious.

Grider leaned back in the rickety chair. "Well, now, as a matter of fact, she hasn't given them the money *yet*. In fact, she doesn't ever have to give it until Congress comes up with the matching funds."

"What do you mean?"

"The Kennedy Center's a creature of the federal government. That's why the chairman and the board members serve at the pleasure of the president. He appoints them. The hundred million dollars Ms. Rinehart has pledged is contingent upon a matching grant from Congress. Provision for that grant is tacked onto the Energy Bill, which is stalled in committee at this moment. I know this 'cause I've been trying to get it passed."

"Wait. . . . You're saying she never has to give the money?"

"Not unless that bill passes."

"What are the odds?"

"Ice cube's chance in Hades."

"So you mean to tell me she's gotten all this publicity and recognition for money that she'll *never* give?"

"That's about the size of it."

I was amazed. "How come people don't know about this?"

"A lot of people do. But Ms. Rinehart also gives a million dollars a year to the center, which is independent of that grant."

"Yes, but she practically spends that on the parties she gives there. And meanwhile, she's making big splashes all over town by donating money, getting a lot of attention, and then finding some excuse to withdraw the funds. Look what she did to poor Constance Morely. The minute Constance introduced her to the prime minister, she reneged on most of the pledge."

"Sometimes it's not so easy to renege on a pledge. Some of these big fellas make you sign a commitment, and they'll sue you sure as shootin' if you try and get out of it."

I shook my head in disgust. "And this is the woman who Grant Bolton thinks walks on water."

"Well, now the Boltons *are* a philanthropic family. They have a big foundation. They do a lot with no fanfare. Old school."

"I know. I told you, Violet's my best friend. She's going to be very interested to hear this. So, would you say that Cynthia's doing anything illegal?"

"Well, now, that depends on if she's violating any regulations."

"What regulations?"

"The regulations governing the status of a 501(c)(3) foundation, which is a charitable, nonprofit, gift-giving foundation. See, now, if you were a little more interested in politics, you'd know that I am very interested in foundations."

"Why?"

"Why am I interested?"

"I mean, why foundations particularly?"

Grider put down his knife and fork and leaned in across the table. Watching him answer my question was like watching a piece of coal warm up and glow.

"Foundations in this country gave away close to forty-three billion dollars last year. Philanthropy is big business. Any time big amounts of money are involved, people are gonna try and cheat the system. It's just human nature. I don't like it when rich people cheat. I don't like self-dealing. I don't like it when the well-off and the well-heeled use a charitable foundation to line their own pockets. I like charity to go where it belongs: to the needy, the poor, the suffering, and the deserving. I've held hearings on foundation abuse. I've called for legislative action to stop it. And yet it continues because people are greedy, and greed fuels greed. There's a dangerous feeling around that once people get theirs, they are free to do as they please, and laws don't matter. Well, let me tell you something, young lady," he said, his eyes burning with indignation, "a country cannot survive on the impropriety of its wealthiest classes."

Grider slumped back into his chair and sipped his beer. He looked sheepish, like he knew he'd gotten carried away. It was the first time I'd seen real passion in the man.

"Wow. You really care about this issue, don't you?" I said.

"Yup. I do. You know in the Bible where it says it's easier for a camel to pass through the eye of a needle than it is for a rich man to enter the kingdom of heaven? Well, that's why rich people invented loopholes—so they can get into heaven without suffering," he said.

"I would not like to have you as my enemy, Senator."

Grider paused. "Like to have me as your friend?"

Chapter 35

Senator Grider and I started "keeping company," as he liked to put it. But that didn't mean we saw each other every day. Socially, Washington was what Grider referred to as "a Tuesday Wednesday town," because so many members of Congress commuted back and forth to their constituencies on weekends. The senator flew back and forth to Nebraska a lot. The arrangement suited me perfectly. Our relationship was decorous, with handholding and a little "smooching," as he called it, but no sex. I didn't really want to sleep with him, and fortunately, he didn't press me.

During this period, I saw much less of Gunner. I figured it was because the case was closed. But then I found out that he was spending quite a lot of time with Violet. The two of them had become great pals all of a sudden. I admit I was a little jealous. After all, Gunner was *my* friend first, and I'd helped him crack his big case. Yet now he seemed more interested in Violet than in me.

One day he called up and asked if we could go for a walk. I'd been cooped up in the shop, and I was ready for some air. I told Polo to mind the store while I stepped out for a while. I met Gunner up at the Oak Hill Cemetery for old times' sake. The grounds were an oasis of tranquillity in the spring, with flowering trees and emerald green lawns.

Gunner seemed very distracted, and when I asked him why he wanted to see me, he said, "It's about the case."

There was only one case in Gunner's life. He was still obsessed with the Beltway Basher murders, despite the fact that the killer was in custody—thanks in large part to my tip.

"Reven, I need you to tell me the truth about something. It's important."

"Okay," I said warily.

"Did you ever tell Violet about me when you first became my snitch?"

"No!" I cried, feigning surprise. I didn't want him to think I'd betrayed him. It was kind of like politics: if I told him the truth, he'd never trust me again.

He stopped in his tracks. "Do me a favor. Don't ever commit a serious crime."

"What do you mean?"

"Because you can't lie worth shit," he said.

I hung my head. We walked on. "Okay, maybe I mentioned it."

"*When?*"

"I don't know."

"From the git-go?"

"Maybe," I said sheepishly.

He shook his head in disgust. "That explains it."

"What?"

"How she knew about Nancy Sawtelle's calendar. She said she read about it in the paper. But it hasn't been in the paper. You told her, right?"

I nodded. "I shouldn't have, I know. But it was all a game to me then, Gunner. I didn't really take it seriously until Amber. I'm sorry. I'm really, really sorry. . . . Anyway, why is that important now? You've got Wardell or Maxwell or whatever he's called in custody."

"There are some other aspects that I still find interesting."

"Like?"

"Like, who was Nancy Sawtelle tracking? I don't think she was tracking Wardell."

"Does it matter?"

"Matters to me. See, Wardell's now admitted to doing three of the women—Bianca Symonds, Maria Dixon, and Amber. But he hasn't admitted to the others. He probably thinks that gives him some bargaining power."

"Why does that give him bargaining power? He admits to killing three women."

"If you were the parents of one of those girls, you'd understand!" Gunner shot back angrily.

I was pretty shocked at how vehement he was on this subject. I guess being a homicide detective, he understood the long consequences of murder a lot more than most people—the grief and the frustration, and most of all, the grand silence the victim's family has to endure.

He saw my startled reaction and softened his tone.

"Look, suppose your child is murdered. She's dead and buried, and part of you as a parent is dead and buried right alongside her. Well, you need to know that your kid's killer isn't still out there, enjoying life, laughing at the cops, maybe killing again. You need to know they've got him, and that he's gonna pay for what he did, for what he stole from her and from you. You need to *know*. Can you understand that?"

"Yes." I thought I saw Gunner wipe a tear from the corner of his eye. "Are you crying?" I asked him.

"No. Just got something in my eye, is all," he said irritably. "So anyway, until this creep Wardell confesses to all six murders, the police are never gonna be sure. We need to be sure. And he knows that. That's his power—his sick, controlling little piece of power in this world. I think he wants to make us believe there's another guy out there violating innocent girls and bashing in their skulls."

"But you don't think that, do you? You think he acted alone, right?"

"You can't be a hundred percent sure of anything until there's proof or a confession."

"Wait. You don't still think Bob Poll's involved somehow, do you?" I said.

"We have no proof whatsoever that he is. And, believe me, they went over every inch of his place and his life with a fine-tooth comb."

"But you think he's involved. I know you do. You always have. So do you and Violet discuss this case ad nauseam?"

"Lemme tell you something. Your friend knows more about serial killers and the way they think than half the guys in my department," he said admiringly.

"Yeah, I can just hear you two discussing the finer points of dismemberment."

"She's had some brilliant insights."

"You know what I think, Gunner? I think you have a crush on Violet."

"I don't."

"Are you sure? I mean, she's very needy at the moment. And you're a big one for damsels in distress."

"I don't have a crush on her," he assured me.

"Well, you certainly see enough of her. She tells me you're over there all the time."

He paused and slid his dark eyes onto mine. "Jealous?"

"No! Well . . . maybe a little. Violet always winds up doing better than I do in life." I sighed.

"Say what?"

"I've told you the whole story about how when we were in school, I was the Valkyrie and she was the troll. Then she wound up on top. Of course, now she's back down again, and we're on more of an equal footing. Don't get me wrong, I don't begrudge her her success—honestly, I don't. But why is she so interesting to you?"

"Violet interests me because she's interested in the same things I'm interested in."

"Yeah—bludgeon, sweat, and tears. You two are a pair of ghouls."

Gunner chuckled. "I think your pal Violet likes to talk about violent crime because it's unexpected coming from someone like her. Makes her stand out. Makes her shine in a weird kinda way."

"Are you going over there this afternoon?" I asked him.

"Thought I might drop by."

"I'm coming with you."

———

Violet was out in the garden when Gunner and I arrived. Since Grant left her, she'd thrown herself into gardening with a vengeance, taking out all her frustration on the earth. Whenever I went to visit her she was either weeding like a maniac or trimming the life out of some poor hedge. Kerry Blockley, her longtime gardener, told me she dug soil fast enough to be a union gravedigger.

Violet greeted us in her usual costume—jeans, a long shirt, a floppy straw hat, and old moccasins. Her hands were covered with dirt. Her face glowed with sweat. She seemed pleased to see us and to take a break from her labors.

The Ancient Maureener brought us a pitcher of iced tea and home-made lemon cookies on a silver tray. The three of us sat out on the patio. I tried to enjoy the lovely weather while Violet and Gunner discussed serial killers who acted in pairs. Violet spoke with disconcerting authority on the subject.

"A lot of serial killers have accomplices," she explained as she sipped her tea. "Sometimes when people get together, they become a lot more violent than they would if they were on their own, right, Gunner? Look at the Moors murderers, Myra Hindley and Ian Brady, or the Hillside Stranglers, Angelo Buono and Kenneth Bianchi, or Leonard Lake and Charles Ng, who filmed their victims being raped and tortured. Individually, those people may or may not have committed murder. But those couples were diabolic. They fueled each other's bloodlust. It's all very psychologically complex. But if you don't believe me, read *In Cold Blood*."

"So you think Wardell might have had a partner?" I said.

"Possibly. I'm not just saying this to be provocative, Reven, because he was such a shit to you, okay? But I wouldn't be surprised if Bob Poll knows more than he's letting on."

Gunner turned to me and said, "See? I told you she was an interesting girl."

"That's because she agrees with you. Gunner's always thought Bob was involved, haven't you, Gunner?" I said.

"Let me put it this way. My soul is not entirely rested."

"Mr. Wardell hasn't confessed to all of the crimes, so I definitely think there's more of a story there. More tea, anyone?" Violet said, lifting the pitcher.

Violet was a different person around Gunner. She played yet another role: ladylike crime buff to his seasoned detective. He seemed to regard her with what I thought was amused wonder, probably because her genteel surroundings were such an incongruous backdrop to her vast knowledge of unspeakable perversions. But he also listened quite closely to what she said, as if he respected her opinion and her observations.

"So how come a nice girl like you is so interested in all this dark stuff?" Gunner said, half joking, half not.

I'd asked Violet that a million times. She never answered me. She always just laughed and told me about some other fiend. This time, however, Violet didn't laugh. She stared at Gunner and thought for a long moment.

"I'm not sure," she began hesitantly. "Maybe . . . maybe it's because growing up, I lived in a house full of secrets. I didn't know what they were, but I knew they were around me—like shadows. And when you're a kid, you imagine the very worst, like goblins hiding in the closet and bogeymen coming to get you through the window. So I guess serial killers are the real-life versions of goblins and bogeymen. You never really outgrow things, do you?'

When we left, I said to Gunner, "Don't you think Violet would have made a great detective?"

"Or a great criminal," he responded with a smile.

Chapter 36

Violet, Peggy Myers, and I had lunch together once a week, mainly to discuss what was now referred to as "the Grant situation." We always went to Café Milano, and we always sat at the same corner table and ordered the same thing. We hunkered down in deep conversation over plates of chicken paillard and grilled vegetables. Marge Horner once told Peggy that we looked like "a trio of suicide bombers."

Although Grant and Cynthia were seemingly inseparable in public, his divorce was going slowly, and not because Violet was doing anything to hold it up. She had a prenup, and there was not much she could do. On the contrary, it was Grant who seemed to be stalling. This gave Violet hope. She had been waiting anxiously for the report from the private detective, and it finally came. Peggy and I were dying to know the results.

"I can't believe you hired an investigator," Peggy said.

"Why should we believe what this woman says about herself, huh?" Violet said.

"No one who courts the limelight as much as the Trailblazer can afford to lie," Peggy said.

Violet waved a dismissive hand at Peggy. "Don't kid yourself. Everyone can afford to lie. They just can't afford to get caught. This would hardly be the first time a big shot has told a big lie in Washington."

Violet knew as well as I did that if she could turn up some really unsavory detail about Cynthia, Grant would abandon her in five seconds flat.

"Grant's always been so careful about who we *connected* ourselves with," Violet said, imitating Grant's supercilious lockjawed tone of voice. "Just imagine if Cynthia actually turned out to be a convicted felon or something. He'd kill himself. Or her. That's why I hired the detective. And I just got the results this morning."

"*Well?*" Peggy and I said in unison.

Violet paused for effect, then deflated.

"Nada, I'm afraid."

"Don't tell me! Well, there goes thirty thousand dollars down the drain," I said.

Peggy's eyes widened. "Is that how much they cost?"

"More," Violet said glumly. "A lot more."

Unfortunately for Violet, Cynthia Rinehart appeared to be exactly who she said she was: a smart, self-made cookie who had made her fortune in the insurance business. She'd never been married, though there was talk she'd had an affair with the married chairman of the insurance company she worked for, and that's how she got her start. But there was no proof, only rumors. That affair didn't matter to anyone except Violet, who said it showed Cynthia had a history of targeting married men.

The only bright side was that although Cynthia appeared to have made her money legitimately, there were questions about how she was spending it. That wasn't covered in the detective's report. But I now knew from Grider that people had to be very careful about how they ran a foundation. Aside from having to give away a percentage of the foundation's assets every year, they had to be scrupulous about how they spent the foundation's money. If they were not careful, they risked being in serious violation of the tax code.

Since putting money into a foundation is a way of avoiding taxes, you can't turn around and squander foundation money on a lavish lifestyle. In other words, you couldn't pay yourself a huge salary, buy a big house, take people on junkets in your private plane, and give expensive gifts, all in the name of philanthropy. There were strict rules and regulations.

Peggy, who was on the board of two Fortune 500 companies and who knew her way around corporate America, pointed out that a foundation had to be very well endowed indeed to own and operate its own plane in the first place, much less fly people around in it the way Cynthia did. It was also unclear what Cynthia's Rinehart Retreats had actually accomplished—except to provide a luxurious venue for networking celebrities.

As Grider said, Cynthia gave a million dollars a year to the Kennedy Center, independently of the hundred-million-dollar pledge she had yet to fulfill. But as Violet was quick to point out, "She spends nearly that whole budget on those ridiculous Golden Key dinners and other events. Meanwhile, the staff sits in offices the size of coffins and the roof leaks. There has to be a better use for that money than food, flower arrangements, and inappropriate entertainment."

The three of us decided that unless Cynthia had a vast personal fortune no one was aware of, what she was doing with her foundation's money wasn't strictly legal, and that she eventually could be held accountable. In that case, she would need a protector—one who was titanically rich. I wasn't the only one who wondered if Cynthia had picked Grant, not for his unscintillating personality, but for his very scintillating pocketbook. God knows this wasn't lost on Violet either, who said to us, "It would serve Grant right if Washington's biggest philanthropist turned out to be Washington's biggest gold digger." And we weren't the only ones asking these questions.

I've found that in this world, you can get away with a lot if people like you. But if you're high-handed and make promises you don't keep—like pledging money and then withdrawing it, or not paying your bills—people start to dislike you. Dislike leads to complaint. Complaint gives rise to rumors. True or not, those rumors will almost certainly reach the ears of a zealous reporter anxious to check them out.

———

Corinna Huff was like a bad cold: there was no avoiding her once you were exposed. I often ran into Corinna at social events around town. She seemed vaguely aware of who I was, but we were not what I'd call friends. When she marched into my shop one sunny May morning, eager to talk to me, I knew she wanted something—and I figured it wasn't a discount.

She said she was writing an article for the *Washington Post*. I was impressed. Corinna rarely wrote articles anymore. She was far too busy with social life. Her marriage to Barkley Huff, the grand old man

of the Senate, had catapulted her to the pinnacle of Washington society, where she reigned with purpose and élan. Few subjects were
powerful enough to lure Corinna out of her semi-retirement as an in-
vestigative reporter. Clearly, she had found one worthy of her fabled
poison pen.

"I'm doing a piece on Cynthia Rinehart," she said, pausing to
appraise my reaction. "I understand you know her."

"And how," I said.

"Can I talk to you?"

It was well known that Corinna's sly ability to put people at their
ease was the way she coaxed them into saying things they would
later regret. But if she was leveling her pen at Ms. Rinehart, who was
I not to pass her some ammunition? I played hard-to-get for a few
seconds—just because I felt like paying her back for all those times
she never remembered my name. But I finally gave in and led her
upstairs to my office, where we spent the next hour and a half drinking bottled water and discussing a subject that was near, but far from
dear, to my heart.

Corinna was all charm and chat. She'd never been so affable to me
before. She had the manner of a sophisticated college girl. Her bobbed
brown hair and youthful looks masked a kind of slithery determination. At first she talked to me conspiratorially, like she just *knew* that
she and I were kindred souls who shared the same slightly wicked
points of view. It was like yakking with a great girlfriend I hadn't seen
in ages. The conversation was easy, effortless, and fun because we had
so much to say to each other on a variety of subjects, and we agreed
on everything, most especially on what we disliked.

Gradually, however, I realized that she was luring me into deeper
waters—getting me to tell her about Cynthia stealing Grant and how
it almost ruined my friendship with Violet. I told her how Cynthia had
stiffed me when I was decorating her house. As I spoke, I knew I was
being indiscreet. But that was Corinna's great gift: she got me to the
point where I didn't care what I said. I just wanted to keep on chatting
with this very clever, very entertaining, very sympathetic woman.

I called Violet immediately after she left.

"You'll never guess who was just here," I said, feeling a vague
sense of unease.

"Corinna Huff," Violet said without missing a beat.

"How did you know?"

"Because she called me up and wanted to see me. But I didn't think it was seemly of me to talk to her, so I told her to call you. I hope you gave her an earful."

That's the thing about Washington: you never know when you're being used.

———

Ten days later, Corinna Huff's article appeared on the front page of the Style section. Once again, there was a large picture of Cynthia standing in front of a great Washington institution—only this time, instead of the Kennedy Center, it was the Folger Shakespeare Library. Silhouetted against the elegant Art Deco neoclassical building, Cynthia stared defiantly at the camera. With her arms crossed in front of her and her chin angled upward, she resembled a defending champion on the eve of a title bout. The headline read: "Much Ado About Rinehart."

The peg for the article was the firestorm brewing around Cynthia's ten-million-dollar donation to the Folger Shakespeare Library. The rumors were true. Cynthia was threatening to withdraw the grant because the Folger had refused to use the funds as Cynthia wished them to. She was demanding the creation of a Rinehart Room, devoted to writers, artists, and film directors of her choosing. The trustees had earmarked the money for other projects, especially "Picturing Shakespeare," the expansion of their online image database of ten thousand drawings, prints, and photographs relating to Shakespeare and his era.

Cynthia's argument was that anyone who gives money to an institution should have a say in how said money is used. The Folger's position was that dealing with the preservation and dissemination of all the priceless books and materials already in their possession was a full-time project. They didn't need another room.

Douglas Reed, the president of the Folger, described by Corinna as "a soft-spoken, scholarly man," was quoted as saying simply, "There has obviously been a very deep misunderstanding."

Corinna went on to chronicle the origins of Cynthia's fortune and her cometlike ascendancy to the top of Washington society through her unparalleled philanthropy. Nothing new there. But then the article got into dicier stuff—like how Cynthia had bought Gay Harding's house and allegedly got into a dispute with her decorator over charges she refused to pay. That decorator would be me! And how she used her foundation's plane for pleasure junkets and personal errands. She apparently sent the decorator who replaced me on a trip to the Maastricht Art Fair to buy antiques and pictures for her house.

The article chronicled Cynthia's early friendship with the Boltons, stating that Cynthia had originally approached Grant Bolton, "the president of the Potomac Bank and the scion of one of Washington's most generous and private philanthropic families," to seek his advice on matters relating to her foundation and which institutions and projects she should support. She described Violet as "a major rung on the social ladder," who took Cynthia under her wing and introduced her to many powerful and important people in Washington.

Corinna went into the scandal in some detail.

"Shortly after Mr. Bolton was honored at one of Ms. Rinehart's Golden Key dinners, he left his wife of fifteen years and took up with Ms. Rinehart. They have not tried to keep their relationship a secret. On the contrary, Ms. Rinehart and Mr. Bolton have become a power couple around town. She recently gave Mr. Bolton a birthday party at the Freer and Sackler Galleries, which drew a stellar crowd."

Then the piece got really delicious. It went into the whole thing about the Kennedy Center and how Cynthia didn't have to fork over the money until Congress matched the funds. And the million dollars she did give every year in a separate grant was used primarily for lavish parties "rather than any enrichment or support of the arts." An unidentified source was quoted as saying Cynthia used these "often inappropriate and over-the-top events to further her influence by entertaining important people and garnering a lot of publicity."

Corinna had somehow gotten hold of the lavish invitation to the Golden Key Awards Dinner, which she described as "a giant fold-out card flecked with red velvet and embossed with gold and silver lettering."

Marge Horner, bless her heart, was quoted as saying: "When I received it, I thought it was an invitation to the opening of a bordello!"

An "unnamed source" at the Kennedy Center called Cynthia "a philanthropic philistine, with a corrugated tin ear." It didn't take a genius to figure out that that "source" was Leonid Slobovkin, the disaffected conductor whose job was now in jeopardy. And although Kyle Michaels, the brilliant and popular artistic director of the center, diplomatically observed that Cynthia's "supreme generosity outweighed any other considerations," even he mentioned that she was sometimes perceived to have "a slightly misshapen agenda."

Corinna listed several examples of how Cynthia had pledged money, only to renege later after she had garnered publicity, given a party, or made an important new contact. "Sources close to the investigation" mentioned Constance Morely's Childhood Lupus Foundation as a case in point. I figured those sources were me and Constance herself.

A famous actor who was a recipient of a Golden Key Award was quoted as saying, "She courted me like crazy until I finally accepted the dinner. Presents, phone calls, trips, the whole nine yards. Halfway through that evening, I looked down at this big gold key hanging around my neck, and thought, 'What the hell am I doing here?' "

It was a scathing profile. But if you really want to hang someone in print, make the noose out of their own words.

Corinna interviewed Cynthia herself and the article was peppered with her quotes. Cynthia admitted that her newfound celebrity was "sweet revenge for all the years of drudgery and being dismissed." She said that philanthropists were "the new rock stars of the planet." She said that her purchase of Gay Harding's house was like "the passing of the torch." She said that people were just jealous of her because she had raised "the giving bar" to a new height, which now meant that everyone had to "dig so much deeper into their old-fashioned pocketbooks."

"People hate parting with money," she was quoted as saying. "It's the reason philanthropy still isn't commensurate with the vast fortunes that have been made in this country in the past twenty years. I made a lot of money, but instead of spending it on myself, I created a foundation to give it away. I've given away tens of millions of dollars and done a lot of people a lot of good."

However, the last line was the coup de grâce. After Corinna inquired whether Cynthia was using her foundation's money to pay for some of the perks she personally enjoyed, Cynthia said: "Everything I do is aboveboard. There are strict rules governing foundations, and I abide by every single one of them. If people don't like the way I spend my foundation's money, they can take it up with Congress!"

That same afternoon, Senator Grider issued a statement: "I'm Congress, and Ms. Rinehart can take it up with me!"

You could almost hear the scaffold trapdoor drop.

Chapter 37

Violet was ecstatic about the article and about Senator Grider's response.

"You have no idea how many people dislike this woman," she said when I spoke to her. "And now they're all coming out of the woodwork, I'm thrilled to say."

Violet and I both agreed that Grant would never in a million years be able to withstand the heat. He was so squeamish when it came to his image in the community that even if he were still madly in love with Cynthia, he'd have to give her up after this. We got a good laugh over what his parents were thinking after having embraced Cynthia so quickly.

"I bet I'm looking pretty darn good to Rainy again," Violet said with more than a little satisfaction.

———

Two days after the article appeared, Constance Morely invited me and Violet to a ladies' lunch at the British Embassy. I was surprised, because ambassadorial wives are scheduled within an inch of their diplomatic lives. It's rare they can make time for a small private meal on such short notice.

It was a hot, sunny July day. Violet and I arrived together. Araminta Upton greeted us and showed us outside to the grand Palladian stone portico overlooking the sprawling back garden of the embassy. Nouria Sahala and Peggy Myers were standing on the terrace, enjoying mint iced teas with our hostess, Lady Morely. We all exchanged cordial hellos. Though it was extremely nice to be there, I kind of wondered why we'd all been asked. My tacit question was answered a few minutes later when Corinna Huff walked out and joined us on the patio.

Corinna, who thrived on the controversy her articles created, looked positively radiant that day. Controversy became her. The fact that her article had stoked the wrath of Congress was a crowning peacock feather in her cap.

Luncheon was served in Lady Morely's private dining room, just off the main hall. The square white room had been used as an office by the former ambassador's wife. Constance made it into more of a sitting room, easily converted to a dining room for small lunches and dinners. We were halfway through the first course of asparagus vinaigrette when Constance got the ball rolling.

"Corinna, any word from Ms. Rinehart about your article?" she inquired in her soft, pretty voice. She sounded as innocent as a Wordsworth poem.

We all perked up like prairie dogs, eager for Corinna's answer.

"I hear she's none too pleased," Corinna said with an air of pride.

"I can tell you who's really upset," Peggy said.

"*Who?*" we all said in bright unison.

"Marge Horner," Peggy replied. "Marge told me you misquoted her, Corinna."

Corinna laughed. "Sorry, Marge, it's on tape. You can't have your quote and deny it too."

"What did Marge say exactly? I forget," I said, not forgetting at all, but rather wishing to pay Marge back for the mean and calculating way she'd broken the news to me about Bob and Melody.

"Oh, you remember, Reven," Violet said. "She described those hideous invitations to the Golden Key dinner as looking like invites to the opening of a whorehouse."

"Bordello," Corinna corrected her. "And she made some other snide comments about Ms. Rinehart that I didn't print."

"Like what?" I asked.

"Oh, just stuff."

"Come on, Corinna. For heaven's sakes, don't go discreet on us now," Violet pressed her.

It wasn't like Corinna to be shy. But she was clearly hesitant for some reason.

"Inquiring minds want to know," I said.

"Yes, we're all friends here. Consider this room a tomb, ladies. Nothing goes beyond it," Constance assured her.

Corinna sighed. "It's not that, it's . . . Okay, I warned you. Marge said that it was amazing how Grant Bolton followed Cynthia around like a lapdog, and you could practically see his tongue drooling."

Corinna flung Violet an uneasy glance. No one quite knew where to look.

"Oh, my God, why didn't you put that *in*, Corinna?" Violet shrieked with glee.

"I was trying to spare certain people's feelings," Corinna said, pointedly. "Always a mistake." She popped an asparagus into her mouth.

"Well, that was nice of you. But I really wish you'd used it," Violet said. "If Grant saw that in print and thought people were talking about him that way . . . ? He'd have a heart attack, believe me!"

"And it couldn't happen to a nicer guy," I added.

Everybody laughed, and the tension was diffused. But I saw that Violet's laughter was forced. I knew she still cared for Grant, even though she pretended not to.

"I didn't put a lot of other stuff in either," Corinna said, pausing for effect. You could have heard a crumb drop.

"Such as?" Peggy asked.

"She rents her jewelry," Corinna announced to collective gasps.

"Don't tell me those klieg-light earrings she wears all the time aren't *hers*?" I said.

"I do believe they belong to Pearce's in New York, and she rents them on a year-round basis. But I only got this from one source, so I couldn't use it. And did you know that she's Pianissimo's biggest customer? She sends their scarves and cashmere slippers to people at the drop of a name," Corinna said.

"Those slippers aren't cheap. Rolly loves them," Peggy said.

"The real question is, does she charge all this stuff to the foundation?" Corinna said. " 'Cause if so, it's bye-bye, Cynthia. . . . But Reven, you probably know more about this than any of us. What does your friend Senator Grider say?"

Everyone knew I was seeing Grider. People just assumed we were having an affair. I didn't dispel that notion because in Washington, it's always good for people to think you have intimate friends in high places. Violet knew the truth, of course, which was that Zack and I enjoyed each other's company, but there wasn't much else going on.

"I really haven't spoken to him since your article came out. He's talked more to the press than he has to me. But you all know he's got a bee in his bonnet about foundation abuse. So if she's done things she shouldn't have, fasten your seat belts," I said.

"I tried to interview him, but no dice," Corinna said. "I also happen to know that Ms. Rinehart is getting tired of Washington. She's referred to it as being 'too provincial.' She may be headed for New York or L.A."

"Not with Grant, she's not. Rainy would kill him," Violet said under her breath.

Nouria Sahala had been uncharacteristically silent for most of the lunch. She'd had a discreet chat on her cell phone, arranging some fête at her embassy, from the sound of it. But other than that, she'd sat quietly, soaking up what the rest of us were saying without contributing any tidbits of her own. I knew she was a friend of Cynthia's, and it occurred to me she might be offended by our conversation. I wondered if she was keeping her mouth shut out of respect for her pal. However, as dessert was being served, Nouria weighed in with one of those sentences that immediately grab attention.

"You know, I used to like Cynthia," she began. The conversation stopped dead. We all leaned toward her like flowers toward the sun. She went on. "Yes, I thought she was a bit pushy, and yes, she was a bit full of herself. But let's face it, there are a lot of pushy people who are full of themselves in Washington."

"They hold the majority," Violet said.

"Being Otanni, I'm very loyal." She paused. "But, honey, cross me and you've had it," she added.

We all nodded; it was so true. Nouria had a reputation for defending her friends when it was inconvenient or even dangerous for her to do so. She famously excluded anyone who attacked a pal of hers. She twisted the famous old Arab proverb, "The enemy of my enemy is my friend," into her own Nouria-esque variation: "The enemy of my *friend* is my enemy."

She went on: "The other night, when Cynthia came to my reception for our foreign minister, she didn't behave at all well. First, in my opinion, it's very bad form to criticize the hostess in her own house. A guest who does that is really not possible."

"Yes, I think we can all safely agree with that," sniffed Constance Morely.

Nouria spoke a fluent, staccato English. No one was eating the raspberry mousse dessert for fear of missing so much as a syllable.

"So Yasmin, the wife of our foreign minister, who is a very old and dear friend of mine, came over to me during the party and pointed to Cynthia and asked me who she was. When I told her, she made a face, you know? I know Yasmin so well. I said to her, 'Why are you asking?' And Yasmin looked me right in the eye and said, 'Nouria, is this woman supposed to be a friend of yours?' And I said, 'Yes, you know, she's not a *great* friend, but she is a friend.' So Yasmin looks at me and says, '*No, she's not.*' Just like that! And I said, 'What do you mean?' Well, apparently, that night Cynthia was going around saying that my chocolate fountain was tacky. Can you imagine? She said to Yasmin that it was 'too Willie Wonka' for an embassy. And Yasmin said to me, 'And what the hell is Willie Wonka?'"

When our collective laughter had died down, Nouria added, "Let me tell you something, girls. You don't criticize a hostess in her own house no matter what you think. That's the *last* time Cynthia Rinehart ever sets foot in our embassy. *Ever!*"

"She'll never come here again either," Constance said.

Violet leaned in and whispered to me, "Grant's such a rabid Anglophile. He'd die if they thought he'd been banned from the Queen's soil."

We had coffee out on the terrace. The mood was jubilant. There's nothing like a good dishy ladies' lunch. We all said good-bye and thanks to Constance, feeling as if we'd just had the full treatment at a rejuvenating spa. As Violet and I were walking out, Nouria pulled us over into the ballroom behind one of the large ocher faux marble columns so she could talk to us alone.

"Violet, I wanted to tell you something," Nouria began in a low voice. "I didn't want to say it in front of the others, but I think I can say it in front of Reven because I know you two are best friends."

"Absolutely. Reven's like my sister."

"Okay. So . . . Grant asked about you at my party."

Violet flushed. "What did he say?"

"He wanted to know if you were coming."

"Oh." She deflated. "That's probably just because he didn't want to run into me."

Nouria shook her finger at Violet. "No, no, no! Trust me. He was looking for you. He was anxious to see you."

"What makes you say that?" she asked.

"I can tell. I'm an Otanni witch," she said with a wink. "So even though I knew you'd regretted, I told him, well, yes, she might come."

"You didn't!" Violet said, obviously thrilled with the mischief of it.

"I did. I wanted to see his reaction. Well, my dear, he stood off in a corner by himself the whole night, just staring at the door. I'm sure he was waiting for you to come in. Really. He hardly spoke to anyone."

"He never speaks to anyone," Violet said.

"Well, darlings, I must go. But I am telling you that woman will never set foot in my house again! Never, ever, ever, ever! Oh, and you're both invited to my party for the new head of the World Bank next month!"

"We love your chocolate fountain!" Violet cried as Nouria ran off. Then Violet turned to me and said in a plaintive little voice, "Maybe there's hope."

I wasn't entirely sure if she was referring to Grant or the fact that Nouria was still inviting her to the embassy.

Chapter 38

In September, the Wheelock twenty-fifth reunion was finally upon us. Like all the milestone—or *millstone*—reunions, as I called them, this one was marked by a big get-together on campus, plus an excursion to another city to see the sights. The twenty-fifth is the one where even the most determined flower child realizes that she is now old enough to be her own mother. There are those who go to reunions, and those who don't. I don't. At least, I never had. I'd missed the fifth, tenth, fifteenth, even the twentieth, for which Violet flew to Boston to the home of Madeleine Pine, our most brilliant classmate, who was a curator at the Isabella Stewart Gardner Museum.

I'd happily managed to avoid all contact with my classmates except Violet for the past twenty-five years. Not that I didn't want to see them. I just didn't want them to see me. I wanted them to remember me for my potential, not for my failed promise. But Violet held me to my word that I would come and help her get through it. Truth be told, I was kind of curious to see what some of my old classmates looked like after all this time.

Nouria's comment that Grant seemed to be pining after Violet haunted my friend the entire week. As we were stringing together the school motto in big gold cardboard letters, Violet said to me, "Do you really think Grant misses me, Rev? Do you think he'll come back?"

It was the zillionth time she'd asked me that question, and I gave her my stock answer. "Of course he misses you. And can you imagine how he feels about Cynthia and this whole scandal? He's probably ruing the day he ever left you."

"Yes, but do you think he'll come back to me? Do you?"

Sometimes Violet reminded me of a child who asks the same question over and over, paying no attention to the response. She was driving me nuts.

We completed the gold-lettered school motto—AD VITAM PARAMUS—and hung it up over the entrance to the living room. It meant, "We are preparing for life." I stared at it thinking that a better school motto would have been: FUCK ALL PREPARES YOU FOR LIFE, AND YOU MIGHT AS WELL KNOW IT NOW. But that would have been too long in Latin.

———

I took more time getting ready for that reunion than I ever had for any date. I wanted to make sure I looked my very, very best and that I was in just the right outfit, so that when the girls saw me, I wouldn't be a disappointment. I put on a chic, form-fitting little black dress and pearls—demure and yet revealing that I'd kept my figure. Just the ticket, I thought.

Against my advice, Violet decided to give a tea party instead of a cocktail party. I knew that was because she wanted to show off the Tiffany tea service that had belonged to Grant's grandmother. But I told her to have plenty of booze on hand. I said, "Believe me, at a twenty-fifth reunion, people don't want tea. They want drugs and alcohol."

I arrived at Violet's house half an hour early to see if I could help with any last-minute details. A bunch of white and purple balloons were tied to the front gate, white and purple being the school colors. Inside, Maureen and a small staff hired for the occasion seemed to have matters well in hand. Lush bouquets of roses and tulips had been strategically placed around the house by Sue Bluford, one of the best floral designers in Washington. I'd insisted that Violet use Sue, fearing she might resort to supermarket carnations just to save a buck. Her impending divorce had made her question little luxuries she'd always taken for granted.

"You want to impress them. Now is not the time to economize," I told her.

A tape of songs from our high-school era was playing softly in the background—classics like "Every Breath You Take," "Ghostbusters," "The Glamorous Life," and what I facetiously dubbed Violet's personal theme song, "Like a Virgin."

Violet hadn't come down yet. I went upstairs to see how she was doing. She was sitting on the bed half dressed, talking on the phone. The
second I came into the room, she cupped her hand over the receiver
and waved me away, saying, "Not now! Please close the door!"

I knew something big was up, because usually Violet never minded
if I listened in on her phone conversations. On the contrary, she liked
to have me there so she could make funny faces to me while being
treacly sweet to the poor unsuspecting soul on the other end of the
line. I can't count the number of times Violet had chatted up someone
on the phone as though she were their long lost friend, then hung up
and turned to me without missing a beat, saying, "God, what a bore
that woman is!"

I walked back downstairs to the living room, where I found Gunner
sitting on the couch, reading. I was surprised to see him there. He was
wearing a pair of thin tortoiseshell reading glasses, which struck me as
an incongruous and rather touching sight set against his dreadlocks.

"Well, well, well, I don't remember you at Wheelock," I said to
him, teasingly.

He looked up. "I was a few classes behind you."

"Chivalry is so dead. . . . What are you reading?"

He held up a little purple and white booklet I recognized all too
well. It was an issue of *Passages*, the school alumnae bulletin.

A few more issues were stacked up on the coffee table in front of
him, and there were several others scattered around on tables throughout the room. Violet had saved every single one of those semi-annual
time bombs. She'd even had a set of purple archival boxes made for
them, with the word *Passages* embossed in gold on the spines. For
someone who had endured near Dickensian humiliation at Wheelock, Violet's devotion to these glossy little odes to school spirit was
touching, if not perverse. I plunked myself down beside Gunner on
the couch and read over his shoulder. He was engrossed in the section
called "Class Notes."

I have to admit that I always glanced at the "Class Notes" before
chucking *Passages* in the garbage. I did so out of curiosity just to see
what my old schoolmates were up to. In the early days, right after
we graduated, a lot of girls wrote in to the magazine, telling of their
college careers, job choices, travels, and marriages. After a while,
the correspondence tapered off as careers heated up and families

"thrived"—the adjective du jour. Then there was that period when contributors wrote about "stopping to smell the roses." It was my impression that people only stopped to smell the roses when they hit a great big rock in the garden. There were far fewer contributors now. The women who wrote in often had sadder, smaller tales to tell.

I pictured our class as a bunch of swimmers battling the tides of life. Some had surged ahead, while others had barely kept their heads above water. A few had drowned—or at least they were never heard from again.

Violet and I were the Class of '84. Our class correspondent was the officious Jenny Tilbert, who took the job no one else wanted and started out all our "Class Notes" with the same bossy exhortation: "Come on, Ladies, let's hear what you're up to! Now! Write!"

Over the years, "Ladies" changed to "Sisters," and "Write!" changed to "Write/Fax/E-mail/Text!"

I was one of the "Ladies/Sisters" who never wrote, faxed, e-mailed, or texted any information whatsoever. Let people imagine what had become of me. I sure wasn't going to tell them. But Jenny could always depend on Violet, who wrote in faithfully twice a year with snapshot accounts of her achievements woven into Jenny's breathy prose. In fact, it was through those alumnae magazines that I'd followed Violet's progress through life way before she arrived in Washington—the schools, the travels, the honors, the months she devoted to working pro bono for various causes. Her brief but informative entries had the cool detachment of real success.

Gunner chuckled as he read aloud from the issue in his hand: " 'Violet McCloud writes: *Graduated with honors from DePaul University for the second straight year. Off to London for my Junior Year Abroad. Wish me luck!* We do, Violet! Good luck!' " He paused and peered at me over the tops of his glasses. "Perky stuff. This how you gals manage to keep tabs on each other?"

"Yup. So, Gunner, are you living here now? You never drop by to say hi to me anymore? Is this how you treat all your CIs?"

He wasn't listening. "So then she went to law school, eh?"

"Who, Violet? Yeah. University of Southern California."

"What were you doing then?"

"Me? I was singing my youth away like the idiot grasshopper while army ant Violet marched on single-mindedly."

I picked up one of the magazines and fanned it to "Class Notes."

"Violet never missed an issue, bless her heart. Look, here she is again . . . Listen to this . . . 'Violet McCloud writes: *The environment is an increasing concern of mine, as it should be of everyone's. I am moving to Washington to try and instigate some real changes on Capitol Hill.* Go for it, Violet. Show them we Wheelock girls can effectuate real change in the world!' That's Jenny Tilbert cheering her on. I think Jenny's coming today. Stick around, and you'll meet her."

Gunner had his nose in another bulletin. He read the entry aloud to me: " 'Violet McCloud is now Mrs. Grant Bolton Jr. Her husband is a vice president of the Potomac Bank of Washington, a family concern. Violet writes to us: *Please come look me up in Washington, classmates. I long to see you. Grant is a wonderful man and we are expecting in August.* We wish Violet and her new family all the best! Go look her up, girls! I know I will if I can ever pry myself away from my consulting practice.' "

Gunner shook his head and said, "Whoa."

"What?"

"I was just thinking what my 'Class Notes' woulda been like."

"What do you mean?"

"The kids I went to school with . . . ? We had kind of a different career path—more like stepping off a cliff," he said with a mordant little chuckle.

"You did okay," I said.

"I was one of the lucky ones. For a while, anyhow."

A wave of sadness suddenly washed over Gunner. He tried to cover it up with a joke.

"Here are my 'Class Notes.' 'Jeff's in jail. Lakisha's working in a burger joint. Oren got shot. Willie's driving a truck. Annie's in rehab. Melvin's out on bail.' . . . Like that. Oh, maybe that's not quite fair. Some of us made it up to a decent pay grade, but not enough."

"I've told you before. Violet was the biggest loser in school. I mean, nobody ever *dreamed* she was going to do so well in life. You wanna know the real reason she wanted to give this reunion?"

"Yeah, as a matter of fact, I do."

"So all the girls who wouldn't spit on her back then could envy her now. You know she gave Wheelock the highest sum ever contributed by an alumna in a single year? Two million dollars."

"Impressive," Gunner said.

"She did it through the Bolton Foundation, of course. When Grant left her, she wanted to call the whole thing off. That's why I'm here—breaking a vow to myself I'd never go to one of these things. But, hey, I had to come and support her."

"That was nice of you. Tell me something. Why do you think Violet did so well if she was so pathetic in school, like you say?"

"I've thought about that. I think it's precisely because things *weren't* so easy for her. Violet had to work harder than anyone for every little thing, which meant she valued the things she got a lot more than those of us for whom things so easily in the beginning."

"Like you?"

"Yeah, like me. I didn't value what I had because I always had it. It was all too easy, too accessible. I never had to fight for things the way Violet did. So I never really appreciated any of the gains I made. I just kinda took them all for granted. I'll tell you a little secret, Gunner—when you don't appreciate something, you eventually lose it. I wish to God I'd been a little smarter and less careless about my life. I admire Violet and what she accomplished."

Gunner patted my hand, as if he sensed my regret. "Don't be so hard on yourself. You've done just fine."

"Thanks." His opinion meant a lot to me.

Seeing all those bulletins there, pristinely preserved in those custom-made boxes, I realized that contributing to *Passages* had been Violet's way of telling a story. The "Class Notes" were her mini autobiography—her résumé, if you will. They left no doubt that the homeliest, weirdest, most unpopular girl in school had bested the lot of us. Her life was a trifecta of revenge, inspiration, and glory. She was like the hundred-to-one shot who comes from behind to win the Kentucky Derby.

"You ever go visit her when Violet was working out in, let's see—" Gunner flipped through one of the bulletins and found the entry he was looking for. "Oklahoma. She writes in: '*I'm tutoring on the Osage Nation reservation in Pawhuska, Oklahoma. My work is both sad and inspirational. I love working with these children and helping them find the skills to discover their own rich heritage.*'"

"See? That's what I mean about her. She just took all of her own sadness and turned it toward helping others. And it paid off."

"So you never went to see her out there?"

"No. I don't know where the hell I was when she was there. Probably in some sort of boyfriend hell. But she called me up the minute she got to Washington. It was so great to hear from her after all those years."

"So you guys didn't really keep in touch."

"No. When she moved here, we hadn't spoken to each other since graduation. But you know what? It didn't make a damn bit of difference. We took up right where we left off. . . . Like with you, Gunner. I mean, here we are all friendly again, even though I hardly ever see you anymore," I teased him.

"And you were the one who introduced her to Grant, right?"

"Yes, indeedy."

"But you went out with him first, right? Why didn't you marry him? Rich, good-looking guy like that?"

"Puh-leeze. I'd rather die of starvation than of boredom. I was much too much of a handful for Grant. Violet's perfect for him. He is, like, the most uptight person in the entire world. And totally insecure."

"He's a good-lookin' guy, he owns a bank, and he's insecure? *Shiiit*," Gunner drawled.

I explained the whole thing to Gunner again, told him what a tyrant old Mr. Bolton was and how Rainy Bolton was the toughest thing in toe shoes.

"Look, the Boltons wanted their only son to marry someone very substantial. Rainy Bolton mistrusts women who don't have certain credentials. That's why they didn't like me. Rainy thought I was frivolous. But they *adored* Violet. Violet was this perfect combination of innocence and worthiness and ambition. She worshipped Grant, and she would let him be the star. If he'd married me, *I* would have been the star, darling!"

"Even if you do say so yourself," Gunner snickered.

"I'm kidding! But I was way too racy for old Grant. He's the biggest prig. At least he *was* up until recently. Back then, the last thing he wanted was a girl with a past, *believe* me. Violet was like the freaking Virgin Mary. And so worthy—unlike *moi*."

"You're not worthy?"

"I'm too chic and cynical to be worthy."

"But Violet's worthy?"

"God, yes! Read those 'Class Notes.' Violet went to law school. She did pro bono work for the Indians. She lobbied for the environment. She's one of those pure people. She was absolutely right for Grant, and I knew it the minute I saw her. Of course, now he's completely derailed with Cynthia. But, frankly, I don't see how that can last. Not now—not with all this terrible publicity. That woman's in a world of trouble. And when the going gets tough, trust me, Grant Bolton will get going!"

"So how come you never wrote in to tell people what you were up to?"

I really didn't feel like going into the whole failed-princess thing with Gunner, so I simply said, "I guess I was just too busy living."

He closed the booklet. "Any more Bob Poll sightings?"

"Actually, yes. I ran into him at the Otanni Embassy."

"How was that?"

"I don't know. He's weird. He doesn't seem too happy, though."

"No? How come?"

"I don't think he likes married life. And I don't care. . . . What's happening with Maxwell? I never hear about him anymore."

"He's going through the process. Enjoying his grisly fame. Playing games."

"What kinds of games?"

"Still not confessing to everything. Kinda hinting someone else was involved in bashing in the skulls of innocent girls and violating them. That's his power now—his sick, controlling little piece of power in this world."

"Oh, my God. So do you think Bob Poll could be involved after all?"

Gunner hesitated. "Look, Reven, I need to talk to you."

"What have we been doing?"

"In private."

"About the crimes?"

Gunner stood up from the couch. "I'll call you."

"I've missed you, Gunner."

"By the way, how's your senator?" he asked as he was leaving.

"Well, I'm happy you're keeping tabs on me, even if you don't call. He's fine."

"Tell Violet I said good-bye. Happy reunion."

I sat there wondering what Gunner wanted to talk to me about. Was Violet right? Could Bob Poll possibly have been involved in these crimes in some way?

Moments later, Violet swept into the room, wearing a chic purple dress and a white patent leather belt—the perfect outfit for this reunion. She looked at me and said, "Well, that was Grant. He wants to come home."

"Told ya!" I leaped up from the sofa and clapped my hands. "That's such great news!"

"Where's Gunner?"

"He had to go. He said to say good-bye. So Grant's coming back with his tail between his legs. You must be so happy."

"I guess."

"Oh, come on!"

"He's behaved so horribly. Humiliated me in front of the whole entire world."

"A second ago you were dying for him to come back. What did he say?"

Violet explained how the Corinna Huff article on Cynthia had sent Grant and his parents into a tailspin. Rainy was now denouncing Cynthia, and Mr. Bolton Sr. feared for the integrity of the bank. Grant admitted to Violet on the phone that he was embarrassed to be seen with Cynthia now that her ethics were coming into question. But he assured Violet that the relationship had been souring in any case.

"I asked him if he'd been looking for me at the Otanni Embassy, like Nouria thought. He said he was. He even admitted that his parents were urging him to go back to me to try and patch things up for the good of the bank and everything."

"Did they mention Tee at all?"

"Not really. I think they're more concerned about the bank at this point because of the publicity."

Was ever a family more concerned with their public image, I wondered?

"Well, I'm sure Tee will be happy," I said pointedly.

"Let's hope. Grant's calling him today. He told me Tee didn't like Cynthia. Thought she was a big phony, even though she tried to bribe him with an iPhone and a lot of other stuff."

Curiously enough, Violet didn't seem nearly as elated as I imagined she would be.

"This is what you've been praying for. Aren't you thrilled?" I said.

"I guess," she replied with an uncertain little smile. "Why does it suddenly feel like such a letdown?"

"Because you're in shock. Come on, have a glass of wine and relax. You won!"

As far as I was concerned, Grant's timing was perfect. Violet could now reclaim her top perch as Mrs. Grant Bolton Jr., the reigning queen of our class. I was happy for her. Honestly. Well, maybe a little envious—but mainly happy.

Maureen came in and announced that the first two guests had arrived. Violet and I took deep breaths and prepared ourselves for the trip down memory lane.

———

Here's the thing: you don't know how old you are by looking in the mirror. You know how old you are by looking at your high school classmates twenty-five years later. I thought I looked really good for my age until I saw what my age actually was. Nobody looks great after forty. We just look better or worse than other people our age.

Every time the doorbell rang, I braced myself for another shock. It was touching how we'd all made an effort to look our best. Still, a few of the girls were totally unrecognizable to me. Twenty-five years is a longer time when you call it what it really is: a quarter of a century, five years more than a whole generation. I kept thinking that some of these girls looked old enough to be my mother. And then I realized we *all* looked old enough to be our mothers, because we *were* old enough to be our mothers!

Many of the women had let themselves go completely. I didn't even recognize the once perky and athletic Jenny Tilbert, our class correspondent. The former lacrosse team captain and basketball star had gotten fat and let her hair go gray. Oddly enough, she didn't seem to care. In fact, she seemed more at ease with herself than the few of us who still wore a size eight. Her face had a disconcerting serenity to it.

I sat down beside her on the sofa, and we talked as Jenny wolfed down ginger snaps between sips of tea. Poor Jenny hadn't had an easy time of it, though she seemed to take hardship in stride. Divorced for a number of years, she lived alone in a small apartment in Providence and worked part-time for the admissions director of Wheelock. Her two children lived in another state and only visited her on holidays. She said that keeping tabs on our classmates was the highlight of her life.

She told me about some of the girls who couldn't make it to the reunion. Just out of curiosity, and because I still felt guilty, I said casually, "By the way, Jen, do you know whatever became of Mary Lou Lindsay?"

Jenny got this horrified look on her face and whispered, "She went to *jail*!"

"What? You're kidding!"

"No. Isn't that the *worst*? A Wheelock girl in prison!" she said with a shudder. "I think she's the first in the whole hundred-and-fifteen-year history of the school."

"Wait! Violet's got to hear this!" I said.

I dragged Violet away from the little group she was showing off the Tiffany tea service to and sat her down between me and Jenny on the sofa. I ordered Jenny to repeat what she'd just told me.

"Well," Jenny began, in the breathy voice of a born gossip, "your old nemesis, Mary Lou Lindsay? She went to jail for check kiting."

Violet shrugged. "I always knew she'd come to a bad end."

"How'd you find out?" I asked Jenny.

Jenny told us that the school had been notified because Mary Lou wanted to get her high school equivalency diploma in prison, and she needed to find out what her credit situation was for the courses.

"Mrs. Lindsay, her mother, wrote a scathing letter to Dean Trow-bridge saying that all Mary Lou's misfortunes in life were on account of her having been unjustly expelled from Wheelock! She said that if they hadn't kicked Mary Lou out, she would have gone to college like all the other girls, instead of becoming a felon! Or words to that effect. Isn't that just too tragic?! A Wheelock girl in jail! I didn't dare put it in the 'Class Notes.' It's just too *too* . . . !" Jenny talked in exclamations, just like she wrote.

Violet sat there with a sullen expression on her face. I wondered if now she felt some remorse for having planted that bottle of gin.

It sure didn't seem that way. In fact, she said primly, "Mrs. Lindsay should blame her daughter, not the school."

"True. Mary Lou was such a bully," Jenny agreed. "Do you think I should put it in the 'Class Notes' as a caution to us all?"

I thought of my own unfortunate role in Mary's Lou's derailment.

"I don't know. I think it's sad. . . . So whatever happened to her?" I asked.

"No idea," Jenny shrugged. "Needless to say, she never wrote in to me. . . . Just like you, Reven, you bad girl!" Jenny shook her finger at me. "Why have we never heard a peep from you in all these years? I trust *you* haven't been in jail!" She laughed.

"Not that much to write about, I guess," I muttered.

"Now, that can't be true! Every story is interesting, no matter how boring it is!" That sentence was pure Jenny. She turned to Violet and said, "But you're my star, of course. You've allowed me to share your exemplary life with your classmates over the years, and I want you to know how much I appreciate it. You've been an inspiration to us all! It just goes to show, you can never predict how people will turn out in the end."

———

Toward the end of the party, who should walk in but Grant. He looked a little stunned to see his living room filled with chattering middle-aged women. Violet rushed over to him, threaded her arm through his, and marched him around the room, showing him off to all the women.

"This is my husband, Grant Bolton," she said, over and over, as if she were claiming him back with each introduction.

When they reached me, Violet said excitedly, "Look who's here, Rev!"

"Welcome home," I said.

Never one to show emotion, Grant managed a facial twitch meant, I supposed, to be a smile. We both understood why he was back, though neither of us was going to say it. He seemed resigned, like a prisoner moving to a different jail.

The reunion made me sad in a way. Not only did it remind me how quickly life goes by, it made me realize that the thoughtless little things we do can have dire consequences. I couldn't stop thinking about Mary Lou Lindsay, wondering if her life would have turned out differently had Violet not planted that bottle of gin in her locker, and I not reported her. I even thought about trying to get in touch with her. But I realized that an apology would be futile. The damage was done. We'd all moved on.

Chapter 39

Grant offered to make things up to Violet in a big way. He arranged to take her to Europe for a reconciliation trip.

"We're going first class, and we're staying in five-star hotels. Can you believe it?" she said.

I couldn't. For a skinflint like Grant, this offer of luxury was the equivalent of a belly-crawl to Lourdes, penitence of a profound nature.

Back on top of the world, Violet now took out her animosity on those who had ignored her when she was down rather than on Grant himself. But she saved the cobra venom for Cynthia. She vowed to "bury Cynthia Rinehart," if it was the last thing she ever did. And I believed her. I wouldn't have wanted to tangle with Violet when she was mad, not after what she told me about planting that bottle of gin. There were layers to that girl I was only just beginning to fathom. However, it looked as if Cynthia was going to bury herself before Violet ever got a hold of a shovel.

———

The aftershocks from Corinna Huff's article just kept coming. Senator Pomador, one of the leading figures on Cynthia's board, was indicted for accepting substantial gifts without reporting them. Indicting a senior senator—particularly one as popular and distinguished as Pomador—is no small matter. Cynthia rallied to his defense, of course. But people wondered if some of the gifts he was accused of taking had come from her.

Senator Grider announced that the Finance Committee would begin hearings to discuss financial abuses by nonprofits, and that those
hearings would lead to stricter laws governing the operation of foundations and other tax-exempt institutions.

Grider issued this statement: "The laws governing nonprofits have
received no serious scrutiny since the 1960s. Over the years, a growing number of people have used tax-exempt entities to fund lavish
lifestyles for themselves and their friends rather than doling out the
money to the people who actually deserve it. This committee intends
to recommend that charity does *not* begin at home."

The first witness scheduled to appear before the Finance Committee was Cynthia Rinehart.

———

The weekend before the hearings began, the Huffs gave one of their
famous parties. This one was to celebrate the twenty-first birthday
of their only daughter, Daphne. Daphne Huff, a studious and ami-
able young woman, was heiress to one of the great names in politics.
Barkley Huff had been an intimate friend of Gay Harding and all the
hostesses in the old Georgetown set. In his day, this witty and patrician man had navigated some exceptionally murky political waters
with probity and skill. He never lost that strong sense of righteousness
that can so easily fade in politicians who hold high office for a long
period of time—Senator Pomador being the current case in point. In
that way, Huff reminded me a little of Grider. However, Barkley Huff
was known for his charm and an appealingly self-deprecating sense
of humor—unlike Grider, who was more like a hunk of peanut brittle
until you got to know him. Recently, Huff had resigned his Senate
seat in order to write a memoir he facetiously entitled *Huff Puffing.*

Corinna Huff was the perfect foil for her urbane, easygoing husband. Acid-tongued, irreverent, and judgmental, Corinna ruffled
feathers easily. Yet she was a lot of fun to be around, especially if you
liked hearing the latest gossip tinctured with her sharp, venomous
insights.

In many ways, the Huffs' parties were what Gay Harding's parties
had once been—a mix of high-level people from all walks of Washington life: politicians, Supreme Court justices, top brass, writers,
artists, famous Washington personalities, and, of course, the media

elite. These gatherings were larger and glitzier than Mrs. Harding's, in keeping with the larger, glitzier spirit of the times. Corinna occupied the throne that Cynthia had once set her cap for and never attained, despite having bought Mrs. Harding's old house.

Grider picked me up at my house. I asked him about Senator Pomador who was on the news smiling and denying all the accusations. Oh, those tombstone teeth! Cemetery row. Grider seemed genuinely sad about his colleague's troubles.

"Pomador used to be a good man. He just let his sense of entitlement get in the way of his judgment. When you're a public servant, you gotta be extra careful not to lose sight of the reason the voters put you there. You're supposed to be doing them a service, not yourself."

"How does this affect Cynthia Rinehart?" I asked him. "He was on her board."

"I can't see that it helps either of them," he said.

It was a balmy fall night, and we strolled to the Huffs' on N Street, only a few blocks away. Their Federal-style brick house, built in the nineteenth century and added onto in later years, was a perfect place for large parties. The entertainment rooms were airy and spacious, with high ceilings, unlike period Federal houses, which tended to be cramped and dark.

Corinna, Barkley, and their daughter Daphne were standing near the front door, greeting guests as they entered. The minute Corinna saw Grider, she broke away from the receiving line and pulled him off into a corner, where the two of them embarked on what looked to me like an agitated discussion. I wandered off into the crowd by myself in search of a friendly face. I saw Peggy and Rolly Myers across the room. They were engrossed in serious conversation with Stephanie Baker, a charter member of what Violet called the "gloom and doom" brigade. Stephanie was a worthy woman who somehow felt obliged to remind people of impending world disasters, particularly when they were having fun. I didn't want to interrupt.

Unfortunately, it was one of those parties where no one wants to talk to someone who is less famous than they are, so there is a constant swirl of expectation coupled with dissatisfaction. The few conversations I had were diluted by the conversant's inability to look me in the eye when we were talking. People kept glancing over my shoulder in an effort to see if anyone more important was coming into view and possibly available for a chat. This grew a trifle wearing. I headed out into the garden, where a huge striped tent sheltered dozens of round tables set for dinner. With candles flickering in the darkness, it looked like a field of tiny campfires on the eve of battle.

No one was around except a waiter filling up the water glasses and a man sitting alone at a table in the shadows.

"Reven! That you?" he called out. I recognized his voice. It was Bob Poll.

I gave him a tepid little wave.

"C'mon over and talk to me! There's too much shock and awe in there! It's a lot friendlier out here."

There's never any harm in being polite, so I walked over for a chat.

"Siddown, siddown," he said, patting the white folding chair beside him. He poured himself a drink from a half-empty bottle of vodka and offered me one. I declined.

"So . . . no chocolate fountains here, unfortunately—just hard liquor. How's the antiques business these days?"

"Fine. How's married life?"

"I wouldn't know. Mel and I are separated." I have to say I was surprised.

He raised his glass, toasted the air, drained what was left, and poured himself another. "Happens to me all the time," he went on. "Happened to me with my first wife. Married her when I should've divorced her. Happened again with Mel. No hard feelings. Just hard cash—although Mel's not greedy," he said with a bitter laugh.

"I'm sorry." I wasn't.

"Why? I'm a free man again. But you're not a free woman, from what I hear. . . . Still going out with Senator Grimface?"

I stood up. "It's been nice talking to you, Bob—"

"Hold on! Whereya goin'? Did I say something offensive? If I did, I 'pologize. Siddown."

"I have to get back."

I turned to go. He grabbed my hand. His face looked demonic in the candlelight, or maybe I just thought that because of what Violet and Gunner had said about him possibly being involved in the murders.

"She was such a pretty girl. . . ."

I looked at him quizzically. "Who?"

"You . . . you're a pretty girl."

"You said 'she.' " I pulled my hand away.

"Oh. Did I? I meant you. . . . You wanna know what people should never be allowed to do?"

"What?"

"Get old."

"Why not?"

"Because they just shouldn't. We should all live fast, die young, and leave a beautiful corpse. . . . Never mind. You're too young to remember that."

He frightened me a little. I was anxious to get away.

"See you," I said, leaving.

"You will, you know! You'll see me! When you least expect it, you're elected! It's your lucky day! Remember that one? *Candid Camera*?"

I hurried back inside the house. Grider ambled over to me.

"Where've you been?"

"Just getting some air."

"Mind if we scoot along outta here?" he said.

"If you like."

"They're not serving dinner for another hour, and I have a big day tomorrow. What say you come over to my house for a bite? My housekeeper left me a nice roast chicken and some salad. I'll cook you up some grits—my specialty."

———

Grider lived in a compact Queen Anne Revival house in Cleveland Park. It had a small turret and a wide front porch with two rocking chairs and a swing. He admitted he hadn't changed a stick of furniture since his wife died, and it looked like she hadn't changed a stick during the entire twenty years they'd lived there. The faded curtains, exposed extension cords, and worn carpets discolored in spots from ancient dog urine were the hallmarks of a shabby gentility that scorned the idea of replacing old, worn things. It was a house that relied on memory, mistrusting change of any kind, a house that ignored the passage of time and its effects, clinging to the belief that what had once been good would always be good, no matter how it appeared now.

I hated it. I wanted to torch the place and redo it from top to bottom. Naturally, I didn't tell that to Grider. Not only did he seem unaware of its shabby state, he was actually proud of the old homestead.

"If Flora had to re-cover anything, she always used the same exact fabric. She was a woman who knew her mind."

The living room was antimacassar hell. Those crocheted white dirt catchers, yellowing from age, were draped over the backs and arms of every piece of upholstered furniture. A batch of family photographs populated a mahogany credenza against the wall. The largest one, front and center, was a picture of Grider and his late wife in their younger days. They reminded me of Grant Wood's famous painting *American Gothic.* They dared the viewer to challenge their lack of humor.

Grider fixed us a nice little dinner made from his housekeeper's leftovers. He also made me grits, as promised. They were quite delicious.

"I thought grits were a southern dish," I said.

"Neighbor of ours in Omaha was originally from Rock Hill, South Carolina. He taught Flora how to make 'em. But hers were so awful I had to learn how to make 'em myself."

We ate in the little breakfast nook, just off the kitchen with its ancient linoleum floor. He offered me a glass of the sherry he kept on hand for company. It tasted foul, but I drank it anyway. I was a little nervous, being there alone with him so late at night. I'd been to the house before, but just to pick him up, and never for any length of time. I hoped he wasn't going to pounce on me and ruin a lovely friendship.

"Corinna seemed very anxious to talk to you tonight," I said as we ate.

"Yup. She had some very interesting information for me. Sharp as a tack, that girl is."

I waited for him to elaborate. When he just kept eating, I said, "Can you share it, as they say?"

"Nope. Well . . . I shouldn't. Senate business. But I s'pose it can't do any harm, since you'll find out about it tomorrow anyway."

He took a swig of milk, which left a thin white mustachio on his upper lip.

"You have a mustachio," I said, pointing to my own lip.

He quickly wiped it off with his napkin. "See now, some gals woulda just ignored that. Then I woulda looked in the mirror later on and felt like a damn fool. But you take care of me."

He stared at me with cow eyes.

I cleared my throat. "So what did Corinna have to say?" That broke the spell.

"Well, see, the Rinehart gal, who's testifying before us tomorrow? She fired her lawyer."

"Is that significant?"

Grider guffawed. "I'll say. She's hired some tough son of a gun from Billgood and Connors. You don't hire Billgood and Connors unless you're expecting some nasty litigation."

"So you think she's worried?"

"If she ain't, she oughta be."

"Grant left her none too soon, I guess."

"So he went back to his wife, eh?"

"Yup. They're in Europe as we speak. The reconciliation tour."

"He should never have left her to begin with," Grider said. "Marriage is a sacred state and should be respected as such."

"I take it you don't believe in divorce?"

"Nope. I think once you make a commitment, that's it. You stick with it, no matter what the consequences."

"You're a better man than I am, Gunga-Din."

"Know that film, do you? Cary Grant—one of my favorite actors. Never won an Oscar. Anyway, I don't say other people have to think like I do. No law against divorce. People only have to think like I do where the law is involved."

"Like Cynthia Rinehart."

"Exactly. . . . Like to talk to you about something else, if I may."

"Sure."

"Let's clear the dishes and go into the parlor."

I loved that he called it the parlor. Grider and I sat on the couch—or the settee, as he said. He didn't look at me. He stared straight ahead through the lace-curtained windows out at the black night, tapping his foot nervously as he spoke.

"Went fishing back home last week, and realized I'm out of practice," he began.

If ever there was a conversation stopper, that was it.

"Really? You didn't catch anything?" I said, feigning an interest just to be polite.

"Nope. Made me think of us."

"Oh?"

"You and I have been keeping company for some time now," he went on. "We've both had a good look-see at each other, and I'd like to get some idea where we're headed."

"I'm not exactly sure what you mean." Actually, I was sure. But I didn't want to go there.

"Like to know if your intentions toward me are honorable," he said, cranking up one of his deep belly laughs.

I laughed too, in an effort to disguise my discomfort.

"What I mean is, I'm not getting any younger—although you're a youth tonic for me. I'm feeling an itch to settle down. I was a happily married man once, and I'd like to be so again. Get my drift?" He glanced at me out of the corner of his eye.

"Is this a proposal?"

"I guess it is. In a way, yes. I guess it is. Not a formal one. But I'll give you a formal one—down on my knees with a ring the old-fashioned way. Promise."

I paused for a long moment. I didn't want to offend him by appearing flip or uncaring.

"Oh, Zack . . . I'm so flattered. Truly I am. But we haven't even, you know—"

"Done the do?" he interrupted. "I know. I'm old-fashioned about that too."

"Well, I know you're not a virgin," I said, glancing at the generations displayed on the credenza.

"Nope. But waiting to consummate a relationship under the sanctity of marriage is not something I'm opposed to."

I just looked at him and shook my head in amazement. "You're so dear and so quaint—like something out of the nineteenth century."

"Not a bad century if you don't count the Indian massacres, which I do. Unforgivable treachery on the part of our government. But I won't go into that now. Did you know they closed the patent office in the 1890s, 'cause they didn't think anything else could be invented?"

Another conversation stopper.

"Look, Zack, I just don't think I'm ready to settle down."

"With me, or in general?"

I hesitated before answering. "Maybe a little bit of both." He bowed his head. I felt bad for him. And for me. I went on, trying to be as gentle as I knew how.

"I'm really fond of you, Zack. I *am*. And I admire you so much. You're such a fine and principled man."

"Oh-oh. When a woman says that, you're a goner."

"It's just that, well, I . . . I'm not sure I feel about you the way I think I need to feel about a husband, that's all."

"That's enough." He rose abruptly from the couch. "Appreciate your honesty. Now, if you don't mind, I'll take you home. Big day tomorrow."

————

We drove in silence back to my house. He parked the Buick and walked me to my door.

"Does this mean I won't see you anymore?" I asked him.

"I'm going to take some time to think about this. You take some time too. They say absence makes the heart grow fonder. Maybe that'll be the case."

"Maybe it will. I hope so."

" 'Course they also say, out of sight, out of mind."

"Somehow, I don't think I'll forget you."

He shuffled his feet. "You ever get into a spot, you tell them you have a friend in high places. Hear me?"

"Thank you, Zack. I'll remember that."

"By the way, I once asked you who you'd come back as if you could come back as anyone. Remember?"

"I remember. You said you'd come back as Teddy Roosevelt and, after that, Fred Astaire."

"What about you? Given it any thought?"

"I'm afraid not."

"Well, I know who I'd like you to come back as."

"Who?"

"Ginger Rogers. So we could dance together forever."

He kissed me on the cheek and ambled down the steps, favoring his right leg. Before he ducked into the Buick, he called out, "Take care now!"

"Good luck tomorrow!" I called back.

As I watched him drive off, a feeling of desolation swept over me. I wished I could be more attracted to him, but passion is like faith: you either feel it, or you don't.

Chapter 40

The Finance Committee hearings were televised live on C-SPAN at ten o'clock the following morning. I tuned in just as Cynthia was taking her seat in front of the committee. She was accompanied by her lawyer, a thin man with sharp features and eyes like razorblades, who kept leaning in and whispering to her. She was dressed in a prim black suit accented with a white collar and cuffs, suggesting the piety of a cleric. Her hair was pulled back in a bun—echoes of Rainy Bolton. She wore no noticeable makeup—not even lipstick—and no jewelry. In fact, she looked so demure that I almost didn't recognize her. It was hard to believe this was the same woman I'd seen over a year ago at the opening of the Symphony Ball, when she'd burst onto the Washington scene as flashy and formidable as a bolt of lightning.

After a brief explanation of why they were all there, Grider began the grilling. Speaking in a slow, deliberate voice, he came at Cynthia with a quiverful of questions, one right after another, aimed directly at the real heart of the matter—namely, income tax evasion.

How much salary did she pay herself? How did she justify the expenses she had charged to her foundation? Had she purchased her house with foundation money? Did she use foundation money to buy her private plane? Were her Rinehart Retreats funded by foundation money, and if so, what did they accomplish, and who did they really benefit? Was more foundation money spent on her lavish Golden Key dinners than on charity? Did she buy the gifts she gave people with foundation money? On and on, like that.

Cynthia answered each of his questions with the same words in the same dull tone of voice: "Senator, on the advice of counsel, I invoke my right to plead the Fifth Amendment." She must have said it at least fifty times.

Grider got fed up. He glared at Cynthia and said, "I understand that you do not wish to incriminate yourself. And that is your right. But it is my right to tell you and others in your position that it's not your right to live high off the hog of a charity, just as it's not your right to donate a sow's ear, call it a silk purse, and claim a ten-thousand-dollar deduction for it. Privileged entities must be held accountable. Otherwise there will be no privilege in this country. There will be revolution."

———

Violet got back from Europe a couple of days later. She called me up and begged me to come over. The Ancient Maureener had TiVoed Cynthia's appearance before the Senate Finance committee, on Violet's instructions. Violet wanted me to watch it with her. I hurried over to her house. Grant opened the door and just stood there, staring at me. Jet lag notwithstanding, he sure didn't look like a man who'd spent the last three weeks lounging around in five-star European hotels with the woman he supposedly loved. He looked like a hostage who'd just been released from a terrorist cell in downtown Baghdad. He had lost weight, and his face was drawn. A wispy little pilot light of apprehension flickered deep within his eyes as he greeted me.

"Hello, Reven," he said stiffly, stepping aside to let me in.

"Hi, Grant. Did you have a nice vacation?"

"Let's just say I hope I won't have to pay nine dollars for a glass of orange juice ever again in my life," he said.

"Oh. Well, I hope it was fresh."

"Not fresh enough. Violet's in the library."

Violet greeted me warmly, but she too looked haggard. I had to wonder if their reconciliation trip hadn't been more like a Himalayan trek. Before we discussed anything, Violet wanted to see the hearings. She switched on the TV. We sat down next to each other on the couch.

"Oh, my God, she looks like the flying nun!" Violet exclaimed at the sight of Cynthia on-screen.

Since I'd already seen the hearing, I was more interested in watching Violet. She sat leaning forward, her eyes glued to the set. Every time Grider asked Cynthia a question, Violet raised her fist and cried, "Go for it, Zack!" or, "That's right, get 'er!"

When it became clear that Cynthia wasn't going to do anything but plead the Fifth, Violet turned to me and said, "Oh, she is so toast!"

Grant walked into the library just as the show was ending. Cynthia was still on camera. Violet didn't say a word. She crossed her arms in front of her and stared at Grant, waiting for his reaction. He watched impassively for a few seconds, then turned and left the room without saying a word. The hearing concluded. Violet switched off the television.

"How was Europe?" I asked.

She didn't answer right away. She was lost in thought.

"How was Europe?" I repeated.

She snapped to. "Okay. Grant bought me a new outfit in Paris."

"I can't wait to see it."

"I have it on."

I looked more closely at the dowdy brown wool suit with its boxy jacket and round collar, wondering what Lisa would say.

"Very pretty," I said, trying to sound convincing.

"You hate it, I know."

"It was sweet of him to buy it, though."

"Not that sweet. He bought it out of guilt."

"How are you two?"

Violet sighed and slumped back on the couch. "Who knows? Are things ever the same after something like this?"

"Did you guys talk about it at all?"

"*Talk? Grant?* Are you kidding? Besides, what's there to say? If you take someone back after an affair, you can't keep rubbing their nose in it."

"I guess. Well, at least your long national nightmare's over. He's home."

She snickered. "Yeah . . . so are the suitcases. He's more withdrawn than ever."

Now that was really saying something.

"Oh, he'll get over it," I assured her. "Just give him time."

Violet shook her head. "No . . . he's changed in some fundamental way. I can't put my finger on it, but this whole fiasco notwithstanding, he's just different."

"How so?"

"I keep thinking about what it took for him to leave me in the first place, knowing the scandal it would cause. Risking his parents' disapproval. Having to face his son. I can't figure it out. Let me ask you something, Rev. You think she was *that* good in bed?"

"You want to know what I think? I think he had a midlife crisis, and now he's come to his senses. It happens."

"I agree with the first part of that. But I don't think he's over it, and I don't think he's over *her*. I think he still loves her. I think he's obsessed with her. I think she'll always be between us."

"Well, if you think that, you should leave him," I said.

Violet looked at me askance. "Are you crazy? You think I got him back just so I could leave him?"

"But if you think he still loves her—"

"That's not the point."

"What is the point?"

"Reven, sometimes you amaze me. You really do. Marriage isn't always about love."

"It is for me," I said, thinking of how I turned down Grider.

"You're not me. I'm much more practical than you are."

"But there has to be love, doesn't there?"

She hesitated. "I guess. But love changes. It becomes part of a larger canvas. And right now, I'm looking at the big picture. Where am I gonna go at my age, huh? I ask you. You think I'm gonna find another guy? A better situation? Dream on. I was lucky to get Grant when I did. I have a wonderful son, a beautiful house, a position in the community, and a date for New Year's Eve. Believe me, I'm much better off *with* Grant than I am without him—even if he does still love her."

Violet looked at me with eyes that begged for contradiction. I had no idea whether Grant still loved Cynthia or had ever loved Cynthia, or whether if he was even capable of love in the traditional sense. But I knew that my friend needed to be reassured.

"Listen, Violet, Grant loves you. And you love him. This has just been a terrible time, that's all. It *will* get better. You must believe that."

"It either will or it won't," she said.

That was something I hadn't heard her say since boarding school.

Back then, I'd say something innocuous like, "Do you think it will rain?" and Violet would respond, "It either will or it won't." It usually meant she was depressed.

"Come on, let's go out," I said, getting up. "I'll show you something that'll cheer you up."

———

Violet and I stood looking up at the blue-and-white Sotheby's For Sale sign planted near the gate in front of Cynthia's house.

"Wow. When did it go on the market?" Violet asked.

"The sign went up the day of the hearing. Peggy told me that Cynthia's selling her plane too. Dumping assets. Probably hoping to make a deal. Feel better now?"

"I do. Revenge is restorative. Thank you, Rev. Come on, let's go get a coffee."

We strolled down R Street toward Wisconsin. It was a muggy, overcast day.

"What will happen to her now, do you think?" Violet asked.

"Depends on if she broke any laws. One thing I'm sure of. She'll be the catalyst for changing some laws. Grider will see to that."

"How are things with you two?"

"He asked me to marry him."

Violet stopped short. She grabbed my arm. "You're kidding! Have you been having an affair without telling me?"

"No! And that's the point. He's so old-fashioned, he thinks it's better not to sleep with someone before marriage."

"The old stick has a point. Who would want to sleep with him voluntarily?"

"He's not so bad. He kind of grew on me. He wasn't a bad kisser."

"Ugh! Reven! How *could* you?"

"I admire him. I wish I could like him in that way."

We walked on. "I wish you could too. I'd love you to be a senator's wife. Couldn't you just close your eyes and think of England?" Violet said.

I laughed. "I'm too much of a romantic, I'm afraid."

"Not me, boy. Romance is just too wearing. . . . I should make Grant buy that house for me now."

"Great idea! Talk about poetic justice."

Violet snickered. "Yeah, right. Look, I may not be the arch romantic of the decade, but even *I* don't have the stomach to live in a place
where my husband cohabited with a vampire."

"Remember when Rainy Bolton told you that house would always
belong to Gay Harding, no matter who owned it?"

"How could I forget?" Violet said.

"She was right."

———

My phone rang at two o'clock the next morning, jarring me out of a
sound sleep. I fumbled for the receiver and said a groggy, "Hello."

"Hey," said the voice on the other end of the line. He said it like it
wasn't two in the morning, and like I'd know who he was just from
that single syllable. I sat up in bed in the dark on alert.

"*Bob?*"

"Shall I hang up?"

I hesitated. "No, I should."

"But you won't, will you? I need to talk to you," he said in a plaintive voice.

"What do you want?"

"To hear your voice, that's all."

"Well, now you've heard it. Good-bye."

"Wait! Please!" he cried.

There's a French phrase, *Nostalgie de la boue.* It literally means, "Long-
ing for the mud." Most people interpret it as slumming, but you can
also interpret it as having an attraction to things that are degrading or
dangerous. In my case, that would be having a conversation with Bob
Poll. Why I didn't hang up on him is beyond me. I guess part of me was
curious to know what he'd say. He sounded sad, not sinister.

"I looked for you again at the Huffs' party, but you'd gone. . . .
Gone away . . . away, away."

"We left early."

"You and Senator Grimface?"

"Bob, I need to go back to sleep."

"I need to wake up from a nightmare," he said.

"What are you talking about? Your marriage?"

"No . . . I don't know. . . . I mean, I *do* know, but . . . I can't talk
about it."

"Talk about what?"

"Nothing. . . . Tell me a story."

Then I got it. Bob was drunk. Really drunk. And he was beginning to sound sinister, not sad.

"You tell me one," I said.

"Okay. . . . Once upon a time there was a beautiful girl who worked in a shop. . . . And a big bad man saw her and took her away. . . . I just wanna tell you again how sorry I am about that beautiful li'l girl. . . . Should've called you when I heard. . . . My fault."

That woke me up with a vengeance. I sat up, on alert. "What was your fault?"

"Not calling after what Maxey did. He's such a bad boy."

Maxey? A bad *boy*? What the *hell*? What was this cutesy term of endearment for Maxwell all of a sudden? Even if Bob was drunk, that was one helluva way to refer to a homicidal sexual psychopath.

I was terrified. Was Bob somehow involved in these murders, like Gunner and Violet suspected? Maybe he wasn't *directly* involved, but he sounded like he knew things about "Maxey" he'd never told the police. Or maybe he had told the police. Maybe he had incriminated himself in some way. God knows Gunner was always hinting around that there was a lot more going on with this case than anybody suspected.

I let him ramble on a while longer, mainly because I was too afraid to hang up on him, but also because I thought he might inadvertently spill some important information, drunk as he was. After he lapsed into incoherence, I gently eased him off the phone.

The second he hung up, I called Gunner. I didn't care that it was so late. I had to talk to him. There was no answer. I left a message on his voice mail and texted him, "MUST SEE YOU. URGENT." I received a text message the next morning telling me he'd come by and see me in the shop that afternoon.

Chapter 41

Gunner dropped by the next day around three o'clock. I told Polo he could take the afternoon off. I closed up the shop. I didn't want anybody interrupting us. Gunner and I went upstairs to my office. I offered him a drink because I was going to have one myself—several, in fact. He declined. I poured myself a stiff scotch from a beautiful cut crystal Waterford decanter, then proceeded to give him an earful about my two a.m. conversation with Bob. He listened without comment. Finally, I asked him point-blank: "Is Violet right? Is Bob involved in these murders?"

"Let's hear your theory," he said.

"Okay. . . . I've really been thinking about this. Bob married Melody very suddenly, right? I mean, he didn't even tell me, and we were pretty hot and heavy. So I've always wondered why. Why *then*? And I was thinking, maybe she knows stuff about him that no one else knows. A wife can't be forced to testify against her husband. Gunner, I wish I had a tape of last night's call. Maybe Bob wasn't *directly* involved, but I'm sure he either knew or suspected what *Maxey*, as he called him, was up to. I don't know. You told me Maxwell's been hinting someone else is involved. Maybe Bob's afraid Maxwell will implicate him. Or maybe he feels guilty and wants to confess. People actually do feel guilt sometimes, I guess—although you'd never know from what goes on today. You know I've resisted this for a long time, but now I think you've been right all along. I think Bob's *definitely* involved."

Gunner nodded as I spoke, appraising me with his sharp dark eyes.

I was certain I'd hit the nail on the head or come pretty close. I have to say, I thought he was damn impressed.

He cleared his throat. "Tell me something. . . . How much have you and Violet discussed your lives right after you graduated?"

The question threw me for a loop.

"What's that got to do with Bob Poll?"

"Just answer the question, if you don't mind. I'm talking about the time after you both graduated up until the time she arrived in Washington. You ever talk about those years with her?"

"Um, yeah. Sort of. I guess." I was irritated he was veering off the subject.

"So what kind of things did you two discuss?"

"I don't know. The usual stuff. I wished I'd been more focused. Believe me, I missed so many opportunities. But you can't look back, right?"

"Did you ever talk about anything but you?"

"Thanks a lot!"

"You ever talk about Violet? Did Violet talk much about herself?"

"Yes! Of course. Believe me, I know *everything* about Violet's stellar career."

"Like what?"

"Okay, smarty," I said, rising to the challenge. "I know she had a Junior Year Abroad and that she graduated magna cum laude from DePaul. That she went to USC law school—stuff like that. Working on the Indian reservation. Being interested in environmental law. No men, of course. She didn't have any men to tell me about. I'm pretty sure she was a virgin when she met Grant. Those two, what a pair! Can't you just see them in bed? Two lacrosse sticks clicking away at each other!" I laughed. Gunner didn't.

"So, Violet came to Washington as an environmental lobbyist, is that right?"

"Yeah. What's your point?" I was growing impatient; I knew I was definitely onto something with Bob Poll, and I thought Gunner was just avoiding that subject because he didn't want to answer any of my questions, as usual.

"You ever go see her up on Capitol Hill?" he asked.

"No. Frankly, I can't think of anything more boring—except a root canal."

"And you know all this stuff about Violet *how* exactly?"

"What are you getting at?"

"How did you know she took her Junior Year Abroad, for example?"

"She told me all about it."

"Where'd she go?"

"England. London University. They have an exchange program with DePaul. She loved London. Like I said, Violet made the most of every opportunity she ever got—unlike yours truly. *What's all this got to do with Bob Poll?*" I cried.

Gunner reached inside his jacket pocket and pulled out a photocopy of what looked like an old newspaper clipping. He folded the bottom half down, so that only the picture was visible, not the caption. He handed it to me. "Recognize anyone?"

It was a picture of an old lady in a wheelchair and a young woman standing behind her. They were on the deck of a luxury liner in front of a row of wooden lounge chairs. Caught in the frame was a passing steward in a white coat, artfully balancing a tray with two glasses and a bottle of champagne on the palm of his right hand.

"My God! That's Violet when she was young!" I exclaimed. "She looked so different then. Is that her grandmother? Where'd you get this picture?"

"Unfold the paper and read the caption," he said.

I did as he instructed. " 'Mrs. Eleanor Pagett and her companion aboard the *QE II.*' Her *companion?*" I was mystified.

"Violet's Junior Year Abroad." Gunner snickered.

I looked at him, uncomprehending. "I don't understand."

"I'll enlighten you. Violet was kicked out of DePaul University her sophomore year for nonattendance of classes. She got a job as a paid companion working for Mrs. Eleanor Pagett, a rich widow from Chicago."

"*What?*" I whispered.

"She accompanied Mrs. Pagett to London in what would have been her junior year of college—if she'd stayed in college. They went first class aboard the *QE II.*"

I could hardly believe my ears.

Gunner went on: "Mrs. Pagett liked Violet a lot. Took her under her wing. Violet seems to be pretty good at playing the victim and making people feel sorry for her."

"I can testify to that," I said softly, thinking back to when she first arrived at Wheelock.

"But when the old lady died on Violet's watch, as they say, there were questions. She left Violet a nice chunka change in her will. I spoke to Mrs. Pagett's niece. She remembers that at the time of her aunt's death there was some talk about pressing charges against her 'companion'—that would be Violet. Nothing ever came of it, though. Hard to prove murder when an old woman takes a bad fall."

I was speechless.

Gunner then related a history that bore absolutely no relation to the one Violet had ever told me or ever written about herself in "Class Notes." She may have lived in Chicago, Los Angeles, and Oklahoma, but she sure wasn't doing any of the things she claimed to be doing in any of those places.

"The University of Southern California has no record of a Violet McCloud as a law student, a graduate student, or any other type of student, for that matter. The Osage Nation Reservation has no record of her teaching or being involved in any way in Indian affairs. And as for her being an environmental lobbyist, deeply dedicated to saving the planet? Pretty near anyone can say they're a lobbyist. Technically, you don't even need a college degree. You can practically fall on your knees, raise your hands up to God, and say: 'I am a lobbyist!' It helps to be a good bullshitter or a good actor, or both. I'm exaggerating, but you get the drift," Gunner said.

By the time Gunner finished, I was reeling. I couldn't take it all in. So much for the sweet innocent roommate I'd introduced to Grant! I felt physically ill. I desperately needed to get some air. I told Gunner I had to get out of the shop. We started walking and found ourselves at the Oak Hill Cemetery. It was still visiting hours, and the big gates were open. I suggested we go in. Somehow a graveyard seemed appropriate for this occasion. There was no one around. We had death all to ourselves.

———

Gunner and I strolled down the path to Usherville. Wispy clouds drifted across a vibrant blue afternoon sky. The leaves were beginning to turn. The chill of fall was in the air. We sat down on the cold stone bench just outside the Hollis tomb. The enormity of what Gunner had just told me was seeping in slowly, like rain on hard soil. I closed my eyes and tried to wrap my mind around this news.

So Violet was a fraud. A total and complete fraud. I just couldn't believe it. I kept asking myself if there'd been any clues, any signs I'd overlooked all these years. I knew she often lied to other people in the interests of social life. How many times had she pretended to like people she disliked and agree with things she didn't really agree with, or complimented someone on a hideous dress, then turned to me and made a disparaging face? But we all did stuff like that. We all wore masks. Other than that, I really couldn't think of anything that would have tipped me off to this extraordinary revelation, except maybe her fascination with serial killers—particularly ones like Ted Bundy, BTK, Gary Ridgway, and Herbert Baumeister—all of whom had led so-called normal lives and fooled everyone close to them, even their wives and girlfriends.

Violet was just like me. We were both basically nice girls from the same privileged sphere of life, with mutual interests and a good sense of humor. Or so I'd always imagined. I knew she lied to others, but I never dreamed she would lie to me, her best friend. I just couldn't get my head around the fact that she wasn't the person she had always claimed to be.

"So what was she doing all that time she said she was involved in those other things?" I said at last.

Gunner shrugged. "That's what I couldn't find out. It'd be very interesting to know."

"You can say that again."

We lapsed into silence once more. I thought back to the day I'd gone over to Violet's house when Peggy was there, and Violet had refused to speak to me or even acknowledge my presence because I hadn't told her about Grant. She was up on her high horse then, looking down at me like I was some peasant in the mud when she said, "If there's one thing I hate above all other things in this world, it's a *liar*!" Those were her exact words. I remembered them like you'd remember the sentence of a judge.

I've always said: tell me what you criticize, and I'll tell you who you are. Violet dared to accuse *me* of being a liar when her *whole life* was a lie! If that ain't the definition of chutzpah, I don't know what is.

Gunner faced me, "So aren't you kind of curious how I know all this?"

And of course, the minute he said it, I thought, Yes, of course! How the hell did he find all this out? And *why*? Why investigate Violet, of all people?

"Yes, of course! What ever gave you the idea to even go there?"

"Nancy Sawtelle. Miss Montrose, as you call her."

"What about her?" I said warily.

"I gotta tell you I never believed Miss Montrose was done by the same guy who did those other girls. I always thought it was a copy-cat."

"Why?"

"For one thing, Nancy Sawtelle was older than the others. She had at least four blows to her head. It looked a lot more personal to me. Her panties were down, but she wasn't violated. The theory was that the killer had been interrupted. But I figured it was something else—like whoever did her staged the crime to make it look like attempted rape. The killer could have learned a lot about the MO of the Beltway Basher just by reading the papers."

"You were the only one who picked up on this?"

"Here's the thing. Treating Sawtelle as a victim of the Beltway Basher ups the manpower devoted to her case. It was a close enough MO for the time being. They figured, lump her in with the serial killer and see what shakes out. There just aren't the resources to devote a lot of hours to one case that looks so similar to the others. And you don't wanna get sued for not giving it your all. I didn't agree with that approach. But they weren't gonna listen to me, so I did some work on my own. . . . You remember her calendar, right?"

"Of course," I said. "I'm sorry I told Violet. I still feel bad about that."

"Yeah, well, they found other things in her apartment too—fake drivers' licenses, a couple of fake socials, a bunch of personal papers, clippings—stuff that nobody really focused on at the time. Not to mention the hundred thou they found in her safety deposit box. They were all focused on that calendar and the fact that she'd worked at King Arthur's."

I couldn't quite figure out where he was going, but I knew I wasn't going to like it when he got there.

"No one appreciates the value of good old-fashioned police work anymore. Everyone wants blood and trace, blood and trace, like the lab can tell you about the life of the victim," he said derisively. "Labs just tell you *how* a person died, not why. . . . Me? I go back to the victim's life, because nine outta ten times it's the life that causes the death. . . . So, on my own, I start to review the evidence on Miss Montrose. I'm going through all the stuff we found in her apartment, and lo and behold, what do I come across?"

"I don't know. What?"

"A stack of little books. Little white-and-purple pamphlet-type books called *Passages*."

My jaw dropped. "*You're kidding!* Wait—Nancy Sawtelle had Wheelock alumnae bulletins in her apartment?" Gunner nodded. "Wow! That is too freaking *weird*!"

"There was stuff underlined in them too. Black, scrawly, angry underlines. Stuff about someone named Violet McCloud Bolton who lived in Washington, D.C."

"*Oh, my God! Violet!*"

"So I find out that Violet turns out to be Mrs. Grant Bolton Jr., wife of the president of the Potomac Bank. And I'm thinking to myself, What's this Sawtelle gal, a drifter and a con woman, doing with these fancy little books? And how come she's so interested in a society lady like Mrs. Bolton?"

"Yeah, *why*? How would she even *know* Violet?" I was fascinated.

"Obviously, I can't ask Nancy Sawtelle, because she's dead. And I don't really want to go ask Mrs. Bolton directly, because I don't want to tip her off right away if there is some connection. And then there's this calendar, which tracks somebody in society. So anyway, I have to find a way to get more information about Mrs. Bolton's life. And I see from the society columns that she's very good friends with a woman who owns an antiques store in Georgetown—a woman I'd briefly met when I was first canvassing the area."

He paused and waited for my reaction. I felt like the wind had been knocked out of me when I realized what he was telling me.

"So that's why you came back into the shop and chatted me up? That's why you made me your *confidential informant*?" I said, putting a sarcastic emphasis on the words. "All this time you've just been using me to get to Violet?"

Gunner didn't say a word.

I shook my head in disgust. "I don't believe it. . . . I really thought you were my friend."

"I *am* your friend."

I was too stunned to move. I just sat there.

"Talk about being set up," I said, after a time. "So you mean to tell me that all this stuff about Bob Poll was just a smokescreen to get to Violet? Is that what you're saying?"

"No. . . . I think Bob Poll may well be involved in the Beltway Basher murders. But you've gotta separate them from Nancy Sawtelle. Sawtelle's another story. Wardell's not confessing to her, and I don't think he did her."

"Has he confessed to those other girls yet?"

"No. But I know he did them." Gunner bowed his head.

"So who killed Nancy Sawtelle, Detective Gunner?" I asked defiantly.

"Don't hate me, Reven. I'm just trying to do my job."

"Of course you are!" I snapped.

"Bear with me, okay? After they caught Wardell, people figured these six murders had been solved. Case closed. I tried to tell them Sawtelle was different, but no dice. But I can't get over the fact that this woman has these fancy little booklets in her apartment. And I still wanna know why she was so interested in Violet. So on my own, I take a little trip to Rhode Island, and pay a visit to your old school."

I let out a guffaw. "You went up to *Wheelock*? Holy crow. This just gets better and better."

"Your old headmaster, Mr. Trowbridge, is retired, but he lives nearby. Looked him up. Nice old guy. Remembers you very well. Said you were the star of the class."

"That and a dime." I shrugged.

"He also remembers Violet. Said he took a chance on her. I asked him what that meant, but he said he wasn't at liberty to go into detail. He told me how you protected Violet and how you two were best friends. He said she was the target of a lot of bullying, and that you'd helped get her chief tormenter expelled."

"He told you about Mary Lou Lindsay?"

"Oh, yeah. He's very defensive about it, on account of her mother blaming the school for all Mary Lou's problems in life."

"Did he know she went to jail?"

"Yup. He didn't want to talk about it. Frankly, he was a lot more focused on the fact that Violet was the biggest single donor to the school in its history."

"I told you. She gave them two million bucks one year. Revenge is sweet, and it's not fattening!"

"I told him about finding *Passages* in the apartment of my murder vic and asked him if he'd ever heard of a girl named Nancy Sawtelle. He said it didn't ring a bell. But he arranged it so I could get a look at the old school records. Which I did. I made a list of all the girls in your class and the states they were from. Most of you gals were from New England—New Hampshire, Massachusetts, Vermont, Rhode Island."

"The provinces! I was the only one from New York."

"So are you aware that we fingerprint all the Jane Does we find and run them through CODIS and AFIS?"

"I know all about CODIS and AFIS from Violet. National DNA and fingerprint databases. They're always running stuff through CODIS and AFIS on her crime shows."

"When we ran Nancy Sawtelle's prints through AFIS, we didn't get any hits. No hits on CODIS either. But sometimes there are glitches— particularly if it's an older crime. Sometimes prints stay in the state system. So just for the hell of it, I called in a few favors and had Nancy Sawtelle's prints run through Connecticut, Massachusetts, Rhode Island, Vermont, and New Hampshire. We got a hit in Massachusetts."

Gunner reached inside his pocket and took out a picture. He handed it to me. It was a grainy old black-and-white mug shot of a woman holding up a card with numbers on it. I gasped when I saw it. I knew that face—that mean, sullen, bullying face with eyes like smoke.

"Recognize her?" he asked me.

"Mary Lou Lindsay," I said.

"That's right. That's her mug shot, taken in 1987."

I stared at it for a long time. Mary Lou looked so young in that picture, just like she looked when we were in school together. It struck me that she looked so young because I was now so much older.

I looked at Gunner, uncomprehending. "But *who's* Nancy Sawtelle?"

"*That's* Nancy Sawtelle."

"No, no, this is Mary Lou Lindsay," I corrected him. "Believe me, I'd know Mary Lou anywhere."

"Yeah. And that is also Nancy Sawtelle," Gunner said. "Mary Lou Lindsay changed her name several times when she got outta prison. You can understand how she might not have wanted people to know she'd been a guest of the government."

"Wait! Are you telling me that Nancy Sawtelle—Miss Montrose—and Mary Lou Lindsay are the *same person*? Are you *sure*?"

"No doubt."

"But you *showed* me a picture of Miss Montrose when you first came into the shop. Her driver's license. That woman didn't look anything like Mary Lou."

"You just went to a reunion. Did you recognize everybody who walked in the door? Mary Lou was a fat young girl. So she lost weight. Dyed her hair. Probably had plastic surgery. It ain't that hard to look unrecognizable after twenty-five years."

Stunned doesn't begin to cover what I was. I leapt up from my seat.

"Wait'll I tell Violet! This is absolutely amazing! *Oh, my God!* Her old nemesis! Violet's gonna *die!*"

Gunner was looking at me a little quizzically at that point. He cocked his head to one side. "You still don't get it, do you?"

"What—that Mary Lou Lindsay wound up murdered? I get it. Trust me! We got it back then. She was a rotten egg. You have no idea. It comes as no great shock that someone might want to kill her."

Gunner cleared his throat. His tone was slightly patronizing. "Sit down, will you?"

I sat down obediently and looked at Gunner, making an earnest effort to concentrate.

"Listen carefully to me, Reven," he began. "Mary Lou Lindsay shows up in town. Let's say she knows your friend Violet isn't who she says she is. Maybe she even knows what Violet was up to all those years she claimed she was doing all this other shit. And maybe what she was up to wasn't so good. . . . Lemme ask you something. If Grant Bolton found out his wife lied about her past, think he'd have a problem with that?"

"A *problem*? Are you *kidding*? Did you see what happened after that article about Cynthia? He left her flat after wrecking his life for her. He just dumped her because of one article. Grant's more terrified of public opinion than a politician. He's a complete coward."

"In other words, you think he *would* have a problem?"

"If he found out Violet wasn't who she said she was . . . ? The mother of his only son and heir to the bank . . . ? He'd go totally ballistic! I don't even want to *think* about what he'd do. I don't even know how *I'm* going to deal with it." I stared at him. "Gunner, you realize we can't tell a soul about this. Violet's life would be ruined if people found out. It has to be kept a secret. Please don't tell anyone."

Gunner was shaking his head in dour amusement. "You're just not getting it, are you?"

"What do you mean?"

"Nancy Sawtelle's calendar . . . What if X wasn't a Mr.? What if X was a *Mrs.*?"

"Huh?"

"Guess who else was at all those society events, along with your pal Bob Poll?" When I didn't answer, he said, "See, I think Nancy Sawtelle, aka Mary Lou Lindsay, was tracking your pal *Violet*."

"No. . . . It's a coincidence."

"*Coincidence?* And the hundred thousand dollars in Sawtelle's safety deposit box? That's a helluva lot of money for an ex-con, out-of-work waitress."

"I don't like where you're going with this."

He went on. "Two women who hated each other since they were kids are in the same town. One knows something about the other that could ruin her life. She blackmails her, and then she winds up dead. You tell me."

"Wait . . . you don't think . . . you don't seriously think that *Violet* killed Mary Lou?"

Gunner didn't answer. He shrugged, then folded his arms and nodded as if it were obvious, as if it had taken me all this time to figure out something that was so plainly in front of my nose.

I narrowed my eyes and glared at him. "*Whoa!* No! You can't seriously think that."

"I do think it. I just can't prove it."

I shook my head over. "No, no, no . . . I can't believe it. I refuse to believe it," I said, as if that would somehow make it untrue.

"Why? Makes sense to me."

"So let me get this straight. You think that Mary Lou somehow found out about Violet's past, and that she came here to blackmail her. Is that right?"

"That's about the size of it. You said it yourself. What was your pal Violet really doing all those years she was pretending to be someone else? My hunch? Mary Lou found out something really juicy about her, and this was her chance to get even."

"Like what?"

Gunner shrugged. "Hell, take your pick of juicy things. Maybe Violet was married before. Maybe she has a kid. Maybe she was a hooker. Maybe she killed that old lady. Maybe she has a record. But from what you tell me, just the fact of her lying about everything would have been enough."

"So Mary Lou just shows up one day, calls Violet, and starts to blackmail her? I can't believe Violet wouldn't have told me."

"Then she would have had to tell you about her past, wouldn't she?"

Gunner had a point. If what he said was true, Violet had lied to me and everyone else for years.

"Mary Lou knew the truth about Violet, and she threatened to expose it. Violet wasn't gonna let that happen," he said.

"But you don't have any proof."

"But I got one hell of a motive. And this is Violet's neighborhood."

I stared at Gunner in stunned disbelief, trying to digest all this.

"You once told me you don't recognize evil if it looks like you," I said at last. "Violet looks like me, doesn't she? Maybe not physically, but we're a lot alike."

"Kinda. Except you're not a killer."

I wasn't a killer, no. But was Violet? Maybe. Now that I knew she'd lied to me about her whole life, I thought her capable of almost anything. I wondered, was it possible that Violet, the serial killer buff, was so attracted to the breed because she might be a killer herself? Could I imagine her murdering Mary Lou if Mary Lou had threatened to expose her past to Grant?

Let me put it this way: It wasn't out of the question.

I thought back to that night at the Symphony Ball when Violet and I sat together, joking about who in that glamorous audience might be a serial killer. Now I realized there was real malevolence behind her mischievous laugh, knowing she'd pulled the wool over my eyes yet again. Because that night, Violet might have already killed Mary Lou. She was certainly first on the scene the next day. And then that time in the park when she took me to see the crime scene, and I'd sensed evil in that place. I thought it was just the echo of a terrible act of violence. But maybe it was the fact that I was standing right next to the killer herself.

Gunner said, "You think you could get her to confess?"

I chuckled grimly. "She's lied to me up, down, and sideways for twenty freaking years. Now all of a sudden you think she's gonna confess to *murder*? You're nuts."

"She might. If you tell her what you know about her. Tell her you found out she lied about her background. Threaten to expose her unless she tells you the truth. Promise her you won't tell anybody. Say you just want to know because you two are best friends."

I let out an inadvertent guffaw. The notion that I'd ever considered Violet my best friend was just too hilarious. But Gunner was so intense, I played it out, just to humor him.

"And when she asks me how I found out all this? What am I going to tell her—that *you* told me? Because if she thinks the police know, she's certainly not going to confess."

"Don't say I told you. Tell her you've known all along, and that you've been protecting her. But now you need to know the truth."

"Why now, all of a sudden?"

Gunner pulled out a photograph of our freshman class at Wheelock. There I was, out front and shining like a daffodil among the weeds. Mary Lou stood scowling three rows behind me. We were all identified by name on the bottom of the photo.

"Show her this. Tell her I just gave it to you, and that I'm on a trail, but I don't really know what's going on. Tell her you've figured out that Miss Montrose was her old nemesis, Mary Lou. Tell her this is your theory, and that you need to know so you can protect her and for your own personal satisfaction."

My own personal satisfaction . . .

I had to admit there was a kind of delicious justice in convincing Violet that I'd pulled the wool over *her* eyes all this time, rather than the other way around. How satisfying it would be to make her think I was the puppet mistress—who had always been in control—rather than the first-class, number-one stooge she obviously took me for.

"Okay. So she confesses," I said. "Then what? It's just my word against hers."

He shook his head. "No. It'll be *her* word against hers."

"How do you figure that?"

"You're going to get it on tape."

He pulled a tiny black tape recorder out of his pocket and played back the last few seconds of our conversation so I could see how effective the little machine was. He handed it to me. I took it reluctantly and stared at it as I thought for a long moment.

"What if she just decides to kill *me*?" I said, flicking my eyes onto his.

"Don't worry. You'll be protected. I'll be right there with you," Gunner assured me.

"Like she's really going to confess with you standing there? I don't think so."

"She won't see me."

Gunner got up from the bench and walked over to the grille door of the crypt. He removed the broken padlock and undid the chain. He opened the door and pointed at the interior.

"I'll be in there," he said.

I peered into the dark, dank mausoleum. The heavy smell of earth and mossy stone mingled with a subtle, putrid smell I didn't even want to think about. A narrow corridor separated the stacked tombs from the walls of the little house of death. Gunner was right. It was a perfect place to hide.

"You just get her down here and start her talking," Gunner said, as if it were the simplest thing in the world.

I told him I'd have to think about it.

"Okay. You call me when you're ready," he said. "And don't you go doing this by yourself. I believe your pal is very capable of hurting you if she feels threatened. Give me your word on this now."

I nodded.

It was closing time. Before we moved on, Gunner peered into the mausoleum one more time. He closed the gate and rewrapped the chain through the grille, then rigged the padlock to make it look secure. We walked up the hill in the deepening afternoon light. I put the tape recorder in my pocket.

"You ever have a really close friend who you thought you knew but you really didn't know at all?" I asked him.

"I don't have any friends," he said.

Chapter 42

I saw Violet a couple of times the next week, once at Amano, a festive china shop on Wisconsin, and once at John Rosselli, Inc., an antiques shop a few doors down the block from me. I chatted with her both times like nothing was the matter, but I viewed her in a jaundiced light. She even looked different to me, like a talking doll. There was something unreal about her now. If she sensed my discomfort, she didn't let on.

I was giving a big cocktail party at the shop in honor of Quentin Partridge, a talented local decorator and an old pal of mine, who had just come out with *Inside Washington*, a coffee table book documenting the houses of prominent people living in and around the city. Polo had photocopied my address book and sent out invitations a long time ago. Naturally, Violet and Grant were invited. Though they'd accepted, Violet called me up the day of the party and begged me to forgive her for not stopping by, but she and Grant were going to a private black-tie dinner for the popular former French ambassador Jean-David Levitte and his wife, Marie-Cécile, who were visiting town. Grant didn't want to go to two events in one night, so Violet begged off. I was relieved they weren't coming.

My party for Quentin went on much later than I expected. By the time I got home, it was dark. I was hunting for my key in the shopping-size handbag I carry with me, stuffed with things I can't do without in case of a terrorist attack, when I heard a low, gravelly voice say, "Hey, there."

Startled, I glanced up and saw Bob Poll, with an eely streak of lamplight shining like a scar across his face. He was wearing a sweat suit—very unlike Bob.

"Jesus! You scared me!" I cried. "What are you doing here?"

"Sorry I couldn't get to your party."

"I didn't even know you'd been invited."

"Aw, and here I thought *you'd* invited me."

I was a little frightened, but I tried not to show it. "What do you want, Bob?"

"Come for a ride with me."

"Do you seriously think I'd ever get back into that car, after . . . ?" I couldn't even finish the sentence.

"It's not the same car. I had to buy a new one. The old one was impounded." He pointed down the block to what looked like yet another vintage Rolls. It was hard to see in the dark. "Navy blue this time. Green seems to be a bad-luck color."

"No chauffeur?"

"Not tonight. Come on. It's a nice night."

"No. I'm really tired. I want to go to bed. So if you'd please move . . . ?"

He smiled that bemused, insinuating smile of his and stood idling in front of the door, making it impossible for me to pass without having contact with him. I smelled liquor on his breath.

"How 'bout a drink, then? Invite me in. One drink, and I'll leave. Promise."

"I think you've had a few too many drinks already."

As I put my key in the lock, he leaned in close.

"I could force my way in if I wanted," he whispered.

I froze. "Are you going to?"

"No." He backed off.

I opened the door, slid into the house, switched on the light, and quickly turned to face him.

"Please don't shut the door," he said. "Just talk to me for a minute. I need to talk to someone."

I closed the door partway and hovered near the entrance, making sure I could shut it quickly if I needed to.

"I'm sorry, Reven. I'm so damn sorry."

"Why? Because your marriage didn't work out?"

"That's part of it. You wouldn't let me come in for a few minutes, just to talk?"

"Better not," I said, clinging to the door.

"You ever have episodes where you can't remember things exactly?"

"What do you mean?"

"Where you can't tell whether something is real or a dream?" he said.

"No."

"Never? You never feel like you're watching yourself doing something you shouldn't do? And you're not really doing it. But you can see yourself doing it. And then, afterward, you say, 'Wait. Did I do that? I never could have done something like that.' "

The light from the hall illuminated him. He raised his hand to wipe his brow. He was sweating. There was dirt under his fingernails. For a man who was always so fastidiously groomed, this was as odd as the fact he was wearing a sweat suit at ten o'clock at night.

"How come you're dressed like that?" I asked him.

"I went jogging."

"At *this* hour?"

"Earlier."

"You usually have three for the road when you jog?"

"Yeah, well, I fell down and kinda blacked out. I'm so fucked up."

"So, you get drunk, go jogging, black out, fall down, and then just decide to get in your car and drive over to see me?"

"I rang the bell. You didn't answer. I decided to wait. You mad?"

"No. I gotta go."

I started to close the door. Bob suddenly stepped forward and put his hand out, like he was going to barge in. I slammed the door in his face and locked it. I stood still in the hall for a long moment, straining to hear what he was doing. My heart was beating wildly. I was terrified. After a few seconds, I turned off the hall light and peered through the curtains of the window facing the street. I saw Bob walking to his car. I was so relieved.

Something was very wrong. I felt it. What was all that baloney about doing things you don't remember doing and thinking you're in a dream?

I called Gunner on his cell. No answer. I texted him: "Need 2 C U

ASAP." I went upstairs and took the shoe box down from the top shelf of the closet. That's where I kept the gun Violet had given me. I loaded it and put it in my night-table drawer. I didn't sleep a wink that night.

———

Over the next couple of days, I tried desperately to reach Gunner. He didn't respond to any of my calls or text messages, which was odd, because I knew he was waiting for me to get back to him on Violet.

Later on that week, another young woman was found bludgeoned to death in the woods—this time off the Little Falls Parkway up in Bethesda. I heard about it in the shop and ran home to watch the six o'clock news.

Jenna Jakes, the local anchor, was standing in the middle of yet another chaotic scene of police cars and milling officers, microphone in hand.

"Police believe that twenty-four-year-old Katrina Hemsford was killed at least four days ago by blunt force trauma to the head, then buried right over there in a shallow grave," she said, pointing back at the woods.

"Sources close to the investigation say the way she was murdered bears an eerie resemblance to that of six other victims of the so-called Beltway Basher. Martin Wayne Wardell, the man they arrested three weeks ago in connection with that case, has only admitted to killing three women. Privately there are questions: Did Wardell act alone? Did he have an accomplice? Or is there a copycat out there? One thing is sure, no one is safe yet."

I picked up the phone.

Chapter 43

The cops at the local area precinct had never heard of Detective Gunner. Neither did they know what I was talking about when I demanded to speak to someone on the Beltway Basher task force. I phoned a couple of other precincts, with the same results.

At this point, I was certain that Bob Poll was involved in this recent murder. The time frame seemed right. I couldn't wait any longer for Gunner to get back to me. I turned to my friend Joy Croft, a Washington fixture who wrote a lively blog about the city called "Capitol Pros and Cons." Joy once ran for the city council, and there was very little about Washington or its denizens in all spheres of life she didn't know. When people got into a jam or needed a favor, they called Joy.

Joy was a good-looking blond divorcée in her forties who managed to be catnip to men without being threatening to women. Her wry sense of humor, coupled with a languid sexuality, made an interesting contrast to her pragmatic, levelheaded nature. She loved antiques, and she'd written about my shop on her blog several times. The two of us often had lunch together, and dished the whole Washington scene. Joy was the kind of cool friend who didn't ask a lot of questions if you went to her for help. She just helped you.

I knew she used to date this policeman named Norman Peterson, who was now an assistant chief in the Metropolitan Police Department. So I called her and asked if I could call Chief Peterson and use her name, because I needed to get in touch with one of his detectives. I told her it was urgent.

"I'll do you one better," she said. "I'll take you to see him myself. I haven't seen Norm in a while."

Joy and I drove out to some godforsaken corner of Northeast Washington that very afternoon. The chief's headquarters were located in a fairly deserted area in a rough section of town. The building looked like a bunker—a great big square mass of concrete blocks, surrounded by a chain-link-fence-enclosed parking lot. Chief Peterson received us in his office, a spacious room with homey touches like trophies, merit citations, and family photographs hanging on the walls. Seated behind a big square desk, piled high with folders and official-looking papers, Peterson stood up when we came in, greeting Joy warmly. Noticeably warmly, in fact. Joy had that effect on men.

Norman Peterson was a tall, handsome man with a kind of fleshy muscularity, like someone who used to be in great shape but wasn't working out anymore. Joy introduced us, and he shook my hand with a zealous grip. A youngish-looking uniformed officer stood beside him, not quite at attention, but almost. He looked like a kid. He had a thin face, a long neck, a protruding Adam's apple, and a blotchy complexion. Peterson introduced him to us as Gary. Just Gary.

Chief Peterson sat down and invited me and Joy to do so as well. Gary remained standing at attention by the chief's side. Joy and Peterson chatted for a while, catching up. I gathered they hadn't spoken in many months. They were flirtatious with each other in that way that former lovers often are, drawing on little private moments with only one or two words, or a knowing laugh. Peterson showed us a picture of his two children, then casually let drop that he was separated from his wife. While he made goo-goo eyes at Joy, I wondered if anyone ever stayed married anymore.

"So, what brings you ladies here?" Peterson finally said.

"Reven has something she wants to ask you," Joy said.

"Ask away," he said.

I hesitated a little at that point, and Joy diplomatically asked me if I wanted her to leave the room. She sensed, quite rightly, that I needed to speak to the chief in private. I took her up on her offer, and she left.

"I'll wait for you outside," she said.

So then it was just me, Chief Peterson, and Gary, the young officer.

"I'm trying to get in touch with Detective Gunner," I began. Peterson glanced up at Gary. "You do know him, don't you?"

"Oh, yeah. We know him," Peterson said. "And why do you want to get in touch with him, if I may ask?"

"I have some important information for him—about the case."

Peterson narrowed his eyes. "What case?"

"The Beltway Basher case. He's on the special task force . . . ?"

Peterson shifted in his chair and glanced up at Gary again. "Why don't you begin at the beginning," he said.

I tried to make a long story short. I explained how I'd first met Detective Gunner and how he'd enlisted me as sort of nontraditional confidential informant who could tell him stuff about the Washington social scene. I also mentioned that I'd gone out with Bob Poll, and in fact it was my tip on the green mink blanket that had actually led to the arrest of Bob's chauffeur, Maxwell, aka Martin Wayne Wardell. As I was talking, Chief Peterson and Gary exchanged uneasy, almost questioning glances at each other.

When I'd finished, Peterson said: "So let me get this straight. You say you've been working for Detective Gunner as a CI?"

"Yes."

"And he told you he was on the serial killer task force?"

"Yes."

Peterson rolled his eyes at Gary. He leaned back in his chair and put his hands in front of his face, with the tips of his finger touching his nose, like he was praying.

"Jesus Christ," he said with a heavy sigh.

"Why, what's the matter?" I asked.

He slapped his hands palms down on the desk in apparent exasperation. "And tell me exactly why you want to get in touch with Detective Gunner?"

"I need to talk to him about the case."

"So he's been talking to you about the case?"

"Yes."

"What's he been saying?" Peterson was growing more intense now, more irritated. I was getting a little anxious. I didn't want to get Gunner in any trouble.

"Well, as I understand it, Maxwell—Mr. Wardell—has confessed to three of the murders, but not to Nancy Sawtelle, the woman they found in Montrose Park and two others. You're not sure if he killed them, right?"

"Go on," Peterson said.

"Okay, well, I guess some people think it's possible that Mr. Wardell may be telling the truth—that he *didn't* kill those other girls—or that he had an accomplice, right?"

"Is that what Detective Gunner told you?"

"Sort of."

"What do you mean, sort of?"

"Yes, he did tell me that."

"And did he have any theories about who this other killer may be?"

Well, naturally, I didn't want to incriminate Violet. But I figured they knew that Bob Poll had once been a suspect, so I proceeded from there.

"Well, I know you all once suspected Bob Poll—Mr. Wardell's employer. Isn't that right?"

Peterson narrowed his eyes. "We all?"

"I mean, the detectives on the task force. As I said, I've been trying to get in touch with Detective Gunner, but he hasn't returned my calls."

"And why exactly are you trying to get in touch with him?"

"Because of that girl they just found off the Little Falls Parkway."

"What's she got to do with it?" Peterson said.

I cleared my throat. "Look, I just had to talk to someone in charge because, well, Bob Poll paid me a visit a few nights ago, and he was acting really crazy. He was drunk. He was in a sweat suit, and he was sweating."

Peterson threw another glance at the young officer, who stifled a laugh.

"That didn't come out right," I said. "What I mean is, it was ten o'clock at night. What was he doing in a sweat suit? You don't know him, but it's just so unlike him. He said he was jogging, but he'd obviously had a lot to drink. I didn't believe him. He was babbling on about all this crazy stuff, like how he blacked out and couldn't remember things. And, well, I think he might have been up to something horrible. Then I heard about that girl. Look, I'm very sure Detective Gunner would be interested in this."

Peterson glanced at Gary again. It was like they had this private joke thing going on between them, and I was getting a little paranoid about it. My nerves were basically shot anyway.

"I'm glad you guys think this is so funny. Mind letting me in on the joke?" I said.

Peterson leaned forward and stared hard at me. He had these really piercing blue eyes. He was a damn good-looking guy, despite the desk-job beefiness. I suddenly wondered why my friend Joy broke up with him and if he was available and if she'd mind if I went out with him, because you know how touchy girls can be about friends going out with their exes. Those things were flitting through my mind—but not for long.

"George Gunner," he began in a slow drawl, "good old Samurai George."

I realized that was the very first time I'd ever heard Gunner's first name. I'd always called him Gunner and thought of him as Gunner, never bothering to inquire what his first name was.

"I've always just called him Gunner, actually."

"Yeah, well, Gunner or George or Samurai Sue or whatever you wanna call him hasn't been active on the force for two years."

I felt a little shock wave run through me. *"What?"*

"He ever tell you anything about himself?"

"Not much, no. Just that he was on this special task force investigating the Beltway Basher. Okay, yes, and one very personal thing—that his daughter had died and his wife committed suicide as a result."

"He told you that?"

"Yes."

"Is that all he told you?"

"Yes. I didn't want to pry any further, because I got the feeling that he really didn't want to talk about it."

"I'll bet he didn't," Peterson said.

"What do you mean?" I was apprehensive.

"Okay. . . . Well, George Gunner *was* one of the best detectives on the force. He *was* assigned to a special task force investigating the Beltway Basher case until his stepdaughter, Dinise Shevette, became the guy's fourth victim."

"What?"

"Yeah. . . . It was one of those freaky, terrible things. It's possible he knew George was working the case and he targeted her. But we'll never know. Dinise was a lovely young woman. Nice, quiet, studying to be a doctor. They found her over in Anacostia Park, dumped near the river. Gunner had to identify her body. I was told he let out this godawful scream when he saw her. Poor guy. And then his wife . . . I feel for the man. I really do. But there are rules."

"But . . . wait . . . Dinise Shevette was white. He showed me her picture."

"*Step*daughter, I said. Lila Shevette, his wife, was white. Dinise's dad was killed in the Gulf War when she was just a kid. George brought her up. He loved that little girl like she was his own flesh and blood. Lila couldn't have any more kids. So Dinise was like their little star. When she was murdered, it just destroyed the both of them. Lila took an overdose of sleeping pills."

I clapped my hand to my mouth. "*Oh, my God. . . . I had no idea.*"

"Naturally, we had to take him off the case, because he was now personally involved. You can understand why. Who's gonna trust evidence we get from the father of one of the victims? It's a defense lawyer's dream. You can't have people working cases they're emotionally involved with. It's tough enough maintaining a distance in cases like this as it is."

I kept shaking my head over and over in disbelief.

Peterson went on: "He was furious we took him off the case. It became a real obsession with him. Not that I blame the guy. His life was wrecked. He had nothing left really. He began to think of himself as this kind of renegade samurai—you know, a warrior who works outside the establishment and dispenses his own kind of justice."

"I know. He gave me a book about that."

"That *Ring* book, right? Yeah, we used to kid him about it because that was the book all those friggin' CEOs were reading back in the '80s. Anyway, he started poking into stuff on his own. Lemme tell you, an obsessed cop is a dangerous man. Or, as a buddy of mine put it, 'An obsessed man is a dangerous cop.' Shit, I warned him to back off—didn't I, Gary?"

"You did. We all did."

"Gary'll tell you. I told him he could potentially do the case a lot more harm than good. But he wouldn't listen, stubborn son of a bitch. So we had to suspend him. An indefinite leave of absence."

"But the blanket . . . I told him about the blanket, and that's how you caught Maxwell—I mean Wardell."

"Yeah. That's right. We didn't stop talkin' to the guy. He lucked out, and we were able to follow up on that lead *precisely* because he was no longer working in the department. We treated it like a tip. It paid off. I didn't say he wasn't a good detective. He was a great detective. But this case derailed him. And by the way, for the record, we believe Wardell did all those girls by himself. He just confessed to Dinise, which is why you probably haven't heard from Gunner. The guy's probably on a bender somewhere. I would be, if I were him."

"Then how do you explain the girl who's just been found?"

"Copycat. Jeez, there's been so much publicity about this friggin' Beltway Basher! They got Web sites describing what he did. Any lunatic who can read could commit a murder that looks like it."

"So you don't think there's any possibility that someone else could be involved?"

"I doubt it. You got someone in mind?"

"I told you. Bob Poll."

"We looked at Mr. Poll very closely. He's not involved."

"How can you be so sure?"

"Why? You got something on him?"

"You don't think the fact he came over to my house the other night drunk and talking crazy and sweating with dirt under his fingernails is significant? It was the same night that new girl was killed."

Peterson chuckled. "If drinking and dirty fingernails were a crime, Gary and me'd be doing life. Right, Gar?"

"Two terms," the young officer said.

"Maybe he was working in his garden," Peterson said.

"No. He has gardeners."

They both snickered. "Oh . . . well, then, maybe he gave the body to one of the gardeners to bury," Peterson said. "Right, Gary?"

"Right. Everyone likes overtime."

"He told me he fell down."

"Sometimes guys tell the truth," Peterson said. "Not often, I admit." They laughed again.

I didn't think this comedy routine was remotely funny, given the sadness and the seriousness of these crimes.

"I guess when you deal with murder and mayhem every day, like you all do, you develop an unfortunate and inappropriate sense of humor to protect yourselves," I said.

Peterson's face darkened. He grew serious. "Look, George Gunner's a great detective and a good man. But he is a severely misguided man at the moment. He knows damn well he shouldn't be talking to you or anybody else in an official capacity because he *has* no official capacity right now. Now, I like George. Life dealt him a bad, bad blow. But that doesn't mean he can go around breaking the law."

He glanced at his watch. I got the hint.

"Well, thanks very much for seeing me," I said. "I appreciate it."

"Listen, if George comes around again, you tell him you've been to see me and that we know what he's doing, okay?"

"And what about this latest murder?" I asked.

"Truth? This gal's murder isn't really like the others at all. The reporters exaggerated the similarities in order to sell papers—as great a shock as that must come," Peterson said. "We're expecting to make an arrest in that case shortly. Not for publication, okay? But just so's you know it's nothing to do with any serial killer. It's a domestic situation."

Just before I left, I stopped at the door and turned to Peterson. "You won't prosecute Detective Gunner or anything, will you? I don't want to get him in trouble."

"I'm sure George didn't say or do anything that broke the law. You guys were just kidding around, right?" He pinned his eyes on mine.

"Right," I said with a knowing nod.

"But it's gotta stop—*now*. . . . By the way, good tip about the blanket. Thanks."

Joy came in to say good-bye to Peterson. I waited outside in the hall. It was clear to me at this juncture that I had a lot of trouble seeing people as they really were—to put it mildly. First Violet, now Gunner. Was anyone close to me *ever* who they claimed to be? Was there anyone I could really trust?

As we drove back from the police station, Joy asked me if I'd gotten everything "sorted out." I said yes, and thanked her very much for setting up the appointment. I wanted her to feel like she'd been helpful. It was the least I could do in return for such a big favor. But the truth is, things were far from "sorted out." If anything, I was more confused than ever.

Joy and I gabbed about the Washington social scene and how the players had certainly changed in the past ten years. Like everyone else in the world, Joy knew the whole story of Grant leaving Violet for Cynthia and then ditching Cynthia to go back to Violet when the bad publicity hit the fan. She'd written about it in a blind item on her blog, in fact. She asked me how Violet was doing, and I told her that she and Grant were back together, working things out.

Joy was no Cynthia fan herself. She revealed that when Cynthia first arrived in town, she'd asked her to do an interview for her blog to talk about being a self-made woman and the art of philanthropy.

"I thought it would make a really interesting conversation. But Ms. Rinehart let me know in no uncertain terms that she wasn't interested in what she called my 'little blog.' She made me feel really insignificant. Hate that, don't you? Bet she'd do an interview now if I asked her," Joy said with a touch of glee.

Joy dropped me off at my shop. I gave her one of my signature scented candles to thank her. As we air-kissed each other good-bye, I told her how cute I thought Chief Peterson was, and she let drop that he'd asked her out.

"Who knows? We might even start dating again, and this time it might work out," she said brightly.

I told her some good deeds *do* go unpunished.

Chapter 44

The next day I was in the garden at the back of my shop, rear-ranging some wrought-iron furniture, when Gunner appeared. He looked beat. His eyes were bloodshot, as if he'd been crying or drinking, or both. But he still took touching pride in his appearance. Everything was neatly pressed and polished.

"Need some help?" he asked.

"No, that's okay. I was just setting up this display. I'm almost done. . . . I've been trying to get a hold of you."

"Yeah, I know. Sorry I didn't get back to you sooner," he said.

"Where were you?"

"Outta town. Checking something out."

"You don't take your cell phone with you?"

He ignored the question. I knew Chief Peterson was right. He'd probably been mourning his stepdaughter all over again in the wake of Wardell's confession. But I couldn't say anything because I didn't want Gunner to know I'd found out about him.

"So, have you decided whether or not you're gonna help me with Violet?" he said.

"I don't know. . . . I haven't made up my mind yet."

"Why'd you call?"

"I read about that girl they found up in Bethesda. And I had this very weird encounter with Bob Poll the other night."

I explained the whole episode in detail. Gunner didn't say a word. He just stood silently, like he was appraising me.

"That all you gotta tell me?"

"Yes. Why?" I asked, trying to be nonchalant.

"Nothing else? You sure?"

"No. . . . Why?"

He pointed at me. "I once told you, you were a lousy liar."

"Why do you say that?"

"Okay, so lemme ask you: If I came into your shop and talked to Polo about you, would he tell you?"

"Sure," I said, uncomprehending.

"So what makes you think that when you come into my shop and talk to people about me, they don't tell me?"

I swallowed hard. "I don't know what you're talking about."

"Yeah, you do."

"No, I—" I stopped myself. It was no use pretending under his withering stare. "Okay. . . . When I read about that girl, I tried to call you, but I couldn't get in touch with you. I really thought Bob Poll was up to no good and that someone should know about it quickly. So my friend Joy took me to see Chief Peterson. She used to go out with him."

Gunner nodded and lifted his brow, "Yeah, I know. Norm called me. . . . Shit, Rev. You really complicated my life."

I stared at him incredulously. "I complicated *your* life? *You've been lying to me this whole entire time!*"

"Listen, a smart French dude once said, 'Treason is a matter of dates.' I *was* on that task force. I'm just not on it now. I rearranged the dates. That doesn't mean I'm not right. Norm told you about Dinise, didn't he?"

"Yes."

"So now you understand why I need to keep doing what I'm doing?"

"I guess. He told me Wardell confessed to her."

Gunner breathed a tremulous sigh. "Yeah. He'll confess to Liza Cooley eventually. He's just holding out for a deal. There's a warrant out for him in Arizona. They suspect him in a murder there. Arizona's a death penalty state."

"Will he confess to Nancy Sawtelle?"

"You know, he just might if he thinks it'll help him. That's what I'm afraid of. And if he does, all my hard work goes to hell."

"And you're still convinced about Violet?"

Gunner bowed his head and shifted his weight from one foot to the other. He seemed nervous, as though what he was about to say was difficult for him.

"Look, Reven, maybe it was wrong me dragging you into this. But, hey, they got Wardell on account of your tip. And they would never have gotten that tip if I hadn't gotten to know you. See, I *need* to find out who really killed Mary Lou. If I can prove that she wasn't Wardell's, it gives me a chance to get back on the force. When Wardell killed Dinise, he killed my wife too. And a part of me. The only thing I got now is knowing I'm a good detective. It's all I have left."

I reached out and touched his hand. "I'm so sorry, Gunner . . . or should I call you George?"

"Nah, George sounds like some nerd accountant. . . . When you decide to help me, just let me know."

"But Chief Peterson says you can get in real trouble if you keep going on with this."

Gunner shrugged. "Yeah? And what are they gonna do? Hang a dead man? They can't hurt me."

Chapter 45

I'm not quite sure why I decided to continue helping Gunner. Maybe it was because I felt sorry for him, or maybe it was because I wanted to prove to him that he was wrong about Violet—at least wrong about her being a murderer. Or maybe it was because I wanted Violet to know that I was onto her at last, that she couldn't fool me anymore, and that if our friendship was to survive, she had to finally start being honest with me. But I needed to see her one more time before I put Gunner's plan into action.

Violet, Peggy Myers, and I resumed our ritual lunch at Café Milano. I was so nervous about seeing Violet again that I got there early and had a glass of wine, trying to prepare myself.

Violet and Peggy arrived, bubbling with fresh news about Cynthia. The whole town was buzzing about the hearings and about how Cynthia was having to divest herself of all her assets.

"Well, I can tell you one person who's very happy about this," Peggy said.

"You mean aside from me?" Violet said.

Peggy just smiled and said, "Leonid Slobovkin. We've renewed his contract. No Nelson Mars, thank God! In fact, everyone at the center is breathing a sigh of relief. Carmen, Kyle, even Jed Jimson—who is stepping down as chairman."

"I heard that Cynthia was angling for that job," Violet said.

"Oh, yes, she was! But now it's been offered to a brilliant guy from New York. Head of the Beaufort Group. I just hope he accepts," Peggy said.

Freed from discretion by Cynthia's downfall, Peggy now filled us in on all the scenes and demands Cynthia had made during her reign at the Kennedy Center. Feasting on the carcass of her enemy, Violet relished every single detail. In fact, she could talk of nothing else. I found it interesting that Grant was somehow secondary in all this. Violet's venom clearly outweighed her victory. I wondered if that had something to do with the fact that Cynthia was not what she represented herself to be—just like Violet.

As Peggy and Violet chattered on, I studied Violet closely, thinking, This is the woman who has lied to me for twenty years. Did she look different? No. Did she act different? No. But she *was* different. Now that I knew the truth, everything about her rang false. Instead of thinking of her as my best friend, I viewed her as an actress playing a part. Had she been playing the part of a best friend too? I wondered, What *was* real about her?

We all ordered the same lunch, as usual. Then Violet took out a small, prettily wrapped package from her purse and put it down in front of me. She put a flat square package in front of Peggy.

"Go on, open them, girls," she commanded us.

Peggy opened hers immediately. It was a scarf—not a particularly pretty scarf, but polite Peggy acted as if it was the most beautiful scarf she had ever received. She unfurled it and tied it around her neck.

I hesitated to open my present. Violet and I were always giving each other little gifts—like girlfriends do. The gifts I gave her had to be chic and well chosen, precisely because they also had to be relatively inexpensive. Violet, on the other hand, had unlimited funds at her disposal. And while you'd think it would be fairly easy to buy a present for a girlfriend when you have all the money in the world, somehow that never stopped Violet from presenting me with some of the most hideous objects imaginable.

A person would have to look long and hard for that sterling silver hand mirror in the shape of a panda she gave me for one birthday. Or that jadeite Statue of Liberty purchased at great expense from a Hong Kong auction in honor of my being from New York. Or that Victorian carved owl clock with a pendulum in the shape of a claw she gave me one Christmas—to name but a few. And of all Chanel bags in all the world—why a pink canvas one covered in clear plastic with the word *Chanel* scrawled umpteen times across it in bright green script? A lot of the things she gave me invariably looked like cheap knockoffs, but they weren't. Unlike Violet, her presents were the real thing. Was money ever so badly spent? And worse, I had to pretend I liked these atrocities.

Today I felt guilty about accepting any present from her at all, hideous or not. But she kept insisting, so I finally opened the little box. Inside was a small burgundy leather jewelry case tooled in gold. When I opened it, I was horribly surprised. I say *horribly*, because for once in her life, Violet had bought me something truly beautiful: an antique crescent moon pin made of ten perfectly graduated rose-cut diamonds set in gold. I didn't know what to say. I just knew I couldn't accept it—at least not before I'd come clean with her about what I knew, and what I suspected.

"Oh, isn't that lovely?" Peggy said.

I was speechless.

"What's the matter? Don't you like it?" Violet asked.

"I . . . I . . . I don't know what to say. It's amazing. Incredibly beautiful. But I can't accept it," I said.

"Are you kidding? Why not?" Violet said.

"I just can't. It's too much."

"Listen, Rev, I understand a lot better what you tried to do for me when you went to see Grant. You were just trying to protect me. You were being a really, really good friend. In fact, you're my bestest friend in all the world, Rev."

She gave me a little pat on the shoulder and a sweet smile. I forced myself to smile back, but apparently as Gunner said, I wasn't that good an actress. Violet looked disappointed.

"You don't like it, do you?"

"No, I love it! But it's much too extravagant." I put the pin back in its fitted case and snapped the lid shut.

Violet furrowed her brow. "No . . . something else is bothering you, Rev. What is it?"

"Nothing. . . . I just have a lot on my mind—with the shop and everything." I pushed the little case toward her.

Violet continued to stare at me. She made me so nervous I had to look away.

"What is it? What's the matter with you?" she pressed me.

"You know . . . I don't feel that well," I said.

Violet and Peggy glanced at each other. "Can we do anything?" Peggy asked.

"No, thanks. . . . Um . . . I'm just not hungry. . . . I think I better go home and lie down. Excuse me, will you, girls?"

"We'll come with you," Peggy said, concerned.

"Yeah, we'll all go," Violet said.

"No, no, that's okay. I'd rather be alone, thanks. Really."

I got up. Violet called after me. "Reven! Are you sure you're okay?"

"Yes! Call you later!"

As I walked out, I heard Peggy cry, "Your pin! You forgot your beautiful pin!"

———

That's when I made up my mind to confront Violet on my own—without telling Gunner. Although my first reaction had been that I needed Gunner there to protect me, I felt I owed it to Violet to do it alone. Besides, now that I knew Gunner was a fraud of sorts as well, it put a whole different cast on the situation. I was as wary of him and his motivations as I was of Violet.

I wasn't afraid of Violet. I needed to find out why she'd lied to me all these years. I wanted to see how she'd react when I told her I knew the truth about her. While I understood I was hardly the best judge of character at this point, I didn't think she was capable of committing murder—not even to protect her position in life, which was so important to her. I didn't think so, but I wasn't entirely sure. I never thought she was capable of making up her whole life either. But she had. So I really didn't know her, did I? And yet, I felt I did know her in my heart. Plus, I still had this gnawing suspicion in the back of my mind that Bob Poll was somehow connected with these crimes, and that maybe he'd killed Mary Lou after all.

I decided to meet Violet alone, just the two of us, on neutral ground. I would bring the tape recorder Gunner had given me so that whatever she said would be preserved. Well, anyway, that was my plan.

Chapter 46

I knew I'd wounded Violet by refusing to accept that beautiful diamond pin. I rang her up to apologize and invited her to come for a walk. I told her I was feeling better. We made a date to meet at three o'clock at the entrance to the Oak Hill Cemetery. I put the small tape recorder in one pocket of my pants, and the picture of Mary Lou in the other.

It was an unseasonably warm fall afternoon. I walked up Thirty-first Street, wondering how best to broach the subject of Mary Lou's murder with Violet. I figured I'd start off by telling her I knew she'd lied about her past, see how she reacted to that, and kind of wing it from there.

Just for the hell of it, I detoured past Cynthia's house to take another gloating look at the Sotheby's FOR SALE sign planted outside. There was something gratifying about the notion that she was selling it, almost as if the ghost of Gay Harding was driving her out. As I looked at the old place from the driveway, I thought about that first day when Violet and I and Cynthia were all there together, and Cynthia announced there was a "new sheriff in town." And then my mind flashed to that life-changing moment when I walked in and saw Cynthia and Grant going at it on the floor. Mrs. Harding must have been dervishing away in her grave at that point. Just goes to show how dangerous it is to thumb your nose at those old grande dames, even today. Maybe they knew something we don't. Like how to behave.

Suddenly a sporty blue Mercedes convertible roared up behind me, made a sharp turn into the driveway, nearly knocking me over, and stopped short. The driver got out and slammed the door shut. It was Cynthia. She marched up to me and stood with her hand on her hip and a look of cool defiance.

"Well, well, well. . . . Happy now, Dream Girl?" she said.

"Hello, Cynthia."

We faced off for a few seconds. False smiles at dawn.

"You know, I didn't do things wrong. I just did things big," she said at last. "When all this stuff dies down, I'll still have a pile of money to do good with."

"I'm happy for you," I said.

"No, you're not!" she snapped. "But that's okay, because I'm gonna win in the end." She glanced back at the house. "I never really liked this musty old place anyway, you know. I'll be glad to get rid of it."

"Why'd you buy it, then?"

She snickered. "As if you didn't know. . . . Washington's too provincial for my vision. You all are about thirty years behind the times."

"If you say so."

"You're smug because you think you've won. You think you've driven me out of town. But you haven't. You know what y'all are *really* objecting to when you object to me?"

"What's that?" I asked with mock earnestness.

"I am the future. Big people doing big things in a big way and making no excuses for it. The world always objects to big change and big ideas at first. But it comes around in the end, because it has to. And here we all are, smack in the middle of things people first objected to: everything from horseless carriages to the Internet. Even women getting the vote and holding high office. You wanna know the great secret of life?" she said.

"Let's see—where to get a good facial in Washington?" I said.

She looked at me with contempt. "You make everything a joke, don't you? It's that damn prep school humor y'all think is so amusing. No . . . the great secret of life is *tenacity*. You just stick to your guns, whatever they are, and pretend like everything's going just fine. Nine out of ten times, things will turn out just the way you want 'em to."

"Well, here's another great secret of life: knowing when you're kidding yourself."

"Funny, I didn't think that was one you were too familiar with," she fired back.

Why did I always set myself up for these people? Anyway, with that, she reached into her purse, pulled out an envelope, and handed it to me.

"I just came from the printer's. These are hot off the presses. Go on. Open it."

It was an invitation—not one of those gaudy, expensive jobs she used to send out, but a nice normal card on a decent ecru stock, engraved in traditional black script. When I read it over, I thought to myself, Some people have no shame, and that's the end of the story. Here Congress was investigating her. She was being forced to sell her house and her private plane. The public outcry against her was growing. Plus she'd just endured a searing romantic humiliation, with Grant leaving her to go back to his wife. Yet none of that seemed to faze her. Because, according to this invitation, she was invited to the White House for a recepion in honor of the Dance Troupe of Morocco. It doesn't get more prestigious than that in Washington.

"Oh, is this for me?" I said facetiously.

" 'Fraid not, Dream Girl!" She plucked the invitation from my hand. "Just thought you'd be interested to know that I am sponsoring this great event. And that the First Lady and maybe even the President will be there, along with all the people *I* choose to invite."

"Did Senator Grider make the cut?" I asked.

"That mangy bad-tempered old coyote? I'd only seat him next to my worst enemy—and since you're not coming, he's not invited."

The little tremolo of rage in her throat undercut her coolness credibility. I think if she could have killed me right there on the spot and gotten away with it, she would have. She turned around, stomped back to her car, and opened the door.

"By the way, your ex-boyfriend Bob Poll is my date," she said.

Birds of a feather, I thought.

With that, she ducked into the car, slammed the door hard, and screeched on up to the house. I doubt that lion's-head knocker had ever presided over a more furious entrance.

———

Violet was standing in front of the open cemetery gates.

"Was that Cynthia you were talking to?" she asked as we entered the grounds.

"She's sponsoring a reception with the First Lady at the White House. She showed me the invitation."

Violet threw up her hands. "God help America!"

We strolled past the chapel down one of the paths leading toward Usherville. Violet stopped.

"Let's go to the park. I don't like all these dead people," she said.

"No, I want to show you something first. Follow me."

I led her around to the Hollis crypt. Before she caught up with me, I surreptitiously switched on the tape recorder in my pocket.

"Why'd you want to come *here*?" Violet asked.

"Gunner and I call this Usherville. We used to meet here so no one would know I was talking to him."

"Lovely," she said sarcastically, peering into the tomb. "Can we go now?"

"I need to talk to you. Sit down, will you?"

"Okay, for a sec." Violet collapsed onto the stone bench. I sat beside her. She took off her jacket. "Christ, it's hot. I hate Indian summer. I never dress right and I always catch cold," she said, wiping her forehead. "Listen, Rev, if it's about the pin—I really want you to have it. I won't take no for an answer."

"It's not about the pin," I interrupted her.

She eyed me. "What's going on with you, Rev? You've been acting so weird lately. You're kind of creeping me out."

This from the woman who once thought seriously of collecting serial killer art.

"Okay, let me ask you something. All that stuff you wrote in the 'Class Notes' . . . is all that true?"

"What do you mean?"

"What word in the sentence didn't you understand? Is all that stuff you wrote in the 'Class Notes' true?"

"Sure," she shrugged. "Why?"

"Just asking."

"Why?"

"You wrote that you went to law school at the University of Southern California. Did you?"

"Well, *yeah*," she said, as though it were obvious.

"And the Indian reservation and the environmental lobbying? All that's true too?"

"Yes," she replied in a warier tone.

I took a deep breath. "So, um . . . if I asked you who Mrs. Pagett was, you wouldn't know?"

She sat up straighter, brightening. "Ellie Pagett? Heavens, yes! She was this really nice old lady I knew in Chicago years ago. How do *you* know Mrs. Pagett?"

I could see that the subtle approach wasn't going to work. I guess maybe if you've been lying for years and years and years, you come to believe your lies on some level. Either that, or Violet was such a good actress there was no point in trying to jolt her out of character. So I just decided to go for it.

"Violet, you're a liar," I said flatly.

I wish I could say that the heavens parted and lightning flashed and the tomb opened. But the truth is, we just sat there on that cool bench, staring at each other in this morbid bucolic setting as the birds chirped and rays of a strong afternoon sun filtered through the shade trees.

"How dare you?" Violet said without conviction.

"If you keep on lying to me, I can't be friends with you anymore. That's the end of the story."

"Well, then I guess we can't be friends." She stood up and started to walk away. I called after her.

"I know you were expelled from DePaul! I know you worked as a companion for Mrs. Pagett and the two of you went to London together on the *QE II*, and that's how you spent your so-called Junior Year Abroad! I know you never went to USC! I know you never worked on an Indian reservation! I know that Mrs. Pagett left you money, and there were questions about her death! And that's just for starters!"

Violet stopped dead in her tracks. She didn't move. She turned around slowly and looked at me with terrified eyes. She swallowed hard.

"How did you find out?" she said softly.

I had debated whether or not to tell her the truth. I knew if our friendship was going to survive, honesty had to be a two-way street. "Gunner," I said.

Violet went pale. "The *police* know?"

"Just tell me: Did you make up all that stuff? *Did you?*"

She hesitated for a long moment. Tears sprang to her eyes. She looked like a four-year-old kid who had just been caught filching cookies. She did not, by any stretch of the imagination, look like a murderer.

"Yes," she said at last.

I felt as if I'd been punched in the stomach. You can suspect something, but until you know it for sure, it's not the same. Now I knew for sure that Violet was a fraud.

"*Why?* Why did you do it?" I asked her.

She shook her head. "I don't know. I did it once just for fun. Just to see how it would feel. It felt so good to be someone I wasn't and tell all those girls who hated me how well I was doing. And then, well, I just kept on doing it. It was like I was making up a story about a girl I admired. And that girl was me."

"Was everything you wrote a lie?" She nodded sheepishly. "So what were you really doing all that time?" I asked her.

"Nothing. . . . Just things . . . I don't know. I want to forget that part of my life."

"What things?"

"I don't know!" she said, throwing up her hands. "Things you do when you have to survive."

"Such as?"

"What are you—the Grand fucking Inquisitor?" she said, in a sudden flash of temper.

"I want to know," I said firmly. She wasn't the only one who was angry. "You've made a fool of me for twenty years. I think I'm entitled to an explanation."

She took a deep breath. "Okay, okay. . . . I'll tell you the worst thing I did. This is the worst thing, I promise. . . . I lived with this guy who had a little business that wasn't strictly legal."

"What kind of business?"

"It was stupid and harmless. A lot of our friends were doing it."

"Doing *what?*"

"He grew marijuana and sold it to people who needed it for medicinal purposes," she said at last.

"*Medicinal* purposes? *Right.*" I scoffed.

"It's *true*. It helps glaucoma. It's even legal now in California. That's not the end of the world, is it?"

"Go on."

"We broke up. He got busted eventually. He went to jail. I never saw him again. That's the worst thing I can think of."

"What'd you do after that?"

"I don't know."

"Come on. *What?*"

"*I don't know!* Mrs. Pagett left me some money, so I didn't have to get a steady job. I just kinda bummed around California and the Southwest. Worked in an art gallery in Taos. Did some stuff for a conservation group in Santa Fe. I lived in Oklahoma City. I knew some people from the reservation."

"But you never worked there?"

She shook her head. "No. But they told me about it."

"Why'd you come to Washington?"

She hesitated. "Truth? I knew you were here."

"So?"

She stared at me. "I don't think you realize, Rev. . . . You were, like, the only person who was ever really kind to me in my life—except for Mrs. Pagett."

"Let's talk about Mrs. Pagett for a second."

"I loved her. I really did," Violet said with great emotion.

"There were rumors that you might have pushed her down the stairs."

She bristled. "You got that from Gunner?" I nodded. "Yeah, well, I know who he's been talking to then—her horrible niece who hated Mrs. Pagett and couldn't wait for her to die. She started that rumor because she didn't get left anything in the will and I did. But Mrs. Pagett's kids knew how much I loved her. Tell him to go ask them. Besides, I wasn't even in the house when it happened. Her daughter and I came home together and found her at the foot of the stairs. Mrs. Pagett was like a second mother to me. Better than the mother I had, God rest her soul."

"That can't be true."

"You don't know, Rev. My parents weren't particularly kind to me. They treated me more like an intrusion than a child. Mom was clinically depressed. You know what she once said to me? She said, 'For me, the glass isn't half empty or half full. For me, there is no glass.' She was such a sad woman. And when I told my dad off for being such a lousy father, he said, 'How can you say I was a lousy father when I was never *there*!' He didn't even come to my wedding, if you remember."

"You didn't want him there with the gym teacher."

"He could've come without her. . . . Everyone always makes such a big deal about family, and how it's only your family that counts in the end. But in my case, it's been my friends who've counted much more than my family. And you've been my best friend, Rev. I thought if I came to Washington and looked you up, you might take me under your wing again like you did in school."

"Right! And I *did*—fool that I am."

"But I'm so grateful to you. . . . I've wanted to tell you the truth so many times."

"Why didn't you?"

"I couldn't. I was too ashamed. I thought I'd put it all behind me."

She sank down on the bench, put her head between her hands, and wept. I just watched her, feeling this weird combination of pity and anger.

"I still don't really understand. Why would you make up your whole entire life?"

Violet looked up at me. Her face was streaked with tears.

"How else was I ever going to get anywhere in this world?" she said plaintively. "A lot of people invent themselves. My God, we live in the capital of self-invention here in Washington! You think these politicians and ambassadors are who they want us to think they are? They all make stuff up. That's how you get elected, appointed, *noticed*! That's how you get anywhere in life if your life isn't handed to you at birth. Just because you've always had it so easy, Rev—"

"I haven't had it so easy!" I protested.

"Oh, no? Well, I've got news for you: you have no idea what it's like to be a *nobody*. A *real* nobody. A person people just look through. You were a star in school. You remember what I was like? I was a target. I had nothing going for me—*nothing!* Even my parents didn't want me. The kids at school didn't want me. Everyone wrote me off. Failure had been drummed into me from the time I was a little kid. If it hadn't been for you, I wouldn't have survived at Wheelock. And for that, I'll love you forever, Rev. But don't you dare blame me for trying anything I could to make something of myself."

"Why did you have to lie?"

"Think about it. Be honest with yourself. If you'd known the truth about me, would you have welcomed me with open arms when I moved here? I doubt it. Not even you, Rev. Would you have introduced me to Grant and all your fancy friends here if I'd just been this nobody who was your old roommate? I don't *think* so!" she said. "You were proud of my accomplishments. You always mentioned them whenever I met anybody. And if you think Grant *ever* would have married me without my credentials—well, then, you don't know Grant—or his parents. You were all so impressed with me and my great record."

"You should have had more faith in me," I said softly.

"Maybe. But you want to know another reason I also wrote all those things? To make *myself* believe them. When I looked at those 'Class Notes,' I was proud of that person I invented. And then a miraculous thing happened. That made-up person actually came to life! When I married Grant, I didn't have to lie anymore. I could actually *be* the person I always dreamed of being."

"Weren't you afraid someone would check up on you?" I asked her.

"In the beginning? Sure. Constantly. But they don't. I mean, it's amazing. People don't check. Rainy made up her mind about me right off the bat. And you know once she makes up her mind there's no changing it unless something drastic happens. No, around here, unless you're running for office or you do something people don't like, you can say you're from the fucking moon and no one will bother to check up on it. You think I'm the only person in this town who's ever lied about their background? And if you get to be Mrs. Grant Bolton, you become Caesar's wife—and then nobody *wants* to check up on you. They're too afraid of alienating Caesar."

"I know Grant Bolton, and he's no Caesar, to coin a phrase," I said.

"Only because Caesar didn't give a damn what anyone thought of him, whereas Grant cares so desperately. I never met anyone who cared more what the world thinks. But most people don't know that about him. They know he owns a bank and he's from a powerful family. That qualifies you as Caesar these days. And when he left me for Cynthia, I was back to being a nobody again. You have no idea how I felt, Rev. It was like being an orphan somehow. I never felt so alone, ever. . . . Then at the first sign of trouble, what does he do? He comes running back to me because he thinks I'm safe and spotless. He would *die* if he knew the truth about me. He would just die. . . ." She started crying again. "I'm begging you, *begging* you, not to breathe a word of this. He'll leave me. He will!"

I felt terrible for Violet. I put my arm around her as she sobbed.

"I won't say anything, I promise. But I need to ask you something. . . . Are you sure no one else knew about your past?"

She looked up at me and cocked her head to one side. "No! God no! I hope not."

"What about Mary Lou Lindsay?"

"What about her?" She seemed genuinely perplexed.

"Violet, please don't lie to me now."

Violet extracted herself from my arm and edged away from me.

"What are you *talking* about, Reven? What's Mary Lou Lindsay got to do with *me* at this point?"

"It's okay . . . I promise that if you tell me the truth, I'll help you in any way I can."

"The truth about *what*?"

"Miss Montrose."

"What *about* Miss Montrose?"

"Are you telling me that you honestly don't know that Nancy Sawtelle—Miss Montrose—is really Mary Lou Lindsay?"

Violet furrowed her brow. "Is this a joke?"

I took the yearbook picture out of my pocket and showed it to her.

"That's our freshman picture from the Wheelock yearbook. Gunner found it in Nancy Sawtelle's apartment. There's me. And there's Mary Lou," I said, pointing us out. "Her fingerprints weren't in the main system because her arrest was so long ago. But Gunner tracked her down. Nancy Sawtelle *is* Mary Lou."

Violet clapped her hands to her mouth. She looked like she was going to be sick. "Oh, my God," she whispered.

"Have you had any contact with Mary Lou?"

Violet sat there shaking her head and repeating, "Oh, my God, oh, my God," over and over.

"What? *What*? You've *got* to tell me. I can only help you if you tell me the truth."

Violet bit her lip. She took several deep breaths to calm herself. She looked at me strangely. Her whole manner had changed. She was more businesslike now, more matter-of-fact. "You'll help me? You promise?" she said.

"I promise."

"You're the only one I can trust."

"I *promise*. Tell me the truth."

Violet stood up. She started pacing around like a caged cheetah. She stopped suddenly, stood squarely in front of me, looked down, and said, "Okay, here goes—" She exhaled fiercely, like she was about to leap into the abyss. "Mary Lou did call me."

I was sitting down. She was towering over me. I don't know why, but I was a little frightened. I stumbled to my feet, and the two of us stood facing each other.

"When?"

"Over a year ago. I'll never forget hearing that voice. I knew exactly who it was, even after all those years. She said, 'Hey, Violet, this is a blast from your past.' In a way, I've always been waiting for that call— for someone to find out I was a fake. It's ironic that someone turned out to be Mary Lou, of all people. It was just destined, I guess . . ."

"How did she find out?"

"I don't know! But she knew all this stuff about me. She'd obviously met someone who knew me back then. She knew for sure that a lot of the stuff I'd written about myself in the 'Class Notes' was bullshit. I think she just figured the rest of it was too. She had me. And we both knew it."

"So what happened?"

"She wanted money. Natch. She knew how much I'd given to Wheelock, so she figured I was a bottomless pit. She said unless I gave her a million dollars, she was gonna tell Grant about me."

"Did you give it to her?"

"Yeah, *right*! I don't have that kind of money personally. You know that. You know what a skinflint Grant is. I gave that money to Wheelock through the Bolton Foundation. I told her I didn't have it. I told her I didn't have any money of my own—that it was all my husband's."

"What did she say?"

"She told me I better get it. She said she was coming to Washington to collect it in person."

"They found a hundred thousand dollars in a safety deposit box."

"Well, I don't know anything about that."

"Did you see her when she came?"

"No! That's just it. She never showed up! This was over a year ago, like I said. I've been waiting for her, dreading the day. It's been like this sword of Damocles hanging over my head."

I thought for a moment. "So you're telling me that the only contact you had with her was those phone calls?"

"Yes! And *she* always called *me*. I had no idea where to call her."

"What if she had shown up? How would you have gotten the money?"

"God, I have no idea! I guess I would have had to tell Grant. But I never heard from her again, and then Grant left me and my world collapsed and I tried to put it out of my mind."

"Why didn't you tell me?" I asked her.

"If I'd told you about Mary Lou I would have had to tell you everything, and I was too ashamed. . . . But you've got to believe me. It never even occurred to me that Miss Montrose and Mary Lou Lindsay were the same person! I thought she'd show up eventually. I swear to you on Tee's life I had *no idea*! *None!*"

"I believe you," I said, more because I wanted to than because I really did.

"Do you? Do you *really*, Reven?"

"I do. But I don't know if Gunner will. He thinks you had something to do with her murder."

Violet let out a little cry. "*No!* He *can't* think that! He *can't*! Anyway, they *know* who killed her, don't they? It was Wardell."

I shook my head. "Gunner doesn't think so. He thinks whoever did it just wanted to make it look like she was one of his victims. And Wardell denies he did it."

"He does?"

I nodded.

Violet thought for a moment. "If I admit that Mary Lou wanted to blackmail me, it gives me a strong motive, doesn't it?"

"Yes."

"Will they arrest me?" she said in a quivering voice.

"Let me see if I can talk to him."

"Yes, please! You've got to convince him I had no idea. I didn't do it, Reven. I'm innocent! Yes, I lied about my past. But I swear to you I'm not lying about this!"

I looked at Violet standing there, so distraught and panic-stricken. In essence, she reminded me of the frightened and fragile young girl who walked into my room that first day of sophomore year at Wheelock and said shyly, "Hi, I'm Violet. I guess you're stuck with me."

I wanted to believe her, but the truth is, I honestly didn't know if she was telling the truth or if she was still lying—like she'd been doing for the past twenty years.

———

The two of us walked home in silence. There wasn't a whole lot to say at that point. When you accuse your best friend of murder, you pretty much exhaust all other topics of conversation. As we parted ways, Violet said to me, "Seems like you're always saving my life, Reven. Thank you." She gave me a little hug of appreciation.

I went home, sat down on the sofa in my living room, and played back the tape. Violet's stunned reaction when I told her about Mary Lou being Miss Montrose seemed so genuine. But I still wasn't totally sure if she was telling the truth or not. I played the recording over again and again, trying to pick up something in her voice to confirm my suspicions one way or the other.

Violet called me an hour later.

"Listen, Rev, I've been thinking," she began in a much calmer voice. "I want to see Gunner myself and explain everything to him. I have to make him understand that, okay, yes, I lied about my background, but I didn't kill Mary Lou."

"Okay, I'll set up a meeting, and the three of us can talk."

"No! I want to see him by myself. I need to talk to him alone."

"Why? Why can't I be there? I could help you."

"Because this is one thing I need to do by myself."

I paused. "Okay. . . ."

She hung up. I called Gunner and said I had to see him right away. He came over to my house. I played him the tape. He sat hunched over with his arms resting on his knees, staring down at the floor, listening with grave intensity. I could tell he was agitated. When the tape finished, he shifted his gaze to me and asked in an exasperated voice, "Girl, didn't I tell you not to try and do this alone?"

"I survived, didn't I?"

"Is that why Violet wants to see me?"

"She called you?"

"Yeah. I told her I'd meet her tomorrow morning, six thirty, at the chapel in the cemetery. We're gonna go for a little stroll, just the two of us."

"Okay, look, Violet admits that Mary Lou was trying to blackmail her, but she denies having anything to do with her death. Listen to the tape. She says she never even knew Mary Lou was in Washington! She's been waiting in dread all these months for her to show up."

Gunner gazed at me in utter disbelief.

"What'd you expect her to say, huh? 'Oh, yeah, you're right. I had to kill her because she was blackmailing me'? She's *lying*. Read my lips, Violet is *ly-ing*! She's been lying to you for twenty fuckin' years! She's good at it! She says she wants to see me? Fine . . . I'm gonna see her. She will not lie to me. I promise you that."

Chapter 47

All night long Gunner's words rang in my ears: *Violet is lying. She's been lying to you for twenty years. . . . She's good at it!* I didn't sleep a wink, wondering why she didn't want me at that meeting, why she needed to talk to Gunner alone. Was there something else my old friend wasn't telling me—yet another secret she didn't want me to know?

When you've been best friends with someone for that long and you suddenly discover she's not who you thought she was, it's not only your friend you don't trust anymore—it's yourself. How could I ever trust my own judgment or instincts again when I lacked the ability to see people for who they really were? Bob Poll, Maxwell, Violet, even Gunner—they'd all fooled me in their own ways. And why was that? Was I so naïve? Or was I just so self-centered that I couldn't see past my own nose? I wondered if I'd ever seen anyone clearly, including myself.

I lay awake all night, obsessing and fretting. Finally, as dawn broke, I decided: whether Violet wanted me there or not, I was going to go to that meeting between her and Gunner. Oh, I'd wait a little, give them some time alone so Violet could have her chance to explain whatever it was she wanted to explain to him. But then I'd show up so the three of us could have a little conversation. If Violet was lying to me again, I had to know it. And it was better to find out with Gunner there.

I knew they were meeting at the cemetery at six thirty, so I got dressed and waited until then to leave the house. I figured it would take me fifteen minutes to walk up to R Street. I put on jeans and a jacket. I made sure the gun was loaded and put it in my jacket pocket. To this day, I'm not sure why I took it. I told myself it was just a precaution. But in hindsight, it feels more like a premonition.

It was a blustery fall morning. The wind churned the fallen leaves in crazy circles. There was a queer gray glow in the air. Witch weather, I called it. I walked briskly up to the cemetery. The side gate was slightly ajar, as I expected. I slipped inside and headed down the path toward Usherville. I was cautious because I didn't want them to see me right away. I confess I was hoping to overhear some of their conversation. It wasn't eavesdropping exactly. Well, okay, maybe it was.

As I drew near the mausoleum, the wind died down. An eerie calm fell over the place. I listened for voices but heard nothing. Only morning sounds broke the ominous silence—the rustling of trees, the occasional chirp of a bird, dying breaths of wind.

When I reached the Hollis tomb, there was no sign of Gunner or of Violet. I glanced at my watch. It was six forty-five. Either they were late, or I'd missed them. But that couldn't be; I couldn't have missed them, I thought. I would have seen them leaving. And besides, this was too important a conversation for that kind of brevity. They must be somewhere around, somewhere close by. They were probably taking a walk, I thought.

"Violet! Gunner!" I called out several times, but got no answer. Then I noticed that the chain on the grille gate of the mausoleum was lying on the ground, and for the first time, I sensed danger.

I opened the little gate just wide enough to peer inside. At the far end of the crypt, I saw a dark shape lying on the ground. I couldn't quite make out what it was, so I ducked my head down and went inside the tomb, where I was assaulted by that dank smell of earth and decay. I edged cautiously toward the far end, but what I saw turned out to be just an old blanket and some leaves. Someone had obviously camped out there—maybe a homeless person, or some kids.

As I turned to leave, I suddenly knew I wasn't alone. Standing in the shadow of the entrance to the tomb was a figure I couldn't really make out at first, because the gray morning light was behind it.

"Violet?" I called out. The figure quickly retreated.

I came out of the crypt and looked around. I saw a familiar figure running off—although it was not the person I expected to see.

"Grant!" I cried.

He stopped in his tracks. He was dressed in his basic weekend uniform: khakis, blue button-down shirt, driving shoes with no socks, and a navy blue nylon windbreaker. He was the picture of an aging preppy. His hands in the jacket pockets, he walked back toward me slowly.

"What are *you* doing here?" I asked him.

He stopped and stared at me with an almost sad, rather puzzled expression. Then he hung his head, as if he didn't quite know the answer to my question. An apologetic smile passed across his face, and he said simply: "I fucked up, Rev."

In all the years I'd known Grant, I'd never once heard him use the F-word. It didn't fit him any more than a zoot suit.

"Where's Violet?" I asked him.

"*You* were the one I should have married," he said.

As if, I thought to myself. But the severe, almost tortured look on his face told me now was not the time to rehash who left whom.

"Where's Violet?" I asked him again.

"Home."

"Why? What happened?"

"What are you doing here? You're not supposed to be here."

"Neither are you."

He hesitated. "Violet told me everything last night."

"Oh? What exactly did she tell you?"

He glanced up at the sky and sighed, as if waiting for some sort of divine intervention. Then his mood switched, and he said rather chattily, "You know, my mother used to tell me this story about a husband who sold his watch to buy a comb for his wife's beautiful long hair. But without him knowing it, his wife sold her hair to buy him a watch fob. Isn't that funny?"

" 'The Gift of the Magi.' O. Henry. It's a very famous story, Grant."

Grant nodded as if he was willing to take my word for it. "I think my mother told me that story to scare me."

"*Scare* you? How?"

"So I'd always tell her what I was up to. It felt like a threat, the way she told it. It was like her saying, 'Don't ever do anything I don't know about, because if you do it'll cause damage and be useless anyway.' "

I didn't quite understand how that ironic little story could be seen as a threat. Then again, I wouldn't put anything past old Rainy Bolton. I nodded as if I understood perfectly. Grant went on.

"But I didn't listen to her. I did a lot of things she didn't know about. I did stuff no one knew about. Remember when we were going out, Reven, and you asked me so many questions? It used to drive me crazy, the way you asked me questions. Violet never asked me any questions. She left me alone. She was the first woman who was completely content with me the way I was. Or maybe she just didn't care to know the truth."

"Grant, please tell me what happened. What did Violet tell you?"

He shifted from one leg to another. "Can I explain something to you?"

There was something about his mood, something unsettling that was starting to make me nervous, so as much as I wanted him to answer my question, I said, "Yes, sure. Go ahead."

"Okay, see, about a year ago, this woman called my office. She wouldn't tell my secretary who she was or what it was about. She said she had to speak to me personally, and that it was important. Maddy buzzed me and asked if I wanted to talk to her. I was curious. I said to put the caller through. This woman said she had some information she thought I'd be interested in. I told her to come to my office at the bank. She said no, she wanted to meet me somewhere neutral. I didn't like the sound of her or of the whole thing, so I hung up. That afternoon, I got a hand-delivered envelope marked 'Personal.' It was—" He paused, as if stung by the memory. "It was a snapshot of Violet holding hands with a man."

I didn't say a word.

"You're not surprised?"

"Go on."

"He wasn't the sort of person I ever expected Violet to be with. He was sort of a hippie type. A very unkempt and unsavory looking fellow. Something told me I better meet with this woman. I had a feeling she could do damage. So we met up in Rockville at a mall. I hate malls—although the bank invested very successfully in one." That was Grant, always needing to prove his worth.

"We had a cup of coffee at a Starbucks, this person and I," he went on. "She told me her name was Nancy Sawtelle. I didn't like her eyes. They were weird, almost like gray holes in her head. Her eyes are the only thing I really remember about her now," he said pensively. "Anyway, she showed me another picture. This one was of the same man in the picture with Violet. . . . Only it was a mug shot. She told me that my wife had once been married to this guy."

"*Married?*" I felt another shock, a deeper one.

Grant nodded.

"Did you know Violet was married before she met me, and that her husband eventually wound up in jail?"

"No," I whispered.

"Imagine! My wife, the president of the Potomac Bank's wife, was once married to a jailbird. This woman wanted a million dollars to keep her mouth shut."

"What did you do?"

"I told her I'd give her a hundred thousand dollars cash the next day, and the balance in a week. The next afternoon, I took a gym bag full of hundreds to a mattress store up on Rockville Pike, like she asked me to. She was in the store, but we didn't talk. I just put it down on the floor and left."

"Did you tell Violet?"

"No."

"Why not?" I was mystified.

"I didn't want her to know that someone was blackmailing my family because of her. I needed to protect her, and to protect us."

This screwy reasoning was so typical Grant. The O. Henry story anecdote now made sense.

"But weren't you curious to know who Violet really was, and why she'd lied to everyone, and, for that matter, who this person was who was blackmailing you?"

Grant thought for a second. "I probably should have been. But what was the point? I couldn't change the past. My job was to protect our future. If I'd confronted Violet, she probably would have told you. You would have told someone. It would eventually have gotten out. Don't you see? A thing like this could ruin us. Tell me something. Did you know Violet had an unsavory past?"

"No. And I still don't. We can't all be judged by our ex-husbands and -wives, Grant. You don't know that Violet's done anything to be ashamed of. A bad romantic choice doesn't make *her* a criminal."

"You're a good friend, Reven. But I don't see it that way, I'm sorry to say."

"So what happened?"

"Two weeks later, I met this woman again in the park at dusk, so no one would see us. I brought her the key to a storage facility where the balance of the money was. Before I gave her the key I told her I wanted her promise that she would leave me and my family alone from then on. But you know what she said?"

"What?"

"She said she wanted more money. *Two million dollars*, or else she'd put those pictures of Violet on the Internet and tell everybody about her past. I couldn't believe it. We had a deal. When I told her I wasn't going to give her any more money, she *laughed* at me."

He said this as though she'd spit on him. For Grant, all laughter was the kiss of the devil. He didn't see it as a joyful or playful expression, but as something shameful or shaming. In this case, he was probably right.

"What did you do?"

"I lost my temper," he said quietly. "She was obviously a terrible person. I knew I'd never be rid of her. People like that have no decency, no honor. They never keep their side of a bargain. You have to deal harshly with them. Very harshly. You must silence them forever."

I suddenly realized what he was telling me.

"Grant, are you saying that *you* killed her?"

He gave me a slow, solemn nod, like a royal assent. "I *had* to, don't you see? I didn't *want* to. She made me. Asking for more money like that when we'd made a deal? It was outrageous. A person like that could irreparably damage the bank. The Potomac Bank is my family's legacy. It will belong to Tee one day. When she threatened me, it was like threatening my child. And, of course, I didn't want Tee to know that his mother wasn't who she said she was. And my parents? They love Violet. My mother doesn't like to have her judgment questioned. She's never wrong. If she found out about Violet, it would just kill her."

It suddenly dawned on me that I was face to face with a certain kind of evil, and that I'd once again failed to recognize it. I had never even sensed it because, as Gunner once said, it looked so much like me. Grant was so familiar that I couldn't see his true nature.

"Jesus, Grant, I can't believe you *killed* her," I whispered.

"You know, sometimes I can't believe it myself," he said thoughtfully. "I don't know what happened. I just snapped. This fury came over me like a madness. It was almost like I was watching another person. When she demanded more money and laughed at me, I hauled off and hit her in the face. I'd never hit a woman before. But she wasn't really a woman. She was an evil thing. I hit her much harder than I thought, because she fell down and didn't get up right away. I stood over this thing, looking down at it. It was looking up at me with those cloudy eyes. I picked up a rock and hit it again and again until the eyes closed. Then I realized what I'd done."

He paused to collect himself, then continued. "I knew all about the Beltway Basher from Violet, so I tried to make it look like those other murders. I thought it was worth a shot."

My mouth was dry with fear. "You took a human life, Grant. Didn't you feel anything?"

"To be honest? I was much more frightened of getting caught. I don't know if I could make a jury understand why that awful woman had to die. There was a fair amount of blood. Luckily, I had on a coat. I turned it inside out to get out of the park. I even took the rock with me. That's what comes of living with a crime buff. I had to sneak into my own house. I drove to Maryland to get rid of those clothes and that rock, even the shoes. I thought I'd feel relieved when I got rid of the evidence, but I didn't." He sighed, sounding vaguely perplexed.

"Were you having an affair with Cynthia then?"

"No. I'd resisted. That day you saw us in the house was the first time we consummated our relationship. I became a different person after . . ." His voice trailed off. "And to be perfectly honest, I resented Violet for putting me in this position."

"You blame Violet for the fact that *you* killed someone?"

"None of this would have happened if Violet hadn't lied."

"So you left her."

"Yes. I needed to think of myself for a change."

I shook my head in disbelief. "So why on earth did you go back to her?"

Grant looked at me as though it were obvious. "How could I possibly stay with Cynthia when she might very well get indicted? Mother told me it would look much better for the family if I went back to my wife and child. I agreed with her."

"So you went back to Violet because *Rainy* told you to?"

"Mother understands what's best for this family. She always has. She took to Violet immediately. I can't believe her judgment was so wrong. You know, Mother meets everyone we employ at the bank. Her instincts are always correct. I couldn't bear for her to find out how wrong she was about my wife."

I'd always known that Grant was a mama's boy, but this took the cake.

"Why are you here this morning? Where's Violet?"

"Last night Violet confessed everything to me. I acted like I didn't know anything. She said that this woman you all had gone to school with found out about her past and had tried to blackmail her. She said this woman was the one who got murdered up in Montrose Park, and that that Detective Gunner suspected Violet had killed her to keep her quiet."

"What did you do?"

"I told Violet I'd handle it. And I have handled it."

When he said this, I got a queasy feeling.

"Oh, my God—where's Gunner?" I looked around in a panic. "*Where is Gunner?*"

Grant's right hand slid out from his pocket. He was holding a gun that he pointed directly at me. He cleared his throat and spoke in a low, even tone.

"I met Detective Gunner here earlier. He knew me, of course. I asked him to go for a little walk so I could explain things to him. I told him that Violet had confessed to me that she'd killed Nancy Sawtelle, and she was home preparing to give herself up."

"Grant! You mean to say you were going to frame Violet for what *you* did?"

He cocked his head to one side and said earnestly, "No. I would never do that. But I had to put him off his guard, didn't I? These fellows are very clever. Trained professionals and all that. I let him think we were going back to the house to get my wife, and that I just needed to talk it through with him before we all went to the station.

He was very obliging, very calm. We were having a nice conversation when I shot him."

"You *shot* him?"

"I don't know if he's dead, though. He was sort of moving when I heard a voice. I came up here to investigate, and I saw you."

I swallowed hard. "Are you going to shoot me too?" He didn't respond. "Talk to me, Grant. . . . You know you can talk to me."

He hesitated. "Yes, I really should have married you, Reven. Then none of this would ever have happened. We might have been happy. But now I think I have to kill you."

"You don't. Grant, you're not in a movie. You can't kill *everybody*."

"I have no intention of doing that. I'm not stupid. You're the last loose end." He squinted as if he were in pain. "Frankly, I don't see another way out."

"I know you don't. Because you're not thinking clearly right now. You're not well. But there *are* other ways, believe me. I'll help you see them."

"I told you. . . . I fucked up."

Grant massaged his temple as if he were disoriented. I could see he was teetering on the edge of sanity. His forehead was wet with perspiration. I felt like every word I uttered from here on in could determine whether he let me live or die.

"Everyone fucks up, Grant. We'll get you help. No one will blame you for what you've done."

He looked at me skeptically. "They won't?"

"No! You *had* to kill Nancy Sawtelle, because she was blackmailing you. People will understand that."

"They will?"

"Killing a blackmailer? Of course they will! Anyone would do that. Especially with the bank at stake. You said so yourself. You had to protect all these people's money and your family's reputation. But killing a policeman's another matter, and right now, we need to find Detective Gunner. What if he's not dead, Grant? If he's still alive, we need to find him and help him. And if he lives, you won't be in nearly as much trouble. It'll weigh very heavily in your favor."

Grant blinked hard a couple of times, like he was trying to sort things out in his mind. All my thoughts were on the gun in my jacket pocket. Even if I was able to draw it, could I shoot him? I wasn't sure.

I took a risk and said to him, "Look, if we find him and he's dead, you can always . . . well . . . take care of me then."

He ordered me to turn around. He shoved his gun in my back and said, "Move!"

I started walking ahead of him. "Put the gun down, Grant. It's just me."

"*Walk*," he commanded.

We headed down the path deeper into the grounds. The gray morning light flattened the landscape ahead.

"Where are we going?"

"Just walk."

His voice was cold and kind of crazy in a dull, determined way. I was terrified.

"Grant, please listen to me—"

"Shut up and keep walking," he said without emotion.

I kept thinking that every step I took was going to be my last. For the first time in my life, I didn't dare utter a single word. We were walking in silence when I heard what sounded like low moans nearby. I felt a little jolt of hope, praying it was Gunner and that he was still alive.

"Hurry up." He sounded more nervous than numb.

We walked around a large stone monument. Gunner was propped up against a nearby tombstone. His shirt was soaked in blood. A cell phone lay on the ground beside him. I ran to his side and knelt down. As I took off my jacket to cover him, the gun dropped out of the pocket onto the mossy ground. I looked up at Grant, and we both glanced at the gun that was within my reach. I wanted to grab it, but I hesitated, fearing Grant would shoot me. Just then, a voice cried out of the mist, "Grant!"

Grant instinctively turned around. I looked past him and saw Violet running toward us down the hill. I screamed at her. Grant turned back to me. I shut my eyes in terror as he aimed the gun at me. A shot rang out. The noise was so loud I covered my ears. Grant dropped his gun, teetered slightly, and fell to the ground. Violet ran to Grant, screaming. I heard sirens in the distance.

Chapter 48

It's been over three months, and Violet and I still haven't talked about that morning. We talk about other things: gardening, politics, gossip. Violet has had her hands full, coping with the media, Grant's parents, and with Tee. I sometimes wonder how she manages to keep up her spirits after all that's happened. Maybe it's her remarkable talent for self-invention that allows her to go on. The other day, I asked her directly, and she replied, "The trick is never to look back."

That's a good trick—one I haven't yet mastered. I look back all the time at that ghastly morning in the cemetery. Everything happened so fast that, typical me, I'd managed to miss the critical moment, even though I was right there. I do remember a few things quite clearly, however—like running over to Gunner and the gun falling out of my pocket. I'll never forget the look on Grant's face as he pointed his gun at me—that mindless, insane gaze that convinced me he was just about to shoot me. And then the shot—which practically burst my eardrums. Who could forget that?

At first I thought Violet had shot Grant. I saw her in the distance, and she'd screamed and run to him, cradling him in her arms. But when I turned to Gunner and saw he was holding my gun in both his hands, I knew that he'd shot Grant with the last of his strength before passing out. I learned later that he'd already called for help on his cell phone.

Grant died on the way to the hospital. Violet was with him in the ambulance. The one thing she did tell me were his last words. He said, "Tell Mother I'm sorry."

I went to visit Gunner every day in the hospital. He's out now, fully recovered. He wasn't wearing all black the last time I saw him, which made for a nice change. He was in a white shirt and a colorful tie. I think that means he may finally be coming out of mourning for his lost family.

"You look almost cheerful," I told him.

"Don't go overboard," he replied with a hint of a smile.

He's back on the force and working hard. Maxwell finally confessed to the murder of Liza Cooley, and Gunner told me that some people think he's responsible for other murders of women in other states, not just Arizona. I believe Gunner is finally satisfied that Bob Poll had nothing to do with the crimes. But he takes pride in the fact that he solved the murder of Miss Montrose all by himself. I don't see him that much, but he's promised to drop into the shop whenever he's in the area. I know we'll stay friends, not only because of what we went through together, but because I think we really, genuinely like each other and maybe even have changed each other's lives. I know he saved mine.

The firestorm of publicity is just now beginning to abate. Let's face it, it's not every day the scion of such a great and powerful family turns out to be a stone cold killer. Reporters dredged up some dirt about Cynthia and her involvement with Grant and the bank. There are those who wonder if the venerable old Potomac Bank will last. Mr. Bolton Sr., has had to step in and take over operations again. So it wasn't only Violet's reputation Grant wanted to protect. The senior Boltons are blaming Cynthia for their crazy son's behavior. I can't say I'm surprised. They have to blame someone. I am surprised that they've forgiven Violet. But they have, probably because Rainy is now investing all her energy in Tee, her only grandson.

I know Violet's a little nervous about her relationship with her son. But Tee and I had a talk when he was home from school, and he said, "I'm actually looking forward to getting to know my mother at last." Isn't that interesting? See, all that time, Violet was playing a part, and Tee sensed it, because children sense everything. Anyway, it'll all work out. Or it won't, as Violet says. I've given up making predictions. Almost getting murdered by someone I knew for twenty years has mellowed me quite a bit.

I haven't seen Bob Poll around town. Ken Corwin, an editor at

Washington Life, informed me he heard that Bob recently gave a birthday party at his house for one of the girls from King Arthur's, and that a couple of married members of Congress were there—without their wives. Maybe Bob is finally following his real heart at last. I wish him well. I did read that he went to that event at the White House with Cynthia and that the evening was a success. The woman is nothing if not tenacious, I'll say that for her—although there are rumors she may not be honoring her pledge to the Dance Troupe of Morocco and they might go out of business as a result.

A lot of people think Cynthia should move away from Washington. Violet keeps asking when she will get indicted. Senator Grider told me to tell her to hold her horses. "The law takes time," he said.

And yes, Zack and I are having another look-see at each other. I'm learning to appreciate him more. He's definitely growing on me. One night we were going to a party and I asked him if Violet could come with us. He didn't hesitate to say yes. It was the first time she'd been out in public since the whole scandal broke. At first, she didn't want to go because she was afraid of what people were saying about her. She didn't want to be snubbed. But I convinced her she had to come with us and face the gossip squad.

"You can't just crawl into a hole and hide for the rest of your life," I told her. "Don't worry. I'll look after you."

And I certainly will. I mean, this is Washington. People survive scandals here all the time.

Things are kind of back to the way they were in school—with me protecting Violet. Only a lot has come in between. So even though it's the same, it's different. But the main thing is, we're still best friends.

———

"Throw me that roll of duct tape," Violet says.

I pitch her the dull silver ring.

As she tears off a long strip, she says, "Remember that anthrax scare years ago? The government warned us about chemical attacks, and there was a run on duct tape to seal up windows. All the stores ran out. Remember that?"

"Vaguely."

"They didn't stop to think that serial killers are the only ones with a ready supply of duct tape, since it's a tool of their trade. So they'd survive while the rest of us died. I bet very few people thought of that."

"I bet you're right," I tell her.

Violet has lost none of her sinister sense of humor, despite her own recent brush with the macabre. She seals the last carton of books, stands up, and claps the dust off her hands.

"There! That's the library done!" She looks around the room. "I won't be sad to leave this house. It was always more of a stage set than a home. . . . Just a sec. I want to show you something."

She reaches inside her pocket and hands me a copy of a letter. It's written on her personal stationery, addressed to "Ms. Jenny Tilbert, Class Correspondent, *Passages* Alumnae Magazine," and it's folded in half.

"Just read the top part for now," she instructs me.

The letter reads simply:

> Dear Jenny, this is to inform you and all my classmates
> that everything I wrote about myself before I moved to
> Washington and married Grant Bolton was a pack of bald-
> faced lies concocted out of vanity, insecurity, and a childish
> need for self-aggrandizement. I apologize to each and every
> one of you for any misconceptions, inconvenience, or envy
> I might have caused as a result of my mendacity. Yours
> sincerely, Violet McCloud Bolton.

I look up at her incredulously and say, "Are you really going to send this?"

"I already did," she replies with a grin. "I'm sure a lot of them know it already—it's been all over the Internet. But can't you just see the look on poor old Jenny's face when she reads that? Provided she doesn't die of shock, she may finally give up bugging people to write in with news! . . . Now read the bottom part."

I unfold the letter. The bottom half reads:

> P.S. I know everyone always says it's family that you turn to
> in the tough times, that it's family that gets you through. But
> I don't have a family, and so for me it's friendship that got
> me through. And I just want to thank my best friend, Reven
> Lynch, for saving my life.

I gotta say, I feel the old tears coming on, but I decide not to ruin the moment.

"So now can we finally talk about everything? And I mean *everything*? Violet McCloud, the lost years?"

"Oh, God," Violet sighs. "Where to start . . ."

Acknowledgments

My deepest thanks to my wonderful editor Marjorie Braman, who helped and encouraged me all through the writing of this book. My thanks as well to Jennifer Barth, who was instrumental in polishing up the final draft; and to Jonathan Burnham, who made it all possible.

I am indebted to Carol Joynt, Assistant Chief Peter Newsham, and Captain C.V. Morris for their indispensible assistance.

Deep thanks, also, to Susan Cheever, Linda Fairstein, and Kathy Rayner, dear friends all, who patiently listened to and read countless drafts of the book.

The following people supported and spurred me on. I couldn't have gotten through it without them: Lily and Lee Hoagland, John, Helen, and Serena Wong, Natalie Linkins, Josh Beach, Richard Braunstein, Jim Fennell, Jane Ellis, Dr. Chand Khanna, Dr. Alexandra Sahora, Ms. Cindy Gonzales, and all the staff at Friendship Hospital for Animals.

And finally, a special thanks to Miss Coco Loco Hoagland, my beautiful little Westie, who was with me all through the writing of this book and who promised she would see it through to the end. She kept her promise. Though she is gone, she is with me still in spirit.

A+

AUTHOR INSIGHTS, EXTRAS & MORE...

FROM

JANE STANTON HITCHCOCK

AND

AVON A

A Conversation with Jane Stanton Hitchcock

Vanity Fair writer-at-large Marie Brenner spars with the author of the new novel *Mortal Friends*, a riveting tale of murder, money, and high society set in the nation's capital.

MARIE BRENNER: *Mortal Friends* is *the* hot summer read. I could not put it down. You have taken us inside a Washington that no one ever sees. Who would ever think that so many feverish plots are being hatched in those grand Georgetown houses? You have guts to write about so many characters who are recognizable to Washington insiders. What can you tell us about these so-called novelists' imaginings?

JANE STANTON HITCHCOCK: I'm a fiction writer, so all the characters in my books are versions of me—including the murderers! But of course I draw from the life around me. I watch the parade until someone grabs my attention. Then I focus in on them and aim my pen at them for better or worse. It's my experience that everybody recognizes someone else, and no one ever recognizes themselves. However, if I never eat lunch in this town again, I'll just have to starve.

MARIE BRENNER: You and I met soon after I moved to New York. I knew and admired your mother, Joan Alexander Stanton— the late, great dame and radio star who was the voice of Lois Lane in the 1940 radio series "Superman"—and observed the intense loyalty and complexity of your very close relationship. Vivian Gornick once wrote a book called *Fierce Attachment*, which I think captured what you had with your mother. You had a childhood of fairy-tale glamour; who else would have had the chance to have Leonard Bernstein sing "Happy Birthday" on her twenty-first? And all this was orchestrated by your mother! Does your mother's influence come into play in *Mortal Friends*?

JANE STANTON HITCHCOCK: My mother was unquestionably the most powerful force in my life. I probably write mysteries because of her. She was a beautiful and very complex woman, an enchantress, often a mystery to me. *Mortal Friends* is a book where everyone is wearing a mask of one sort or another. My mother wore a mask for much of her life.

MARIE BRENNER: To me and your many fans, you are our Patricia Highsmith—the author who wrote, among many other superb mysteries, *The Talented Mr. Ripley*. You cut through the diabolical essence of your characters—and *Mortal Friends* is especially compelling. One of your gifts to your own friends is that dark, comic genius for seeing underneath surfaces. What was it about Washington and your first days there that inspired *Mortal Friends*?

JANE STANTON HITCHCOCK: When I first arrived in Washington, I knew very few people. It was pathetic how little I knew about my own government. I remember I was at a dinner at the British Embassy and I met a man who said, "Hello, I'm Warren Christopher." I said politely, "Your name sounds familiar to me. What do you do?" He looked at me in absolute awe, and said sweetly, "I'm the secretary of state." This happened to me several times, I have to admit. But once I got to know the players, I could go to a party and sense the undercurrents like a swimmer in an ocean. Social life here is where a lot of important business gets done—sometimes more than in Congress, or so it seems. Unlike other places, in Washington a friendship or a feud can affect national or even global events.

MARIE BRENNER: If you could tell the Obamas five guidelines for successfully navigating Washington, what would they be?

JANE STANTON HITCHCOCK: The Obamas don't need any tips, from what I've seen so far. They are navigating these treacherous waters with a lot of style and substance. However, since you ask:

1. First, read *Mortal Friends*, because my book will show you how things work behind your back. Communication between federal agencies is like pulling teeth, but the gossip mill goes like greased lightning.
2. Trust but verify, as Ronald Reagan said. Always get at least two sources before you act on information.
3. If you do get into trouble, never forget that the cover-up is often worse than the crime.
4. Remember that an omission can sometimes be as dangerous as a lie.
5. Take good care of the dog.

MARIE BRENNER: In the Kennedy years, the Georgetown cave dwellers were the power center. Is this still the case? There seems to be transformation in the air, with all the rules being rewritten. True or false?

JANE STANTON HITCHCOCK: The Old Georgetown set passed away forever with the late, great Kay Graham. Things are much looser now. There is no one presiding eye. There are many. It's called the Internet. Listen, in an era where textbook history is being questioned and anyone with a blog can have an opinion, there are no more guidelines. The transformation seems to be that anything goes, and it goes like lightning on the Web.

MARIE BRENNER: What does America and the world not understand about the power grid of Washington?

JANE STANTON HITCHCOCK: That women are more powerful than they appear. Wives of ambassadors and Cabinet members and congressmen may wear pastel suits and smile and nod alongside their husbands in public like obedient spouses—but they are actually artfully concealed weapons of mass destruction when they want to be. A whispering campaign started at a ladies' lunch can be almost as dangerous as having Bob Woodward on your trail.

MARIE BRENNER: You excel at raising delicious grudge-holding to an art form. How did this affect *Mortal Friends*?

JANE STANTON HITCHCOCK: I'm half Lebanese, and as far as letting bygones be bygones and kissing and making up is concerned—well, just take a look at the Middle East. As the heroine of my last book, *Social Crimes*, was fond of saying, "I may not remember, but I never forget." *Mortal Friends* explores how old grudges come back to haunt you. Having said that, I rather like holding grudges. And hey, I may not exactly see the heads of my enemies floating down the river just yet—but I am starting to see some of their clothes go by.

MARIE BRENNER: If someone were to write your biography, what would be the title? Subtitle?

JANE STANTON HITCHCOCK: *Writing Well Is the Best Revenge.*

MARIE BRENNER: When did you know you would be a writer?

JANE STANTON HITCHCOCK: I was a lousy student, and writing was always a great solace to me from the time I was a little girl. I didn't choose writing; writing chose me.

MARIE BRENNER: It has been observed that life is high school. So is Washington similar to your alma mater, Brearley—or in other words, a cloistered girls' school of elite backstabbers? Is there a TV series here?

JANE STANTON HITCHCOCK: In *Mortal Friends*, I describe life as "high school with wrinkles." I believe the enemies of the past come to haunt us in interesting ways—and since *Mortal Friends* is as much about female friendship as it is about murder, the past plays a big role. As far as a TV series? There seems to be a TV series about everything these days. So let us hope.

MARIE BRENNER: Here's a question suggested by Powell's bookstore in Portland, Oregon: Writers are better liars than other people: true or false?

JANE STANTON HITCHCOCK: Mystery writers are serial killers at heart. We are God one day, the devil the next. I wouldn't say we are better liars; we are just more concerned with the way a lie works. How do you get from point A to point B? Churchill once said that the truth was so precious it had to be surrounded by a bodyguard of lies. In writing fiction, the lie within the lie is what's interesting to me. So I amend the great Mr. Churchill and say that in writing, the lie is so precious, it must be surrounded by a bodyguard of truths or half truths to put the reader off guard.

MARIE BRENNER: What is your idea of absolute happiness?

JANE STANTON HITCHCOCK: A quiet weekend by the sea with my husband, my dog, and a fabulous idea for a book.

MARIE BRENNER: Another question suggested by Powell's: Have you ever made a literary pilgrimage?

JANE STANTON HITCHCOCK: Yes, to Edgar Allan Poe's grave in Baltimore. Poe is my absolute hero, because he wrote about the raw insides of obsession. He spun every human fear into literary gold.

MARIE BRENNER: What do you want readers to take away from *Mortal Friends*?

JANE STANTON HITCHCOCK: A great beach read and a sense of how Washington—and female friendship—really works.

Courtesy of Marie Brenner for wowOwow.com
  http://www.wowowow.com/entertainment/crimes-misdeameanors-conversation-new-york-times-author-jane-stanton-hitchcock-323794?page=0%2C0

Len DePas

JANE STANTON HITCHCOCK is the *New York Times* bestselling author of *The Witches' Hammer*, *Trick of the Eye*, *Social Crimes*, and *One Dangerous Lady*, as well as several plays. She is married to syndicated foreign affairs columnist Jim Hoagland. They live in New York City and Washington, D.C.